BLOODRING

BLOODRING

FAITH HUNTER

A ROC BOOK

ROC
Published by New American Library, a division of
Penguin Group (USA) Inc., 375 Hudson Street,
New York, New York 10014, USA
Penguin Group (Canada), 90 Eglinton Avenue East, Suite 700, Toronto,
Ontario M4P 2Y3, Canada (a division of Pearson Penguin Canada Inc.)
Penguin Books Ltd., 80 Strand, London WC2R 0RL, England
Penguin Ireland, 25 St. Stephen's Green, Dublin 2,
Ireland (a division of Penguin Books Ltd.)
Penguin Group (Australia), 250 Camberwell Road, Camberwell, Victoria 3124,
Australia (a division of Pearson Australia Group Pty. Ltd.)
Penguin Books India Pvt. Ltd., 11 Community Centre, Panchsheel Park,
New Delhi - 110 017, India
Penguin Group (NZ), cnr Airborne and Rosedale Roads, Albany,
Auckland 1310, New Zealand (a division of Pearson New Zealand Ltd.)
Penguin Books (South Africa) (Pty.) Ltd., 24 Sturdee Avenue,
Rosebank, Johannesburg 2196, South Africa

Penguin Books Ltd., Registered Offices:
80 Strand, London WC2R 0RL, England

First published by Roc, an imprint of New American Library,
a division of Penguin Group (USA) Inc.

First Printing, November 2006

Some scripture quotations taken from the Amplified® Bible, copyright © 1954, 1958, 1962,
1964, 1965, 1987 by The Lockman Foundation. Used by permission. (www.Lockman.org)

RoC REGISTERED TRADEMARK—MARCA REGISTRADA
LIBRARY OF CONGRESS CATALOGING-IN-PUBLICATION DATA:
Hunter, Faith.
  Bloodring / Faith Hunter.
    p. cm.
  ISBN 0-451-46108-8 (trade pbk.)
  I. Title.
PS3608.U5927B55 2006
813'.6—dc22   2006014334

Set in Filosofia • Designed by Elke Sigal

146122990

To my Renaissance Man

Acknowledgments

Many thanks to:

My Renaissance Man, for encouragement and the right word at the right time.

Kim, for support, for friendship, for making three great suggestions, and for tea breaks.

Mary, Fazelle and Nova, and Kipper, for the stones and the great time "prospecting."

Ben, for the martial arts stuff.

Matthew, for keeping my Enclave bearable.

Ken and Don Waldroup at Peoples Furniture and John Wellborn in Spruce Pine, NC.

My agents:

Lucienne Diver, for believing in me and in this bizarre world I created, and for saying, "This is the sexiest book. . . ."

Jeff Gerecke, for guiding me in the right direction.

Finally and profoundly, to my editor, Liz Scheier, for making me think—and write—darker, faster, and leaner. This has been the *most* FUN!

Then I looked, and behold, in the firmament that was over the head of the cherubim there appeared above them as it were a sapphire stone, as the appearance of the likeness of a throne.

And the sound of the wings of the cherubim was heard even to the outer court, as the voice of God Almighty when he speaketh.

And I looked, and behold, four wheels beside the cherubim, one wheel beside one cherub, and another wheel beside another cherub; and the appearance of the wheels was like unto a beryl stone.

As for the wheels, they were called in my hearing, the whirling wheels. And every one had four faces: the first face was the face of the cherub, and the second face was the face of a man, and the third face the face of a lion, and the fourth the face of an eagle.

And when the cherubim went, the wheels went beside them; and when the cherubim lifted up their wings to mount up from the earth, the wheels also turned not from beside them.

—*Ezekiel 10:1, 5, 9, 13–14, 16*

BLOODRING

Chapter 1

I stared into the hills as my mount clomped below me, his massive hooves digging into snow and ice. Above us a fighter jet streaked across the sky, leaving a trail that glowed bright against the fiery sunset. A faint sense of alarm raced across my skin, and I gathered up the reins, tightening my knees against Homer's sides, pressing my walking stick against the huge horse.

A sonic boom exploded across the peaks, shaking through snow-laden trees. Ice and snow pitched down in heavy sheets and lumps. A dog yelped. The Friesian set his hooves, dropped his head, and kicked. "Stones and blood," I hissed as I rammed into the saddle horn. The boom echoed like rifle shot. Homer's back arched. If he bucked, I was a goner.

I concentrated on the bloodstone handle of my walking stick and pulled the horse to me, reins firm as I whispered soothing, seemingly nonsense words no one would interpret as a chant. The bloodstone pulsed as it projected a sense of calm into him, a use of stored power that didn't affect my own drained resources. The sonic boom came back from the nearby mountains, a ricochet of man-made thunder.

The mule in front of us hee-hawed and kicked out, white rimming his eyes, lips wide, and teeth showing as the boom reverberated through the farther peaks. Down the length of the mule train, other animals reacted as the fear spread, some bucking in a frenzy, throwing packs into drifts, squealing as lead ropes tangled, trumpeting fear.

Homer relaxed his back, sidestepped, and danced like a young colt before planting his hooves again. He blew out a rib-racking sigh and shook himself, ears twitching as he settled. Deftly, I repositioned the supplies and packs he'd dislodged, rubbing a bruised thigh that had taken a wallop from a twenty-pound pack of stone.

Hoop Marks and his assistant guides swung down from their own mounts and steadied the more fractious stock. All along the short train, the startled horses and mules settled as riders worked to control them. Homer looked on, ears twitching.

Behind me, a big Clydesdale relaxed, shuddering with a ripple of muscle and thick winter coat, his rider following the wave of motion with practiced ease. Audric was a salvage miner, and he knew his horses. I nodded to my old friend, and he tipped his hat to me before repositioning his stock on Clyde's back.

A final echo rumbled from the mountains. Almost as one, we turned to the peaks above us, listening fearfully for the telltale roar of avalanche.

Sonic booms were rare in the Appalachians these days, and I wondered what had caused the military overflight. I slid the walking stick into its leather loop. It was useful for balance while taking a stroll in snow, but its real purpose was as a weapon. Its concealed blade was deadly, as was its talisman hilt, hiding in plain sight. However, the bloodstone handle-hilt was now almost drained of power, and when we stopped for the night, I'd have to find a safe, secluded place to draw power for it and for the amulets I carried, or my neomage attributes would begin to display themselves.

I'm a neomage, a witchy-woman. Though contrary rumors persist, claiming mages still roam the world free, I'm the only one of my kind not a prisoner, the only one in the entire world of humans who is unregulated, unlicensed. The only one uncontrolled.

All the others of my race are restricted to Enclaves, protected in enforced captivity. Enclaves are gilded cages, prisons of privilege and power, but cages nonetheless. Neomages are allowed out only with seraph permission, and then we have to wear a sigil of office and bracelets with satellite GPS locator chips in them. We're followed by the humans, watched, and sent back fast when our services are no longer needed or when our visas expire. As if we're contagious. Or dangerous.

Enclave was both prison and haven for mages, keeping us safe from the politically powerful, conservative, religious orthodox humans who hated us, and giving us a place to live as our natures and gifts demanded. It was a great place for a mage-child to grow up, but when my gift blossomed at age fourteen, my mind opened in a unique way. The thoughts of all twelve hundred mages captive in the New Orleans Enclave opened to me at once. I nearly went mad. If I went back, I'd go quietly—or loudly screaming—insane.

In the woods around us, shadows lengthened and darkened. Mule handlers looked around, jittery. I sent out a quick mind-skim. There were no supernats present, no demons, no mages, no seraphs, no *others*. Well, except for me. But I couldn't exactly tell them that. I chuckled under my breath as Homer snorted and slapped me with his tail. That would be dandy. Survive for a decade in the human world only to be exposed by something so simple as a sonic boom and a case of trail exhaustion. I'd be tortured, slowly, over a period of days, tarred and feathered, chopped into pieces, and dumped in the snow to rot.

If the seraphs located me first, I'd be sent back to Enclave and I'd still die. I'm allergic to others of my kind—really allergic—fatally so. The Enclave death would be a little slower, a little less bloody than the human version. Humans kill with steel, a public beheading, but only after I was disemboweled, eviscerated, and flayed alive. And all that after I *entertained* the guards for a few days. As ways to go, the execution of an unlicensed witchy-woman rates up there with the top ten gruesome methods of capital punishment. With my energies nearly gone, a conjure to calm the horses could give me away.

"Light's goin',' " Hoop called out. "We'll stop here for the night. Everyone takes care of his own mount before anything else. Then circle and gather deadwood. Last, we cook. Anyone who don't work, don't eat."

Behind me, a man grumbled beneath his breath about the unfairness of paying good money for a spot on the mule train and then having to work. I grinned at him and he shrugged when he realized he'd been heard. "Can't blame a man for griping. Besides, I haven't ridden a horse since I was a kid. I have blisters on my blisters."

I eased my right leg over Homer's back and slid the long distance to the ground. My knees protested, aching after the day in the saddle. "I have a few blisters this trip myself. Good boy," I said to the big horse, and dropped the reins, running a hand along his side. He stomped his satisfaction and I felt his deep sense of comfort at the end of the day's travel.

We could have stopped sooner, but Hoop had hoped to make the campsite where the trail rejoined the old Blue Ridge Parkway. Now we were forced to camp in a ring of trees instead of the easily fortified site ahead. If the denizens of Darkness came out to hunt, we'd be sitting ducks.

Unstrapping the heavy pack containing my most valuable finds from the Salvage and Mineral Swap Meet in Boone, I dropped it to the earth and covered it with the saddle. My luggage and pack went to the side. I removed all the tools I needed to groom the horse and clean his feet, and added the bag of oats and grain. A pale dusk closed in around us before I got the horse brushed down and draped in a blanket, a pile of food and a half bale of hay at his feet.

The professional guides were faster and had taken care of their own mounts and the pack animals and dug a firepit in the time it took the paying customers to get our mounts groomed. The equines were edgy, picking up anxiety from their humans, making the job slower for us amateurs. Hoop's dogs trotted back and forth among us, tails tight to their bodies, ruffs raised, sniffing for danger. As we worked, both clients and handlers glanced fearfully into the night. Demons and their spawn often hid in the dark, watching humans like predators watched tasty herd animals. So far as my weakened senses could detect, there was nothing out there. But there was a lot I couldn't say and still keep my head.

"Gather wood!" I didn't notice who called the command, but we all moved into the forest, me using my walking stick for balance. There was no talking. The sense of trepidation was palpable, though the night was friendly, the moon rising, no snow or ice in the forecast. Above, early stars twinkled, cold and bright at this altitude. I moved away from the others, deep into the tall trees: oak, hickory, fir, cedar. At a distance, I found a huge boulder rounded up from the snow.

Checking to see that I was alone, I lay flat on the boulder, my cheek against frozen granite, the walking stick between my torso and the rock. And I called up power. Not a raging roar of mage-might, but a slow, steady trickle. Without words, without a chant that might give me away, I channeled energy into the bloodstone handle between my breasts, into the amulets hidden beneath my clothes, and pulled a measure into my own flesh, needing the succor. It took long minutes, and I sighed with relief as my body soaked up strength.

Satisfied, as refreshed as if I had taken a nap, I stood, stretched, bent, and picked up deadwood, traipsing through the trees and boulders for firewood—wood that was a lot more abundant this far away from the trail. My night vision is better than most humans', and though I'm small for an adult and was the only female on the train, I gathered an armload in record time. Working far off the beaten path has its rewards.

I smelled it when the wind changed. Old blood. A lot of old blood. I dropped the firewood, drew the blade from the walking-stick sheath, and opened my mage-sight to survey the surrounding territory. The world of snow and ice glimmered with a sour-lemon glow, as if it was ailing, sickly.

Mage-sight is more than human sight in that it sees energy as well as matter. The retinas of human eyes pick up little energy, seeing light only after it's absorbed or reflected. But mages see the world of matter with an overlay of energy, picked up by the extra lenses that surround our retinas. We see power and life, the leftover workings of creation. When we use the sight, the energies are sometimes real, sometimes representational, experience teaching us to identify and translate the visions, sort of like picking out images from a three-dimensional pattern.

I'm a stone mage, a worker of rocks and gems, and the energy of creation; hence, only stone looks powerful and healthy to me when I'm using mage-sight. Rain, ice, sleet or snow, each of which is water that has passed through air, always looks unhealthy, as does moonlight, sunlight, the movement of the wind, or currents of surface water—anything except stone. This high in the mountains, snow lay thick and crusted everywhere, weak, pale, a part of nature that leached power from me—except for a dull gray area to the east, beyond the stone where I had recharged my energies.

Moving with the speed of my race, sword in one hand, walking-stick sheath, a weapon in itself, in the other, I rushed toward the site.

BLOOÐRING

I tripped over a boot. It was sticking from the snow, boot-laces crusted with blood and ice. Human blood had been spilled here, a lot of it, and the snow was saturated. The earth reeked of fear and pain and horror, and to my mage-sight, it glowed with the blackened energy of death. I caught a whiff of Darkness.

Adrenaline coursed through my veins, and I stepped into the cat stance, blade and walking stick held low as I circled the site. Bones poked up from the ice, and I identified a femur, the fragile bones of a hand, tendons still holding fingers together. A jawbone thrust toward the sky. Placing my feet carefully, I eased in. Teeth marks, long and deep, scored an arm bone. Predator teeth, unlike any beast known to nature. Supernat teeth. The teeth of Darkness.

Devil-spawn travel in packs, drink blood and eat human flesh. While it's still alive. A really bad way to go. And spawn would know what I was in an instant if they were downwind of me. As a mage, I'd be worth more to a spawn than a fresh meal. I'd be prime breeding material for their masters.

I'd rather be eaten.

A skull stared at me from an outcropping of rock. A tree close by had been raked with talons, or with desperate human fingers trying to get away, trying to climb. As my sight adjusted to the falling light, a rock shelf protruding from the earth took on a glow displaying pick marks. A strip mine. Now that I knew what to look for, I saw a pick, the blackened metal pitted by ichor, a lantern, bags of supplies hanging from trees, other gear stacked near the rock with their ore. One tent pole still stood. On it was what I assumed to be a hat, until my eyes adjusted and it resolved into a second skull. Old death. Weeks, perhaps months, old.

A stench of sulfur reached me. Dropping the sight, I skimmed until I found the source: a tiny hole in the earth near the rock they had been working. I understood what had hap-pened. The miners had been working a claim on the surface—

because no one in his right mind went underground, not anymore—and they had accidentally broken through to a cavern or an old, abandoned underground mine. Darkness had scented them. Supper . . .

I moved to the hole in the earth. It was leaking only a hint of sulfur and brimstone, and the soil around was smooth, trackless. Spawn hadn't used this entrance in a long time. I glanced up at the sky. Still bright enough that the nocturnal devil-spawn were sleeping. If I could cover the entrance, they wouldn't smell us. Probably. Maybe.

Sheathing the blade, I went to the cases the miners had piled against the rocks, and pulled a likely one off the top. It hit the ground with a whump but was light enough for me to drag it over the snow, leaving a trail through the carnage. The bag fit over the entrance, and the reek of Darkness was instantly choked off. My life had been too peaceful. I'd gotten lazy. I should have smelled it the moment I entered the woods. Now it was gone.

Satisfied I had done all I could, I tramped to my pile of deadwood and back to camp, glad of the nearness of so many humans, horses, and dogs that trotted about. I dumped the wood beside the fire pit at the center of the small clearing. Hoop Marks and his second in command, Hoop Jr., tossed in broken limbs and lit the fire with a small can of kerosene and a pack of matches. Flames roared and danced, sending shadows capering into the surrounding forest. The presence of fire sent a welcome feeling of safety through the group, though only earthly predators would fear the flame. No supernat of Darkness would care about a little fire if it was hungry. Fire made them feel right at home.

I caught Hoop's eye and gestured to the edge of the woods. The taciturn man followed when I walked away, and listened with growing concern to my tale of the miners. I thought he might curse when I told him of the teeth marks on the bones, but he stopped himself in time. Cursing aloud near a hellhole was a sure way of inviting Darkness to you. In other locales it might attract seraphic punishment or draw the ire of the church. Thoughtless language could result in death-by-dinner, seraphic vengeance, or priestly branding. Instead, he ground out, "I'll radio it in. You don't tell nobody, you hear? I got something that'll keep us safe." And without asking me why I had wandered so far from camp, alone, he walked away.

Smoke and supper cooking wafted through camp as I rolled out my sleeping bag and pumped up the air mattress. Even with the smell of old death still in my nostrils, my mouth watered. I wanted nothing more than to curl up, eat and sleep, but I needed to move through the horses and mules first. Trying to be inconspicuous, touching each one as surreptitiously as possible, I let the walking stick's amulet-handle brush each animal with calm.

It was a risk, if anyone recognized a mage-conjure, but there was no way I was letting the stock bolt and stampede away if startled in the night. I had no desire to walk miles through several feet of hard-packed snow to reach the nearest train tracks, then wait days in the cold, without a bath or adequate supplies, for a train that might get stranded in a blizzard and not come until snowmelt in spring. No way. Living in perpetual winter was bad enough, and though the ubiquitous *they* said it was only a *mini*—ice age, it was still pretty dang cold.

So I walked along the picket line and murmured soothing words, touching the stock one by one. I loved horses. I hated that they were the only dependable method of transport through the mountains ten months out of the year, but I loved the beasts themselves. They didn't care that I was an unlicensed neomage hiding among the humans. With them I could be myself, if only for a moment or two. I lay my cheek against the shoulder of a particularly worried mare. She exhaled as serenity seeped into her and turned liquid brown eyes to me in appreciation, blowing warm horse breath in my face. "You're welcome," I whispered.

Just before I got to the end of the string, Hoop sang out, "Charmed circle. Charmed circle for the night."

I looked up in surprise, my movements as frozen as the night air. Hoop Jr. was walking bent over, a fifty-pound bag of salt in his arms, his steps moving clockwise. Though human, he was making a conjure circle. Instinctively, I cast out with a mind-skim, though I knew I was the only mage here. But now I scented a charmed *something*. From a leather case, Hoop Sr. pulled out a branch that glowed softly to my mage-sight. Hoop's "something to keep us safe." The tag on the tip of the branch proclaimed it a legally purchased charm, unlike my unlicensed amulets. It would be empowered by the salt in the ring, offering us protection. I hurried down the line of horses and mules, trusting that my movements were hidden by the night, and made it to the circle before it was closed.

Stepping through the opening in the salt, I nodded again as I passed Audric. The big black man shouldered his packs and carried them toward the fire pit. He didn't talk much, but he and Thorn's Gems had done a lot of business since he discovered and claimed a previously untouched city site for salvage. Because he had a tendresse for one of my business partners, he brought his findings to us first and stayed with us while in town. The arrangement worked out well, and when his claim petered out, we all hoped he'd put down roots and stay, maybe buy in as the fourth partner.

"All's coming in, get in," Hoop Sr. sang out. "All's staying out'll be shot if trouble hits and you try to cross the salt ring." There was a cold finality to his tone. "Devil-spawn been spotted round here. I take no chances with my life or yours 'less you choose to act stupid and get yourself shot."

"Devil-spawn? Here?" The speaker was the man who had griped about the workload.

"Yeah. Drained a woman and three kids at a cabin up near Linville." He didn't mention the carnage within shooting distance of us. Smart man.

I spared a quick glance for my horse, who was already snoozing. A faint pop sizzled along my nerve endings as the circle closed and the energy of the spell from the mage-branch snapped in place. I wasn't an earth mage, but I appreciated the conjure's simple elegance. A strong shield-protection-invisibility incantation had been stored in the cells of the branch. The stock were in danger from passing predators, but the rest of us were effectively invisible to anyone, human or supernat.

Night envcloped us in its black mantle as we gathered for a supper of venison stew. Someone passed around a flask of moonshine. No one said anything against it. Most took a swallow or two against the cold. I drank water and ate only stewed vegetables. Meat disagrees with me. Liquor on a mule train at night just seems stupid.

Tired to the bone, I rolled into my heated, down-filled sleeping bag and looked up at the cold, clear sky. The moon was nearly full, its rays shining on seven inches of fresh snow. It was a good night for a moon mage, a water mage, even a weather mage, but not a night to induce a feeling of vitality or well-being in a bone-tired stone mage. The entire world glowed with moon power, brilliant and beautiful, but draining to my own strength. I rolled in my bedding and stopped, caught by a tint of color in the velvet black sky. A thick ring of bloody red circled the pure white orb, far out in the night. *A bloodring.* I almost swore under my breath but choked it back, a painful sound, close to a sob.

The last time there was a bloodring on the moon, my twin sister died. Rose had been a licensed mage, living in Atlanta, supposedly safe, yet she had vanished, leaving a wide, freezing pool of blood and signs of a struggle, within minutes after Lolo, the priestess of Enclave, phoned us both with warnings. The prophecy hadn't helped then and it wouldn't help now. Portents never helped. They offered only a single moment to catch a breath before I was trounced by whatever they foretold.

If Lolo had called with a warning tonight, it was on my answering machine. Even for me, the distance to Enclave was too great to hear the mind-voice of the priestess.

I shivered, looking up from my sleeping bag. A feasting site, now a bloodring. It was a hazy, frothing circle, swirling like the breath of the Dragon in the Revelation, holy words taught to every mage from the womb up. "And there appeared another wonder in heaven; and behold a great red dragon. . . . And his tail drew the third part of the stars of heaven, and did cast them to the earth: and the dragon stood before the woman. . . . And there was war in heaven: Michael and his seraphim fought against the dragon; and the dragon fought, and his seraphim." The tale of the Last War.

Shivering, I gripped the amulets tied around my waist and my walking stick, the blade loosed in the sheath, the prime amulet of its hilt tight in my palm. Much later, exhausted, I slept.

Lucas checked his watch as he slipped out of the office and moved into the alley, ice crunching beneath his boots, breath a half-seen fog in the night. He was still on schedule, though pushing the boundaries. Cold froze his ears and nose, numbed his fingers and feet, congealed his blood, seeped into his bones, even through the layers of clothes, down-filled vest, and hood. He slipped, barely catching himself before hitting the icy ground. He cursed beneath his breath as he steadied himself on the alley wall. *Seraph stones, it's cold.*

But he was almost done. The last of the amethyst would soon be in Thorn's hands, just as the Mistress Amethyst had demanded. In another hour he would be free of his burden.

He'd be out of danger. He felt for the ring on his finger, turning it so the sharp edge was against his flesh. He hitched the heavy backpack higher, its nylon straps cutting into his palm and across his shoulder.

The dark above was absolute, moon and stars hidden by the tall buildings at his sides. Ahead, there was only the distant security light at the intersection of the alley, where it joined the larger delivery lane and emptied into the street. Into safety.

A rustle startled him. A flash of movement. A dog burst from the burned-out hulk of an old Volkswagen and bolted back the way he had come. A second followed. Two small pups huddled in the warm nest they deserted, yellow coats barely visible. Lucas blew out a gust of irritation and worthless fear and hoped the larger mutts made it back to the makeshift den before the weather took them all down. It was so cold, the puppies wouldn't survive long. Even the smells of dog, urine, old beer, and garbage were frozen.

He moved into the deeper dark, toward the distant light, but slowed. The alley narrowed, the walls at his sides invisible in the night; his billowing breath vanished. He glanced up, his eyes drawn to the relative brightness of the sky. A chill that had nothing to do with the temperature chased down his spine. The rooftops were bare, the gutters and eaves festooned with icicles, moon and clouds beyond. One of the puppies mewled behind him.

Lucas stepped through the dark, his pace increasing as panic coiled itself around him. He was nearly running by the time he reached the pool of light marking the alleys' junction. Slowing, he passed two scooters and a tangle of bicycles leaning against a wall, all secured with steel chains, tires frozen in the ice. He stepped into the light and the safety it offered.

Above, there was a crackle, a sharp snap of metal. His head lifted, but his eyes were drawn ahead to a stack of boxes and firewood. To the man standing there. *Sweet Mother of God . . . not a man. A shadow.* "No!" Lucas tried to whirl, skidding on icy pavement before he could complete the move. Two others ran toward him, human movements, human slow.

"Get him!"

The first man collided with him, followed instantly by the other, their bodies twin blows. His boots gave on the slippery surface. He went to one knee, breath a pained grunt.

A fist pounded across the back of his neck. A leg reared back. Screaming, he covered his head with an arm. A rain of blows and kicks landed. The backpack was jerked away, opening and spilling.

As he fell, he tightened a fist around the ring, its sharp edge slicing into his flesh. He groaned out the words she had given him to use, but only in extremis. The sound of the syllables was lost beneath the rain of blows. "Zadkiel, hear me. Holy Amethyst—" A boot took him in the jaw, knocking back his head. He saw the wings unfurl on the roof above him. Darkness closed in. Teeth sank deep in his throat. Cold took him. The final words of the chant went unspoken.

Chapter 2

I curled deeper, savoring the muted pulse of power in the heated springwater. It swirled around me, a dull flush of stored creation energy, slowly released from the smooth stones on the porcelain bottom of the antique bathtub. The heat soothed childhood scars that traced up my limbs, puckered and pale. Scars that still throbbed each long winter, aggravated by the cold. Warmth seeped into my bones, easing winter's ache.

Feeling totally safe for the first time in nearly two weeks, I let my neomage attributes slip free and sipped a Black Bear Brew, the label on the ice-crusted beer bottle blurred by rising steam. A full moon shimmered through the stained-glass window at the back of the loft, and wavering heat rose all around me. Soft light cast by the outer ring of candles whitened the protective ring of salt enclosing me, keeping me safe as I recharged energies exhausted by the Salvage and Mineral Swap Meet and the trail.

A year ago, Lucas would have slid into the big tub and wrapped his arms around me, cradling me against him, kissing the pale length of the few scars my amulets allowed him to see. We would have celebrated my success with wine and passion.

"Dragon bones," I said, pushing away the memory. I refused to spend another second grieving over the woman-chasing cheat I'd had the bad taste to marry.

I drank again and slipped lower into the potent bath, finishing off the beer. On my empty stomach, it went straight to my head. I had done well at the swap meet, appearing as little more than an anonymous shadow in the security monitors. The rock hounds and salvage miners selling their wares would remember only a mild-mannered, nondescript, middle-aged woman who bartered in a lethargic voice for trinkets, not Thorn of Thorn's Gems, a woman for whom the costs would have soared. Our recent success had instantly bred price increases.

Most of the folk who had traded with me, bargaining for all last year's remaining rough stock, wouldn't remember me at all. I had released a rune of forgetting at the conclusion of each deal and come away with fabulous buys. But I'd done it fairly, so no one would have the need to search for a young witchy-woman, accusing me of haggling with unlicensed enchantment.

While selling and trading for rough stock for the next year, I had found and purchased some exquisite cabochons I could use as is, and three charged stones from the time of the beginning of the neomages. They contained wild magic that tingled against my fingers and were likely dangerous, but I hadn't been capable of passing them up. The seller hadn't known what he offered and they came to me for a song.

I had done so well that I should be having a party, singing and dancing and discharging bursts of rowdy wizardry. But as that would get me tossed out of my home, likely in bite-sized, cube-shaped pieces, I was happy to settle for a moment of quiet revelry, even if I did have to celebrate alone. Humans were such spoilsports.

The doorbell rang, a low-pitched chime. A slow, spiraling dread twisted through me. The bell echoed in the hollow of my loft, insistent. Evil happened when callers came after midnight.

BLOODRING

Life had taught me that early. I jerked when it chimed again and stood, too fast.

Water surged over the rim of the tub in a tiny tsunami. Almost in slow motion I saw the power-charged water splat on the earth-made tile, swirl, and melt into the salt ring, paralyzing the protection for a moment before it broke the circle and opened a pathway. A hard tremor gripped me as power flowed back into the water around my calves. I slipped, regained my balance, and stepped from the tub to the dark tile. Force rippled up from the baked clay into me, an electric sizzle of might that actually hurt.

"Sweet seraph!" I swore softly. The bell rang again as I dried off, chilled and miserable. Leaving the gas logs and candles burning, I belted on a robe and slid my feet into suede slippers. I was halfway out the door when I remembered the omen of the bloodring.

Surely not . . . Still moving fast, I raced to the back windows and pushed aside the draperies. A bloodring swirled around the full moon. I choked off a second curse. I'd never heard of a bloodring appearing twice in as many days. Only omens and portents of great significance came more than once. I paused, hands on the jambs, hanging half in, half out of the loft as icy air swirled under my robe. Reaching back inside, I grabbed the walking stick and swept the blade from its sheath, gripping the bloodstone hilt in my right hand, the guard curving over my fingers. I slipped it through the robe's belt, angling the blade down along my robe, hiding it. Into my tight left sleeve I slid a shortsword I kept at the coat rack.

With a swipe at the amulet set into the doorknob, I damped my neomage attributes so I'd stop glowing and ran down the stairway. It was chilled and damp, the treads creaking under my padding feet. At the foot of the stairs I found the keys to Thorn's Gems on their ring and tightened the robe's belt, securing the longsword at my side.

Slowing to human speed, I ran into the display room, to the shop's front door, silhouetted by moonlight through the glass. I flipped on a light, unlocked the door, and gripped the hidden hilt of my blade. I threw open the door, the bells overhead ringing jaunty, clashing notes. Icy air blasted in, chilling my bath-wet skin, carrying with it a scent that rocked me back a step. The unexpected smells of caramel and vanilla, a hint of brown sugar, and beneath it all something peppery, like ginger.

My body clenched in reaction, then went slightly limp, my hold on the sword hilt lax. I looked up. Glacial eyes stared at me, the greenish blue of the ocean in spring. Shaggy red hair fell over his brow. Full lips were stern above an almost square chin, shadowed with a red-gold haze. And the smell. I breathed it in, the scent as rich as a candy shop.

"Are you Thorn St. Croix Stanhope?" he asked, shifting into the light. His coat gapped open with the movement, exposing a sigil pinned to his lapel. A badge of office, half hidden in the folds of cloth. *He's a cop. Seraph stones! I'm caught.* Hand sweaty, I stepped back again, gripping the sword's hilt to draw it. I had left my amulets at the bathtub. I had no defenses without them. Adrenaline whipped through me, fear throbbing in my veins.

Yet he didn't attack. He was alone. A single human cop would never attack a mage. We were too dangerous.

Indecisive, I drew in a breath, all movement arrested by the smell, rich and sweet. Oddly disorienting. And then I felt the tug of blood, the pull of earth and sex. I felt him flow into me like a wraith, as heated as the stones in my bath, as potent as the springwater I had charged with their stored power. And I knew what the smell meant. This man, this cop, this stranger on my doorstep in the middle of the night, was a child of the seraph Baraqyal, a third- or fourth-generation descendant of the winged warrior and a mage. This was a kylen. I shook my head to clear his scent. At the gesture, the skin over his cheekbones tightened; his eyes narrowed.

Fear rushed through me, chased by doubt. A kylen on my doorstep? A kylen who wasn't drawing his weapon and taking me into custody, or ripping off his clothes to mate? Time, always fluid, slowed to a sluggish honey-thick construct with the flush of fight-or-flight instincts, endorphins and hormones. *He isn't here to mate, as a kylen would come to a mage. And he isn't here to arrest me.* And then I realized. *He doesn't know I'm not human. Stranger still, he doesn't know he's not human.* Time snapped back to its accustomed speed. My brain kicked into gear and I released shortsword hilt, trusting the tight sleeve to hold the kris blade in place.

What had he asked? I gestured to his sigil with a jut of my chin. "What's happened? Why would a cop ring my bell after midnight?"

"I could be a rapist," he said with a faint smile, "or a thief here to clean out your shop." Involuntarily, unaware of the power of his breeding, he called to me, his blood promising a touch I recognized and craved but had never known.

Holding on to the door frame with the other hand, seeking the balance that had fled from me, I pointed to his badge. "No. You look like a cop. Mean." And wished I could pull the words back out of the air.

He laughed and unclipped the black sigil with its State Police Department emblem of a hand and open book on one side and a holographic ID on the other. "Insulting, but correct. Thaddeus Bartholomew, detective with Carolina State Law Enforcement."

He was a Hand of the Law, not an Administration of the ArchSeraph Investigator. Okay. That offered me a measure of safety.

"May I come in, out of the cold?"

Instantly, I saw my bed, silk covers tossed back for the

night, an antique novel on the comforter, the pages curled and brittle, the book nestled into the deep, thick down. My bed and a kylen in the same room. Warmth spiraled through me. I'd heard tales about mages and kylen and their attraction for one another but had never really believed them. Until now. An icy draft swept up my robe and I clutched the lapels close. The cold helped, brought me to myself enough to see that he was staring at me.

Crack the Stone of Ages. I'm going into heat. With a cop. Very *bad idea.* "Yes. Come in. I have a fire." I took a deep breath to settle myself. This sucked Habbiel's pearly toes.

I pressed my palm against the bloodstone handle of the blade along my side. A sizzle of power from the mineral shot up my arm, into my heart, into my mind. Suddenly I could reason. I stepped back from the doorway, my mind clearer as the cop entered Thorn's Gems.

Something was wrong with this. There was a child of Baraqyal in Mineral City, a thousand miles south of where he belonged, a kylen living outside of a Realm of Light, a kylen whose mind was sealed to me. So far as I knew, the mind of any mage within miles was an open book—hopes, dreams, fears, hatreds, petty irritations—my problem living in Enclave surrounded by others of my kind. But here was a part-mage, part-seraph, part-human who was as sealed to me as a full-blood human being.

Had Lolo known that was possible? Had she sent him? Or were the state cops working with the AAS, looking for fabled runaway neomages? Or looking specifically for me? Fear roiled through me, clearing my head, and I reached out with a silent skim, little more than a whiff, hoping he was head-blind. He had no blood scent, but I could—almost—hear the cop's thoughts. He believed I was guilty of something. I dropped the skim fast. What did he think I'd done?

He stamped his feet free of snow and closed the door, sealing out the cold, sealing us in, alone together. His eyes fell to my shin, exposed between the lengths of velvet, scars whiter than white. One-handed, I pulled the robe close, tightening the knot, my palm firm against the bloodstone prime amulet. The blade pressed against the flesh of my lower leg through the robe.

"Are you Thorn St. Croix Stanhope?" he asked.

I nodded, an idiot puppet, staring into his eyes, shivers running up my spine, weakening my limbs, the mage-heat he had stimulated beginning to grow. I had been a Stanhope until I took back my maiden name. But those words didn't come.

"Is there a place we could talk?"

"Yes." Talk I could handle, as long as it was general—the weather, the state of the union under the new president, the military's readiness to combat Darkness. But if it became personal, if I gave myself away, I would be in trouble. Within days I would be either dead or insane; neither option was appealing.

I led the way up the steps to the second story, the former hayloft of the two-hundred-year-old livery that had become both Thorn's Gems and my home. His footsteps followed close behind me. Heat wrapped around me like a warm fist as I entered the loft, covertly lifting the walking-stick sheath and hiding it in the robe beside the sword. Bartholomew stopped just inside the door. I could feel him scanning the open space as I crossed the width of the vast apartment and stepped behind my dressing screen.

Dropping the robe, I strapped a blade sheath to my lower left arm and inserted the blade, pulled on silk undies, slacks, and a bulky sweater over a silk tee to hide the curved blade of the shortsword. Fuzzy socks protected my cold feet and ankles, suede slippers went back over them. Silently, I resheathed the longsword in the walking stick. I could feel his apprehension from across the room, his assessment. He didn't like my being out of sight. He was thinking about his weapon.

The phone rang. I came out from behind the screen, picked it up from the worktable near my bed, knowing it was Lolo. Not assuming it or guessing it as humans would have done, but *knowing* it. Knowing it in the way of my people, in the way of the neomages. The phone rang again as I carried it to him, the cord trailing. I thought I had been sent far enough to disappear, to hide from them all forever. But here was a kylen in my apartment, a man filled with questions and judgment, and I *knew* Lolo was on the phone. *Gabriel's tears!*

"You going to answer that?"

I lifted the hard black plastic receiver and said hello. A moment later I handed it to the cop, not liking Lolo's command, but helpless to refuse. *The old witch.* "It's for you."

A strange look crossed his face. The heavy black base cradled in one hand, he lifted the receiver and said into it, "Bartholomew."

I walked to the back of the apartment, knelt at the bathtub, pulled up my right sleeve, and plunged my arm into the charged water. Power shocked to my shoulder, deadening the fear and the heat that was beginning to prickle and burn in my bloodstream. Arm in the water, I directed into the garnet-studded hilt of the kris some of the stored energy I had released into the bath, while I absorbed more into my own body. I pulled it into me the way I would before battle, had I become the battle mage Lolo once envisioned for me, long before the attack that had ended my usefulness. Long before the blossoming of my awareness that ended my tenure in Enclave and began my outlawed presence in the human world.

Steadier, calmer, my energies more balanced, I pulled the plug. Water gurgled down as I picked up one of the wet stones and stood. I scattered the salt ring with my feet, lifted my necklace of amulets and slipped it over my head, beneath the sweater, and pulled down my sleeve. The stored power in the bath stone and in my necklace soothed me.

BLOODRING

I glanced at the cop as he listened to the phone. He hadn't arrested me on sight to deport me to Enclave. He was a cop, but not an AASI. And while it seemed impossible that he didn't know what he was, impossible that he hadn't scented what I am, it was also true. If I could keep him from the tub and the scattered salt, he might never know. My secret would be safe. Thorn's Gems would be safe. My friends . . . *Fire and feathers!* I had to protect them. No one would believe I had kept my secret all these years. They would be arrested as accomplices.

The urge to fight, to draw blood, rose in me, but I tamped it down. *Not now. Not yet.* But the memory of the bloodrings sang in me, a descant of terror.

Kicking off the slippers, I curled on the big, deep cushions of the couch in front of the gas logs and pulled a green afghan over my feet as I watched Bartholomew's face. Those green-blue eyes flicked over me and stared.

"And who or what is a Lolo?" he asked into the phone.

Near the tub, my wedding ring glistened in the candlelight. The hue of the red-gold band with its spray of rubies and emeralds appeared rosier than in bright light. It had been beautiful once. Now it was ruined, the gold beaten flat, the gems shattered. Beside the ring was a damaged prime amulet, the one I had worn day and night while married. It had kept the neomage glow of my skin damped, and most of my scars hidden, even in the throes of passion, allowing me to marry a human. It was the most powerful amulet I had ever owned, one of two keyed to me at my birth, by Lolo, and I had accidentally damaged it. When I learned of Lucas' infidelity, I took a five-pound steel mallet to my wedding ring. In my rage, I'd chipped the amulet, rendering it useless. The amulet and my ring glistened in the soft light. Portents?

"Ma'am, I—"

Flames glimmered from the gas logs, their heat rising in waves, as curvy as the blade against my arm. By feel, I wrapped the bath stone in a corner of the afghan and set it by my toes. Listening, I pulled my gaze back to Bartholomew's strange-colored eyes, the exact shade of chrysocolla.

"Who gave you that information?" The cop's face was a gathering storm. "Ma'am, I—. Thank you, ma'am. I may consider . . ." He glared at the ugly black phone and hung up. I figured Lolo had broken the connection. She hated phones.

Except for me, and the few licensed witchy-women living in human lands, no neomage used technology. The presence of so much mage-power in Enclave had a deleterious effect on technology. Meaning the stuff didn't work. To make a call, Lolo had to dress for the weather, get on a horse, ride several miles to the general store near old I-10, and trade for the use of the phone. Because the store owner knew he had something valuable to Enclave, such calls were costly in terms of bartered neomage power. Very costly. Yet Lolo had done that, at just this time. She knew he was here.

"She claims to know I'm a cop and why I'm here. She's telling me there's a bloody moon. Want to tell me what's going on?"

I wasn't going to risk an outright lie but couldn't offer the complete truth. "Lolo is a licensed witchy-woman." Which was the truth as far as it went. "She was my mother's friend and I've known her since I was a baby. She knows things. She said there's danger. And a bloodring has circled the moon for two nights. To Lolo that's a strong portent."

The cop stared at me, face impassive. I resisted the impulse to squirm. Thaddeus handed me the phone and our fingers brushed. A small electric jolt kicked its way up my arm. He inhaled sharply, as if he felt the quiver of heat, and stepped back.

Mage-heat coiled and spread through me. I had felt passion with Lucas. A lot of really, really good passion. But this was different. Hotter. Something untamed and fierce. Need swam in my veins.

As he withdrew his hand, I noted his nugget ring, a large, sky blue turquoise in a massive silver setting, the band shaped like seraph wings. I set the phone on the table and pulled the afghan closer to me, hiding beneath the velvety yarn.

"Lucas Stanhope is your husband?" Thaddeus asked, towering over me.

"Ex. My divorce was final two months and three days ago." I looked at the black pig wall clock and almost added, "And thirteen hours, twelve minutes." But I didn't.

"When did you see him last?" he asked as he pulled my rocking chair close and sat, one hand draped over the carved lion-claw arm, his dark suit made even darker by the soft dun-colored upholstery. He flipped open a thin spiral notebook and uncapped a pen.

My eyes were drawn to the working of his hands, the knuckles prominent, his fingers long and tapered, with elongated index fingers. If he brushed my stomach with a closed fist, the knuckles would feel like lustrous, polished wood. I curled my toes into the stone to block the growing pull and licked my lips, which felt swollen, as if I'd been kissed. Yep. Lucky me. I was going into heat. Had to be, though I'd never gone through one before. "He dropped Ciana off for a visit the Friday morning I left town," I said. "Ten days ago."

"Ciana is your daughter?"

"His daughter by a previous marriage. I'm guessing you know all this, so why ask?"

A faint smile touched his mouth. "Procedure, ma'am. Was the divorce acrimonious?"

I closed my eyes, feeling the familiar pain. "Isn't it always? I was—justifiably—angry at him for sleeping around on me, but I managed to put it behind me for Ciana's sake. We talk off and on, mostly about her. Are you going to tell me what's happened?"

I opened my eyes and found him staring around the

apartment, up into the rafters and the lazily turning fans that pushed heated air back to the floor, around the four-foot-thick old-brick walls, some of which I'd had plastered and painted rich greens and blues. His eyes settled on my sleeping area, the armoires open, clothes hanging out, the bed turned down. The fluffed teal comforter was mounded, pillows in lavender, ruby, and turquoise, the sheets a ruby red silk. Mage-heat surged through me, offering an image of throwing him on the covers and—

"Actually"—he turned back to me, his gaze penetrating and merciless—"we have a report that Lucas was attacked in an alley and dragged off."

The words were like a blow to my stomach. My fingers curled into fists, my reaction surprising to me. I was supposed to be over Lucas. "Is he hurt?" I whispered.

"We don't know, ma'am."

My breath stuck in my throat, throbbing, as I tried to make sense of it. "He's missing?" And then I knew. The bloodring. "He's been kidnapped."

The cop's eyes were steady, watching me. "It appears so. But no ransom demand has been delivered."

"When did it happen?"

"Monday at dusk. But we learned of the attack only this morning."

Monday. While I was eating stew on the trail from Boone. Misery throbbed along the length of my scars, their sensory pathways laden with pain and blanked luminescence.

"Does Ciana know?" I asked.

"I spoke to her and Marla earlier this evening."

I should have been there for Ciana. I should have checked my messages. Shame and a feeling like grief lashed my nerve endings. "Are they all right?"

"As well as can be expected."

And then the pieces clicked into place. I knew why

Bartholomew was here in the middle of the night. Warrior instincts flung anger heat through my limbs. My muscles tensed with battle readiness. "Let me guess. I'm your 'woman scorned' suspect."

Thaddeus' brow quirked slightly and when he spoke his words were careful. "There would seem to be an awful lot of women in that category."

My anger vanished in a whip crack of laughter, the sound shaky with adrenaline overload. "You could say that. Lucas is charming and beautiful, and he sleeps around. A lot." But I noted that he hadn't discounted the idea that I might be a suspect.

I looked from the clock to the phone and answering machine, which blinked a tiny red light. I hadn't bothered to listen to the messages. It was so late. If I called now, Marla would have a hissy fit.

I couldn't sit still. Throwing off the afghan, I walked across to the kitchen, poured water into a kettle, and lit the gas stove with a match from a box on the table. The lighting mechanism on the stove had died ages ago and I had never bothered to replace it. A fire amulet worked well enough, and I had matches for when there was company. I set the kettle on the burner.

Ciana would be mad with worry. Marla would only make things worse. I could almost see Lucas' first wife joking about the incident, finding humor in his being hurt, laughing about it in front of Ciana. "What happened? Can you tell me?" I asked over my shoulder as I got out two mugs and a jar of herbal tea. Chamomile, passion fruit, and rose hips for their calming properties. I dumped four tablespoons into the pot, needing a powerful draught.

When I turned around, the cop was right behind me. He was wide, tapering to a narrow waist, taller than any mage, who are small and trim. Much taller than I, at my four feet ten inches. One hand was in his pants pocket, the cashmere suit coat pushed back, exposing the silver and turquoise of his belt buckle and, surely accidentally, a gun, reminding me of the danger he represented. Yet he looked so right in my home, as if he'd been there forever. "Nice house," he said.

"It was the town livery," I said, an inane comment, but the silence was charged, my emotions in a snarl. I had a powerful desire to slide my hand between the buttons of his shirt and touch his chest. Would he arrest me for assault? A witless laugh tittered in the back of my throat and I chattered to cover it. "It was built for the horses and mules used to build the railroad back in the early twentieth century. The wooden parts are post and beam, hand-hewn logs, twelve-by-twelve supports, and ten-by-ten beams for the roof structure," I pointed over his head, his eyes following my hand. "Exterior walls are four-foot-thick stone and brick." It was a charming mishmash of materials I loved, a style unique to Upper Street.

When I looked back to him, his eyes were on my hair, which was still piled high in a scarlet tumble from the bath. Then his eyes trailed down, over my ear, my jaw. My neck. To my mouth. I shivered, need purling deep inside. "Where have you been the last two days?"

I hadn't expected the question. I had expected him to say something else entirely, or hoped he would. The heat he generated quivered in my belly. "At a Salvage and Mineral Swap Meet."

"At the market in Boone?"

"Yes," I said, surprised he knew about it.

"Can anyone substantiate that?"

"I was seen by a few people I know. I have receipts for purchases—" I stopped. I had released a rune of forgetting after most of my sales, and I had been disguised for almost all the purchases. I had to be careful. Few would remember me, and the cop would think that strange. "I had coffee with Fazelle and Nova Henderson, owners of Henderson Shielded Mine. I had a spa day Sunday afternoon, after kirk services were over and locals were allowed out to work. I left for home on the Monday morning mule train, with Guide Hoop Marks. Spent the night on the trail. I got into town tonight after eight p.m. You can check."

"I will. Will you provide me the names of the people you remember from the show?"

My first stubborn instinct was to refuse. It wasn't his business whom I had seen in Boone, but Lucas was in trouble. Which shouldn't have bothered me—shouldn't, but did. I gave him the names and addresses of people with whom I had bargained while not wearing my glamour disguise, including Audric, and he copied them down in his little notebook, seeming not to note that one address was right next door. The kettle sang and I poured out two mugs of tea, straining the loose leaves with a silver strainer, and handed him a cup. He asked a few more questions that seemed to slide right out of my memory the second I answered.

And then he was leaving. I followed him down the steps to the outer door of Thorn's Gems and locked the shop behind him. Standing in the shadow, I watched as he moved through the snow across the sidewalk toward the town's only hotel.

The last hour was a blur of nothingness in my mind, a fuzz of sound and need, and when he was gone, I made it back upstairs, where I fell against the closed door. *A kylen! Had Lolo sent him? Why hadn't I been inside his mind? Was it his human genes?* I had to stay away from him. But if mage-heat kicked in full force, I'd be hard-pressed not to take him in the streets.

Dizziness and need rocked me. I stripped and pulled on flannel pajamas, but heat and cold, sexual attraction and fear, seemed to have invaded my body. I couldn't get warm, couldn't get comfortable. I pulled three more bath stones from the tub and huddled with them under the down duvet on my bed, drawing from their power. When I had myself under control, I listened to messages while sipping cooling tea, hitting the button until I heard the sound of Ciana's voice. She was crying, begging me to call.

Knowing she wouldn't be able to sleep after learning her father was missing, I dialed her number. Of course, Marla answered and wouldn't let me talk to Ciana, though I could hear the child of my heart begging in the background. Instead, Marla called me a few names banned just after the start of the Last War and hung up on me. Frustrated, my last nerve thoroughly stomped on, I replaced the receiver and sipped my cold tea.

Chapter 3

†

I slept with the charged bath stones, still warm from the water and leaking power that I absorbed as I rested. The radiance healed the effect of two days of rigorous riding and of having been in a city surrounded by technology and strange people, of bathing in water collected from both sky and earth, pooled stream water augmented by snowmelt, which confused my senses and drained my neomage gifts. The stones restored energies spent hiding what I was under almost constant glamour, a glamour hard to maintain now that I no longer had my strongest prime amulet. When I woke, I felt healed, though my bath had been interrupted and snow was piled high beyond the windows. I'd have to sleep with charged stones more often. The princess and the pea, I wasn't.

In the dull light of early morning, as roosters in the surrounding area crowed up a racket, I stretched before moving into the flowing exercises of savage-chi, the martial art created by the earliest neomages when they came under attack by frightened humans. The movements turned violent as I whirled and slashed, kicked and blocked, channeling and expending the leftover fear and sexual energy stirred by the kylen cop.

After I worked up a sweat, I took up the swords. Holding the ebony walking-stick sheath, I slipped the longsword free with my right hand and fully extended the blade. In my left I took the twelve-inch kris and sweated another ten minutes, executing savage-blade, concentrating on prime moves, not graduating to secondary moves. Though calmer, I was too shaky, too heated, for more advanced forms. I might accidentally draw my own blood.

Refreshed, I washed in cold springwater, made the bed, and dressed in teal, ocean green, and a turquoise scarf to accent green chrysocolla jewelry I would display in the shop. My outer clothing was layered against the cold, slim underleggings against my legs with wool-and-silk-blend trousers. Winter made it easier to blank the glow of neomage flesh, as there was so little of it exposed. I dulled the pearl sheen and the whiter glow of scar tissue with an amulet charged for that purpose. Every scar still showed, had, ever since I damaged the prime amulet, but I could still pass for an injured, long-healed human. I looped my necklace of amulets around my waist under my clothes.

I had fallen asleep with my hair up and it still looked good, so I dropped it, ran my fingers through the strands, and smoothed my tumble of red curls back into a twisted mass, securing it with an oversized butterfly clip. I added a bit of makeup, which I seldom needed to use, letting the amulets do the work of expensive products. Today I added lipstick and blush.

I didn't examine why I wanted to look my best today, but thoughts of Thaddeus Bartholomew fluttered deep in my belly. A kylen was in town, next best thing to a seraph—a winged warrior—also longed for but denied. Not that I'd ever even seen a seraph up close.

Except twice a decade, seraphs and neomages aren't permitted to be in close proximity. Once every five years, a dozen seraphs chosen by the Seraphic High Host, the ruling council of seraphs, fly over each of the Enclaves and hover long enough to stimulate mage-heat. As soon as mage-heat comes on the Enclaves, signaling that mage females have ovulated and are capable of breeding, the seraphs chosen for the duty are forced to depart, their own desires unsatisfied. Mages and seraphs can't resist each other, and physical interspecies relations between them had long been disallowed by the ArchSeraph Michael. The flyover concession was allowed by the council so that mages could breed.

Neomages had never been prophesied, but our extinction seemingly wasn't in the plans of God the Victorious. Clipping on my jewelry, I took the stairs to Thorn's Gems, the jewelry shop I owned with my two best friends.

We had started as a poor and struggling jewelry store, producing stone, metal, and glass items for retail shops across the East Coast. Because Mineral City was fairly remote, we concentrated on the Internet, with a complete online catalogue, but we barely made enough to survive the first few years. When Chamuel, the seraph called "God's pure love in winged manifestation," wore one of our necklaces on television, our star rose fast. Because of the seraph, Thorn's Gems was thriving, our designs sought after by the rich and famous, as well as by seraph chasers, the groupies who followed seraphic updates as if they were scripture.

Downstairs, I lit the gas fire, put on water for tea and ground beans for coffee. The winter-month minutia of the shop eased me. I had no time for dark fantasies, only to prepare for customers.

The scent of fresh hazelnut coffee drifted from the tin percolator. The Mr. Coffee had died last year, and this time the town's handyman had been unable to revive it. I still missed the ease of its use. The last twenty-five years had seen a resurgence of technology, but household items hadn't yet reappeared.

Water sizzled in a copper kettle resting on the cast-iron top of the gas fireplace. I poured cream into a tiny pitcher and scooped carefully hoarded honey-sugar into a crystal bowl, then stacked china cups and saucers. Ancient silver spoons Audric had dead-mined from his abandoned town under the aegis of the Salvage Laws were stacked on folded napkins. As I worked, my desire faded to a dull thump deep in my bones.

"Dearie, you look . . . diff-er-rent," a voice said. "My, my, my. Who is he? Give papa details."

"Can it, Rupert," I said, bending over the huntboard we used for refreshments. I hadn't heard him enter and kept my back to him, pouring a cup of the rich brew as an excuse not to look up. "I heard about Lucas," I added as a distraction.

"Have you seen it? He made the morning news."

I looked up as Rupert turned on the television mounted high in the corner. The connection buzzed, warming.

"And of course, Gramma called, all in a dither, demanding that I *do* something, that I ride to her favorite's rescue, that I come stay with her until all this 'unpleasantness is resolved,' as she put it." Rupert shivered delicately. "That is sooooo not going to happen."

Rupert, who had fallen in love with Pre-Ap musicals, claimed he had been born in the wrong century, believing he was made for the stage. Today he was in a dramatic, full-blown theatrical mode, wearing indigo blue in an Arabic cut, flowing robes and silky textures that complemented his pale skin. Navy liner and a heavy coat of mascara circled his black eyes. Dangerous if the kirk elders came around, though his Pre-Apocalyptic thespian style brought in many of our big-paying clients.

The picture cleared and he tuned the TV to SNN. Three digital video feeds ran simultaneously, two stacked rectangles on the left with the events of the day, and a long, narrow one on the right of a reporter dressed in purple robes made fashionable by the seraph Uriel last year in his appearance at the White House. Three text messages raced across the bottom of the screen. Everything in threes.

The television blinked and brightened. With the first instant of video feed, I was reminded of the holiday. This was the hundred and fifth anniversary of the start of the Last War, and the eighty-seventh anniversary of the last great battle.

"This date marks the commemoration of both the first and the final battles, the date when all mankind celebrates the end of the world," the announcer intoned. I snorted. Only humans could celebrate the death of six billion people. "Here, the modern world first saw the death seraph Azrael as he lifted his sword over the city of Paris at the start of the first of the three great plagues—"

Rupert muted the sound and placed a hand on my shoulder. On the screen, the ancient handheld video camera captured the first ray of scintillating light, the bursting prism of power as a seraph of death appeared in a cloud of fire, alighting on the very tip of the Eiffel Tower, golden wings outspread, sword held aloft. Azrael, the harbinger of the end of the world.

Well, sort of. Things hadn't quite worked out like the great prophets had expected.

In the famous video, the shot tilted as the camera fell and bounced, landed, still running, but resting on the former photographer's body, the seraph framed as he lifted his sword. The photographer's hand appeared at the bottom of the field of view, twitching, changing color to ruby red, then bleeding as capillaries swelled and burst. The twitching stopped. The seraph turned and faced the camera, as if he knew it still recorded him. I didn't have to turn the sound up to remember the famous words as Azrael cursed the city in the name of the Most High. Only one thousand people in the whole of the city of Paris survived the first plague. One thousand.

The screen changed, displaying the customary three shots

of SNN. In the largest, I saw the mushroom clouds of the few nuclear explosions, the first detonating in what had been the Koreas and in China, followed by the three on the West Coast of the United States, eight in Russia, two in the former Holy Lands, and ten on the continent of Africa.

In the stacked footage on the left of the screen were the twin seraphs, Mordad and Murdad, swords raised over Jerusalem and Mecca, respectively. The center screen mutated to the arrival of Metatron over Washington, D.C. Metatron, raven feathered, the seraph of death. Not one person in the most powerful city on the face of the planet had survived the first plague, all dead in less than twenty-four hours, though the president and his cabinet had escaped into a bunker somewhere and survived. Then shots of the Kremlin, St. Petersburg, Tokyo, Singapore, Bombay, Frankfurt, Geneva, and on and on as hundreds of thousands, as millions, died in the streets, all on the first day of the first plague.

The second plague followed, wars, pestilence, death, all displayed on the three screens, fast-tracking the end of the world as it once was. Not once did the Most High appear. As always, the announcer would be careful not to voice the fact that God the Victorious had never been caught on film. The only time a reporter had commented on the fact, she had fallen dead on the set, suffering a massive pulmonary embolism and cardiac arrest. All quite natural, or so they'd said. No news analyst since had been brave enough to test the theory.

Each of the three screens depicted storms, as the earth's climate underwent terrible change from mild global warming to ice age in months, the result of nuclear bombs, volcanoes, and earthquakes, just as scientists had long predicted. Not that there were many scientists around to gloat. Nine in ten had died, in proportion to the rest of humanity, the wrath of the Most High, God the Victorious, sparing no one in any socioeconomic, intellectual, or religious group.

BLOODRING

The screen shifted, showing rioting in the streets as fanatics from every major religion claimed the end of the world and the ascendancy of their own belief system. The seraphs reappeared, this time not glowing and beautiful, but dark, faces carved with anger. The third great plague had punished the rioters doing violence in the name of the Most High. Rioters dropped where they stood. Then the plague moved on to the rest of the human population, striking mostly rural areas. In this plague, called the Plague of Punishment, no children under the age of six had perished.

To appease the seraphic host, governments appointed elders authorized to prohibit religious violence, to mete out punishment, to organize different believers in each locale, and to force them to cooperate. Many elders also had secular, political aspirations and ran for public office on county councils, in state legislatures, even for president. For a hundred years there had been little separation of church and state. Elders were cop, preacher, referee, judge, and hangman.

As SNN chronicled the end of the world, the three screens showed the arrival of the Angel of Darkness in a cloud of hornets, locusts, hail, and fire. Devil-spawn poured up from the ground and devoured dead and dying humans in a scene so grisly, I always closed my eyes against the sight of blood, brimstone, and tearing teeth. Cold chills raced up my arms. Nausea rose. My hands were tingling, breath too fast. My nostrils flared, scent searching. My heart raced. I longed for my blades, needing the comforting warmth of the bloodstone hilt in my hand as my blood raged.

Dragons, later identified as Major Powers, directed battles against seraphs, their centipede or spider or snake bodies, with human hands and serpent heads, crushing entire towns. The stuff of nightmares. Because the seraphs turned against this new evil with swords raised and voices booming, many humans fought with them against the common enemy.

As the war progressed, the ice caps grew, Darkness became more bold, and bands of seraphs and humans took the war underground, where the Powers lived and bred. Finally, in the last great battle, seraphs, mages, and humans fought side by side against the Darkness, driving evil into the deeps, though announcers seldom mention neomage contributions.

I looked away from the death of the old world and the violent, bloody birth of the new. The world that followed the end of the Last War had become a world of peace, of political and religious accord, at least on the surface. But mage priestesses had prophesied that war would come again soon; it wasn't over. Not that humans listened.

The announcer appeared in the center screen, mouth moving. The footage of the hundred and fifth was done. The top screen went dark and a murky scene emerged, a jerky digital feed, distorted. A man was walking fast down a dark alley, a knapsack slung over his shoulder. The figure was lit for a moment in the edge of a security light, a peaceful aftermath to the historic videos, yet my heart thudded, stuttered once, and started again. I put a hand to my chest against the pain. It was Lucas, shadowed by a growth of beard, his deep-set eyes only dark holes until he lifted his head to reveal his face. My gut tightened. He was still beautiful. Far too beautiful.

We have a report that Lucas was attacked in an alley and dragged off, Bartholomew had said. Not a report. A security-camera video.

On the screen, boxes and a woodpile stood to one side, scooters and a tangle of bicycles half visible at the extremity of the circle of illumination. A shadow slithered in the dark, disjointed and stiff. A second shadow flitted, resolving into the shape of a man moving forward fast. A third shadow joined the rush and the two collided with Lucas. He went down to a knee and one hand.

Arms reared back and slammed down, feet kicked viciously. Lucas fell, covering his head, shielding his face. Blows punched on the hazy screen, the silence adding to the horror as my mind waited for the sound of impacts, grunts, the echo of screams. There was only silence. The violence depicted in the anniversary video was far more bloody, but this was personal, intimate. Chills raced up the back of my neck. Lucas' face was covered in blood. I gripped my wrists, wishing I'd worn blades, feeling naked, vulnerable.

The body on the ground was dragged away, leaving the ruptured knapsack pushed to the side, its contents scattered. A smear marked the path the assailants took as they pulled him out of the camera's view. Blood. Lucas' blood.

Coffee was forgotten. Chills whispered down my arms, lifting the fine hairs. Horror danced along in the icy wake. Rupert raised the level of sound as the announcer spoke.

"This vicious attack is similar to those shown on television in Pre-Apocalyptic times, a memory of violence the human race has put behind us, unsuccessfully, as we see all too often. This assault reminds us once again that the final judgment has not taken place and evil still lives in the hearts of humans—" Rupert muted the sound again on his falsely pious voice.

"Violence we've put behind us?" Rupert mused. "There's a scene of a mob attacking a woman convicted of black magic in the lower screen. A mutilated body was found in the outskirts of Atlanta last week, a 'crime of passion,' they're calling it. The disappearance of a mule train outside Knoxville, evidence of bloody conflict buried in the snow. Might be human, might be spawn. Drained bodies near Linville. Violence is everywhere." Rupert braced himself on the huntboard. "And the media caters to the propaganda of the Administration of the ArchSeraph in hiding it all." It was a dangerous sentiment, should a kirk elder overhear. But there was worry in Rupert's voice. I could smell a trace of fear on the air. "The cops came to the door last night," he added. "They think I had Lucas kidnapped and killed to get at his part of the inheritance."

I sat slowly on the worn heart-pine floor, my legs giving
out, weakness rising through my bones, turning them to water.
On the TV, the upper video feed began again. Lucas walking
down the alley. I felt sick, the taste of toothpaste in my mouth
replaced by a sour tang, my stomach burning. The pull of the
snow outside was a weakness in my bones. Lucas looked up,
eyes flashing. Shadows twisted and undulated in the dark.

On the screen, shadows resolved into humans. They attacked. Bludgeoned Lucas. His body was dragged away. The feed
began again, a continuous loop. Lucas walked down the alley.
Looked up. Shadows moved.

"How can you be so . . ." I swallowed, unable to finish, and
clasped my knees. *This is his brother.* I rocked slowly on the cold
planking.

"I've been looking at it all morning." The words hid whatever Rupert was feeling, but his body was stiff as he stared at the
screen.

After a long moment and three more replays of the attack, Rupert fluffed his sleeves and said, "Oh, for pity's sake.
You can't just sit on the floor." He bent over and lifted me with
a grunt into the soft, cushioned chair I favored. Adding cream
to his coffee, he stirred in honey-sugar with soft tinks of silver on china, then poured heated water into my cup. He added
a silver strainer filled with tea leaves and set the cup in my
chilled hands. "Don't make me hover. That's *so* déclassé for a
gay man."

"Turn it up," I said, ignoring both his worry and his attempt to make me smile.

As Rupert turned the volume up again, a reporter's voice
rose slowly, his face centered on the long screen reserved for
live feed. "Again, Satellite News Network has obtained special
permission from the Federal Satellite Broadcast Administration to air the video of human-on-human violence you see
rolling in the left corners of your screen. This is Oliver Win-

ston, live on the scene in Mineral City, Carolina, with Jane Hilton, the victim's new wife."

I jerked with the word, sloshing my tea. *Wife?* "No ..." Rupert stood at my back, a hand on my shoulder as the woman lifted her head. She was breathtaking, with blond hair and vivid eyes, a sculpted, anguished face.

"I just want him back," she whispered. "That's all. Please bring him back. Please. I love him." She dropped her head into her hands and wept a moment before lifting her face again to the reporter. Her eyes hardened, frightened but determined.

"Seraphs," Jane said, "I call on you to help." Her voice caught, as if she were strangling, and when she spoke again, she had to force the words out. "Help my Lucas. I'm begging you! Surely there is a winged warrior, a seraph somewhere, who would help against this evil. Please. Heed my call!"

"Very dramatic." Rupert fell into the plush chair beside mine, his hand still on my shoulder in comfort. "She didn't even smear her mascara."

"Hush," I said, my attention on the scene and the warmly dressed reporter.

Winston, the microphone held at his mouth, was still speaking. "Will a seraph answer her? In the last twenty years, humans have seldom seen the seraphim," he said, using the formal political designation rather than the casual "seraphs." "Since the last great battle, few have been seen outside of war videos, only in rare sightings as they depart and enter Realms of Light. The last significant seraph update was over seven years ago, outside the Realm that was once Manhattan Island. And no non-seraph, except for the kylen, half-breed seraphs themselves, have ever entered a Realm. Will that change? Will the Seraphic High Host help this distraught woman find her husband?

"This is Oliver Winston, SNN reporter at large, live in Mineral City, Carolina, with the latest on the attack of local citizen Lucas Stanhope. Updates and residents' responses to this most unusual crime as they happen. This is SNN. Glory to the Victorious."

Winston's face was replaced with the face of a familiar anchorwoman. She was recapping the event as Rupert again turned down the sound.

"Don't worry. The police will find Lucas. Drink your tea." When I didn't comply, my eyes on the scene in the upper corner of the screen, Rupert lifted my hands with his, carrying the cup to my lips. "Drink." This time it was a command, and I sipped, the taste of rose hips and blackberry in a strong black tea sweet on my tongue.

On the screen, below the replay, was a different scene, the stoning of a woman taken in the act of black magic the night before. As she fell, she cursed the attackers and exposed her breasts. There was no sound as the rocks fell. And again, blood. Human blood. Human violence. Public access stations airing footage.

When had it begun, this sudden relaxing of the standards and rules imposed on the media so long ago by the High Host of Seraphim? Surely the president or Congress would demand a halt. If they didn't, I wondered how long it would continue before the High Host intervened and wholesale slaughter brought the human population back under control. The High Host didn't ask for things to be done. They didn't confer. They just punished humans when they didn't follow the rules.

Chapter 4

†

I checked the clock over the door. I had half an hour before opening. It might be enough time. "I have to go back upstairs." I was running, taking the stairs to my loft with renewed energy dancing through me. From below I heard Rupert call a muffled "But Thorn, we—" as I slammed the door and clicked the latch. I fell against the door, taking in the apartment.

My pulse was thrumming, a basso tone in my ears. This was dumb. I didn't even know whether I could actually do it. I might hurt myself. I might expose myself, but I had to try, didn't I? If I could find and rescue Lucas, then no seraph would have to come to Mineral City and intervene. And find me.

I shoved my body from the door and flew to the tub, grabbing candles and the bag of coarse salt. Not sea salt, but salt mined from the ground. Salt of the earth, of power I could draw upon. I dropped them at the edge of the dark turquoise tile floor in the kitchen area, added stones from the bath, the bed, the windows, and the tables, piling them in a pyramid of pink marble, white quartz crystal, agate, others. From pebbles to fist-sized rocks, rounded smooth with my grindstone, not by river water and nature.

I added some jewelry imbued with wisdom and sacrifice: a jade netsuke on a silver chain, three antique crucifixes, two hung with the Christ in agony, a free-form fire opal wrapped in silver wire, and my own half-drained, blackened-steel-mail amulet necklace, which I removed from around my waist. On the necklace were stones keyed to my central nervous system.

I dumped artificial greenery from a heavy silver bowl; flowers and leaves scrolled around the rim. The bowl was Pre-Ap, sent to me by Lolo ten years ago but never used for neomage purposes. Lastly, I took up my damaged wedding ring, symbol of commitment and betrayal, its stones the tint of blood and living things, rubies and emeralds.

I shoved the kitchen table against the cabinets, exposing the floor. The tiles were poured stoneware from clay collected in Mexico, near a battlefield where seraphs, humans, and demons had once fought an earth-rending war. The glaze was composed of mineral pigments Lolo had charged to my protection before shipping to me on a summer train. Taking up the bag of unused salt, I poured a heavy ring in a circle six feet in diameter, leaving a foot of space open for me to enter.

I positioned candles around the outside of the ring, dithering about the number until I settled on just three. There was both power and risk in numbers. If a nearby seraph found me, then he found me. I filled the bowl at the sink and set it in the exact center of the salt ring, springwater sloshing gently. I set my ceremonial knife, hidden in plain view in the cutting block, to the side of the stones. Lastly, I pulled the *Book of Workings* from the shelf beside my bed, finding the incantation I needed in the index and placing the open book on the floor by the bowl. Three empty stones went into the bowl, bringing the water lapping to its top.

I sat within the circle, at the open space in the salt ring, crossed my legs yogi fashion, and closed my eyes. Spine erect, I blew out a tension-filled breath and drew in a calming one.

Again. And again. Serenity fluttered just out of reach, distanced by fear. I didn't know what I was doing.

I'd been removed from Enclave for my health and sanity long before I would have learned how to do this. I knew the theory. I knew how it was supposed to be done. But I'd never practiced a skill I thought I'd never need.

I breathed, calm just beyond my reach. The silence of the loft settled about me. A brittle tranquility finally rested on my shoulders. My breath smoothed. My heart beat slowly, methodically. All glamour fell from me. Behind my closed lids, my own flesh was a gentle radiance, the brighter glow of my old scars tracing down my legs and arms. I opened my eyes, seeing now with mage-sight.

The loft pulsed with power, a place of neomage safety I had created in the humans' world. Stones were everywhere, at bath and bed and gas fireplaces, every window and doorway, the floor. From them, every aspect of my home glowed with pale energy, subtle harmonious shades of lavender, green, rose, red, yellow. The great human scientist, Einstein, had once reasoned that mass and energy must somehow be different manifestations of the same thing. Mage-sight saw that energy in everything.

As I closed the circle with two handfuls of salt, power seized me. Power from the beginning of time, heard as much as felt. It hummed through me, a drone, an echo of the first Word ever spoken. The first Word of Creation. The reverberation was captured in the core of the earth for me to draw upon, a constant, unvarying power of stone and mineral, the destructive potency of liquid rock and heat. I trembled as vibrations rolled through my bones and pulsed into my flesh. I could *see* the thrum of strength, the force, the raw, raging might of the earth, a molten mantle seeking outlet. Finding me. I was a crucible for incandescent energy, mine to use.

Power. The need for it, the lust for it, rose in me. Waves of lava bowed my spine, clawed my hands into weapons. *I can take what I want.* I *was* the strength of the earth, the might of the core, the power of its creation. A scream built deep in my chest.

Dis de moment of absolute choice, Lolo's voice rang within my memory, *of ultimate danger. What you do with all dis might?*

With a single motion, I slid the necklace of amulets over my head. The scream withered unreleased.

I pulled in a breath burning with freedom from the power crave. A breath that refreshed and satiated, yet ached deep in my lungs. I could breathe; I could think. I returned to myself.

The loft was unchanged. There was still a pulsing glow to the room, but now the power appeared distilled and clarified to my mage-eye. A sharper vision to remind me that I had stepped close to the abyss, stared into its depths, and conquered myself.

The *Book of Workings* was constructed of blackberry ink on handmade paper. Unlike the rest of the room, the book and its pages contained little luminescence. The book itself wasn't a thing of power. At the top of the page was written in ancient calligraphy, "Scrying for a Human." Not a spell, not really an incantation, nothing so mundane; only a guide, a map of sorts, showing me the way to use my gifts. Strangely, the directions were in the final third of the book, the section dedicated to warfare, and required mage-blood and three candles.

I studied the recipe and my arrangement for the invocation. Lucas was taken with violence and blood. Those facts led the way. I hung the crucifixes around my neck, in contact with my amulets, and took the fire opal pendant in my left hand with the netsuke, the two stones connecting with each other. A soft resonance of energy gathered each time stone met stone, as crystalline matrix touched matrix.

I swiveled on my backside and faced the bowl, took up the knife in my right hand and slipped the wedding ring onto my left little finger. I stared into the water and improvised.

BLOODRING

Dangerous. The muted warning slipped through me, unheeded memory. From the Old Testament, I paraphrased lines suggested in my book for finding a human.

"And the revenger of blood find him," I chanted. "And the revenger of blood find him. And the revenger of blood find him." With the point of the knife, I sliced my finger. The sting shocked through me.

"We send, and they shall search out the land and bring us word again. . . ." A trail of blood slid down my finger and collected in my palm, a growing crimson pool.

"Then shalt inquire, and make search and ask diligently." I dropped the netsuke and amulets into the blood, smearing both before dangling them on their chains from my wrist. "And behold, if it be truth, and the thing certain, that such an abomination is wrought among you"—this was the dangerous part, the creative words I tossed into the mix—"that evil has been done to this man, in the spilling of his blood. That ye seek Lucas Stanhope to save him." Setting down the knife, I pulled the ring from my finger and placed the gold circle into my blood. My shivers became a hard shudder, a quake of energy that roared through me in a heavy wave. "Find me such a one as Lucas."

I dropped the gold band into the water. Three drops of blood followed, soft, distinct splats. Three candles, three stones, three drops of blood. Three and three and three. My blood swirled into the charged water. "Show me Lucas." Blood diluted, spreading, as it spun lower. "Show me Lucas." My blood touched the stones in the bottom. The water stilled, darkened. Power rose from the earth. My blood thrummed in my ears. The stones on the bottom of the bowl wrenched energy from the depths of the land. They heated. A thin mist of steam rose.

As he slipped a ring onto my finger, I saw Lucas, his face, full of love and tenderness. The vision dissipated in a surge of mist.

In its swirling whiteness a form took shape. Lucas, naked, on our bed. He was laughing, his beautiful blue eyes blazing with passion. Lips swollen with kisses, his body full with his need. He held out his arms, the wedding ring I made for him on his finger. A woman came to him, draped by a diaphanous gown, a floating gauzy thing that slipped from her shoulders.

Pain slithered through me. *How could he . . .?*

Lucas moved up her body in a sensual glide, his face between her breasts. Her head fell back and Jane Hilton laughed low, the sound lost beneath the resonance of energy humming in my mind.

The power of truth steamed up from the water. The certainty of history.

A tear slid down my cheek. He had given himself to me. And then he had slept with that woman. Slept with Jane Hilton while married to me.

I was seeing history. Two histories. One of my marriage and the vow of eternity together. Then this one of Lucas' betrayal. The memory of my wedding ring as I picked it up had been of commitment and betrayal. I hadn't performed a scrying. I had miscalculated. I had performed a truth vision.

I blew on the steam, blinked away the vision, and wiped my face on the scarf at my shoulder, smearing my makeup. Dangerous indeed, but not as I might have expected.

Blood was still liquid on my hand. I would try again. Lifting three more stones from the pile, I placed them in the water, which had evaporated in the steamy visions, leaving just enough space. When the water settled, I plunged my hand into it, the netsuke and fire opal tinking on the stones at the bottom.

"Let me find grace in your eyes," I quoted from Genesis, still trying to banish the memory of truth. I bounced around, paraphrasing the Old Testament, choosing verses that seemed appropriate, my words soft and slightly slurred. "Can we find such a one as this is . . .? Thou shalt find Lucas if thou seek him. . . . Come and I will show you the man you seek," I finished.

The mist swirled, revealing the back of a man's head. He was bent over a bowl of oatmeal on a table, eating. Reddish hair, shaggy and long, curled over his collar. He sat up, spoon bouncing into the bowl without a clatter. Thaddeus Bartholomew looked around the room, his strange green eyes taking in every patron and server, wary, on alert. But he saw nothing suspicious.

Heat sparked in the pit of my stomach, coiling, expanding. An image of Thaddeus, naked on my bed, took shape in my mind, separate from the vision, vibrating with a different kind of power. A look of perplexity crossed his face, followed by a deeper kind of shock. His pupils widened. He half stood. The mist faded on the vision, thinned, and was gone.

The water was glowing to my mage-eye, but no longer hot. My hand rested in the water on top of six stones. An imperfect number giving me an imperfect vision. Or had it? Hadn't I asked to be shown the man I seek? The man who sought Lucas?

Pulling my hand from the warm water, I dried it on my scarf and looked at the clock. I was late. I broke the salt circle, releasing all the stored power, returning the loft to its mundane appearance, and myself along with it. I dumped out the water and swept up the used salt, pouring it into a separate plastic bag, which I labeled TRUTH/LUST. I placed the pile of stones at the fireplace where they belonged, heated stones for warming my bed at night. I stowed all my other neomage equipment—bowl, book, and candles—in its place, even sweeping up last night's used salt from the tub, which I had forgotten.

I bandaged my finger, knowing scar tissue would pucker it slightly, a remembrance of today, before refolding my scarf to hide the makeup smear I could wash out later. I damped my skin from pearly to human, and freshened my makeup, all in three and a half minutes. I was almost out the door, only a bit late, when the phone rang. And I knew it was Lolo.

With trepidation I picked it up. "Good morning, Lolo."

"*C'est le fol de mon sang?*" the Cajun woman raged.

"Fool of your blood?" I felt my own blood drain to my feet.

"*Oui! Le fol! O, c'est tous les soirs, moi, je me couche avec des larmes dedans mes yeux—*"

"In English, Lolo," I interrupted. "I can't—"

"You makin' trouble, gurl! De police, dey trouble. Les seraphs, dey trouble what to come. Trouble in de sky, trouble in de deep. Danger come, and you make blood sacrifice on de full moon, scream you power to heaven. All hear. *Fol*, fol *de mon sang*, you."

My pulse pounded in my ears. The moon was full. I had forgotten. Forgotten that, for a stone mage, Luna in her glory resulted in malformed incantations and attention from on high. I sat slowly, my couch cushions sighing softly.

During the Last War, the full and new moons were when practitioners of black magic, humans who had joined the Dragon of Darkness, the Big D, had done blood sacrifice of innocents and attacked seraphs, wounding many to the point of death. Even now, seraphs remained on hyperalert during the full and new moons, watching for a resurgence of blood sacrifice and black magic. And I, the only unlicensed neomage living outside of protective Enclave, hiding in plain sight, had just spilled my own blood in the full moon. *Glory and infamy.* What had I done? Can one even perform black magic by accident? Doesn't intent have to be part of the ritual? Or is spilling blood enough?

"I make a protection aroun' you. But dat no enough. I fear. I fear fo' you."

"I'll be careful, Lolo."

The call was disconnected without good-byes, as always, and I slowly replaced the receiver. What had I done?

"Did you see?" Ciana burst through the door of the shop and slammed into me, enveloping me in a hug that crushed my waist and forced out a grunt of pain. "My Daddy got kidnapped." The words came muffled from my clothing as I caught my balance.

My heart clenched and I wrapped her in my arms. "I saw. It was awful. But I'm here, darlin'." What could I say? Should I lie and tell her everything would be all right? It might not be, even if we got Lucas back. He had been injured, maybe pretty badly. I remembered the boots kicking him.

"He's dead, isn't he?" she asked, her tone wounded, perfumed with fear.

"Oh, Ciana, no, I hope not." I rocked her, tears gathering in my eyes.

"I'm praying about it. After school, I'm going to kirk and praying to God the Victorious to save him. Will you come?" she begged.

Shock tightened my hands on her shoulders. *To the kirk?* Dangerous thoughts overlapped about Lolo's warning, about my fear of the High Host, about human whispers that their cries were no longer heard, or that the Most High might have turned against the earth and the life he created. And the secret blasphemies that no one had seen God, not ever, that he might not exist, might not ever have existed. About the danger I was already in, and that I shouldn't call attention to myself by going to kirk too often or too seldom, all washed through me as I opened my mouth to answer. In the end nothing could stop me from helping Ciana. "Of course I'll go with you. If Marla doesn't mind."

"Mama thinks it's funny," Ciana whispered into my waist, her arms tightening. "She keeps watching the TV when daddy falls. And on top of that, she called me a liar."

I rocked her against me, finding Rupert on the far side of the store watching us, his eyes filling with tears. Rupert loved kids, and Ciana especially. He worried because she was being raised in loveless, chaotic, emotionally tumultuous homes, by parents who lived apart and hated each other. He held up a mug, mouthed *cocoa*, and pointed at the seating area. "Well, that sucks Habbiel's pearly toes," I said to Ciana, nodding at Rupert. Of course we would part with a small serving of the shop's fantastically expensive, imported chocolate. "I'm sorry, darlin'."

Ciana sobbed and hiccuped into my clothes.

"Come on." I pulled her toward the small kettle where milk now simmered. "Let's get some hot cocoa into you and get you calmed down enough for school. And I'll be here at five for the trip to the kirk," I promised, dread already building in my heart.

"Tell Thorn why Marla called you a liar," Rupert said softly.

"You won't laugh, will you?" Ciana looked up at me, her dark hair mussed, her blue eyes—so like Lucas'—wet with tears. She sat in my favorite chair and curled her legs under her, legging-covered knees and leather shoes sticking out beneath her school uniform tunic. Ciana was eight and very bright, far too intelligent to lie to successfully. My dread grew.

"Never," I said, stirring cocoa and sugar into the steaming milk.

Her face a careful blank, Ciana said, "I saw a devil-spawn yesterday."

I stopped stirring the cocoa, swirls of clumped chocolate rising and dropping as the milk whirled.

"I was in the hills at the base of the Trine and he came up to me." Her voice grew challenging as she spoke, ending on a mutinous note.

I put down the mug and bent over her, shoving her hair back and inspecting her throat. Lifting her wrists, staring into her eyes.

"Stop that." Ciana pushed me away, a half grin replacing the defiance, knowing my inspection meant I believed her. Devil-spawn made a mockery of the sacrament. Children of a Dark seraph and a human, born in litters like rats, they drank blood and ate human flesh, among other abominations.

"He didn't attack. He just talked to me and took off. Like, vanished." Her hands made little finger snaps as if scattering water. "Poof, you know?" She wiped the last of her tears.

"I know." Everyone had seen video feed of captured devilspawn. "Poof" was an accurate description of their speed. "Why were you out on the Trine at night?"

"It wasn't night." Ciana took the mug and stirred, the tinktink of silver against stoneware the only sound. "It was Monday, before sunset."

My eyes flew to Rupert's. "Before?" He shrugged, uneasy. Spawn came out only at full night. No wonder Marla had called Ciana a liar.

And then the meaning of a daytime sighting sank in. Daylight meant she had seen a daywalker. The stuff of legends. "It talked to you?" I asked, fighting to keep my voice steady.

"He. And he was way cool. He had green eyes, not the red you always hear about. And he was *gorgeous*." She paused to blow on the cocoa and drink. "Really long black hair, you know? Braided down his back, but some had got loose and flew in the wind. Way, *way* cool. He wanted to know about you."

The words fell on the room like a box of stone dropped from a great height. Lolo's warnings sank into me, bloodrings, portents of danger. "Me?"

Rupert pursed his lips.

"Yep. He wanted to know all about you. Where you lived, where you worked, what you did for a living." She looked slyly up at me. "If you were married or a virgin. I told him right off you were *not* a virgin."

"Ciana!"

"Spawn only want virgins, right? And he kissed my hand."

When it came to mating, spawn captured human virgins for their masters, but any neomage flesh was prime breeding material for the Dark Powers. And spawn would eat anything. I didn't share this with Ciana. Little was known about daywalkers; they were near mythical, their origins unknown, perhaps the issue of a mating between a Darkness and a captured kylen. They supposedly could pass as human, and had the power to glamour their appearance. There were rumors about them, but nothing concrete. Scholars debated whether they had ever existed, had been eradicated, or had gone underground at the end of the Last War.

"He kissed your hand?" Rupert said, his body very still. I watched as he worked to cover deep emotion with casual curiosity. "You didn't say that when you called. How?"

"Like a Frenchman in one of your Pre-Ap movies. Like this." Ciana hopped to her feet and took Rupert's hand. She bowed over it, hovered, and smacked her lips into his knuckles. Then she hopped back into the chair and drank more cocoa. I watched Rupert, his eyes going dark before he turned to the percolator and freshened his cup, blue robes fluttering.

"Did you feel his breath on your hand while he kissed you?" he asked. "Was your skin cold after? Or wet?"

Ciana shrugged, watching us over the rim of her mug. "Gramma says Mama is a convert to some Dark Power hiding in the hills."

"You called Gramma?" he asked, suppressed dread in his voice.

"I called her and my friends. A spawn is way cool. You think the spawn is the Power she's talking about?"

Rupert groaned. "Gramma is . . . not . . . actually one who should be talking about Marla or anyone else. Gramma has problems of her own."

"Very diplomatic," I murmured, wondering what he thought he was hiding from Ciana. I bent over the chest where I kept the pendants I had already imbued with power, my right hand hovering over each, searching for one charged with protection from supernatural evil. I chose a slab of agate with bright bands of purple and lavender and removed it from the case before stringing it on a silver chain.

"Is that for me?" Ciana asked, coming up behind me, leaning over the case. "It's way cool." She touched the stone, sending it swinging on its chain.

"Yes." I looped it over her head and tucked it beneath her uniform tunic. "Way, way cool," I said, mimicking her Pre-Ap TV slang. "Keep it out of sight at school, but wear it when you go outdoors and at night."

"It's beautiful." She fished the pendant out and held it up to the light. "Is it magic?"

"There's no such thing as magic," I said, sticking it back out of sight. And there wasn't. Not really. No matter what the humans called it. "The foul neomages make magic," she said, clearly quoting someone else.

I nearly choked. Rupert replied, "Neomages draw upon the leftover force of creation to imbue things with power. More like prayer, not magic, no matter what the orthodox say about it. And we don't believe in mage hating." He thunked her head like a melon and she grinned up at him. "Remember that."

"Gramma says all neomages make black magic and should be burned at the stake."

"Grampa had to have been spelled when he married her," Rupert grumbled under his breath. "She's more orthodox than a kirk elder. Maybe she should be burned at the stake."

"If it isn't magic, why do you want me to wear it when I go out?"

"Just . . . wear it. Please."

Ciana shrugged again and tucked it into her shirt, out of sight. "It's pretty. Mama will want it if she sees it."

"Tell her Thorn made it. That'll change her mind," Rupert said. Ciana laughed, shrugged into her coat, and swung her backpack on. "Bye, guys. I'll see you after school." Her face fell and her eyes sought me. "How will I know if something bad happens to Daddy if I'm at school?"

"We'll keep the TV on," Rupert said. "If anything happens, Thorn'll come get you."

"Promise?"

I touched three fingers of my right hand over my heart in a seraphic gesture. "Promise."

"Okay. And we'll go to kirk together?"

"Yes," I said. "Together."

"Cool. Bye." And she was gone, shoes crunching on snow.

"So." I faced Rupert, his eyes shadowed and still. "Why did you ask the questions about how the daywalker kissed her hand?"

"If it was a daywalker." When I didn't reply he said, "It was important to know if the daywalker breathed on her or licked her skin."

"Why?"

"Why did you flinch when Ciana asked if the pendant was magic?"

Touché, I thought. "Because it is." Rupert blinked. He'd clearly not expected that answer. I was glad I had chosen the agate, because I couldn't lie to him worth angel bones. "The agate was from a batch I picked up last spring at an estate sale. Paid a pretty penny for it too. Supposedly it's neomage stone from the early Post-Ap days. The heir said it was charmed against evil. I'm hoping she was right, but I didn't want Ciana to accidentally blurt that out to Marla. That witch might take a hammer to it out of spite. Your turn."

Rupert looked apprehensive. "Well. Nothing. Just old wives' tales."

"Reeeeally?" I drew out the word, watching as Rupert squirmed. I knew every old wives' tale ever told. Tales, yarns, fables, and parables were part of the earliest neomage training, and there was nothing about daywalkers in the instruction.

"If a daywalker takes your scent, he learns all about you. If he licks you, he's marking you as claimed territory. For sex or food."

"Not good." I didn't think I'd gotten the whole truth. We were both dancing around full disclosure this morning. "If she really saw one," I added, testing the waters.

"If," he agreed, uneasy, pushing back a lock of black hair, busying himself arranging the high-end display pieces of Mokume Gane, known as wood-grained gold, formed of gold and copper with precious stones. He uncovered small stone sculptures I had carved, and polished one of Jacey's chrome and glass sculptures. The silence built between us. Rupert believed Ciana, and he was rattled. Worse, Rupert was frightened. I'd never seen my best friend afraid of anything.

"If what?"

We both looked up at the fresh voice and took the interruption as a sign we'd gotten close enough to the truth this morning. Other revelations could wait. Perhaps forever.

Chapter 5

†

"I said, 'If what?' " Audric stood in the open doorway to his minuscule shop next to Thorn's Gems, his bald head and dark-skinned face reflecting the snow-bright light from the windows, his silver lightning-bolt necklace glistening.

"If Ciana really saw a daywalker," Rupert said.

Audric's eyes narrowed and he gripped the door header, arms bent though the opening was eight feet high. Audric was a seriously big man. He studied Rupert, who was hunched over a display case that needed no reorganizing. "Where did she see this daywalker?"

"On the Trine," I said. "Yesterday afternoon. It may have sniffed or licked her hand, but it didn't bite her. She said *he* was pretty, with green eyes. And he went poof."

"Gorgeous. Not pretty," Rupert said. "You opening today?"

When he was in town, Audric manned a ten-by-twelve-foot storefront he leased from us. In it, locals could come and view some of the smaller items he had mined, or photographs of larger ones, and bargain for them—anvils, axes, china, car parts, gold, anything that survived the destruction of Sugar

Grove and the hundred years since. Audric made an indelicate noise at the obvious change of subject.

An uncomfortable silence filled Thorn's Gems as we each considered the shaky conversational ground. Kirk and secular law both required us to report any rumor of Darkness. But if we did, Ciana would be questioned, at the very least. At the worst, she would be taken into custody and disappear. Probably forever.

The tinkle of the door chimes saved us as Jacey blew in, late as usual, her long dark hair blowing in a wind that was billowing loose powder down the street. "More snow on the way," she said, dropping her walking stick beside mine in the two-foot-tall ceramic umbrella stand and unwrapping her voluminous black wool cloak. She slipped out of hobnailed boots and into suede ballerina slippers she kept by the door, scattering snow on the wood boards at her feet, scuffing the melting flakes with her heel in lieu of mopping them up.

"I heard about Lucas. You guys seen it yet?" she asked.

"We saw," Rupert said, sounding stiff.

"Your business partner's been in a dither ever since," Audric said, crossing to her and catching her up in a bear hug that dwarfed the tall woman.

"I missed you, big man." She hugged him fiercely. "Sure you won't leave that tacky hag and come be my love? You can teach me how to dead-mine and I'll teach you hetero. I can do queen almost as well as Rupert."

"Hey, you two," Rupert said, fists on hips, fighting an unwilling smile. "I'm right here."

"Will not happen, sugar-pie," Audric said, releasing her with a quick kiss to the top of her head and a swipe at her flyaway hair. "My heart is taken. And your husband—remember Zed?—has a very big shotgun. Plus, his sons are big enough to give even me pause."

Setting her patchwork satchel on the counter, Jacey

opened it and removed four wide-cuff bracelets made with flameworked beads and delicas, stitched into intricate patterns with floral motifs. Beside them she added a half dozen necklaces to match, some needing pendants, which I would apply. Lastly, she lifted out a beaded chrome sculpture in the shape of a winged warrior, wings outspread, toes pointed, shield in place, sword upheld and looking realistically sharp. "The cops know anything they're not telling the media?" she asked.

Audric lifted the seraph with a soft whistle. She grinned at him. "Glad you like it. It's Chamuel, our guardian angel."

"Nothing they're telling us. Only the video they keep showing. Violence on SNN, with government approval. Maybe seraphic approval too. Who knows?" Rupert said.

"Spooky." Jacey added earrings that could be sold with bracelets as sets or separately. She had been busy while I was out of town. Jacey's most productive time for finishing work was after hours and days off, as she liked to work in front of a roaring fire, surrounded by her large and ever-growing family. She had married a widower with five boys and promptly started giving them half-siblings. The total count of kids in her house was up to nine now. "I'm in the front this afternoon, right?"

"Right," Rupert said.

"I'm in the back now, then. In Friday's shipment, I got some stellar stock, and I want to see what I can come up with. Pure flame," she said as she disappeared into the workroom in back, her granny dress floating behind her. "Pure flame" was Jacey's trademark saying, both greeting and blessing, pure flame being what turned glass and ore into things of beauty.

Rupert began arranging the new pieces in the glass counter. I paused before I put on the chrysocolla creations I had decided to wear as display, realizing I had chosen the day's wardrobe to match a certain cop's green-blue eyes. I restrained a moan. I needed to look in my reference books and find out how long neomage heat lasted. Clipping on the stone jewelry, I turned to greet an early customer.

"Yeah, I'm open today," Audric finally answered Rupert's question. When neither of us responded, he vanished into his showroom.

Outside, snow swirled with the wind, turning the world white, obscuring the buildings across the street. Overhead, Lucas continued to be attacked, assaulted, and dragged away.

Wednesday's business was seldom brisk, and it slowed as snow piled up another three inches and temperatures fell. After lunch, which we shared around the gas fire in the center of the shop, we decided to close Thorn's Gems and Audric's showroom to work in the back. Larger metropolitan centers farther south or at lower altitudes had massive snow-moving equipment or snow-melting mage-devices, allowing commerce to continue all winter. But Mineral City, at over three thousand feet, and with a population of only four thousand, couldn't afford either. In blizzards, the town and surrounding hills closed down until the weather system moved on.

Jacey and Rupert had talked about moving to a warmer clime, a bigger city, where our client base could grow, but with the help of the Internet, we really didn't *have* to uproot Jacey's family and move. And I couldn't go. I was safer in the backwoods, though I just said I liked it here whenever the question came up.

I changed into work clothes, pulled a jumpsuit over the layers, and met my partners in the workroom. Such times were my greatest joy, when we worked together, the smell of solder or hot metal fouling the air as Rupert heated gold or copper or silver; the scent of gas and the blue flame from Jacey's torches as she melted and blew glass, fusing bits of found materials into beads, or welding a hunk of salvaged steel into sculpture. The faint stink of sweat as we expended energy in the warm room. The roar of my wet saw and diamond-tipped drill tools shaping stone, and the soft clicks Rupert made, nipping and cutting sheets of metal according to templates. It was a raucous multi-sense symphony.

Occasionally, music flowed overhead if we could all agree on the artist and style. Rarely, when we could afford the gas to heat the small kiln Jacey sometimes used, it was even steamy. All the smells, sounds, sights, and movements blended together and spoke of warmth and safety and home, my home since I had turned fourteen and was smuggled out of Enclave.

I was working the hunk of bloodstone I'd carted all the way from Boone in Homer's saddlebags, not waiting for the next mule train or freight train, fearing winter weather would delay it. A diamond-tipped blade roaring in the wet saw, I slowly excised large beads in rectangles, squares, rough ovals, and free-form shapes. If the matrix proved stable, each would be a focal stone for a necklace, the red heart bleeding into the dark green outer area.

It was a remarkable rough, and as I worked, I sent a skim into the heart of the stone and felt an unexpected hum of resonance, an echo of power. Lifting my safety glasses out of the way, I raised the remaining rough and considered it with mage-sight. The bloody heart of the stone was dark fuchsia, bordering on crimson when tilted into shadow. The very center of the stone would make a great amulet that would nest perfectly in the palm of my hand, heavy and smooth. Something carved into a sleeping cat, a sleeping bird, or a shell, and hung from a lace of leather thongs strung with dark green glass beads swirled with scarlet and gold. It would be an amulet hidden in plain view. I turned the remaining stone into the light. I could make my amulet and still get a dozen exciting focals from the double fist of rough. Pulling my glasses into place, I went back to work.

Even with snow outside, the room grew warm, our extra layers tossed over chair backs or onto the floor. My head was filled with the acrid stink of Rupert's copper and pickling solution, and the cleaner smell of Jacey's torch melting, turning, and blowing glass. Today she was flameworking blue glass globes into small droplets, fusing in gold dust.

As we bent over our tasks, a CDS of an ancient rock singer was playing, above the sound of my saw. Elvis Presley, long saved in crystal digital storage, blared overhead, crooning in a sexy, smooth voice. Rock and roll had been removed from the banned listing in the last year and was back in fashion, though we had listened to it for several years before it had been permitted. Elvis' mellow voice seemed tailor-made for the work we did, and he was one artist we could all agree on, though we also liked the Eagles, Patsy Cline, the Allman Brothers, and Tina Turner. We even liked Mercy Me, Avalon, and Casting Crowns, which we played when a kirk elder was expected to make an appearance.

Fifty years ago, when the orthodox had been at the peak of their power, holding both houses of Congress, ruling with the consent of the High Host, the music had been prohibited. As the old-timers died off and their edicts were challenged in the Supreme Court, many were being stricken from the records. No one knew whether seraphs hated rock and roll or the religious Right did, but the loosening of restrictions was a result of the recent seraphic disinterest in the affairs of humans. Regardless of who had once hated him, Elvis now crooned overhead.

When a dozen stones were ready for the grinding wheel, I took a break and peeled out of my jumpsuit, which was crusted over with stone dust. From the icebox in the unheated back hallway, I got us each a juice and sat at my workbench watching my partners on the tasks that had made our designs a success.

Rupert set down metal snips and a sheet of stiff copper he was cutting to the contours of a necklace I had designed. With tongs, he took a copper oval from the brazier and doused it in a heated pickle solution before twisting the top off his drink and taking a long swallow. He wiped the icy bottle over his sweating forehead, nodded to me, and returned to work. Jacey, her granny dress tucked under a thick leather apron, swiveled the welder's mask up off her face and rolled her shoulders before drinking. No one spoke. I stretched, flexing numb muscles that tended to paralyze in position when I worked stone. I was tired, as much from the energy-sapping snow accumulating beyond the walls as from the long trip and stonecutting.

I was restless. Taking my bottle, I rambled in front to check the weather, which was still horrid, and back into the workshop, down the hallway, past some deliveries that made the passage even more narrow, and into the stockroom. Stacked haphazardly, blocking easy entrance, were shipping crates showing rope scoring, the singular evidence of mule train transport. Heavier stock came by the intermittent freight train and was never secured with rope.

I set my juice bottle at the door. While we hadn't assigned jobs when we formed the partnership, we had each taken on certain tasks, the chores that went beyond the purely creative and sales parts of Thorn's Gems. My jobs were the art of working stone, design, and stock, which needed serious attention. With hammer and chisel, I opened the crates blocking the door and updated the inventory folder, which had been misplaced. When I left town, the stockroom always got cluttered, and when I was gone an extended time, I returned to chaos.

Thorn's Gems had been my dream, started with the money left me when my foster father, Lemuel Hastings, died just after my eighteenth birthday. Uncle Lem had been a rough, taciturn, coldhearted, rock hound who had loved only one thing in his life until I came into it—stone. Thinking me wholly human and orphaned, he had opened his home to me, and eventually his heart, teaching me that humans were pretty okay, and to love rocks.

Setting aside the tools, I put away Jacey's quarterly scrap

metal order for salvaged gold findings, melted jewelry dead-mined from war zones, and old, broken glass. One box held rusted parts from Pre-Ap cars and trucks for her sculpture.

I stored the stock in bins and stacked empty crates in back for recycling. Two boxes were mine, filled with rough I had bought sight unseen online, in a rare moment when the computer worked without crashing. We needed a new one, but they were costly. Parts were getting harder to find, though there was a thriving cottage industry for computer repair, and the Internet was still the best place to get neat stuff.

An SNN reporter had claimed there were new companies on the northwest coast creating new PC parts and producing new units, which required high-quality quartz. Mineral City's main exports were guns, feldspar, and quartz crystal. We had seen an upsurge in quartz exports, so it was possible. There had been such claims in the past, however, and nothing came of them. I'd believe it when I saw a new computer.

Opening crates, I shelved some online stock and stacked the rest in a bin identified with big question marks. There had been a photo in the Internet ads, but if I didn't get to handle rough, I had no idea how fragile or frangible it was, so I'd have to study it later.

I cleared space, making the room accessible again, but even with my layers of clothing, it was cold in the unheated room. I thought I could empty a few more cartons before the temperature forced me out. Stepping into the hallway, I considered metal shipping containers that constricted the traffic pattern. It was rare for deliveries to arrive boxed in anything except wood and paper, as salvaged metal had become more valuable to the exploding human population. Usually, metal was used for more important purposes than transport, especially this much metal. The boxes were approximately fifteen inches deep, eighteen long, and nine high, with handles on top and sides. Metal strips looked as if they had been added later, crisscrossing back to front, secured with brass padlocks. It was a lot of metal.

I glanced at one address label and stopped, surprised, then looked at the address on another box. The metal ones were from Linville, Carolina, to Rupert at Thorn's Gems. There were no names on the returns, but the street address belonged to his gramma.

Well, that was just dandy. No telling what the old bat had sent, except that it would be a chore or a problem or a demand. And no matter what it was, Rupert would be ticked off. I slipped my fingers under the handle.

Stone . . . The cold in my flesh was replaced with a frisson of heat, a whisper of power, the touch of mage-perception. Slick sweat broke out on my arms and tingled down my spine. *There is stone here.* Stone imbued with *power.* Straining, I lifted the metal box to the floor. Uncertain, I touched the second box. It too contained stone. And behind it was another box, similar to the first two. I studied the boxes in the dim hallway light. They were an ugly green, painted with pale white pigments, words hidden under the crisscrossed security strips. A number 6 was clearly visible on one, the number 2 in a different place on another. I recognized Pre-Ap U.S. military ammunition boxes. Had the Stanhope matriarch sent these? And why to Rupert, her least favorite grandchild, rather than to her best beloved Lucas, or even to Jason, their older brother? And why stone delivered in metal ammo boxes?

I sent a skim into the box under my fingertips. The stone inside seemed to elongate, like a cat arching under a caress; then it swirled around me in an eddy, testing, toying. I sent a tendril of thought deeper into the box.

Something touched my mind, recoiled a bare instant before it wrapped around me, seized me, and pulled me in. My mind fell into the rock inside.

Shattering, fracturing, sundering might. *Such power.* It

beat into me, demanding. I moaned, breathing in limitless, boundless energies. My head whipped back, my spine arched.

A small, lucid, prudent part of me wrenched away from the might, the mage-torque of stone. I watched as it wrapped barriers around itself, sealing itself off from the stone, the force thrumming against my brain. That small, safe part of me vanished from my own sight.

The desire to rip open the boxes heated my blood. I gasped as I pulled at the lock. It didn't give. Securing the hammer and chisel under my arm, I hefted one of the ammo boxes by its thin, rounded handles. The mage-torque from within burned my palms, singing, calling to me. Unsteady, I walked into the workroom.

Audric watched as I entered, his eyes alarmed as if sensing something wrong. He nudged Rupert, who looked up, irritated. Jacey raised her head, shoved up her welding hood, took us in, and turned off her torch, the blue-flame cone vanishing with a soft pop.

"What is it?" Rupert demanded.

"A lot of stock came while I was gone?" My voice sounded strange.

"Yeah," Jacey said, laying aside her hood, stripping off padded gloves, and untying her heavy apron. "A lot, all week. Why? Hey, I'm sorry, I know I should have stopped and put some of it away. I'm a lazy slob."

I swiveled to Rupert, who moved closer to Audric as if seeking comfort from an expected blow. "Your gramma sent you some presents. They're in metal ammunition boxes in the hallway, each nearly identical to this one. There's stone in them." I realized that sounded strange, so I added, "Maybe."

He glanced at Audric and rolled his eyes, shoulders relaxing. "It's no big deal," he said, crossing the room, steel tongs at his side. "It's just stuff from Grampa's desk. I've been expecting it. Gramma's been cleaning out the papers for probate and sending on anything that needs legal attention. And Lucas was going through Grampa's storage house, sorting estate things and sending on—"

"It's stone," I interrupted, striding past him. There was a resonance in my blood that only mineral could produce, that low, slow hum of something near craving, a hunger close to passion, that only stone recently mined from deep in the ground could demand of me. Ordinary stone, stone that had been exposed to the elements, scoured by water and wind, contained little usable power until after I recharged it with creation energy. But this stone was different, a beating heart of might. This stone was charged with something . . . strange.

I hefted the box and dropped it onto Rupert's worktable. It landed with a weighty thump that rocked the sturdy bench. The stone inside the carton was charged with something I had never felt before, something that was almost—but not quite—creation power. And it fed its hunger into me, hunger that translated into euphoria. I don't know what he saw in my eyes, but Rupert stepped back. "This box is *not* holding papers," I said.

"Touchy, touchy," Rupert murmured. But he set down his tongs and turned off the torch and brazier. Everything that caused fumes was off, so Audric flipped off the ventilation fan, silencing the low rumble just beneath the level of normal hearing, and ejected the CDS. Instantly, quiet pressed in, marred only by the tick and ping of cooling metal.

"Did she send a key to this?"

Rupert's face went blank as he took in the padlock. "Uh. No. Jacey?"

"Yeah, maybe. Hang on." She ran to the front, smoothing her dress, its fabric crushed into long wrinkles by the apron and the heat of her body. In a moment that seemed like an eon, she was back, carrying a manila shipping envelope. "I forgot. This came in the post on Saturday. I didn't know what it was for." From the envelope, she shook a small brass key.

Rupert inserted it, and the padlock clicked. Blood raced through my body, a beat of tribal drums. *Open it,* I wanted to shout. Rupert set the key aside and removed the metal strips, one by one, creating soft twangs that hung on the air, dull notes of off-key sound.

But when he tried to lift the lid, it didn't budge. "It's been soldered shut," Audric said. Rupert pressed his fingernail into a thin line of metal in the seam. The lead solder gave under the faint pressure.

"You want I should open it?" I indicated the box with the chisel and hammer, the need to demolish it nearly making me shake. At his acquiescence, I stabbed the narrow chisel into the seam between side and lid and whapped the blunt end with the hammer three times, three ringing chimes of steel, and beneath them, the dull notes of lesser metals yielding. Working the rod out, I inserted it a few inches to the side and struck again, three solid blows. Audric spun the ammo box and I repeated the steps on the other side, hearing the quiet groan as lead released from the tight seal. A crack formed in the solder. From within the box, something reached out to me, enveloping my mind.

Muscles bulging, Audric pulled the hinged lid and it opened with a shrill squeal as he stepped back, allowing Rupert access to the box. Though I was breathing too heavily for the amount of exertion, the aggression I was fighting had abated with the attack on the crate, and I put down the tools, watching as Rupert pulled out wads of newsprint, exposing sawdust. The pounding in my blood called for him to hurry, to get inside, get inside fast.

Chapter 6

†

He woke to a pounding head and a sharp pain in his wrist. The pounding was more than blood moving through his rattled brain, it was the sound of a steel maul pounding a steel spike into the stone beside his head. Chips of rock shattered and flew, and he covered his head with his free arm, jerking it from the other thing in the dark. Teeth ripped his flesh as he pulled free. A roar sounded, a blow landed, and something screamed close by. Sulfur burned his breathing passages with each breath; cold and pain traveled through his body with each heartbeat. Terror wound around him, the smothering coils of a serpent. He was underground. *Gabriel's tears.* He was underground.

Something rattled like metal and pulled unmercifully at his torn flesh. Unable to help it, he groaned. The thing near him stopped at the sound. It lifted his hand and he heard it sniff as it scented his blood. A moment later something cold and wet slithered around his wrist, burning. He heard a sigh, as of pleasure. And then his hand was dropped. It landed with a boneless flop, but the pain was, seemingly, less. The thing dragged itself away, the sound of its movement growing indistinct.

A moment later, he felt something else touch his hand, and he flinched.

"It's all right. I brought water," it whispered. Lucas felt something heavy hit the stone floor by his head. Iron, a shaped instrument, as cold as death, was placed in his open palm. With his other hand he discovered its shape. A dipper attached by a rope to a stoneware jug. By feel, Lucas dropped the dipper into the jug and brought the cup to his lips. Half expecting something horrible, he touched it to his mouth and tasted water. Sulfur tainted, but water. Desperately thirsty, he drained the dipper and then another.

"I'll bring more tomorrow," it whispered.

"Wait. What are you?"

The pause was fraught with indecision. Then it answered. "I call myself Malashe-el." And it was gone.

Audric's biceps bulged. From the sawdust came a cloth-wrapped packet that blazed, blistered, burned, in my mind. It called to me, a siren song of might so extraordinary, I wondered the humans couldn't see it. He placed it on the workbench; the wrapping fell away.

A lustrous lavender stone pulsed. Cried out. Shock surged through me, a jolt of power from the first creation. But, *no, not quite that. Not quite.* The thought seemed to disintegrate and fall away. My reasoning clouded. The stone summoned. My flesh ached, my skin, blood, muscles, the beat of my heart, every cell in my body, wanted to join with this stone, mate the beat of my heart to it, and glow with power. Instinctively, that safe part of me, the part set aside only moments earlier, resisted the attraction, drawing on a black-and-green-jade bear amulet beneath my clothes. The bear stored strength, keyed to mute my physical neomage attributes. I could *not* start to glow. Simply could not. The need to embrace the lavender stone and claim it as my own, the need to bond with it, eased.

"What is it?" Jacey asked.

"It's amethyst," I said, my lips slightly numb. "Gem quality, unless I miss my guess." Incomplete answer, but the safe one. Of their own volition, my hands reached out and enfolded the stone. Power smashed through my palms, the force of a mighty engine, the flare of a rocket lifting into outer space. I shuddered.

"Be careful. It's heavy," Rupert said, misinterpreting my reaction.

I held the jagged stone to the lights overhead, letting the crystalline center of the rock capture illumination and throw it back. It was dirty on one side, smooth where it had lain for long ages, buried in contact with the ground. But the other sides were crystal spires or cragged and irregular where it had broken from a much larger stone. Along the smooth side, the crystal curved in a strange shape, like the curve of a closed eyelid. *A larger stone with this power is out there. And I want it.* A shiver of warmth threaded along my nerves below my flesh. Heat like mage-heat, like sex, chocolate, whiskey, and wood smoke.

"Thorn?"

I snapped back, aware that I had slipped away from the reality of the shop. I was holding the heavy amethyst over my head, staring into its depths, connecting with it as if the stone had eyes in its heart, eyes that stared back with longing. The weakness caused by snow falling and collecting had vanished. In its place was this incredible . . . bliss. Desire. Hunger.

"Bond with me. Choose me," the stone sang. *"I am lonely."*

I shook the thoughts away and set the hunk of rough with three other stones on the table. Each had been cleaved from the same mother rock, though the others showed darker, oval shadings on one side. Their power held a fragrance, an incredible flavor, like lilac blooms, nutmeg, hyssop, something I could almost taste. It was like, yet unlike, mage-heat.

Suddenly Lolo was in my mind, her voice shocking me

awake. She hadn't been in my mind since I was fourteen, when all the mages in Enclave had been there as well. *"What you got, gurl?"* she cried. *"I feelin' power. C'est trop. Ça c'est de trop. Dem angels, dey hear! Ge' away from there. Run!"* Instead I caressed the double-fist-sized hunks of stone, lifting each for inspection, seeing less with my eyes than with mage-sense.

"Danger, dis. Run, gurl!" I blocked out Lolo's warning. She wasn't here. She didn't see, didn't feel this ecstasy, this rapture. She wasn't a stone mage. She couldn't understand. Vaguely, I knew I hadn't been able to block voices when I was fourteen. No mage should be able to hear another a thousand miles away. This was new. But that thought too slid away.

"There are more boxes in the hallway outside the stock room," I said, my tongue feeling thick and flaccid. "You might want to check them out."

In what seemed only a second, two more boxes were on the workbench, hammer and chisel ringing as they were opened. Power flowed from them.

"What's wrong with her?"

"Looks like she's having an intimate psychic rendezvous with that rock. Seraph struck, angel awed by a boulder."

I didn't know who had spoken, but the words brought me back from the faraway place the stone had taken me. This was the danger Lolo spoke of, that I could be swept away and consumed. I forced the silly smile off my lips as I fought for a sensible reply. And then that still, small part of me, safe in the back of my mind, unfolded with words, clear and concise, as if planted in my mind by another, but generated by years of familiarity with stone and with running the shop. Logic. Business.

"Just trying to figure out how many focal stones I could get out of this if it was cut free-form, and how much more profit we could make if we sent it off to be faceted." I stroked the stone, warm against my palm. "We'd lose carat weight but gain value if we sent it off."

"If it's gem quality," Jacey said.

"It's gem quality. I know it." I held a rock from another box up to the light. Their pulsing energies had achieved a harmony once the stones were close together again. They whispered and sang. I held the stone to my nose and sniffed, but the fragrance wasn't physical, not something my nose could sense. Not something humans could detect.

"Here's a letter," Audric said, "in with these papers." His voice was the mellow tone of an ancient brass church gong. He handed a slim packet to Rupert. My best friend brushed off the sawdust, and the motion of his hand was lissome, exquisite beyond bearing. His grace moved me to tears; they gathered in my eyes, dazzled in the gleam of the rocks.

My mind again retreated, hiding. I watched as Rupert tore an envelope, his fingers strong, dirty with the smut of solder and fire, Stanhope indexes longer than the middle ones. When I dragged my eyes to his face, I saw that his flesh glowed with heat and vivacity, as if I saw the cadence of his lifeblood beneath. His mouth moved, speaking, and I fastened on it as his sculpted lips shifted, poetry made flesh. "Thorn?" The word was drawn out, the last note in a plaintive song. As it fell on my ear, I heard beneath it the call of Lolo singing a nursery rhyme, her voice a cross cadence to the beat of the life force in Rupert. The drums and flute of her acolytes were penetrating rhythm in the childhood ditty. *Break dat call of siren song. Ring dat bell and right dat wrong. Blood and bone and seraph fire, drag her back from dangerous mire.*

Deep in my skull I heard a crack, another, again and again, the sound of stone being split, broken, battered into dust. Suddenly I was free. The world spun and I swayed, catching myself before I fell. I was sitting on the workbench. *Crack the Stone of Ages! What happened?* I placed the rock on the table and jumped down, landing hard. My bones rattled, my joints stiff. My face burned.

BLOODRING

Words bubbled out from that logical, protected, liberated part of me. "It'll cost us more than fifteen thousand dollars to have them cut and faceted, without a guarantee the resultant stones will have a value commensurate with the expenditure. And while we won't make as much if we work them as focals following the stone's natural contours, we'll retain a larger total carat value from each fist. As nuggets and free-form, we can work them into our existing lines, creating an upscale, high-end product that I think will sell well in today's market. I already have some ideas on designs." My babble clipped off abruptly. "What?"

"That's where you've been?" Jacey asked, her tone incredulous. "Doing math and cost-profit analyses? Designing a high-end line?"

I looked at her, my mind locked firmly away from the overpowering stones, buried in Lolo's sweet harmonies, the music of her distant mind balanced and bolstering. "What?" *What have I been doing? How long?* Between the mage-heat and the stone—

"I've been calling—" She spluttered, starting again. "For five minutes, you've been—were." She gnashed her teeth and ground to a stop. I was certain I had never seen anyone gnash her teeth. "I slapped your face," she said. "Hard." I touched my cheek. It stung.

"You were gone," Rupert said, his face normal again, without the otherworldly life it had possessed earlier. But he was worried. Over his shoulder Audric watched me, not falling for the innocent expression I forced onto my face. I didn't know what had happened, but now wasn't the time to consider it. Now I had to cover, guard, and protect them from what I was. I knew my comments about the value of the stones were dead-on.

Audric handed me a letter marked with Lucas' distinctive, crabbed handwriting. While I couldn't read it all, I did make out a few lines and read them aloud. " 'I found this in Grampa's . . .'

something I can't make out. 'It was marked with a plat-map of the Trine. Ask Thorn what it is. I think it's . . .' something, something, something . . . 'valuable.' Two lines of gibberish are followed by 'If I disappear . . .' and more gibberish. Farther down the page are the words, 'Don't go . . .' something, something . . . 'police and elders. There's a new Power in the hills . . .' some more gibberish, then 'and I think some went over to it. All the Stanhopes are in danger. Keep . . .' something . . . 'safe.' " *L* followed by a slash was Lucas' hurried signature.

"The Trine. That's where Ciana saw her daywalker," Audric said.

"Daywalker?" Jacey said, alarmed.

"Tell you later," Audric said.

"Cops I can see, but elders involved with a Minor Power?" Rupert said. "No way."

"You saw the video," I said. "Something happened to him, just like this letter warns."

I set the sheet down and wiped my fingers as if it had left an oily residue. Audric lifted the page. "Does this say he's called for a seraphic investigation?" he pointed to a line.

I couldn't see words in the squiggled text, except for a single *s*. "Maybe."

"Why would the Stanhopes be in danger?" Jacey asked, tucking a strand of sweat-damp hair behind her ear. She was no longer watching me, but I wasn't fooled that she had forgotten my fugue state. I'd hear about it later. My face smarted where she had struck it.

"The Mole Man," Rupert said, taking back the letter and tracing two new words. "Something here about the Mole Man."

"And?"

"The Mole Man was our great-grandfather, Benaiah."

"For real? You got a warrior in your family line?" Jacey seemed to comprehend the term, drawing conclusions I didn't understand.

"Mole Man?" I asked. It wasn't a heroic-sounding name.

"The name they gave Benaiah Stanhope after a not-so-small mopping-up operation in the hills at the end of the Last War. He went with a group of winged warriors underground, into the earth, in the dark," he emphasized, "and the Cherokee named him that. He went in after a Major Power and its human helpers and half-human offspring, the Dark humans. Some say the Power was holed up beneath the Gunthor's place in a cavern. Others say it was beneath the Trine." Rupert shrugged and quoted, his voice acquiring the singsong of scripture. "Bright light shone from the earth, three days and three nights. And the mountains cracked open, and Light and Darkness spilled out over the land in battle dire. The townspeople prayed. Seraphs came back out. Mole Man never did."

"They left him?" I couldn't keep the horror from my voice. "Underground?" With the exception of salt mines and three shielded mines in North America protected by seraphic decree, including Henderson Shielded Mine, no one went beneath the ground. Not ever.

All minerals except for salt, which Darkness hated, were strip-mined, the only way to keep the miners safe. Darkness ruled underground, just as Light ruled above. It wasn't hell and heaven, but parallels for places the seraphs insisted existed elsewhere, or elsewhen.

"I remember that from grade school," Jacey said, her brown eyes bright. "A warrior of the Host claimed that Benaiah died to save the High Host's second in command, offering himself in human sacrifice to bind the Major Power." Jacey reached out and took a fist-sized slab of amethyst in her hand. "The demon was supposed to be a massive being with the head of a lion and the body of a lizard, with human hands. And the usual stink of sulfur and rot. Legend says the town reeked of it for weeks. The beast—a dragon—was given to the Host, bound in chains that were drenched with Benaiah's blood. So they say."

"But it was reported that several lesser Powers got away, vowing vengeance on the Mole Man and his progeny, unto the everlasting," Rupert said softly.

"Yeah. I remember that too," Jacey said.

"And seraphs were seen entering the earth for weeks after," Rupert finished the story. "No one knows why. Or so they say."

"Or so they say" was one of the usual disclaimers after any war story, because at the time no one wrote anything down. Only those things captured and recorded by the film media had been preserved, broadcast across the world via satellites and stored with crystal digital technology. At the time, seraphs didn't bother with public relations. They didn't explain what was happening or what they were doing. Explanations were the guesswork of witnesses. To the current day, no one knew what had happened in many parts of the earth. No one had bothered to keep a written, linear record of the end of the world. Supposedly, it was the end of time.

Except it hadn't been the end of the world. Time still dragged on, and much history had been lost. Earlier technologies hadn't survived, leaving only newer CDS recordings. Rock and roll, soul, R & B, some rap and hip-hop, and religious and gospel music of the twentieth and twenty-first centuries had been kept in storage, along with many films and old TV shows. And of course, the video of the Apocalypse, plagues, and battles of the Last War, which were still replayed every year on the anniversary.

"The Trine still belongs to your family, right?" I asked. When Rupert nodded, I said, "Your great-great-grandfather bought a lot of land after the Last Battle, paying pennies on the dollar. And Ciana saw something on the Trine that might have been a daywalker."

"Or might not," Audric cautioned.

"And these stones came from the Trine."

"Maybe," Audric said, the voice of reason, the devil's advocate, though that phrase was fraught with meaning.

I ignored him. "So the Trine may be the glue in all that's happening, including Lucas' attack. Does anything else about the Trine come to mind?" I asked, proud that I sounded reasonable and calm, though I was still half aware of Lolo's chant just below my normal hearing, an insulation from the stone.

Rupert thought a moment. "I remember mining companies offered to buy land or mineral rights, back when Grampa was young, before the ice made it all inaccessible. Far as I know, he turned them down and we never heard anything else about it."

He tapped an ear, sending a silver earring swinging, and met my eyes. "The Trine didn't always look like it does now," he explained. "Once it was a single rounded hill with a lower elevation. Its trees were harvested to build the railroad in the early nineteen hundreds. It was farmed, stripped bare, and left fallow several times. At the first plague, it was a residential area. In Mole Man's war, the peaks blasted up from the earth, raised by the battles underground. With the ice cap so thick, it would be dangerous to try to get up there."

I had seen ice caps up close on the trek home from the swap meet, miniglaciers, sheets of ice hundreds of feet thick. Caps had formed on all the highest peaks of the Appalachians, and recently, one had caused a disaster. Midsummer, unexpected temperatures in the sixties had undermined the caps. One had shifted and slid, burying an entire town, killing everyone. No one had even attempted to dig the town out from the thousands of tons of ice and debris.

Now there was talk of solutions. So far, there were three possibilities. The first two involved getting seraph help or neomage help to melt ice caps that threatened towns. The third method was evacuation. Acquiring seraph assistance might be impossible, due to their current lack of interest in human affairs. Contracting with mages was going to be expensive. Very expensive. One town, upon hearing the cost of neomage help, had simply packed up and moved, abandoning everything. Evacuating had left its well-off citizens nearly penniless refugees. Saving Mineral City could leave us equally broke.

The elders had held several town meetings but a course of action hadn't been decided upon. If accord was reached to get mage help, I was hoping I had time to get away before anyone came. An extended vacation to a tropical isle sounded a lot better than almost certain death.

"Lucas wants to buy neomage help," Rupert said, "using our inheritance to pay for it. He wants to offer the town a loan they can pay back over twenty years. Jason wants to sell it to the highest bidder and run, and let the new town owners worry about the ice. He needs money, as usual, and sees saving the town as wasting his nest egg. And then there's this one town leader who wants to buy the town at pennies on the dollar."

"What about you?" Jacey asked, settling into a cushioned chair with needle and thread. She began beading a patterned, punctured strip of leather with glass seed beads.

"I sided with Lucas in paying for mages."

Unable to help myself, I picked up a lavender stone, one side almost fuzzy with crystalline shavings. Light from bulbs and from the high alley windows seemed to be trapped in the stone. Power called to me from within it, pulsing with something close to life. That something was almost creation power, but wasn't, not quite. Lolo's block insulated me from it, but still, the might stored in the stone pulled at me, singing a haunting melody.

"Mineral rights, huh?" Audric said. "Bet a mining company would love to have the rights to this. For that matter, I'd like them, but I'm tapped out for the next five years with the salvage of Sugar Grove. If a big mining company knew about this much stone, they'd strip the mountain bare to get it. And they could pay for neomage help to do it too."

A spurt of possessiveness wrenched through me at his words. *This is mine!* I turned the stone again to the light, one palm cupping it tenderly. This piece was larger than my two hands, a flame-shaped rock, its light spilling out between my fingers. Warmth ran down my arms like honey.

"There's only one question that really gets me about all this," Rupert said, "and that's why, if Grampa knew the stone was on the Trine, he didn't mine it himself. And why is it in lead-lined boxes, soldered shut? Lucas had to open them, and then had to figure out how to solder them shut again, and my brother isn't the most handy man. And where did Lucas find them? I've been over that house with a fine-tooth comb several times since Grampa died."

"That's more than one question," Jacey said complacently.

"Maybe you should call your gramma and ask her all that," Audric suggested.

Rupert shivered dramatically at the thought. "Over my cold, dead, and decaying body."

"Okay. I see that point." Audric grinned. "So start with your grampa."

"He's dead," Rupert said, being deliberately difficult.

"Start with his papers," I said. "He never threw anything away. You could try to get all of them and search them first."

The three glanced at one another, a shared look of warning and worry that concerned and excluded me. Jacey's eyes were positively accusing, and way too speculative. She stabbed the piece of leather with special force. "What?" I asked.

Audric tapped one of the metal ammo boxes on the work-bench. "That's what's in this one. Rupert's grandfather's estate papers. Lots of them. We were talking about them while you were . . . elsewhere."

Oops.

"We could call for a seraphic investigation," Rupert said. "If enough of us make the call, like Lucas' *new wife* did, then they'd have to come. And then we can ask about the peaks and the ice caps too."

No seraphs. Not in Mineral City.

"You think he really married her?" Jacey asked, redirecting the flow of conversation.

"No. Jane's a head case. Lucas knew that."

"We have an alternative," Audric said. "A state cop." The two men shared a glance.

"Thaddeus Bartholomew," Rupert said. "We met yesterday. I didn't particularly like him, but of the cops who stopped in after Lucas' attack, he was the least obnoxious. He's a Hand of the Law, which gives him more contacts than the local cops have, so maybe . . ."

I overlooked the hesitation in Rupert's voice, set down the stone, and took a deep breath, the first breath I remembered for hours. Calling in the kylen was dangerous for me, but the alternative was a death sentence. "Call him. He's staying at the hotel, he isn't seraphic, and he can help."

"And why don't you want to call in a seraph?" The look of suspicion on Jacey's face was unwavering.

"Because if a seraph makes a proclamation, we're stuck with it even if we don't like it. And because a seraph, if one comes, might decide that Mineral City deserves punishment," I said. When a seraph pulled a sword in punishment, people died. Lots of people, nearly half of them, all of them over the age of six. And a seraph would recognize me in a heartbeat. But I kept that part to myself. I had given something away today, something about me, about my heritage.

"No seraphs. Not yet." Audric sided with me, but he too had a certain speculative look about him.

I pulled the jumpsuit back on. "You may want to wrap that rock up and put it in the storeroom," I said, casual words and casual tone, giving away none of the discord I felt at the thought of the lovely rock being put away in the cold and dark. "It's valuable enough that it shouldn't be left lying around."

From a bag of rough, I pulled a hunk of moss agate in soft shades of green. I had last worked the rough six months ago, but now held it to the light and turned on the wet saw. The roaring whine shut out my friends. I settled safety glasses on my face and chose a triangular segment to crop free. Securing the rock in clamps, I maneuvered the whirring blade and began the tedious drudgery of cutting small beads.

I was aware the moment the others wrapped up my amethyst and put it away. Pretending I was free of its call was a fool's lie. I longed for the stone. Hungered.

Chapter 7

†

When I opened my *Book of Workings*, I was upstairs, eating a bowl of thawed, sliced peaches. The stone downstairs and rising mage-heat had me feeling distinctly uncomfortable, which was ridiculous. There had to be a way to control it, to put a lid on heat, or Enclave would become an orgy every time a seraph flew within a hundred miles.

For the first time, I read the warnings and explanations in the front of the book and discovered something I must have been taught in the early years of training but had forgotten. Only in warfare should I use scripture in incantations. That explained why none of my conjures worked exactly as planned. Clearly, I should have studied the book as Lolo demanded. There was some neat stuff in it. I could almost hear the witchy-woman scold me.

I was halfway through when the cop arrived. Even a story up, even with snow blanketing every stone for miles around, I knew the moment Thaddeus Bartholomew walked onto the premises. Instantly I understood that asking him here had been a big, big mistake. His first footstep below was like a gong of flaming need, resonating through me.

As the kylen stepped into the store, a gale of lavender light raked through my mind like a hurricane wind. Mage-sight glared and my skin blazed alive without my consent. I gripped my amulets, my flesh aching as energies lashed me.

All I wanted in life was below—the kylen and the amethyst. My knees weakened, breasts tightened as the lavender power merged with erotic heat, doubling it, tripling it. *Oh, sweet seraph.* Gasping, I dropped to the floor and forced my liquid bones into a meditative posture, sitting, knees bent, spine almost straight. My hands clenched the amulets tied beneath my work shirt as I attempted to slow my breathing, dampen my libido.

But employing the amulets had a peculiar effect. The amethyst stone sought to blend with the creation power I was drawing on, attempted to whirl into the energy currents established and stored in my amulets. I had never heard of this, yet instinctively, I understood what was happening. As if with intelligence of its own, the amethyst was piggybacking, bolstering each amulet's incantation. I had handled the amethyst and my mage-sense had recognized its power. As a result, the amethyst was trying to combine with my energies, trying to bond my blood to itself. My amulets were focal points, lenses of convergence, concentrating the effect of the kylen. Demanding that I utilize the power or mate. One or the other, if not both at the same time.

Though I was only half trained, I knew that using a new source of power would come with a price. Probably a price I wouldn't want to pay, especially if the cost was tied to sex. *But it would be really, really, really great sex . . .* I broke contact with my amulets, releasing them in a single negation, as if they burned. But I was the one who burned. For the kylen. For the amethyst.

I slid prone, pressing my body against the tile, my cheek against the cold glaze. Desperate, I chanted a child's mantra, one taught to all neomage children, almost the first words we learned in the Enclave version of nursery school. "Stone and fire, water and air, blood and kin prevail. Wings and shield, dagger and sword, blood and kin prevail."

I said the phrases over and over, breathing deeply with each repetition. The incantation drew on the oldest, most holy protection of the neomages, the defense offered by the High Host when they set my ancestors apart. The power for the liturgy resided deep in the earth below the Enclave where I was born, and I drew on it in times of extremis, of danger. The link was stored in the figure of an arctic seal carved from white onyx, tied around my waist. My fingers found the seal and held it, a lifeline.

Minutes dripped, slowed, frozen, as I fought the tides of need and heat. Finally, I could breathe easily again, could feel the muscles as my ribs expanded and contracted, could feel my skin, though it ached, could see reality, rather than a haze of energy and desire. "Wrath of angels," I swore under my breath, wiping my mouth. I had never believed the old tales about neomages and our reactions to certain bloodlines. Never really believed that a female in the presence of a seraph or a kylen went into heat like a mare in a field, demanding to be mounted by the nearest randy stallion.

I pulled myself upright and to my knees. A wave of nausea rushed over me, dizzying weakness. I fought that too. Little by little, I won.

When I could stand, I considered the food on the table, ripe, succulent fruit. In the wake of the sensual mistrial, the peaches in the stoneware bowl lost all enticement. I placed the bowl in the refrigerator and closed it up in the dark, drinking a quart of icy spring water before applying lipstick. Again, I didn't look too closely at why I used cosmetics. Desire for the kylen still surged, muted by the protection of the childhood incantation and by the stored power of the arctic seal. I stuck huge gold and silver hoops in my ears, and a wide cuff on one wrist.

The metal was Rupert's signature Mokume Gane. Before I left the apartment to join my friends, I plucked up an arm sheath and strapped on the kris, sliding the curvy shortsword on. Lipstick and a blade. I was in trouble. Oh, yeah.

Thaddeus Bartholomew was not beautiful like Lucas. Where Lucas was lissome and lithe with hair as black as night, Thaddeus was kylen tall, broad shouldered, and muscular, his hair bright with reddish tints from the glint of outside light. He moved with the grace of the kylen, and when he extended an arm, I could almost see vestigial wings move beneath his jacket.

I was drunk with the amethyst's power. Distressed, despairing, and if I was perfectly honest, horny as a bunny rabbit, I walked past them to the icebox in the workroom and opened a beer, downing it in one long swallow. On my empty stomach, the alcohol hit like a freight train, and the attraction for the kylen dulled. Great. I'd have to stay drunk to keep from tearing off his clothes and having my way with him in the middle of the display floor.

Laughter at my predicament, at the absurdity of my being in heat—with a cop—bubbled up, and I returned to the group carrying bottles of Black Bear Brew and wearing a grin that made Jacey and Audric do double takes before glancing at each other, one of those *significant* looks passed by people who have recently been talking about you. A lot. In the central sitting area of the shop, I set drinks on a table and toasted them before I sat down.

There had been conversation while I was gone to the back, and it had left eddies of emotional strife swirling in the room. I didn't know what had been said, but Audric was tense and watchful; Jacey, quiet. Rupert was tight-lipped with restrained wrath. His hostility helped stabilize my unsteady emotions and further dull my reaction to the kylen as I curled into an oversized wingback with velvet upholstery, my left knee bent up to hold my elbow while I drank. Overhead, the video of Lucas being attacked was still rolling.

"Why do you think they knew what he was carrying?" Audric asked Thaddeus, folding his muscled arms across his chest, cradling the beer, looking like an African prince.

"SNN agreed not to show it, but one of the men came back for the knapsack exactly seven minutes and fourteen seconds after they dragged Lucas off. At seven minutes and twenty seconds, the camera went dead. Local cops are using that time frame for determining the search for Lucas." The kylen, his tone curt, spread a city map on the low table in front of the gaslog fire, bent, and pointed. "The theory isn't bad. If the subjects were on foot, then the assumed range is accurate. If they had horses, they could have reached the second circle."

Mineral City was a divided town, the religious and commercial half on the north bank of the Toe River, the residential and civic half on the south. A suspension footbridge connected the two halves. The map was marked with a yellow circle enclosing the north half, a radius from the point of attack indicating foot traffic. The second circle, marking the radius the attackers could have reached if they had horses, was blue, enclosing areas both south and north of the Toe. There was no third circle for mechanical transport, El-cars, or trucks.

"Cars?" I asked.

"No vehicle tracks." Thaddeus turned those odd blue-green eyes on me, and my belly did a little dip and curl that I felt all the way down to my toes. I managed not to moan. The cop seemed unaffected.

Audric was watching me and I didn't want to meet his eyes, not knowing whether I would see speculation there or humor. I'd be ticked off if he was grinning. "And you discovered shattered rocks at the scene?" Audric asked, his tone asking for clarification.

I sat up straighter. "Rocks? What kind?"

Thaddeus shrugged. He moved as seraphs move, the shrug a curl of shoulder blades rather than a lift of collarbone and ball and socket. When seraphs are uncertain, and their wings are folded out of the way, they raise them, touching what—in arms—would be the wrist bones together. It's a strangely unemotional gesture, as if being uncertain doesn't bother them. "Does it matter?" he asked.

I dragged my thoughts away from his muscled back and what it might look like naked if he lifted a bale of hay overhead. In summer. After a hard workout. I wondered what he was talking about for a moment before I realized he was responding to my question. Jacey looked back and forth from the cop to me, a slight tug on her lips telling me my attraction wasn't a secret. *Great. Just great.* I drank the rest of the beer and took another before speaking. "Because if it's purple stone, we may have some info," I said. "Lucas mailed some amethyst rough to Rupert before he was attacked. Rough from his grandfather's estate."

Thaddeus straightened to his full height, flipped open a small notebook, and poised a pencil on the first page. "What's rough?"

"Was it purple?" I bargained.

Thaddeus' attention settled on me and he waited a beat before answering. "Yes."

"It's stone before it's cut, shaped, and polished," Jacey said, as she watched the cop watch me. And watched me flush. Just a hint of color, but that was enough for my best gal pal. She had a definite "well, well, well," look on her face. "And the stone he sent Rupert is probably gem quality, which he claimed to have found on . . . around here somewhere."

She amended the location on the fly at an almost invisible tightening of Rupert's face. I had a feeling Thaddeus caught the exchange. He didn't miss much, to my chagrin. On the heels of her words, questions rose, like, why Rupert didn't want him to know where the stone had been found. And what caused the animosity flowing between my friends and the cop? Rupert hadn't said a word since I came down the stairs, and there was a part of him that thrived on conflict. A quiet Rupert was very unusual.

"How much of this rough did he send? When, from where, and by what post? And is it valuable?" the kylen asked.

Speaking slowly, taking cues from Rupert's body language in my peripheral vision, I said, "A lot, a week before he was kidnapped, postmarked Linville, where his gramma lives, sent by mule train. And yes, pretty valuable, unless I miss my guess." Pretty valuable, all right—the most powerful stone I'd ever heard of, even in legends.

"So *someone* found the stone *around here*," Thaddeus placed a faint emphasis on the last two words to show he had caught the previous hesitation, "carted it off to Linville, only to have Lucas ship it back here. And Grandma knew all about this."

"Oh," I said. Put that way, it didn't make sense.

"*Gramma,*" Rupert corrected, sounding surly. "Not *Grandma*. And Thaddeus knows about *Gramma*." Rupert's eyes were on the cop, his tone rancorous. "*All* about her. And he's decided that if I'm not behind Lucas' disappearance, you are."

"We discussed his 'woman scorned' theory last night. I'm on his list of suspects. So is every other woman Lucas has been with in the last few years. Right?" I asked the cop. "And how does he know about your gramma?"

Rupert said, "He neglected to mention we're cousins. His mother is my aunt, long lost and all, found by the investigators Lucas hired for probate. Gramma sent him up here to *pry*." His tone was insulting, claiming there was nothing worse than a busybody.

The malice in the room suddenly made sense. Gramma was the paternal grandmother to Rupert, Lucas, and Jason. She lived along the Linville River, in the same house where the

Stanhope patriarch had died last fall. She was a sour woman, full of old anger and unfulfilled hopes that had turned her soul bitter. She also kept secrets. Forbidden knowledge floated in her eyes. Being a keeper of secrets myself, I had spotted it. On top of all that, she was a snoop, a meddler, a woman who delighted in creating animosity among her own family, pitting one grandchild against the other. The old hag.

"Mrs. Stanhope sent you up here? Not the state police?" I asked.

Bartholomew seemed to realize he'd made an error in judgment at some point. His face went through a fast series of emotions, ending with uncertainty. "I had just discovered the Stanhope branch of my family, so I was killing two birds— looking at an opening with local law enforcement, and taking the opportunity to meet my relatives, starting with Gramma." The word sounded curious on his tongue, as if he'd never said it before. "Then Lucas was attacked, and because I'm on the scene, I accepted a temporary liaison position with the local cops." He looked back and forth between us.

"Which you didn't bother to explain when you were questioning me as if I was a fugitive from some hellhole," Rupert accused, both fists on his hips, head thrown back. "Thanks. It's great to meet you too."

Thaddeus sighed, flipped the little notebook closed, and sat down, choosing a small, pink tapestry chair with delicate, turned legs. Each move, from the chair choice to the sigh to his posture after he sat, was calculated to bring down the level of animosity. He went from interrogating bad cop to nonthreatening, just-one-of-the-guys good cop in a heartbeat. "I can see I handled this all wrong. I'm sorry."

That was a nice surprise, I thought, liking him against my better judgment.

"I should have just come to see you and introduced myself. Should have told you who I was up front. Get acquainted the usual way." He dropped his elbows to his knees and laced his hands together. I pulled my eyes away from his long, limber fingers, Stanhope hands, I realized, set off by the impressive ring. His body language was honest and sincere, but I didn't quite buy it. Neither did Jacey or Rupert, but Audric seemed complacent. Odd.

"Gramma acted like I was the savior of the family. Said her other grandsons were quarreling, fighting about the inheritance. She claimed you'd never accept me as anything but a money-grubbing interloper—her words, not mine—if I just came to visit. With the kidnapping, I figured being a cop might give me an entrée I might not get otherwise."

"The old bat set him up," Audric said, with a bark of laughter.

"She set us up too," Jacey said. "Why?"

"It's her nature. Like scorpions sting and lions eat their prey," Audric said, lifting a brow at Rupert.

Rupert pursed his lips, clearly making a judgment. Finally he stood, walked over, and extended his hand. "Let's start over. I'm Rupert Stanhope, your long-lost cousin. I'm a metal smith, a partner in Thorn's Gems. My associates and I design and make jewelry. My brother Lucas is missing. Jason, my other brother, is probably drunk, and if he knew you were here, he'd be trying to borrow money."

Thaddeus stood and took Rupert's proffered hand, his face slightly wry. "I'm Thaddeus Bartholomew, Hand of the Law of the state police. Good to meet you, cousin. Call me Thadd. I'd like to meet your ne'er-do-well brother and offer my services to find Lucas." Instantly the ambience in the room mellowed.

"Okay, Thadd. And Gramma?" Rupert asked, his hand still clasping Thaddeus' as the men measured each other.

"Gramma appears to be a poor judge of character. And a . . . contentious woman."

"Didn't like me much?" Rupert asked.

"She didn't like anyone much."

"Bingo."

I thought about the stone in the back room, the pull it had on me. And about the stone Lucas had been carrying. Over my head the scene of Lucas being attacked still played, and I watched it again, focusing on the dark smear on the alley floor. Without exactly knowing why, I asked, "The alley where Lucas was taken. Was there any blood left when the cops got there?"

The kylen froze and turned penetrating eyes to me, his face a cop mask. I had asked something important. Suddenly I knew that something had happened to Lucas' blood at the scene of the attack. Something bad.

Thadd's eyes narrowed, holding mine. "Why do you ask that?"

Oops. I had just moved back up a notch in the list of potential bad guys. Choosing my words carefully, I said, "Yeah, I thought so. And you found a shattered piece of amethyst in the alley, didn't you? And the other cops don't know about it."

His eyes narrowed farther and he moved slowly closer, to tower over me.

I craned my neck up at him. "You took it from the scene because you knew it had to be important. Can I look at it?"

"Why don't you have the stone Lucas sent evaluated by a geologist?" he deflected.

"I can do that. I have a friend here in town and another in Boone."

"I'll bet you do." His tone was bland, obscuring a measured note of satisfaction.

"Now, wait a minute—" Rupert said.

"I'm a lapidary," I interrupted with a vulpine smile. "A maker of, and dealer in, stone jewelry and sculpture. I have to know people who evaluate its quality."

"Convenient. But if we can come to terms, I'll see about

letting you have access to a bit of the stone from the alley. For comparison purposes."

My smile widened, showing teeth.

"What terms?" Audric asked.

"Our strange little friend here introduces me to her Lolo," the kylen said.

I was thrown off base. In this convoluted conversation, that was one subject I hadn't expected at all.

"What's a lolo?" Jacey asked.

Thadd answered without taking his eyes from me. "A difficult old woman who somehow found out where I was staying. She called my room about ten times. And then she found my secure police sat number, which I was furnished only last week, and she's calling that. She's an annoying, irate old woman who keeps calling, and whom I can't seem to block, though I've tried twice. And she keeps telling me I have to help Thorn."

"My adopted grandmother. Sorta," I said.

"What's a sat?" Jacey asked.

"Well?" he asked, ignoring Jacey.

I couldn't tell him Lolo lived at Enclave, not without going to die there myself. So I lied. More or less. "She lives in southeast Louisiana. You want to visit a licensed witchy-woman, I'll give you her address." He didn't seem to read the partial omission.

His eyes considered. "I was born in Natchez. Maybe my mother knows her."

"Stranger things have happened," I said. Like the confluence of events that resulted in a kylen being related to Rupert, having family in spitting distance of my Enclave, and arriving in Mineral City near the time his cousin was kidnapped. Then coming to Thorn's Gems and interrogating me. I didn't believe in coincidences. Either Thadd orchestrated it, or it all was Lolo's machinations.

"What's a sat?" Jacey asked again. "Wait. You mean a portable phone? Like a Pre-Ap satellite phone? Can I see it?"

Ignoring Jacey, he said, "May I look at the stone? Or do I need to get a subpoena?"

At the implied threat, I stood and led the way. Throwing open the storeroom door, I stood back and allowed the others to enter. The cold of the unheated space rolled out in an icy wave. I opened the small icebox and pulled out another beer. Was it the third today? The fourth? I'd be drunk at kirk and have to confess.

The cop stepped in. I clenched the bottle to keep from running my hands across his backside. The curves were taut, moving beneath the fabric with a rapid, smooth flex. I downed the beer, drowning my need in alcohol.

He flashed me a look over his shoulder and saw the direction of my gaze. I felt his answering heat and knew suddenly, finally, that he wanted me too, though his interest was tempered by suspicion.

A sense of drunken triumph flooded me, until I remembered that sex between us would come with a death sentence at seraphic decree. No kylen and mage may mate. Ever. There may never be another mixing of seraph and mage genes. I wanted to laugh. After all, what was one more death sentence? They could kill me only once.

Audric and Rupert opened a case of the amethyst rough, handing a sample to Thadd. He lifted the stone as light danced through it, diffuse and sultry. I wanted to grab the amethyst, *my* amethyst, out of his hands. Desperately, I slid fingers beneath my tunic and touched the amulet. Lust for man and rock receded and I could breathe.

"All these are full of this?" Thadd asked, kicking a metal box with his leather-clad toe. When Jacey said yes, he asked, "Are you going to trust me enough to tell me where this came from? More than 'around here.' "

My eyes on the stone in his hand, I said, "From the Trine."

I could feel the reactions of my friends, their shock, their incredulity that I had allowed a near stranger in on the truth. I explained to them, "Lucas said local cops and elders are involved with Darkness. The Stanhopes are in danger. Thadd isn't a local cop. He's a Stanhope, and he's here, against all odds, at this particular time. We have to tell him."

"You just want to get in his pants," Jacey murmured into my ear as she whisked out of the room, pulling me away from the men. "You just want him in your bed and if you don't get yourself under control, we won't be able to help you."

Help me what? I blinked and put down the bottle. My fingers were white where I had cut off circulation, gripping the beer. I released the amulet and sighed, not knowing how to salvage this. The ammo box lid clanged shut. The power of stone and cop waned as Jacey pulled me across the workroom, shook me once and shoved me toward my loft. "Go upstairs. And don't come back down until time for kirk. Go."

Exhaustion swamped me. I took the stairs on leaden legs, entered my cold apartment, stripped off my clothes, and slid between the sheets, beneath the feather duvet, my shortsword on the pillow near my head. Sleep fluttered downy wings over my flesh, tantalizing. Just as I slid beneath its lure, I had a moment to wonder about Thadd. He had seraphic and neomage genes mixed with his half-human structure. Why didn't he react to the amethyst?

Chapter 8

†

Ciana's knock woke me. I crawled from warm blankets, tossed on my robe, sheathed and hid the kris, and opened the door. The sleep had done me good. I was myself again, clearheaded, as Ciana came in and plopped into a chair.

She kept her eyes downcast, her mouth in a firm pout, more angry than sad. I didn't try to draw her out; she would talk when she was ready. I poured us juice and put sliced, thawed fruit and cookies on a plate.

Without speaking, I put the treat on the table beside Ciana and gathered up my clothes from this morning so I didn't have to think about my wardrobe. I added heavy underclothes, boots, and a scarf, and tossed my leather cloak over the stand near the door. Taking the clothes, I moved behind the screen, strapped on the kris, and started dressing.

"Seraph stones," she swore, her tone cross. "It's cold as devil blood in here."

I didn't tell her not to curse out loud. Not now. "I hadn't noticed," I fibbed, shivering in the icy air, pulling on thick underleggings, waiting, knowing she wasn't finished. Not by a long shot.

Her tone growing more quarrelsome, she said, "Don't you ever start a fire?"

"Yes." I pulled on the loose outer pair of leggings, securing my amulets around my waist, settling T-shirts and tunic atop them.

"No one will tell me anything!" she shouted, her voice thick with tears. "What's happening to my daddy?"

I stepped around the screen and sipped from a glass of juice. Plum and peach, and colder than the air in the apartment. It made my teeth hurt. "I'll tell you everything I know."

Ciana's blue eyes, so like Lucas', were drowning in grief. I knew for a certainty that fear left unchecked could warp a child. I remembered my own pain and fear when I was a neomage tot, cold, bleeding where talons had raked my flesh, in pain, alone, Dark sorceries swirling about me. And again when I was a little older and my long-awaited gift came to me, ripped me open, and laid me bare. I wouldn't let her suffer.

"I expect you to keep all this to yourself," I said. "No friends, and not Marla." When she agreed, I said, "Your daddy sent Uncle Rupert some metal boxes of amethyst rough. Some documents suggest it came from the Trine, but we don't know why it would have been gathered here, sent to Linville, then sent back here. And it's possible your daddy had some of it in his backpack when he was attacked. If so, the attackers took it. He's alive as far as I know, but he's probably hurt. The police and your new uncle Thadd are going to find him if they can. Uncle Rupert, Audric, and I will help."

Ciana stood when I finished the summary and wrapped her arms around me. "I hate it when I cry. It's sissy and silly and dumb and makes me feel like a baby."

I lay my cheek on her head and smoothed her dark hair. "I hate to cry too, but sometimes we need to."

"Did you cry when Daddy left you?"

An electric shock zinged through me and I drew a breath of cold air. "Yes. I did."

"Me too. You were the best thing he ever did. Then he started acting weird and left you, and I had to go back to Mama. She's my mom and all, but she's not very nice. I miss living here with you and Daddy and Uncle Rupert."

"I miss you too," I said, my own tears gathering and falling. Wisely, I said nothing about the Marla complaint. Never step between a child and her parent. "You ready for kirk?"

"Yeah." She breathed and pulled away, handing me my walking stick. "Let's go."

Hand in hand, we walked into the cold, into a world locked in perpetual winter. Some summers the snow hung around until July and came back by the end of August. In mid-winter, piled snow reached the tops of display windows. The streets and sidewalks were cracked and broken, last repaired over half a century ago when a winged warrior was due to arrive for a ceremony lauding a great battle fought here. I guessed that Mole Man had been honored, but I could be wrong. I hadn't learned local history, my own was enough to keep me occupied.

My boots and walking stick clicked on the ice. From up ahead and behind us came other clicks as the townsfolk braved the cold for kirk, their own boots and walking sticks sharp on the ice. The kirk-goers were somber, most wearing dark wool suits, long dresses, capes, and hats, and sporting the perpetual frowns of most dogmatic orthodox fundamentalists.

After the Last War, when the seraphs didn't pick a religion and validate it, when there had been no sighting of a One True God, religious violence had erupted across the globe. Angels of Punishment had appeared on the scenes, swords raised, and humans had died by the thousands. Since that time, the differing religions had built an uneasy alliance. As long as no blood was spilled in the name of the Most High, the unseen God, the seraphs didn't intervene.

However, if an undocumented mage was discovered, they

would direct the proceedings and lead the pack in tearing her—me—to pieces.

I nodded to an elder's wife and she waved back gaily. Polly was the spouse of Elder Jasper, the youngest elder in Mineral City. She took the hand of an older woman who slipped and nearly fell, and they walked on together.

The cold seeped into my boots, through their hobbled soles and fur insoles, into my tripled socks, to my feet. Though the fur industry was closed down, proclaimed inhumane and cruel, interdicted by seraphs, there were still fur clothing items made every summer when animals who had died in the blistering ice or through starvation were exposed by snowmelt, thawed, and gathered for use. My boots were lined with beaver. So were Ciana's, and even with the thick fur, the temperature was deadly dangerous should we remain outside too long.

After plowing a half mile through crusted snow, we reached the kirk, a stone building with no heat, no electric lights, no padded seats, no comforts of any kind. Under the arched porch, we stamped our boots clean before we entered the incense-scented, candlelit dark. Inside, we paused, allowing our eyes to adjust. I put my walking stick in the stand near the door and moved to the walls where frescoes of the last local battles had been painted—seraphs and humans depicted fighting a Major Dragon as light blasted up from the deeps.

With the new knowledge of the Mole Man, I studied the frescoes closely, noting in one the beast being pulled from the ground bound in bloody chains. Mole Man's sacrifice. A disembodied face in one corner had Lucas' eyes. A polished brass plaque beneath it read, BENAIAH STANHOPE—MOLE MAN.

It was true. And now the Stanhopes were in danger. One was missing in a trail of blood. One had seen a daywalker. Another had been brought a long distance. In the fresco, rock avalanched down three mountainous, raw rock peaks, towering into the heavens, newly created from the original, single hill. Dark smoke poured from the ground of the Trine.

An elder moved from the shadows and sprinkled us with holy water, flinging his hyssop branch, the water icy, miserable. The water had come at great expense from the Dead Sea, and had been perfumed with essential oil of rosemary and stored in quart jars. It was considered a great blessing to be splattered. I could have done without it.

Kirk services are different in every town. In primarily Jewish communities, the Sabbath of ancient times is still observed on Friday night and Saturday. Muslims answer the call to prayer a traditional five times daily. Orthodox Christians worship daily, though reformed and progressives worship less. In the United States, Hindus, Buddhists and other Eastern religions tend to worship at home due to the dearth of temples.

After the Last War, it was clear the Christians' Christ hadn't made it back to earth or lifted them to the heavens in a Rapture, yet the angels had come and so had the plagues and the wars and the destruction of the world as the church had long predicted. Deciding that the Second Coming was delayed, survivors had created worship practices unique to each town.

In Mineral City, elders had been authorized to promulgate the religious continuation of Jews, Christians, and the local Indian population. Jewish services are held in the kirk building on the Sabbath, and Sunday services are Christian, though very different from Pre-Ap ceremonies. According to rumor, many of the local American Indians have returned to the religious practices of their ancestors, building their own places of worship deep in the hills.

Neomages don't have souls, yet my parents had been reformed Christian, attending services in the tiny Enclave church, with the few other soulless mages so inclined. Churchgoing had seemed a waste of good playtime to Rose and me, but if there was one chance in a billion that the seraphs had it wrong, or any hope that the Most High might change his mind and give mages souls later—allowing us into heaven along with the human elect—our parents were going to see to it that we were prepared.

At the front of the kirk, we knelt on the hard stone floor. Ciana bent her head and folded her hands, her beautiful hands, so like Lucas', like Thadd's, that I was brought up short by the sight. I should have realized Thadd was a Stanhope the first time I saw him.

My own square, worker-woman hands stole beneath my cloak and tunic to my amulets and gripped handfuls as I followed her lead and bowed my head. And because I had promised her, I prayed for Lucas. To live. To find safety. To be saved.

I felt nothing. I always felt nothing when I prayed, but I wasn't human, and prayer was for humans. There was nothing in the holy scriptures about neomages. We had not been prophesied, not in any religion mankind had ever professed. The Administration of the ArchSeraph had proclaimed us soulless at some point after the mage-war, eliminating us from the elect. So it did no real good for me to pray. If God the Victorious existed, he wouldn't hear me.

Did he exist? Had God the Victorious known mages were coming? Had he cared? Blasphemy, all my thoughts, and blasphemy was always a prelude to disaster, a prelude to a seraph with his sword raised and humans dying. If I prayed for nothing else, I always prayed to avert such a disaster for Mineral City, prayed just in case he was real and might hear me. And this time, I concentrated on Lucas, fearful for the first time in ages, that I'd bring the wrath of angels down on the small town.

When we left the kirk, my knees were aching and dusk was settling onto the earth as the sun fell below the mountain peaks. I lifted a hand in greeting to Elder Culpepper; he nodded once, censure on his face. I hadn't been to kirk in three weeks and two days. I knew he knew that. And I was leaving before the Jubilee.

Even though having a child to remove before the holy revelry began was a proper excuse, he would remember.

Fortunately, his attention was drawn to a man outside in the cold, leaning against the stone porch column. The man was wearing rags, a patched hood, a fur coat so ancient the hair was falling out in clumps, the soles of his worn-out shoes tied to his feet with straps and padding. Layers of threadbare pants and gloves. Kirk brands for cursing and blasphemy disfigured both cheeks. The beggar blew clouds of mist as we exited, eyes half mad. The elder pushed me aside in his rush to reach the man. I grabbed Ciana's hand and sprinted away from the kirk, nearly dragging her, glancing back at the altercation that was breaking out between elder and beggar.

The elder raised his staff and brought it down across the beggar's back. "Get out. Get out of here," he shouted with each whap of the rod. "Get out or I'll call a seraph."

The man laughed, defeat, abandonment, and derision all mixed in the anguished sound. "What, Father. No pity? No alms for the poor?" He danced beyond the six-foot staff and raised his voice. "And why call a *seraph*? Even you know they aren't angels."

"Blasphemy!"

"Truth," the beggar shouted. "You fool. They didn't come from God; they came to invade our world. And more and more humans know it. The EIH knows it! You know it, if you only search your heart for the truth!"

A second elder appeared in the doorway and the beggar ran for the creek bed near the kirk. "Stop him!" Elder Culpepper shouted. Robes flapping, they chased him down the depression.

I pulled Ciana harder, moving as fast as the slick surface allowed, my walking stick digging into the ice.

"What's EIH?" she asked when we were out of earshot.

"Earth Invasion Heretics," I said softly, not wanting the

elders to overhear. "And you will *not* speak of them in public, understand?"

"I'm not stupid," she said, expression lofty. "We got taught about anarchists and antigovernment groups in school. But everybody knows that angels and seraphs are the same thing. Right? And God will show himself when he's good and ready. Right?"

I looked back over my shoulder. The two elders were standing in the snow looking down the frozen streambed, righteous breath billowing. "Right. Sure."

"You sound like you don't believe it."

"I believe it. And I agree that God will show himself if he wants to, when he wants to." I looked down at Ciana and managed a smile. I wasn't going to be a stumbling block to her budding faith. She would suffer enough if she ever discovered that her ex-stepmother wasn't human and didn't have a soul.

"But?"

But they call themselves seraphs, not angels, not messengers. And none appeared to punish that man for blasphemy. "It's not something I can prove one way or another."

"You just have to have faith. Right?"

"Yeah. Faith." *Can a soulless being have faith?* As we crunched back up the half mile to the shop, Ciana's hand in mine, I ventured, "Do you feel better?"

Ciana turned to me, eyes calm, face peaceful. "Daddy's okay. He'll be saved. God the Victorious promised." The breath left my lungs in a single harsh whoosh, and Ciana smiled. "And you're supposed to help rescue him. God told me so."

"God the Victorious talked to you?"

"Yep."

"Ciana." I stopped, though she pulled free of my hand and continued up the path. How did I tell my stepdaughter that the Most High didn't tell me the same thing? Words froze on my tongue and, like usual when humans talked about a faith I was genetically incapable of sharing, I chose the coward's path. Agreement. "Okay."

I paused a long moment before catching up to her. "I'll do my best." And that was absolute truth. But, as I wouldn't have a chance to help Lucas, I changed the subject. "About the devil-spawn you saw. You know that devil-spawn don't appear in daylight."

Ciana shrugged, her face serene. I was going to save Lucas. She believed it totally. *Glory and infamy.* My amulets warmed my waist as I drew on them in unconscious fear.

"The thing you saw," I persisted, "may have been a daywalker."

She shrugged again, her eyes turned into the dark, and I felt the cold seep up through my bones. "Ciana, a daywalker is dangerous. Have you seen it again?" When she didn't answer at once, I knew. She had seen the creature again.

The thing finished with him, pulling its teeth from his flesh with a pain like acid and steel, dropping his wrist again. He heard the sound of it spitting his blood into a container. Why didn't it just drink it? Wasn't that what Darkness did? Drink human blood?

Exhausted, too drained of blood and life to fight, Lucas lay in the dark watching where the thing that carried his blood scampered and disappeared. The cavern seemed less dark now and he saw a brighter rectangle nearby. Slowly, he sat up. It was a doorway. A doorway into a larger hall, indicated by a dark, dull glow.

He scooted across the cavern floor to the pale red glow and put out a hand. Cold burned him. He jerked back fast, sticking blistered fingers into his mouth. His fingers screamed with pain, and he gasped. Only now did he see the bars. Demon-iron, spelled and rimmed with ice, barred his way. He remembered the sound of mauls as they locked him in. An echo of iron on iron still rang in the distance, Darkness working metal.

Out there, something moved. He heard the splash and knew the sound was his blood being poured out. A soft gurgle of something swallowing followed.

They were using his blood for something, he knew that. Something different from the usual slaking of spawn lust and hunger. But for what?

Chapter 9

✝

"Ciana. Talk to me, please. Has that thing appeared to you again?"

"He said you'd know."

My toes were ice and agony, but I stopped on the frozen walk, gripped Ciana's shoulders, and turned her to me. "Tell me everything. Please."

"He said I could take you there, where he meets me." Finally, her eyes lifted to mine. Something swam in their depths, something hidden and fearsome.

A secret. *Saints' balls.* Ciana had a secret about a daywalker.

"It's behind the shop." With a little tug on my hand she pulled me back the way we had come, then sharply to the left, into a little alley between two buildings. The cloud-shrouded dusk dimmed even more and shadows closed in on us tightly.

The dark held secrets more fearful than the ones in Ciana's eyes, and my own past roared up, memory clamoring for attention. Pain lanced through my old scars, a wrenching fear. Skimming, I swept behind and ahead at the alley opening and overhead at the rooftops, flexed the fingers of my free hand around the bloodstone walking-stick hilt, longing to pull the blade. But the path ahead was clear. Clouds were breaking above us and a star peeked through. I forced the memory of my own childhood shadows away. We cleared the alley and stepped up the hill at the foot of the Trine.

Little stables and outbuildings were scattered along the flat area, hip deep in snow. I scented horses, mules, and domestic fowl in the deep dusk. As though she could see in the dark, Ciana pulled me beyond the stables, higher up the hillside, into the edge of the woods. A single footpath led through the trees, across what had once been Walnut Avenue, up the base of the Trine, as if it had been well and recently trod, though snow had fallen this morning. My breath sped up; I gripped Ciana's hand more firmly. If attacked, I would throw her behind me, pulling my blades at the same instant. *Glory and infamy.*

I opened my senses and sent out a hard skim, not trying for silence. If a daywalker or an early-rising spawn was here, it already knew we were too. But there was nothing, only the well-worn path and the cold and the sound of night creatures waking. A bird called, a single owl hoot, lonely and longing.

Ciana led me west and north. She stopped at a circle of large rocks piled nearly waist high, sticking out of the snow, as if brushed clean. Water tinkled. We were at my spring.

From a copper pipe between two stones water gushed into a stoneware and plastic cistern. I had spoken words of power over the system, charging the fired clay and plastic to resist cracking as temperatures changed with the seasons, then released a rune of obscurity over it to shield it from human notice, passing warriors, or the rare, unexpected seraph. The spring and cistern had worked flawlessly for years.

"This is where he meets me." The words had a tone of confession to them. "Meets me" meant more than once. Ciana knew she shouldn't have come here.

"Did it kiss you? Taste you with its tongue?"

"No. Not exactly."

"Then what *exactly* did it do?"

"He put his head here." She held her hand near her neck. "And he sniffed a lot. He said I smelled good."

Yeah. Like a slab of raw meat, dinner, or worse—a virgin. I gripped my walking stick. My eyes swept the surrounding trees as my mage-senses scoured the hillside. Nothing. Nothing there at all. "But it didn't lick you?"

"No. He said you'd ask that. He said you knew about people like him."

I did know, memories half forgotten, buried deep, only now beginning to unfurl in a deadly blossoming. "Did it sit? Where?" I asked when she nodded.

Ciana pointed to a stone, larger than the others. Pulling her with me, I walked around it and bent, pretending to look closely. There was no snow on the stone. It had been brushed to the ground. Drawing air in, I sniffed with nose and mage-sense, sending out a powerful skim, half challenge, defiant.

The fetid spoor of devil-spawn slammed into me and I rocked back, nauseated, remembering the scent of foulness from my childhood, from my time of terror. A fainter hint of something else, something unknown, lurked beneath the smell, perhaps the subtle stench of daywalker. Two species of Dark beings had been here. Recently. The spawn pack before dawn, the daywalker when the sun was high. Fear crawled up my arms and legs. Devil-spawn had found me. Again.

"He said you would be afraid, but that you didn't have to be."

"It isn't a he. And it isn't a person; it's a beast." Two kinds, spawn and something else. I threw my senses into the dusk, following the older spawn scent as it moved uphill before vanishing. The spawn pack had traveled north, up the center peak of the Trine, then angled west. "What did it ask you, this thing that sniffed you? What did you talk about?"

"He said you had been hurt when you were a little girl and that made you afraid of people like him."

I swallowed hard. Only a very few knew of the attack when I was a child. Except for Lucas, all of them were at Enclave. "I was injured by devil-spawn when I was a little girl, smaller than you are now. I nearly died." I stared up the hills, breathing deeply, remembering a deeper dark, the dark of underground where I had been taken, stuffed into a crevice, and left to die, left for my body to cure to the palates of a Major Darkness. Too young for mating, I had been a tasty morsel for a special event. Bleeding and cold and dying. So cold.

"I got away," I whispered through a throat that didn't work right. "I got away" wasn't the full and complete truth, but I didn't remember my escape; it was all foggy, like a nightmare the morning after waking. "Have you told me everything?" I asked.

"Yep. Except his name."

I jerked, almost drawing my blade. No Darkness willingly gave its name! And daywalkers were supposed to be far more intelligent than spawn. If one gave her its name—

"He said you'd know what to do with it. It's Malash—"

I slapped my free hand over Ciana's mouth as she spoke, cutting her off. Her shocked eyes met mine above my thumb. "Shhh. Never say it aloud. Promise." Her head bobbed slowly. "To say its name is to call it. And devil-spawn are following it, tracking it. If you call it, a spawn pack may come too. And then the spawn would know its name and yours and have power over you both. I don't know what kind of strength a daywalker has, but I know for a fact that at night, the spawn would have their full strength. And they would be hungry. They're always hungry. Understand?"

Ciana pushed my hand from her mouth. "Your fingers are frozen. They feel like icicles. And I'm hungry."

My throat working, I swallowed down my fear, an icy shaft stabbing as it went down.

Her hand still in mine, I led the way around the spring-head, back down the hill. Words were still painful. "Let's go inside. I'll fix dinner and call Marla. Tell her you're staying with me tonight."

"Cool. Can I play with your dolls?"

"Yes," I said, scarcely hearing. "Anything you want."

We ate onion soup and cheese, toasted olive loaf with herbed olive oil drizzled over it, and fried apples for supper. Two girlfriends on a sleepover, we munched while curled in comforters in front of the fire, talked about clothes, her friends, school, her father, horses—anything but daywalkers—played with my dolls, the ones given to me by my foster father, and strung beads to replace items sold over the winter.

We kept the old radio on the news channel for any word on Lucas. There was no new information, but Ciana wasn't perturbed or frightened at the lack. She was peaceful, resting in the assurance granted her by God the Victorious that her father would return. That *I'd* find him. I tried not to think about any of it, keeping my fingers busy with my work.

Near nine, I put Ciana to bed in the middle of my huge mattress, covered by mounded down comforters wrapped in silk duvets. I turned down the flames, placed my walking stick, its hidden blade loosed, on the floor close to hand, and curled up beside her, spooning her with my body heat. Worried by the name Ciana had almost spoken, I didn't sleep well, rising at every little sound, checking the position of the blade in readiness. Agitated, I went twice to the narrow back windows flanking the stained-glass one to stare past the springhead. But devil-spawn never came, nor the daywalker whose name I could guess. *Malashe-el*, a name taken from a fallen seraph. Perhaps he hadn't heard her aborted call. Perhaps we would be safe a little longer.

* * *

Thursday morning dawned dark and cold, the sky hidden by heavy clouds. The weather was so bleak, even the roosters stayed in bed late. I helped Ciana dress, fed her fruit and bread with honey and milk, and kissed her forehead, promising to come for her if there was news of Lucas. Through the dim light, I pointed out Jacey across the street, taking her youngest to school, and scooted Ciana into the steady stream of mirthless, sullen, early-morning populace. I watched her trudge across to Jacey and take her hand.

Upstairs, I rushed through twenty minutes of savage-chi, took a skimpy, cold shower, and, because Ciana had eaten the last of the bread, lit the stove with a handy-dandy fire amulet that sparked a steady flame when I thumbed it. It was useful for starting a fire in wet wood while camping too. If I was ever stranded outdoors, I wouldn't go cold.

I cooked and ate a breakfast of oatmeal with honey while dressing in the outer clothes I had worn yesterday. Because of the snow, they had been seen only by my partners and the elders. To alter the look, I used an ocean green scarf and wore huge silver hoops and one of the necklaces I had made the night before. Over my sleeves I clamped wide, silver cuff bracelets studded with green—malachite, chrysoprase, and emerald.

The cuffs were ostentatious, but beneath each I wore blades strapped to my forearms. I had designed them myself, and they weren't for sale, though Thorn's Gems had similar ones on display. Flamboyant, but it all looked great when I was carrying a walking stick. Very stylish. It gave me three blades: one for throwing, two for wielding. With Darkness nearby, asking questions about me, I wasn't taking chances. I packed a small bag with necessities, specially loved items, and battle clothes and set it by the door, half hidden by my long, silk-lined, insulated leather cloak. The cloak, my battle boots, and gloves were mage-made, conjured against most minor weapons of Darkness. If I had to run, I could be ready in moments.

Lastly, I put away the handmade porcelain dolls, storing them in the armoire in the sitting area. I had seven: three adults in fancy outfits, and four babies with padded bodies and lacy christening gowns, all gifts from Uncle Lem. If I ran, I'd be leaving them behind, along with the life I had built in Mineral City. Ineffable sadness rose up in me, and I blinked back tears. I had been so lonely when I first came, the only mage in a thousand miles, hiding what I was even from my foster father. Uncle Lem had known me only as an orphan and had worked hard to fill the void of family in my life. Though I was fourteen, I had been small for my age, as all mages are, and he had begun the tradition of giving me dolls on special occasions. Four birthdays and three Christmases, until he died in my eighteenth year from a rare fast-acting cancer.

I held a baby doll in a long silk and lace gown close, and breathed deeply before putting her away and closing the door. I fancied I could still smell Uncle Lem's scent on her.

I lit the fire in the shop, heated water, and made coffee, preparing to open. At just after nine, as the last town bell announced the hour, the beginning of kirk, and the orthodoxes' morning prayers, I turned the key in the front door. I stood there, my face to the wan light, looking out at the ugly weather, watching the final stragglers dash into kirk or into work, smelling the coffee perking, wishing for spring.

From down the street Rupert came, appearing in a break in the last of the pedestrians, carrying a canvas bag of groceries with a long loaf of bread sticking out the top. My partner was wearing black: black denim, black boots, a black coat with wide tails flying out behind. Denim lapis stones in his ears, around his neck, and clipped to his black hat were the only spots of color. He looked spare, dark, and solemn, while I looked colorful and flamboyant. We'd clash. He'd hate that, which made me smile.

From the alley at his side, a gray form darted. Another.

They crashed into Rupert. Flung a gray cloth over him. He was gone.

I blinked. Stared at the spot where Rupert had been, his groceries in a pile. Traffic moved on as if nothing had happened. As if no one had seen. Breath and fear blasted from me. I screamed. And ran, the walking stick in my hand.

Cold bit through my clothes. Ice beneath my shoes ripped at my balance as I rounded the corner. I loosed the blade. Shadows swirled at the back of the alley and I dove at them, screaming, *"Rupert!"* It was a battle cry.

I rammed into the first one, catching him unbalanced, flinging him across the alley. A solid thunk sounded, his head hitting the wall. On its echo, I flowed into savage-blade.

The walking-stick sheath whirled. My blade sliced across, beneath it, and down. Tore into the other assailant's coat at his hip with a ripping shush. Swept along my body as the sheath blocked his out-thrust arm.

Mage-vision blazed. The alley came alive with color, with energies, with the might of stone and mortar composing the buildings to either side. In a whir of speed, I clipped him on the side of the head. He blocked the stick. It landed on his shoulder with a crack.

I pressed the attack, stepping over a squirming body on the snow-packed alley floor. Rupert. "Be still," I shouted. The body ceased its struggles.

Behind me, the other stirred and stood. Shook his head. Sluggish. No threat yet.

Fingers shaped in *the claw* whipped by my head. *Neomage move.* A leg swept out at me. *Swan-wing,* human strong, but human slow.

I hadn't been thinking, had just been hitting, not using my brain. These were humans, which meant they had more muscle mass, more strength, but less speed. They would hurt me if they actually landed a blow. Badly. I had weapons—three blades and the sheath—my body, and speed. I altered my response to the claw and swan-wing moves.

Twin whacks of the walking stick reacted to them. A single fist glanced off my ribs. Breath grunted out. My blade cut along his damaged shoulder. Drew blood.

A black aura filled the sliced flesh and flowed toward me with the blood. *He was spelled.*

Instantly, my palm drew on the power stored in the bloodstone. Linked to my amulets. All of them. Heat and force gathered, crackling around me. A simple, basic sphere of shielding snapped into place at my feet. Force rose from the earth beneath the snow, called by the amulet. He couldn't see me, flinging blows against my shielding. Mage-sight glared with energies. I shouted an incantation, the words scripture-strong and fast, though they sounded almost languorous. Sonorous.

"Their defense is departed from them!" Stored power coalesced. I shaped it into a talon with my mind. "Be thou my strong rock, for an house of defense, to save me." A spur of might, it pierced into the rock wall at my shoulder. The shield blocked the Darkness flooding through the attacker's blood.

"The place of defense shall be the munitions of rocks," I shouted. The talon of power twisted inside the stone. A huge crack blasted the alley. Dust flew. The other attacker launched at me. And I paraphrased from Joshua, chapter six, "And the wall of the alley shall fall down flat!"

The talon I had shaped curled into the stone, lacerated the mortar, and pulled. The wall gave way with a roar. Rocks that were mine to call, stone that became mine to use, blasted out. Sought out the man before me like an avalanche. Bounced off my shield. Pummeled the man behind me.

His eyes glowed an angry red. He shot out his hand. Power rocked me, black and murky against my shield. He turned and ran.

The man behind me cried out, staggered beneath the

heavy stone, and followed, limping, out the alley mouth into brighter day.

"He set a mark upon Cain," I said, pulling in the wild energies dancing on and within the stone at my sides and below the snow. "He shall be a fugitive and vagabond in the earth. Up, follow after the man, to mark the place where he shall lie."

My might swept after them, stealing the energy that formed the shield, draining me to power the conjure—a flaming fireball of purpose. Through the air. *Idiot! Demon horns!* The attackers rounded the corner, out of sight. Gone.

With a near-silent pop, the conjure fell apart and splashed down. The power of the seeker chant ruptured, falling back to the earth, into the walls at my sides. Into stone. The snow all around me and down the length of the alley melted in a rush. I dropped to my knees, sucking air. The power I had called dwindled into nothing, a dissipating fog.

"Thorn?" The voice was muffled.

Gasping, I wiped the last of the attacker's foul blood onto the gray cloth covering Rupert. With a metal-on-leather grating, I sheathed the blade, knelt, and unwrapped my friend. His face was bloodied, a purple-red bruise beside his right eye. "What happened?" he asked, his words slurred.

"I don't know," I said. And then I caught the faint afterstink. The black aura smelled, leaving a trace of its origins. A hint of Powers and Principalities. *"Glory and infamy,"* I whispered and then wished I hadn't cursed. They had used neomage moves, which meant a rogue mage had been training them. A mage had gone over to Darkness.

Chapter 10

†

Footsteps crashed at the mouth of the alley. I whipped halfway to my feet. Audric stood there, bare chested, framed in the opening like a black godling staring down the mouth of hell. A katana longsword and a wakazashi shortsword were crossed at groin level. A fighting stance. In an instant, I drew on my drained amulets to blank my skin, damped my mage-sight, and dropped back to the alley. Melted snow soaked into my pants. My indoor shoes were dripping. Shivers gripped hard in the aftermath of adrenaline loss. I was freezing, skin aching, teeth chattering.

Knees flexed, Audric advanced at an angle, allowing him a partial view of the street behind, repositioning the longsword to cover the entrance as he moved. He inspected the length of the alley, the wet cobblestones even now freezing over, the rock wall exploded out, revealing the webbing of ancient wood slaths. He looked at me.

I gathered up the gray cloth that had been tossed over Rupert. It carried the reek of Darkness in the smear of blood, and my hands ached when I touched it, but I balled it up and tucked it beneath my tunic as I helped Rupert to sit. He was groggy, confused, and the bruise at his temple was a rising lump.

A screech of wood echoed in the alley and voices sounded from above. Audric lifted the katana as if to ward off attack, before instantly lowering both weapons and hiding them along the lengths of his legs. Over our heads, two mostly bald octogenarians started speaking at once. "You folks okay?"

"That wall jist fell right on out."

"Dang, woman, I see it."

"I tolt you that wall needed attention. The mortar was rotten. Now them people are hurt. You folks need a medic?"

"Yeah, you tolt me. You always telling me something or other."

"Rupert?" When he shook his head, I said, "We're fine. No one's hurt. But your wall needs repair." Actually, it now needed to be replaced, but I didn't point that out.

"Fine, then. Glad you're all okay. And we got us a son what's a stonemason. You change your mind, you need help, you bang on the shop door at front." The couple, still bickering about the mortar, lowered the window with a second screech. Only after the window closed did I recognize the proprietors of the bakery. It was the bakery's wall I had destroyed. I scented yeast and fresh bread on the morning air.

Audric relaxed his stance and rested his weapons as he advanced the rest of the way to us. His skin was puckered with cold, steam radiating off his chest. "Rupert? Are you okay?"

"Yeah. Woozy." He braced his arms and looked down his body. "I'm all wet. What happened to the snow?"

"Thorn happened."

The blood in my veins froze. What had Audric seen? He hadn't been here—

"The wall can be rationalized, but we need to get you two away from this spot before anyone notices the melt. Can you walk?"

"Sure. Help me up." Rupert raised his hand.

Audric slid the wakazashi into his belt and lifted Rupert. I stood up alone. "Audric—"

"Not now."

"Yeah. Later." *Much later. Like never, maybe?* The swords disappeared into the folds of Audric's pants leg for the short walk. No one looked out a window to see two wet and wretched people and one nearly naked man. It was as if we moved beneath a cloak of invisibility or as if the light of the rising sun bent around us and vanished.

Heat blasted us as we entered Thorn's Gems. I shuddered hard, slipping off my shoes. My feet were so cold even the floor felt heated.

"Get dry and warm," Audric ordered. I ran upstairs and locked myself in. What had he seen? What had Audric meant when he said, *Thorn happened*? I unsheathed my blade, recoiling at the stink on the steel. Wiping it hadn't removed the microscopic traces of blood.

Mage-fast, hoping to generate body heat, I pulled a bag of salt to me, one that had been used often, mostly to close circles of power, and plunged the mage-made steel into the bag. Brimstone burned my nose as the blood was cleansed. When I pulled the blade free, salt clung to the cutting edge. I held it beneath springwater in the sink as the final traces of blood were neutralized. I quickly opened a bottle of lightweight oil and wiped down the blade. It needed more attention, but the oil would hold it temporarily. To remove traces of spelled blood from the sheath, I poured salt inside and touched a little-used amulet at my neck. There was barely enough strength left in the stone to clean the inside of the walking stick. When I banged the sheath, pouring the salt down the sink, it had grayed, losing its savor.

The smell of evil was still in the cloth the attackers left behind. I could use it to track them. I could use it to scry. And so could they to me. It wasn't safe to keep or use.

I knelt and turned the fireplace flames up high. With my ceremonial knife, I cut the fabric, removing the bloodiest sections, and tossed the contaminated cloth on the flames. The stink would rise and be swept away by winter winds. Let them try and track it to me. It wouldn't be possible unless they had planned well in advance. The stink of evil wafted up the chimney.

The rest of the cloth, still tainted but less powerful, wasn't something that could be tracked easily, though I smelled brimstone and knew it contained traces of blood. I stuffed it into a stone jar, sealed the top, and wedged it into the bag of salt. It was effectively insulated until I needed it. No one could track it, not through the salt. I marked the bag with a black X.

Only then did I strip out of the wet clothes, hanging them in front of the fireplace to dry, re-dressing in warm underleggings and slacks. I wore navy this time, which wouldn't clash too badly with the teal tunic and ocean-toned scarf. My hair was mussed and I braided it hastily. I was shaking. A pale glow seeped from my skin.

My amulets were almost barren. I had panicked and drawn on them, all of them, wasting their power. I was shaking with after-battle fatigue, cold, even after moving with heat-generating speed. I was too drained to restore both the amulets and myself. Audric had seen me glow.

Because tainted salt wouldn't affect every incantation, I picked up the salt marked TRUTH/LUST and formed a small circle on the kitchen floor, not bothering to move the table, but sitting half under it in my exhaustion. I didn't have the resources to call on the power of the deeps, or to fight the temptation to steal power and force for my own if I did. So I settled on recharging the amulets I needed most.

Neomage amulets can be set up as empty vessels waiting for any incantation one might need, as if formatting a hard crystal disc for information storage. Or they can be adapted with a permanent matrix, as if an incantation or computer program is permanently etched in the crystal matrix of the stone or shell or whatever is used to hold the conjure. Such amulets are preprogrammed for only one purpose and can be refilled after each use. The latter version of amulet making is time-consuming, requiring several days, sometimes even several mages, to make one, but they hold an incantation and the power needed to fuel it much better.

Most of my amulets are the latter sort. I live alone. I require greater protection than a neomage living in Enclave, and when blizzards blow in, isolating us for days at a time, I have the freedom to make them. In Enclave, a mage might have hundreds of lesser amulets, each charged for a different use. To keep my secret, I made do with a few major ones. I dropped my necklace of amulets at my ashen blue toes with a clatter. My feet were an agony, but I could immerse them in warm water later.

With an effort of will, I called up mage-sight and added the last of the salt, closing the circle with a soft pop. The loft glowed, but dimly, as my own depleted forces dulled my perception of other energies. Too tired to think, I tried to pull energy from beneath my feet. Instead, a seductive lavender heat throbbed at me, pulsing power that soothed and enchanted. The amethyst in the storeroom.

It flowed up my body like a lover finally allowed an intimacy, heating my chilled limbs, even my frozen feet, my aching hands. Too fatigued to refuse the easy lure of such readily available power, I let it touch me, a sultry warmth. I didn't have to pull in the energy; it simply flowed in, like my own blood returned to me, my own strength, power, and life force. It quickly restored my strength, heated my cold body, then passed into the amulets at my pinkening toes. As I watched, my mage-sight swirling lavender and gold with tints of fuchsia, the stone in the stockroom recharged my amulets: the fish that held my shield, the elephant carrying the basic charmed circle, the black-and-green-jade bear that was keyed to mute my physical neomage attributes, the larger bear I called on when I needed power from the deeps for some crisis, the cougar carved from red brecciated jasper that offered the glamour I had hidden beneath at the Salvage and Mineral Swap Meet, others. Usually I required a whole day of intense recharging to achieve such restoration, and another two days to fill the amulets. Drawing on the amethyst, I was renewed in minutes, the amulets only a few minutes later. And still the power flowed, as if begging me to take it, so tempting.

I should stop. There was something wrong with all this power so easily given. But I was empty, empty to a bone-cold depth. So I yielded and filled all the empty amulets in the loft. All the stones that protected and served me. I drew in enough excess energy to recharge the bloodstone hilt of my walking stick. And then a bit more. Just a bit, to warm me, feeling myself expand to contain it.

Immediately I was unsteady, mentally inebriated, physically nauseous. It was more than a psychic reaction. A lot more. My skin, muscles, torso, felt heated, engorged. I swallowed heavily and put out a hand to stabilize myself. I had pulled in too much, yet the amethyst energies still demanded to be used, an external pressure. A faint headache started, my blood beating with an irregular cadence of pain. When I looked around, my loft was a bower of blissful might, pulsing with color as if I could see the energies of every atom.

A knock sounded. I groaned. It had to be Rupert and Audric. With a sick moan I shut down my receptors and broke the protective ring, kicking aside the salt. Wavering as if drunk, I blanked my skin, tied the amulets beneath my tunic, called out that I was coming, and swept up the salt, dumping it into its bag. Movement made me want to throw up. Yeah, I was drunk, as drunk as a skunk, power drunk. I heard myself giggle and stifled it.

BLOOÐRING

Taking up the walking stick, I felt power flowing through the bloodstone hilt, deep within the stone's crystal matrix. The handle was a prime amulet, one of two Lolo charged to my genetic code the week after I was born. After I damaged the other one, the bloodstone handle was my best defense. Barefoot, warm, I walked to the door and opened it.

Audric was alone, dressed in a loose and flowing black martial uniform, a scarlet belt of status tied, just so, at his waist, his blades at rest, hilts toward the floor. Though many humans practiced the art form and fighting techniques, I hadn't known he was a practitioner of savage-chi and savage-blade until I saw him in the alley only minutes ago. Now it seemed he not only wanted me to know, he wanted to grind my face in the fact that he was a master. His dark eyes met mine from his great height, and when he spoke, his tone was formal. "Are you well?"

His words held a hidden meaning. *Thorn happened.* He had seen my flesh in the alley, had to know I was a supernat. But did he know what kind? I sighed. "You want to talk here or downstairs?" My way of asking who knew besides him.

"Here. Rupert is cleaning up. Jacey has an early customer."

I stood aside and he entered, his bulk dwarfing me. Audric was bigger than the kylen. A lot bigger. "Who were they?" he asked.

"I never saw them before. They were waiting in the alley." As I talked, I moved to my armoire and pulled on a pair of socks, planting my story. "When Rupert reached the mouth of the alley, they rushed him. Threw a cloth over him and he was gone before I could blink. I grabbed my walking stick—because it was the only thing resembling a weapon—and ran after them. I bumped one into the wall and hit the other with the stick several times. They dropped Rupert and the wall fell. Probably because its mortar was rotten and the guy hitting it dislodged enough to . . ." At the expression on his face, I let my words fall silent.

Audric's gaze was deep, grave, with the Zen-like silence of his training. And something more. Prickles traced up my spine, helping dispel the sense of drunkenness. *Thorn happened.* I gave up the pretense and dropped onto my cushy couch, pulling up my feet and wrapping my arms around my knees, a defenseless pose, but with my walking stick secured between knees and chest, blade loosed. And I still had the kris strapped to my forearm. "Okay. Let's talk."

Audric settled onto the couch, but he didn't look relaxed. He lay his blades across his lap, prepared for battle. "You are neomage, out of Enclave, hiding. I assume you ran following an infraction. Or banishment. This I have suspected for some time."

I should have attacked. Audric tensed as the thought crossed my mind. Not good. I had telegraphed my intent; no human should have been able to pick up on neomage battle reactions. I had become sloppy. I had been away from my people for too long.

Against my training and instincts, I loosened the autonomic muscles that had given me away. Audric mirrored my slight relaxation. I should have thrown everything I had at him, mage-power and blade, hurt him badly, then run. That was what Lolo had prepared me to do if my origins were exposed and I was accused. But Audric hadn't accused me. I hesitated. A conundrum. I had no prearranged plan for this situation. And I didn't want to run, start over somewhere else, as someone else. I had roots here. I had Rupert. Jacey. *Ciana.*

How had Audric known? I opened my mage-sight and examined him. He appeared human, smelled human, moved human slow. As I looked, he touched the lightning-bolt pendant at his throat and relaxed from warrior readiness. Something indefinable slipped aside, as if he dropped shields, as if he had been glamoured, as if a strong conjure had been countered. A glow seeped from Audric, soft coral, like me. Or almost. *"Seraph stones,"* I breathed. "You're a crossbreed."

"The common term is mule, I believe." Audric sat relaxed, peaceful, waiting.

I closed off mage-sight and looked at him, astonished. He wasn't in my thoughts, driving me insane. I hadn't been tested against half-breeds before I was sent away, and clearly I should have been. Lolo would have sent one or more with me into hiding. Surely.

Joy budded in the depths of my heart, tremulous, half disbelieving. *I'm not alone.* When I spoke, my voice was breathless, scratchy, and I had to stop and clear it. "Not even a human would find you common, Audric. And the term is insulting."

"Indeed," he said, his tone and words still formal. "We call ourselves the second-unforeseen. Or—for the neomage-human crossbreeds who desired to sire children or enjoy the full physical delights of mating—the cursed." He canted his head. "I too am in hiding, for an incident which I will not discuss."

"Are you a seraph-bound warrior or mage-bound?"

"Neither," he said simply.

I looked at him in surprise. A free half-breed was a rare being, almost unknown. When he didn't elaborate, I asked, "What will we do now? Who else knows?"

"Your scars have been noted at times over the years, while you were working in back. They are"—he paused carefully—"distinctive."

Unconsciously, I smoothed my sleeves along my arms, aware of the spawn-claw shapes, uniform, three fingered and deep.

"Rupert and Jacey have speculated that you are half-breed. Neither have guessed about me. But if Rupert remembers the melted snow in the alley or your unglamoured skin, he will realize, as I did, that you are fully neomage." Rumors had always abounded about neomages hiding in the human population, though to my knowledge, none had ever been substantiated. Until now. It suddenly occurred to me that I was proof the rumors were true. I considered carefully, knowing my power-drunk judgment was suspect.

"The two in the window saw the broken alley wall. It affected them personally, so it was likely all they saw. The wall was old; its falling made sense. The clouds outside hold frozen rain, which could easily create the frozen mess there now. I think Rupert was knocked loopy. And the melt will have refrozen by now, partially hiding my error," I said, watching his serene eyes. "May I suggest we do nothing? Keep each other's secret from the humans?"

Audric relaxed even more and a hint of amusement crossed his face. "A neomage and a crossbreed living in the same town? One of us divorced, the other living with a human man? What would they say?"

"If the humans knew? Too much. But Rupert has to know. If you've been"—I searched for a polite term and felt my face burn—"intimate."

"We're not all totally without physical characteristics. He believes my differences are the result of an accident when I was a child."

"Oh." That sidestepped the issue nicely, which made me even more curious, but I couldn't think of a polite way to ask what he looked like naked, so I changed the subject. "I've never met an unforeseen," I said, using the new designation.

"Second-unforeseen. Neomages were the prime-unforeseen."

That generated another question, and before I considered whether it might be rude, I asked, "Do you have souls?"

He inclined his head, the lights gleaming off his bald pate. "It is said that we do."

Sorrow pricked at me, sharp in my drunkenness. Striving to be as formal as he, I said, "I may have met another like you today. One in the alley appeared human, but he knew savage-chi." I thought back to the alley, parsing each sensation. "I cut him. His blood smelled wrong, not entirely human. And he was spelled with Darkness."

"Ahhh," Audric breathed. "Living in Enclave is the only way for second-unforeseen children to be truly safe. The war art is taught to all of us before we leave Enclave as adults, to find and bond with a seraph, to battle minions of the Darkness. Most of us are not fortunate enough to find a winged warrior for war partner, and we either return to Enclave to bind with a mage or enter the human world, often teaching chi as a way to survive." He worried his jaw back and forth, thinking. "It is perfectly legal to teach humans the art, as long as no Dark humans receive instruction. A Darkness may have drawn in unbound ones. Or perhaps a neomage teacher is in rebellion."

"Lolo would have heard if so."

"You are of the New Orleans Enclave. I originated in Seattle Enclave," he said. "The one you sensed might have been conscripted by a Power, but we cannot assume no primes have joined them unbeknownst to the mage council. Or perhaps a captive was bred to humans kept by the Darkness."

I shrugged. "It's getting complicated."

"It's always complicated. Let's consider the threats we face." Audric bent, crossed his blades on the floor before him, and settled into the cushions, resting his hands on his knees as if meditating. "Lucas sends Rupert stone from Linville. While carrying some of the stone, he's attacked. His blood is spilled. He disappears along with the stone except for small fragments, found by happenstance, by a Stanhope cousin. One who shares the same genetic structure. This stone, and this man, affect you in a peculiar way."

"Noticed that, did you?"

"With the stone is a letter claiming Lucas found it while cleaning out his grampa's belongings, but the original discoverer is unknown, and it is possible we may never find out who discovered it."

"The old man was a notorious money-grubber. His own grandson can't see him not exploiting an opportunity to mine it himself." I set aside my weapon, reached into a basket at my feet and pulled out a pad and pen, flipped past several jewelry designs to a blank page and sketched a globular outline of the relationships and events so far.

"A previously unknown Stanhope cousin is in the mountains," Audric continued, "and is sent here just at this time, by the matriarch."

"Coincidence?"

"Is there such a beast?" Without waiting for an answer, he continued. "The blood spilled in the alley where Lucas was attacked was removed, indicating devil-spawn were present, or close enough to be drawn by the scent. In the hills of nearby counties, spawn are drinking blood. In Linville, where Gramma lives, where the stone was stored, a family was drained. I asked a few questions when I heard of it. They were Stanhopes, distant relations."

I didn't like the direction this was taking, but it was making an awful kind of sense. "They were looking for the stone?"

"Or for Stanhopes. A daywalker has spoken to Ciana, also a Stanhope," he said, worry lines growing at his eyes. "Now a second-unforeseen has attacked a Stanhope. Because he was spelled with Darkness, we may consider the possibility that a Power, seeking that bloodline, was involved with Lucas' kidnapping. Lucas' letter stated that Stanhopes are in danger, and though we don't yet know why, it must be related to Benaiah Stanhope. I had thought the focal point of this conundrum was the amethyst, but it could be Stanhope blood." He thought a moment more. "I will escort Ciana to school each day and back here or home. She and Rupert must be protected."

Relief flooded through me. "Thank you."

"And now we have to go to the cops," he said, dropping the formality.

I looked away from him but saw the smile he smothered.

"I'm not particularly fond of them myself. No unforeseen is. But the Stanhopes need the police to be involved. If we don't go to them and Ciana or Rupert is taken or killed, we couldn't live with it. Up, mage. And dress appropriately for the weather this time."

"At least I wasn't half naked."

"I am a specimen of great beauty. You are privileged to have looked upon me."

I snorted, and Audric laughed. I was no longer alone.

At the LEC, Officer Litton listened to our story as sleet fell in the streets and alleys. It took an hour to fill out all his papers and another until his superior could meet with us. Captain Durbarge met us in the Law Enforcement Center's cafeteria, and as he entered, I felt Audric disguise a flinch in a small yawn, and stretch as if he had been sitting too long, the denim of his shirt and jeans too tight. As he moved, he touched his necklace, the amulet hiding his neomage genetic heritage. That meant Audric sensed something about the cop.

I sent out the faintest skim and withdrew instantly. *Sweet seraph!* An Administration of the ArchSeraph Investigator! I drew on my bear amulet to double-damp my skin as the small man sat across from us, and then realized that wasn't smart. AASIs, called *asseys* by the disrespectful, sometimes recognized the use of power. The investigator had hooded, droopy eyes, giving him a deceptively somnolent look. He wore an old-fashioned, black wool suit with a starched white shirt and a fringed black scarf looped around his neck. Durbarge opened a black leather case, revealing an AAS ID sigil, wings and halo, the clear crystal glittering with archseraph energies. I was careful to keep my neomage paws away. It was said such sigils would sometimes glow in the presense of a mage. "I'm Captain Durbarge with the AAS. What can you tell me about the attack you just reported?"

"We are honored to have the Administration of the Arch-Seraph show an interest in the case," Audric said, cutting off my response. "Are you in Mineral City because of the disappearance of Lucas Stanhope and the violence shown on SNN?"

The cop held Audric's gaze. "That and a related matter. What can you—"

"So the violent attacks on Lucas and Rupert are part of something larger."

"It's possible. The matter today? Please?" He still looked sleepy, but Audric's questions had snared his interest.

Audric glanced at me. My turn. I described what I had seen and done. Well, the sanitized version Audric and I had concocted before we came to the station. Durbarge laced his hands together on the table in front of him. When I finished, he asked, "And you raised your hand against another?"

Fear plunged into me like a spike. I almost bowed my head, taking refuge in humility and repentance. Instead, the fear did a somersault in my chest and came out as anger. I met his eyes. "In defense of another life. I took no joy in my actions."

The assey cocked his head as if he found me a curiosity. *Not what I wanted.*

I reined in the irritation seething beneath my skin. "Before the next Jubilee I will confess my sin of violence at kirk and ask God the Victorious for mercy."

"A chaste and humble reply."

His tone made me want to kick him. *Chaste and humble my neomage backside.* He didn't believe me. He didn't believe Audric. Somehow, we had slipped and generated his special attention.

"What can you tell me about Jason?"

That was unexpected. "Lucas' brother?" I asked. The assey didn't reply. He simply stared at me, waiting. I resisted the urge to draw on my amulets. "Not much. I met him at my wedding and again at my divorce."

"Have you done business with the man?"

"He's never been in the shop."

"I see. And your impression of him?"

"It isn't kind."

Durbarge quirked his lips into a small smile. I had a feeling that for him it was the equivalent of howling laughter. "Humor me. You can confess this small sin today too."

Cheeky. "Jason wants money. He doesn't care about family or children, or anyone except himself. He isn't capable of committing to a long-term relationship, much like Lucas, but with Jason, there's an element of cruelty in his flitting from woman to woman. With Lucas, it's more that he can't seem to help himself."

Again that small smile. "Weakness in one brother, cruelty in another, and a catamite in the third." Smooth words, like a sharp blade one doesn't feel until the blood starts to fall. I was stunned into silence.

"The Most High is merciful," Audric said, his face as still as stone, eyes flinty.

Durbarge nodded once. "So he is. And just. His vengeance will not be hindered."

"There are those who depend on his mercy more than others."

"And those who look with joy for his justice and retribution."

"And all are part of his body," Audric said quickly. The two had now established that they were well trained in opposing schools of study on the nature of the Most High, Durbarge a practicing orthodox, and therefore a mage-hater, and Audric a student of the reformation. Wasn't that just dandy? I wondered what other secrets Audric was hiding.

Each nodded once, signaling his recognition of the other's theological position. I wanted to slap them upside their thick skulls and shout, *Focus! Rupert is injured and Lucas is missing!* But I kept my expression serene and seethed inside where they couldn't see it. I hoped.

"You are Audric Cooper, dead-miner, man with a salvage claim for the entire city of Sugar Grove," the assey said. "Tell me what you saw today."

Without reacting to proof that his background had been researched, Audric told of the dustup in the alley, our version. The assey listened, motionless, taking in each small gesture, each shift of expression, depositing them in his brain with information we didn't have, and correlating them into an interactive vision only he saw.

When Audric stopped speaking, Durbarge sat silent, fingers laced. A clock ticked somewhere close, a door opened and closed, the smell of scorched coffee filtered into the room. We waited. "I don't usually tell interested parties about an investigation, but I'm making an exception." He looked directly at me as if I were an insect and he a collector. "A Power has been operating in nearby counties. We believe citizens are working with the Darkness. Jason is associating with those we suspect. He's being investigated."

I remembered the stink of spelled blood, the proficient savage-chi moves. I wanted to ask about neomage involvement but settled for a question that might not get me carved up. "How does that relate to the violence against the Stanhopes?"

"It relates quite well if there is a blood-demon involved."

I looked at the small man, horror seeping through my veins. A blood-demon was a Dark spirit, incorporeal, incapable of physical manifestation but able to use the bodies of humans. They traveled from human to human through bloodlines. Some speculated they had the capability of recognizing similar genetic properties and traveling through families by accessing genes themselves. Ciana and Rupert were in mortal danger. Devil-spawn roamed the hills. A blood-demon was in the mix, and a Power. A daywalker was loose. I opened my mouth to tell the assey about the beast when Audric placed his foot over mine beneath the table in warning. Instead, I said, "Thank you for telling us. We appreciate that the Administration of the Arch-Seraph is on guard to protect the Stanhopes."

Durbarge's brows rose in amusement and he stood with a scrape of chair legs. "We aren't here to protect your family, Thorn Stanhope. We're here to investigate a major Power and its minions. Then to summon warriors to subdue it and bring to justice its cadre of slaves and followers. Whoever they may be."

Officious little snot. We stood as well, and the big man took my arm. Another warning. Or he noted my rising color and knew what I was about to say. "We thank you," he said to the little man, who definitely didn't like having to look up into Audric's eyes.

Audric pulled me out of the LEC. Cold clamped down, trying to freeze the anger simmering inside me. I shoved my hands into my pockets. "You should have let me sock him," I said as Audric guided me into the sleet. He chuckled deep in his chest and led the way past the new city hall and Waldroup's Fine Furniture, owned by the baker's brother. The Waldroups were a large, prosperous clan.

"Which would have given him the right to search you. He would have found your amulets and you would have been taken off in handcuffs to the AAS, interrogated most painfully, then turned over to the nearest Enclave. Or he might have kept you, used you, and given you to the elders," he said, his tone pleasant. "I would have been arrested and sentenced to the winter. Death by freezing and starvation is quite painful, I imagine, but nothing compared to cold steel and human wrath."

"You're getting a kick out of all this, aren't you?"

Audric grinned happily. The half-breeds were warriors who trained for, and loved, a good battle. Most were bound to the High Host, participating in the mopping up of the remaining Powers and Principalities of Darkness. Heavy fighting. Mighty battle. Blood, guts, and glory, huzzah! Nothing one could have in peaceful Mineral City, in the middle of nowhere, a city where no

Darkness activity had been seen in generations—until now. Co-incidence piled on coincidence. Or something planned by an unseen hand. Audric hadn't said why he first came to Mineral City. And he hadn't asked why I was here. Don't ask, don't tell. Was I lucky or what?

We came even with the Blue Snail Café and Diner. I turned from the window, then quickly back again. Sitting in a booth was Jane Hilton, Lucas' *new wife*, having lunch with three men, including Derek Culpepper. I risked a second glance, nudged Audric to look, and we moved on.

"Distraught, isn't she?" I asked.

"Well, well, well," Audric chuckled again.

The Culpepper family had big bucks and was politically powerful, and the family patriarch was a kirk elder. Jane looked beautiful, delicate, weakly feminine, and positively beseeching, blond hair loose across her shoulders, green eyes huge. It was revolting. I couldn't see the other men, whose faces were turned away from the window. There was red meat on the plates, burgers cooked rare, oozing with thin blood. Colas and french fries. An expensive, fancy Pre-Ap meal. "Now, what could Lucas' *new wife* want with the likes of him?" Audric asked. I had no answer.

Chapter 11

"**D**erek wants us all to abandon the town because of the ice caps," Rupert said, holding an ice pack to his temple. "Privately, a few months back, he approached Lucas, Jason, and me about supporting the decision to move. He promised he could get the seraphs to resettle us elsewhere, which would mean we would be slightly better off financially than refugees, though not much."

"And where was I during all this?" I asked.

"You were going through a divorce, not speaking to Lucas, and have never been interested in politics. Remember?"

"Oh. Well, I'm interested now."

"He didn't say why, but purchase of the Trine was part of the deal, though no one said anything about mineral rights. When we turned him down, he left with no hard feelings."

Audric smoothed the lightning-bolt pendant at his neck, thinking. We were in Rupert's apartment across from mine, my injured friend lying on an ancient and worn leather sofa Audric had dead-mined from his salvaged city. Audric and I were sitting across from him in wingback chairs. A small gas fire danced merrily in the fireplace, casting warmth over peach-painted walls and windows hung with heavy tapestries.

"Jason saw dollar signs out of the deal and was ready to sell. He was pretty unhappy when Lucas and I turned him down." Rupert stretched his left arm as if it ached. It was the side he'd been dropped on when I rammed his attacker.

Audric's voice was almost dreamy when he said, "Culpepper could be involved with the people who took Lucas, I suppose. He has ties to town and kirk government through his father. He has money. If he wants the land, then that gives him motive."

"He's smarmy enough to get involved with a Dark Power," Rupert said. "And so is that woman. Maybe they're in it together. Just a thought." He grinned at me slyly. "So go to your policeman and tell him they were talking. Let Bartholomew figure it out."

"He's not *my* policeman."

"Whatever. Pass me the aspirin?"

"I think that would be a precipitous action," Audric said carefully, as he passed the bottle. "The meeting between Culpepper and Hilton may have been innocent. She may have thought such a powerful and wealthy man could call seraphs."

"The woman, like all the women my brother attracts, is a harpy."

"Thank you so very much," I said.

He waved away the insult, downing two aspirin with water. "Except for you. I never did figure out what Lucas saw in you. You have a brain; you have morals; you're built like a ballet dancer rather than a cow." I looked down at my chest. Small boobs. Right.

"There's a meeting after Jubilee," Audric said. "If Culpepper is involved, if he took Lucas, knows about the amethyst, and wants the land, he'll attend. And he'll eventually contact the remaining Stanhopes. So we'll go too. See how the wind blows."

"Questions," I said to Rupert. "Now that you know what we think, and what the AAS thinks, what if Jason *is* involved with a Darkness in the hills? What if he intends to kill off all his family for reasons we haven't uncovered? What if there is a blood-demon?"

"Jason's blood is so saturated with liquor that nothing could use it to track us."

Audric made a clawing motion at Rupert and hissed, but he was laughing. It wasn't an answer. Perhaps there wasn't one.

He rolled over in the dark, the stink of sulfur waking him again, burning the delicate membranes of his sinuses. He reached out and touched the walls of his prison. Coarse rock, brittle and broken. The faint stench of old urine and rot reached him. He knew he had gangrene on the frostbitten dead flesh of his exposed wrists, fingers, mouth, and ears. The smell would soon bring the spawn to him, hungry, eyes gleaming and impatient. He could only hope Malashe-el showed up again to protect him.

He almost laughed, but the single deep breath brought on a spell of coughing that racked his chest. His life wasn't worth devil spit if he was dependent on a Darkness for survival.

The faint red glow in the opening to his prison was brighter now. He could see the rocks that made up the boundaries of his small cell and the corroded iron bars that blocked off the only entrance. Could see the pale white of his living skin against the black of dying flesh where he'd touched the iron bars. Could see the stone jar that held the measure of water allowed him each day.

Air moved through the cavern like the breath of many beings, a soft soughing sound. The things they were bringing to life with his blood would soon wake, and the Stanhopes would die, every last one. Followed quickly thereafter by the remaining inhabitants of Mineral City.

"You're awake!" The voice was delighted, the breaking

tone of an adolescent human boy, the same voice that had identified itself as Malashe-el.

Lucas knew it was important that he had been told the
name. There was something about Powers' true names, but he
couldn't remember what. His brain was mush. He turned his
head, the stone beneath his cheek tearing his skin. The boy
sniffed at the fresh blood, then ducked his head, abashed.
"Sorry. Mama tells me that's really rude."

Lucas chuckled. "You could say that. Humans don't like to
be thought of as food."

"But you *are* food."

His amusement faded and he shuddered at the statement
of fact, the only reality to the Darkness. Such simple logic. It
meant death—and soon.

"I brought you a blanket. And some fresh bread."

Lucas rose on one elbow and regarded the boy at the opening, his gangly body silhouetted by reddish light. "Why?"

"Mama said I had to."

"Why?"

"She doesn't want you to die just yet."

Lucas chuckled again, the sound rasping and bloated with
despair. "That would be my hope too, but it isn't very likely. Just
who is your mother?"

"She said you knew her." The boy sat on the cavern floor,
his movements demon-fast, his tone puzzled. He handed Lucas
a blanket and a loaf of bread. The blanket was silk, soft and
warmer than seraph wings. Lucas wrapped the length of it
around him, luxuriating in the heat, a near-human warmth he
had never thought to feel again.

Holding the blanket with one hand, he took the bread. It had
a peculiar glazed texture, a scent like honey. His fingers trembled
as they broke off a piece and stuffed it in his mouth, crumbles of
crust flying. An unknown seasoning flooded his mouth, reminiscent of anise and nutmeg, as sweet as cake. The bread softened

and he swallowed easily. He imagined he felt strength and healing flowing out to his limbs from the single bite.

"I don't know any Darkness, boy. Not one," he said after he
swallowed.

The boy flipped his black braid out of the way. "Mama's
not a Dark One. She said you know her as the Mistress. And
she's not finished with you yet."

Despite himself, Lucas felt hope wash through his bones like
a warm flush of life. "The Mistress?" he breathed. "Here? How?"

The boy shrugged. "She's always been here."

But that wasn't possible. The Mistress was a Being of Light.
Not a seraph precisely, but similar. Unless . . . He felt the flicker
of hope quiver and die. He had been deceived.

"The meeting will bore the pants off you, I warn you," Rupert
said.

"There's no way to learn what Lucas was involved in before
he was kidnapped, without going. And I promise to keep my
leggings on," I added dryly.

The real reason I wanted to appear at the Save Mineral City
meeting was to do a mind-skim on all present, but this other
excuse worked pretty well too. I hoped I'd be able to tell
whether any of the humans present had gone over to a Dark
Power. I wasn't certain I could parse out a specific Darkness, or
that I could recognize Darkness on a human who wasn't bleeding, but I wanted to try.

The day was half gone, squandered. I had completed
nothing on the spring lines, no stone cutting, no stringing.
Once again, I was totally involved in Lucas' life, just as when I
had first set eyes on him, fell madly in love, and could think
only of his blue eyes, firm chin, and full lips. I had wasted my
time and desperate emotions on the man, but love is blind,
deaf, dumb, and stupid. Now I was doing it for Ciana. Or so I
told myself.

Afternoon was plunging into a false dusk of lowering clouds and a cold so intense, it penetrated my layered clothing and my insulated leather cloak. Walking sticks in hand, Rupert, Audric, and I trudged over rutted snow, our hobbled boots gripping the slick ice. Rupert was still wan, a painful-looking, purple lump in his hair above one ear, bruises on his chest and arms, but he was determined to stick by me, having decided that from now on we would travel in groups, for protection. Jacey was running the store, being watched over by her eldest stepson, Zeddy, a big, strapping kid.

We entered the old Central Baptist Church, passing between the double-wide doors into the sanctuary, a cavernous room, and took seats midway back. There were about two hundred people gathered, most up front where they could hear, the church's loudspeakers having given out before I was born and never been replaced. Its heating system was on the fritz too, and the collective breath of the crowd was a faint mist three feet off the ground.

At the front, on the dais, stood Derek Culpepper, the developer wanting Mineral City to move. Rupert said, "He presents himself as a philanthropist with no thought to profit."

"A humanitarian? All motives altruistic? How novel," Audric said.

The lady in front of us swiveled in her pew and hushed us; chastened, we fell silent. Culpepper was short and bowlegged, and had more money than taste. He was wearing a lemon yellow suit and mustard green tie, a perfectly hideous combination with his carrot orange hair, purple shirt, and orange socks.

"Do you think he dressed himself or had it done by mob vote?" Rupert whispered, drawing another irritated glance from the stout woman. We all sniggered softly, trying to keep silent. Up front, Culpepper strode across the stage and preened, posing in a three-quarter view, chest out, like a rooster ready to crow. "This town faces the most frightening challenge since Mole Man went into the earth and gave himself as a sacrifice, both for us and to save the seraph. The ice cap has grown larger every winter for the last three decades, and hasn't melted completely in over seventy-five years.

"At the last meeting, I offered to buy out the town property at fair market value, and to provide land and loans for rebuilding, well below the frost line, in the foothills. Three of the town fathers have visited the site, looked it over, and testified to its beauty and bounty, flowing with two streams, ample water for wells and farming, and lush with growth four months out of the year. Four months!" he shouted, throwing an arm skyward, much like a jaundiced John Travolta in an old Pre-Ap movie. The film had played for months on satellite TV and had many of the young men dressing in tight clothes and learning how to dance. Rupert stuck a finger in the air and smothered a chuckle.

"How long will the town fathers wait to act on my offer? Until snowmelt? Until the ice cap starts to slide? Until the danger grows more menacing? If they do, the buying price drops drastically, or the offer may disappear from the table entirely."

"Thank you, Derek," said a bored voice from the far side of the dais. "I think all us dumb mountain folk understand you made a fair offer on our town. Fair, that is, considering the ice cap that could shift and crush it flatter than one of my competitor's biscuits."

Everyone laughed and I craned my head, spotting a tiny black man, bald and ancient, in the row of elders and elected political officials. It was the baker from across the street, the baker who now had a wall to repair, thanks to my uncontrolled use of energy this morning. Shamus Waldroup, a man with family ties to the town for over a hundred and seventy years. I sank down in my seat, hiding from his line of sight.

"Now, listen you here, Waldroup," Culpepper said. "I'm not finish—"

"Nope, you listen. Lessen you got some new information to

add, you can sit down. You took up mostly the whole meeting last week, and we got a lotta business to cover. So sit down and shut up." The crowd laughed easily, as if used to Waldroup's abrasive tones. "Next speaker on the list is Esmeralda Boyles. You here, Essie? Essie?"

"I'm here, I'm here. Give a old woman a chance, will you?" a voice croaked. To my left, an elderly woman moved down the aisle, talking even before she got to the stage. "I'm old, I'm tired, and I ain't selling," she shouted as she shuffled. "I ain't moving. I ain't going nowhere. Soon's Lucas Stanhope is fount, I'll take his advice to hire mages to melt the ice cap in a controlled melt. It'll cost the town less money and I can keep my family land. That's all." She hadn't even reached the dais before she turned around and moved back to her seat.

Some of the crowd burst into applause and the rest shook their heads. The crowd was split fifty-fifty on selling. Waldroup, who seemed to be in charge, called another speaker, Elder Culpepper. If I could have sunk lower in the pew without sliding to the floor in a boneless sprawl, I would have. It was the kirk elder who had given me the withering look when I took Ciana to pray.

Culpepper took the stage wearing brown robes like a prophet of old, and bowed his head a moment before siding with his son. Big surprise. Personally, I thought appearing in his robes of office at a secular, political meeting was cheating, but nobody asked me.

After his opening statement, I closed off my mind and relaxed, settling on the hardwood pew, head rocking against the shaped, curled back. I breathed in, first smelling the massed bodies, wet wool, old wood, the damp of melted ice and snow. With my second breath I took in the scent of soap, varied perfumes and lotions, and the underlying alcohols and oils that composed them, along with dim tangs of excitement and adrenaline. My sense of smell was acute, surprising me, but maybe a heightened olfactory sense was a mage-trait. It wasn't like I practiced in public. Until now, my gifts had been private.

I breathed out worries, fear, and the discomfort of the bench beneath my thighs. Breathed in calm and peace and the faint smell of leather from my cloak and from all the boots, the oils and tannins that had been worked into them. Breathed out the awareness of the gathered crowd. Breathed in the strength and stillness of stone. Old, quiet stone. Stone that still carried the strength of the deeps.

The old church's outer walls were made from stone, hundred-pound rocks blasted from nearby hills. The sanctuary stood on a single huge stone, the heart of an ancient mountain. The roof was newer, some sixty years old, made of local slate. Stone above and around and below. Stone surrounded me, rich and deep and cold and solid. I relaxed and fell into the serenity of stone.

Sighing, a half smile on my lips, I reached beneath my cloak and tunic and took hold of the small amulet that offered calm and peace. I didn't often draw on the small carved rose, as the pale pink quartz was tied too closely to memories of my sister. Rose, ever the peaceful, gentle twin, had worn a curved, sharp, black onyx thorn, for a fierce fighting spirit.

The rose deepened my sense of tranquility yet again, and on the fifth breath I was so relaxed, I could have slept. My eyes still closed, I opened my mage-sight, seeing the roseate glow of my lids, the brighter network of capillaries through the thin flesh like a map of a river system, flowing with my blood. I could hear the drone of the elder, the shuffle of boots on scarred wood, the breath of the crowd like a soft summer wind. I opened my eyelids.

With mage-sight, I looked at the crowd. There was nothing, no taint, no blemish of Darkness. I pushed harder with my sight, sending out a vigorous probe. And still nothing.

I sat up in the pew. The room glowed softly with life and heat. The breath of the gathered was still a mist, but now it glowed a soft green, the color of new leaves. The walls, long in need of paint, glowed warm peach with delicate blue tracery, looking much like my eyelids until I realized the peach and blue were the colors of stone and mortar behind the wallboard. The inner walls had stood in contact with the outer for so many years that the ground-up gypsum, paper, and paint had taken on the strength of the rock. The inner walls glowed, picking up the colors of the stained-glass windows, seven of which remained, even after the clash that had rocked nearby mountains in Benaiah Stanhope's battle. I turned my sight to the crowd.

Beside me, Audric looked strangely lifeless, like a mannequin, the only one in the room who didn't glow with power of some kind, his flesh appearing untouched, wholly plastic, except for a pale glow at his neck, centered in the lightning bolt, hanging bright and silver. All the others in the room glowed with energy, their flesh unglamoured and human, a soft, fragile, fluctuating light of life, in shades of yellow, green, brown, soft orange, and blue, the colors of their auras in mage-sight. I turned back to Audric and then looked down at my hand. Below my glamour, my own flesh glowed with the pearled nacre of mage-power. But of Audric's gift and nature, I could see nothing. The lightning bolt was a powerful amulet.

On my other side, Rupert was muddy gold swirling with rivers of blue, rose, and green, like ocean jasper. He twitched, trying to stay awake, and sat up straight, forcing his thighs onto the ungiving wood, pain keeping him alert. I didn't wonder how I knew what he was doing. I knew Rupert better than I knew myself.

As unobtrusively as possible, I swiveled my head and let my gaze flow across the crowd like a breeze. There were no shadows, no places of Darkness or even of simple darkness. Every place in the old church glowed with power, with light. But then, Audric had hidden his true nature beneath a glamour even a mage couldn't penetrate. There had to be a way to see more, on a deeper level. Neomages had long used their gifts to protect themselves, to fight evil, standing beside the second-unforeseen. There had to be a better way to seek out Darkness.

When my neomage training was interrupted at age fourteen, when I was sent away from my kind for my own sanity's sake, my training had been interrupted as well. I had never finished any part of my mage studies and had never seen a reason to continue them all alone in the hills. I would never be allowed to use my gifts except for survival against humans, the survival of trickery, deceit, or violence. There was so much I didn't know.

But what if I could combine a mind-skim with my neomage-sight? Perhaps that was what trained mages did. I released the quartz rose and found the distinctive shape of the black-and-green-jade bear, strengthening the incantation that kept my flesh damped. I opened my mage-sight wide and skimmed hard, blending the two senses.

And nearly fell off the pew. The world rolled and sloshed as if caught in an eddy. I was inundated with sight-smell-*otherness*. For a long moment I thought I might lose my last meal. Finally, the new world I was sensing settled, and when I wasn't overwhelmed with my body's reactions to the otherness, I sent out a deeper, more comprehensive scan. The images and the smells pounded like a stiff uppercut, knocking me for a loop. A wave of vertigo slammed me. I swallowed hard, closing my eyes, holding the breath tight inside, unmoving. A hand took my wrist, offering stability, Audric, a solid tree of endurance and strength. I held my breath a long moment, both the breath in my lungs and the neomage breath that moved through me with a heartbeat of its own. When I released them, easing them out between my lips, the world steadied.

I considered the blended scan and realized I had just

pulled in a new combination. New for me anyway. I'd have probably learned how to do it years ago if I had stayed at Enclave. Okay. So combining senses was possible, if disorienting. I'd take it slow this time.

I opened my eyes and skimmed slowly. Gradually, I reopened my mage-sight, drawing on the bear to keep me hidden, and using its stored strength to help balance my gifts, like opening a dam through a sluice gate instead of dropping the dam walls all at once and getting inundated. Audric tightened his grip on my wrist to steady me.

Carefully, I sniffed around the room, seeing the life beat of each being, blood flowing in blood vessels, a collective breath stirring the soft mist. Heat and life writhed and glowed, matter vibrating with intensity. Audric was no longer glamoured to my sight. He glowed with a warmth of purity and purpose, as steady as a boulder, a tested strength. He smelled of strength too, a familiar mage-strength. That seemed important for an instant, but the thought skittered away, overpowered by the brighter images of the crowd.

I smelled deeper scents as I breathed: mold in a far corner, bat droppings from the attic, peppers, onions, and moonshine on the humans. The water at my feet was snowmelt, not from a well, not from the earth, purified by stone and pressure, but water that had passed through the air and was useless to me. And then I caught it. The fainter-than-a-shadow-at-night hint of sulfur. I swiveled my head. The smell was coming from the doorway, carried on wind wisping under the front door. It was moving. I followed it with my mind as it shifted from the door to a window along the side wall. It had to be nearly night outside. *Spawn!*

My hands clenched, reaching for my blades. Audric's grip tightened, stopping the motion. I turned my gaze to him and his mouth moved in a silent *No*. I shuddered with the need to fight, to draw spawn blood. I broke out in a hot sweat. My heart rate doubled. I forced myself to relax under the pressure of Audric's fingers. Against the compulsion to battle, I turned my scan to the crowd. I could do this. I could. But a dull ache in my temples foretold a killer of a headache. The stink of evil faded.

Pushing the fatigue and pain away, I reached into the crowd and instantly felt several *somethings*. I identified some as stone I had worked, each filled with an incantation for a specific need. One was for freedom from mild pain, another was for peace, a third was for protection, and there were others as I counted. Seven amulets altogether, most of them well drained, but still leaking a bit of comfort. Amulets I could sense with the blended scan. Could other mages and seraphs sense them as well, proof that a witchy-woman was nearby, operating without a license? Not good. I'd been stupid. But I hadn't thought about leaving tracks of my gift in and on the townspeople. I'd have to consider how to hide myself better.

Even if it means not using my gifts in stone I work? How can I not use my gifts?

The thoughts of covering my tracks I pushed aside, and centered myself again, reaching out to the gathered, scenting and searching. I caught a bit of magery not my own. It was earth magery, the gift of life and all things growing. It smelled warm and green, like sunlight on spring leaves. I turned my head, placing the scent, and saw a brightness at the front, on the pew where many of those who had signed up to be speakers sat. I narrowed my concentration, focusing down on the left, on the man on the aisle seat. In a yellow pocket, Derek Culpepper carried a freshly charmed object. His fingers caressed it as I watched, his bones glowing with the power it pulsed into him.

The ache in my head expanded, as if I had stared too long at the sun, and I pulled my eyes away from Culpepper, knowing I should stop, but needing to scan the rest of the room.

I moved my senses to the other speakers, finding nothing of interest. Scanning the seats behind the developer, I stopped, surprised. It wasn't a Darkness—not exactly—more like a phantom of a shadow overlaying an aura. The shadow shifted lazily back and forth, as if searching to gain entrance through the aura into the body and soul beneath, but not in a hurry to do so. It danced over the woman in a slow waltz of menace. I blinked, recognizing Jane Hilton. She was scowling, her eyes fixed on Derek Culpepper. I held my scan on her a long moment, considering. Was she under threat by a Darkness? Flirting with a Power, hoping for some gain? Had she been involved in Lucas' kidnapping? Bargained with a Darkness, hoping to save him?

A stab of pain pulled me back from the scan. With the last moments of power, feeling the drain on the bear amulet, I raced my eyes over the remaining crowd. A second shadow hovered over the pew to my right, near the tiny old woman who spoke while she walked, but to her side. I bent forward and craned my neck.

The scan snapped off with a blinding flash and a spear of agony right in the center of my head. I gasped and crumpled, and Audric pushed me into my seat before I fell into the aisle and had to claim womanly vapors or some such excuse.

I lay my head against the pew and Audric released my wrist to slide his massive arm around my shoulders, cradling me. Tears sprang to my eyes with the pain and with the knowledge of what I had seen just as the scan failed. Marla. Sitting beside Elder Culpepper. Marla, polluted with Darkness.

It was no big surprise that Marla was helping the people who wanted to move the town when her ex-husband wanted to keep it where it was. Marla Stanhope would do anything, bond with any faction, if it meant she could stick a blade into Lucas. Anything to damage the man who had hurt her, and continued to hurt her, by no longer loving her. But moving the town? Losing the money that moving would mean? Bonding with a Power?

And then I realized. If Lucas died, Marla would have control of lots of money, in the form of Lucas' estate. Money that was intended to provide a good future for Ciana. For her, Lucas' disappearance and possible death created a win-win situation. That was the dark I was seeing—the dark of avarice and cruelty. Her enemy dead, and his money at her disposal. Now wouldn't that be just ducky.

Chapter 12

✝

Between the pain of the headache and the worry over Marla, I didn't pay much attention to the rest of the meeting, stirring myself for only three speakers: Fergus Yardley, Randall Prentice, and Jason Stanhope. Yardley and Prentice sided with Culpepper about moving the town, citing the instability of the ice caps and the resultant flooding should the caps be melted by mages or seraphs. A flash flood in the Toe River running through the middle of town could result in damage equal to that caused by the ice cap sliding and burying us. Of course, because Yardley and Prentice were on the Culpepper payroll, their testimony was suspect at best.

Though I could have sworn he hadn't been in the crowd when I ran the scan, Lucas and Rupert's brother took the stage. I was recovered enough to pay attention. Jason appeared to be mostly sober for once, shaved and dressed in a business suit that had fit him before he crawled into a bottle and forgot to eat. According to Rupert, Jason had been handsome once upon a time, dynamic and charismatic, but it had been years since he was completely sober. I wondered who had dried him out, cleaned him up, and dressed him for the meeting. Not Culpepper, as Jason's suit was gray and business dull. I didn't expect much from the recently drunk man, but this was a Jason I had never seen before.

"Lucas was my brother."

His first words made me sit up and lean forward to hear better. *Was? Past tense, as in dead? Did he know that Lucas was dead? How could he know?*

"I loved him. But Lucas was shortsighted. Foolish. And Lucas trusted people way too much. Let me tell you how." Jason leaned forward and braced himself on the podium I hadn't even noticed until now. His blue eyes roamed the crowd, touching a face here and there, smiling slightly at several, cocking a finger at someone. "First, he wanted us to use our hard-earned money to melt the ice caps on the Trine and the surrounding peaks, which sounds great on the surface. But we haven't had a thaw in nearly seventy-five years."

I saw several people nod.

"The cap is hundreds of feet thick. It will create a flood endangering every single person and town between here and the ocean. It will put a strain on small dams that our brothers and sisters downstream have built to create electric power, to build pools for capturing water for drinking, fishing, watering crops in the dry month of summer." Jason leaned closer to the audience, dropping his voice. The crowd automatically leaned in.

"And then next winter, the ice cap will start to rebuild." More heads nodded, thoughtful. A stillness settled on the crowd. Even the old woman, Esmerelda Boyles, seemed to pause. She pursed her lips, sucking on a front tooth as if it pained her.

"The second thing my brother was wrong about was the ice cap. Lucas claimed it wouldn't rebuild for fifty years. But unless the weather warms, by the estimates of a geologist and a climatologist I consulted, the ice cap will be back to a dangerous thickness in *under twenty years*." The crowd stirred.

"The loan to the mages for this melting won't even be paid off by then. *Mages . . .*" His tone dripped with scorn and something like dread. A collective flutter of fear swept the crowd. Audric retook my wrist and tightened his grip as if afraid I might stand up and speak against the humans' fear. I scowled and shook him off.

Jason propped on one elbow. "And if the temperatures continue to cool, it will happen faster. We'll be destitute and still in danger. We'll still have to move, and our children will be stuck with that financial burden. And we will yet owe *mages* money."

The crowd moved uneasily.

"Yes. Have you thought what it might mean to be beholden to *mages*? That's the third error in Lucas' plan. Mages would come here bringing their unnatural acts, their orgies and their *heat*, their easy use of energy and power, their profligate lifestyle and the wealth they have amassed by the sweat of *our* brows, selling us trinkets and amulets and things we think we can't live without." Jason adjusted his jacket.

"So it's up to you. Are you willing to have your children's future held in the grip of mages, who might require even more of them than mere money?" He looked over the crowd, giving them time to imagine such requirements. He nodded, speaking slowly. "Perhaps mages will demand the use of their bodies in the orgies we all hear so much about. Or perhaps they'll turn their magic and spells against us, as at the battle of the Mage War." The crowd murmured, totally with Jason now.

Beside me, Rupert shuffled his boots. Audric again gripped my wrist hard, bruising. I pulled on it and he released me as if he hadn't realized what he was doing.

"You decide. It's up to you."

"Oh, please, brother, dear," Rupert drawled. "Orgies? Wild sex in the streets? Wine, women, and song? You'd *loooove* that." The crowd relaxed and several chuckled. Rupert stood and tossed his coat away, resplendent in dark blue robes and tunic, the newest style among the hip crowd. He turned and addressed the town fathers. "Permission to be added to the list of speakers."

"This is highly irregular," an older woman said before anyone could reply, "but I move to accept the speaker. You will rebut the comments, I assume?"

"I am a fantastic *rebutter*," Rupert said, all glam and batting eyelashes. The innuendo generated more chuckles and a frown or two. "Yes. I am refuting my brother's statements."

Shamus banged his gavel, acknowledging Rupert's right to speak. Head back, shoulders broad from savage-chi practice with Audric, Rupert moved down the aisle between the pews and onto the dais. There was no sound except his boots, slick on the old floors, and the crowd settling again for what appeared to be the start of a good show.

Jason moved away from the lectern, his blue eyes shooting fury and loathing, but he didn't leave the stage. Rupert took the podium and turned his back on his brother. He made an impressive figure, robes picking up the dim light of dusk coming through the windows, long hair thrown back behind his collar, brushing his shoulders, the purple bruise hidden in his hair.

"It's customary that a missing person not be presumed dead unless we've seen a body." Rupert glanced back at Jason, who looked away, realizing he'd made a mistake. "My brother is only *missing*." Rupert tilted his head, focusing on those assembled below. He gripped the narrow stand and said, "Lucas and I had decided to loan our inheritance to the town for mage-help to melt the ice caps." The crowd drew in a collective breath.

Jason's face darkened and he looked into the group, as if searching out one person.

"You was gonna use your own money? At what percentage rate?" Esmerelda Boyles called out.

"That was negotiable based on how long the town fathers

wanted the loan to run. But according to probate, the money has to be invested in bulk, all the brothers investing jointly. Between the three of us, it was two to one in favor of the loan."

"Now it's one to one," Jason shouted, balling his fists, "and I'm not signing over my inheritance. Not for something as useless and impossible as mage-help to save this town. Mineral City is going to die." He was sweating profusely, breath heaving. I attempted to open my mage-sight, but a lance of pain stabbed through my head. "Die! And there's nothing we can do to stop it. The best we can hope for is to buy a reprieve, not a salvation. And we'd be selling our souls to deal with *mages*."

"Mage-help is fully sanctioned by the seraphs," Rupert shouted back, whirling to face his brother. "I won't abandon this town based on unsubstantiated rumors circulated by narrow-minded zealots—especially ones who would profit by abandonment."

Jason drew back his arm, hands fisted. Rupert raised his chin and opened his arms, daring him.

"Order. Order, you two," Shamus Waldroup said, banging a gavel. "This ain't a free-for-all, boys. You done had a chance to talk, Jason, so sit down and get yourself in hand. We ain't having no violence. Go on," he ordered when Jason paused, his body rigid. "Go ahead, Rupert. Talk. I want to know if you got any proof that you and Lucas was planning a loan. 'Cause if there is, then we might have us a way to salvage the loan even though Lucas is gone. Missing, I mean."

Jason hadn't moved. "Jason Stanhope, you sit down or I'll have you sat down," the bald baker said. Two robe-clad elders stood and stepped forward, staring hard at Jason. His hands trembled; his face was beet red, sweat pouring in steady trickles, soaking his collar. He turned on his heel, walked down the steps to the aisle, and flung himself into the first pew.

"I have the documents where we sketched out a plan," Rupert said. "It's all handwritten, pencil on paper, Lucas' and my handwriting. Of course, if it's proven that my brother really is dead"—he paused, as if surprised to hear the words on his lips—"then his estate goes for the care of his child. It'll be up to Marla Stanhope to decide if the loan goes through. I'll be happy to show the paperwork to the elders and elected officials. Just give me a time and place, and I'll be there."

"So will I." Marla stood, smiling. "But I'm not inclined to loan away my baby's money and future unless it's financially beneficial. For her," she added quickly.

"Fine." Shamus banged the gavel again. "Any more speakers? No? Meeting's adjourned. Let's get home before full night." As he spoke, the shadows lengthened and the room fell dark, as if night had been waiting to fall until the last word was spoken.

After the meeting, I lingered, waiting on Rupert. Audric and I walked slowly from the old church while my business partner talked to passersby. The delay allowed the entire crowd to walk by me, and I was able to perform a mind-skim on each person. While an aborted attempt convinced me not to try mage-sight, I was still able to do the most basic exam, skimming for use of mage-power and for unglamoured supernats. Audric moved patiently at my side, one hand on my elbow. I didn't get anything I hadn't picked up before, and my head hurt worse, but the skim made me feel better on a purely safety-first level, and the spawn, if that was what I'd sensed from inside the church, was gone, leaving only a faint residue.

Except for Rupert chatting to Shamus Waldroup, the walk home from the meeting was accomplished in silence, small groups sticking close together for protection. The last streetlight had burned out before I was born, so Upper Street was lit only by the moon and by light spilling from shuttered windows onto the street.

"Did you get anything?" Audric murmured.

"Not much. I got a whiff of sulfur blowing in under the doors at the start of the meeting. Marla's hatred has blackened her aura. And I caught power leaking from a hidden amulet on Culpepper the younger."

"What did you try?"

I grimaced. "A mind-skim and mage-sight all at the same time, a sort of a blended scan, or something." In the dark I couldn't tell, but I thought he looked at me strangely.

"I didn't know that was possible."

"I nearly fell on the floor. Nearly hurled on the old biddy in front of us. Nearly made a spectacle of myself."

"Too bad you found such self-control," he chuckled. "Headache?"

"Oh, yeah. It's better now. But I won't try blending scans anytime soon. The world is a little too intense that way."

"I'll bet. You see the two just ahead? Fergus Yardley and Randall Prentice, Culpepper's underlings? Did you get anything special on them?"

"No. Just plain old run-of-the-mill humans. Nothing special about them."

"Lucky them," Audric said. He cleared his throat, his tone toughening. "Fergus is a geologist, in town trying to get the remaining feldspar strip mines and surface mines opened up and producing again. Randall is the moneyman behind the plans. Handles investments. Some say he even has a seraph or two as clients."

"You think?"

"No. I don't. There's no evidence that seraphs understand or care about money. I think he lets it be said because it makes him sound more trustworthy and respectable."

I thought about the necklace worn by Chamuel, the necklace that had rocketed Thorn's Gems into stardom, had made us a household name. If seraphs didn't handle money, how had Chamuel purchased the necklace? And when? Or had it been bought as a gift? They were questions I had asked myself often over the last few months; I had never found satisfactory answers. The records of the sale showed the purchase had been made by a traveler, a male, for cash. If Chamuel had come in human guise, then clearly I had been out of the shop, or we would have been pawing each other on the floor, my first heat stimulated in an instant. But none of my partners remembered the sale, the man who purchased it, or even much about the day in question. Weird. And where my safety was involved, weird wasn't good.

At that thought I looked into Audric's face, a half-seen dark sheen in the night. "I didn't see any cops tonight. Not even Thadd. Wouldn't you think they'd be there?"

"It crossed my mind. Several times."

Another weird event. They were starting to pile up.

Chapter 13

I could feel the warmth through the covers and reached across the sheets, moaning as dawn waked me from an amazing dream. I was trying to hang on to its remnants. And then my eyes popped open. Either the streetlights had all been replaced or the sun was shining. I tossed the covers and raced to a window, throwing back the heavy tapestry covering the glass. Friday morning had dawned bright and warm, the sky blue with lacy clouds, the air clear. We had an early thaw!

I raced through a shower, layered on a purple T-shirt over a dark teal one, with turquoise boots and jeans, clothes I could wear indoors or out, added my amulets and a primitive-looking necklace of tribal beads and citrine, grabbed a corduroy jacket, and flew downstairs. At the bottom, I ran headlong into Rupert, bounced off his chest and hit the wall before rebounding into his arms. He set me upright, talking fast. "Early thaw! It's sunlight!"

"I see it! Come on!" I grabbed his hand, pulling him through the shop and out the door into the day. We turned left and stopped in the walkway, blinded by the brightness of the rising sun. Eyes closed, I inhaled, pulling in the scent of sun on snow. I concentrated, feeling the warmth on my face, gentle, like my mother's hands, tender and warm. A sun reminiscent of Louisiana, not the pallid, clouded-over sun of winter mountains at high altitudes, but warm like my childhood, my last memories of complete safety and joy. The sun of spring, so fresh it didn't leech away my strength.

For an aching, heart-wrenching moment, I mourned Enclave, the heat, the humidity, the soft susurration of the Gulf, the night roars of gators and the cries of birds, the scents of salt, fish, rotting vegetation. Mourned the wonderful sense of belonging. Of being loved. Tears gathered and spilled down my cheeks.

"Heaven," Rupert said. "Pure heaven. Someday I'm moving south, where there's a real summer and heat and rain, and winter is a few months of tepid cold instead of a frozen misery."

I moaned, the sound close to a sob, eyes still closed, face turned to the sun. "Mosquitoes, gnats, roaches, wild pigs big enough to wreck an El-car," I said, trying to remember that the South had had its drawbacks for me, the worst of which was a slow death by insanity. "Birds that start screaming before daylight, gators with teeth like razors, snakes—big poisonous snakes with huge fangs—panthers, skunks— You think mountain skunks stink? You have no idea how bad a skunk stinks until it lies dead under a hot sun for a day or two."

"Sounds like you've been there."

Heat like the worst of a Louisiana summer reared up in me. Blasted its way up my body, through my muscles, along my nerves, and into my skin. Every cell of flesh ignited. Thaddeus Bartholomew, kylen, a Hand of the Law. Fear followed the heat, a flare of adrenaline making the heat sharper, sweeter.

I angled my face higher and sighed. "Once, for a summer. My mother and father took a cabin on Lake Ponchartrain," I said. Truth. All truth. "I was about four? Five? I remember everything about that summer. I remember catching fish, the smell of them frying." *Back when I ate meat . . .* "I remember the crows, the alligators, the lilies. Did you know that flowers can grow in the water? Beautiful flowers." I opened my eyes and turned to Thadd. *Anael, help me. My body burns . . .*

My voice dropped, and when I smiled, it was with all the heat in my eyes, in my voice, in my body language. "It's so warm there, the natives go nearly naked for six months of the year." I widened my smile, letting my words slow to the pace of life so long denied me. "Baring their toes, their arms and wrists, their necks, to the sun."

"Sounds wonderful," Rupert said, voice lazy, unconsciously matching my tone, the pace of my words. "You told me about that place. Remember? We're going there someday, you and Audric and Jacey and her family. All of us. For a vacation."

I opened my eyes and dropped my arms, which had risen toward the sky. Rupert was watching me, warning in his eyes. *Oops.* "Yeah. I remember," I said. But I knew full well I had never told Rupert or Jacey a single thing about my youth. Rupert was trying to protect me from whatever he had seen in me just now. Mage-heat was making me stupid. I had to get control or I was in trouble. But I'd rather get hold of Thadd.

He stood bareheaded in the sunlight, dressed in browns and greens—brown business suit, dark green tie, green shirt, green scarf loose around his neck, long brown coat unbuttoned. His hair glistened like polished red gold. His eyes glowed, filled with the heat of the earth. I think my mouth was hanging open. Maybe I drooled.

Beside me, Rupert jutted his chin, the gesture drawing the cop's attention across the street. "Once or twice a winter we have a rare, early thaw, a sun-day. The entire town turns out for a few hours to enjoy it, to appreciate that winter will eventually end, and warmer, better times will come."

Across the street, the bakers were on the sidewalk in their

shirtsleeves, old man Shamus doing a little jig. He danced toward his wife and they linked arms, feet kicking. His wife laughed aloud and the sound of their singing caroled across the street, a song I half remembered from town dances. Her name was Do'rise, I recalled. I'd like to dance with Thadd, a horizontal rumba with lots of turns and dips.

As my awareness of Thadd increased, the mage-heat rose, and the call of the amethyst in the storeroom woke. A purple splendor sang through my blood, begging to be taken.

"What are they doing?" Thadd asked.

"Clogging," Rupert said. "A dance with its roots in the Highlands of the British Isles. What can we do for you? After two p.m., of course. You couldn't buy an egg or get a newspaper until then."

"I hear you were at the council meeting last evening, and offered to make the town a loan for mage-help to melt the ice caps."

Rupert shrugged. "Word gets around. It's worth considering. If the town officials and Lucas and I can work out an acceptable business arrangement."

Thadd nodded, his eyes following the activity down the street. My gaze followed his. From every doorway, the townspeople emerged, lifting faces and arms toward the sun, some singing, some praising the Most High, some kissing passionately and disappearing inside to reemerge on porches or roofs, then dropping from sight for a session of lovemaking in the sun. Some called out psalms of glory for the sunlight and the warmth; others hugged their children, ran into the street, and started snowball fights with melting snow.

Behind us, Audric stepped from the doorway, dropped a canvas bag, and stretched high before bending and dropping his hands slowly to the ground, knuckles scraping the crusted snow. I wanted to see Thadd do that. Maybe without the business suit.

"The town fathers just hired a plane to take a look at the caps," Thadd said. "I hear you're footing the bill."

Rupert shrugged again. "Why should I offer to pay for mage-help if the caps are so unstable there's no time to get a mage here? It's good business. Now, go away. My partners and I need to play."

"One last thing," Thadd said, "strictly personal. Should it be proved that Lucas is deceased, what happens to that portion of Grampa's estate?"

"It's complicated. But we'll work something out. Or maybe your mother will make the investment with her portion."

An elder stepped from a house down the block, his brown robe open, exposing long johns, boots loose on his shins. He began to sing, face raised to the sun, a hymn about all things bright and beautiful. Others joined in, four-part harmony echoing off the buildings.

Rupert and Audric and I clasped hands and meandered toward the Toe River, following a line of people already heading that way, leaving Thadd behind. I tried to turn and go back to him, but Audric put an arm around my shoulders and so did Rupert, effectively trapping me between them.

"See?" Audric said.

"Weird," Rupert said. "Like she's seraph struck."

"Yeah," I breathed. "Sorta like that."

He scooped up water in the dipper and drank sparingly. His thirst wasn't so bad, now that he was being fed. The bread brought by Malashe-el tasted better than any bread he had ever eaten and seemed almost magical in its restorative properties. He could tell, even in the dark, that the flesh of his wrists and hands was healing. The stink of gangrene was almost gone, and he had never heard of anything that could reverse gangrene. The bread had to be responsible. Ergo, it wasn't ordinary bread. It was something new.

BLOODRING

Lucas lay on the thin mattress in his prison cell, ankles crossed, one arm behind his head, his gaze locked on the bars, barely visible in the faint red haze from the passageway. Six bars ran vertically from the rock at the top and into the rock at the bottom. So far as he had been able to tell, there was no door. And no lock. So how was Malashe-el able to enter the cell? How was the other one, who tapped his blood, able to come and go? Before he was fed, he had been too drained to think, to ask questions, or to watch. Lately, he was always asleep when they came and went. Were they drugging him?

Something flashed by in the passageway, demon-fast. Several others followed, feet scurrying, brushing the passages, leaving behind the stink of burned things. He caught a wisp of sound, hollow and atonal, "Mage-heat. Mage-heat. Time, time, time . . ."

Together we forded the Toe to the old Pinebridge Complex. The river, only a trickle in winter, was already growing stronger in the fast melt. The complex's parking lot had been plowed, leaving huge mounds of snow and ice at the periphery. Melting slush trickled across the exposed blacktop. From both sides of the Toe, cars began to roar in: trucks, snow-Elbile, and El-cars—the battery-solar-powered vehicles that had proven so efficient since the reduction of the petroleum industry. People appeared from everywhere for the traditional, impromptu party, held when winter took a break from torturing us.

Tables were pulled out of the complex buildings and, like magic, food appeared, heaping platters of bread, muffins, salvers of bacon, jellies on one table, canned vegetables and sweets on another. Wonderful food, brought to be shared. A side of beef, freshly slaughtered, turned on a spit.

A table was set aside for surplus foodstuff. Hoarding was a sin, punishable by kirk sanctions, but over the course of the long winter, everyone ran out of something, and early thaws allowed us to bring out whatever we had in surplus. From Audric's bag came jars of strawberry preserves, a box of dried mushrooms, raisins, and three quart jars of canned pumpkin. Five women manning the surplus table descended on the offerings and laid them out with the others. As the crowd increased, people gathered around the food, eating their fill.

School had been called off and children were sledding in their shirtsleeves, joined by some of the younger adults. Story-telling had begun, and in a far corner, dancing. I saw Ciana and Marla, holding hands, laughing as they watched a teenager wearing a red clown nose trying to juggle. Ciana spotted me and waved before pulling away from Marla and running to a group of her friends. One girl had a long sled and the group raced up a nearby hill, pulling the sled behind them with a cord. Dogs barked.

Crafts and household items were set up in a flea market. A table appeared with fresh-baked pies; barkers carrying trays sold beer and meat-on-a-stick. We ate and visited with old friends and ate some more. Competitions started between groups of men, throwing cabers and a beer barrel filled with concrete. Mage-heat made me drowsy and itchy, made all the sweaty men appear so much . . . more. I basked in people watching, man watching, ignoring Audric's eyes on me. Hours passed as the sun beat down. Eventually, we ended up at the edge of the dance floor—the cracked and abraded parking lot. I leaned into Rupert as couples formed up, toes tapping to the beat of bag-pipe, fiddle, and guitar.

The mage-heat was lessening as distance from the kylen persisted, and I could breathe easier, though my memories of the early morning were pretty blurry. Rupert said nothing else about my strangeness, so I was pretty sure I hadn't tried to take off my clothes and attack Thadd in the street. I also assumed

Audric had given him a convincing story to explain my actions. Weirdness on top of weirdness. The story of my life.

The dancing started, a dozen couples whirling into a high-stepping clog, the beat of the dancers' feet like forty-eight drums on the frozen pavement. The music began to flow faster, and the dancing took on the air of a contest. My senses stirred. The sun continued to climb, warmer and brighter, glaring off the piled, packed snow. The townspeople and those from the rural hills continued to gather, a brightly dressed crowd in a holiday mood. Even the orthodox were dressed in light gray—a spring treat.

I caught the scent of beer and wine and a whiff of moonshine; the smell of roasting meat drifted over it all. The dancers' sweat was ripe in my nostrils, and when Audric put a package of dried fruit in my hand, I smelled raisins, apricots, bananas, berries, and apple. My friends smelled of roasted meat. My sense of smell was sharper than I ever remembered it. A side effect of mage-heat? Of taking too much amethyst?

The music raced, and the speed of the steps eliminated the less athletic. Couples fell away from the dance floor, exhausted. One man, slim and delicate, only a few inches taller than I, caught my attention as he twirled his partner into a fast spin. He was dark haired, with odd, amber-colored eyes. He wore a day-old beard on a deeply tanned face and moved with a grace that was almost more than human, fast and elegant. He looked like an Internet ad for men's cologne, wearing tight-fitting jeans and navy cowboy boots, a flannel shirt open at the collar, chest hair curling out. I wanted to curl the hair around my fingers to see whether it was as soft as it looked.

Seeing the direction of my gaze, and maybe my mouth hanging open, Rupert nudged me. "Eli Walker. Got a profitable feldspar mine a little south of here. Does some tracking for the kirk and the cops. Pretty, huh."

"Oh, yeah," I whispered, picturing the man at a different kind of dance.

When the sixth number finished, only four couples were left standing, including the miner, Eli. They all bowed, and the gathering, which had grown to nearly a thousand, cheered the winners. I stood on the edge of the dance floor, silent, unmoving, staring. As he stood, I caught his eye and he paused. A woman handed him a cowboy hat, and Eli turned his attention to her a moment, flashing her a smile that I felt all the way to my toes. I wanted him to look at me like that, dangerous and tough, self-assured, just a little cruel. I wanted him to bite me, oh so gently, with his strong white teeth. *Oh, yeah.*

The sweating dancers left the floor and Audric moved closer. "Can you dance, little mage?" he asked softly. "Do you know the dances of Enclave?"

I remembered the beat of Enclave drums in my blood, the wild, almost violent, music. "It's been so long," I murmured, eyes half closed with desire and memories. And the underlying pull of the amethyst. And the kylen. Eli. My blood thrummed.

Audric raised his voice to the musicians. "Can you pitiful excuse for a band play 'The Dragon's Demise'?" The other dancers laughed at the challenge in his voice and gathered around the floor to watch. Audric thrust out his chest and paced the floor. I began to wake up, as if I had been trapped in a dream.

The fiddler called back, "We can play anything, mister. But you have to be more than just a dancer to keep pace with us on that one. Big man like you would collapse in a faint just trying."

"Wager!" Audric shouted.

"Think you're up to it?" The fiddler swept into a glissando, sharp and piercing, and the bagpipe player put his disjointed instrument on a stand and picked up a guitar, following the passage with flying fingers. The banjo player retook her seat, and a mouth organ sounded a train whistle.

"The little woman and I can outdance you all," Audric replied.

"A gamble, then!" the harmonica player called.

"Ten pounds of beef and a keg of the best beer if we outlast and outdance you."

"And if you lose?"

"We'll not lose. But if we do, I have five Pre-Ap hammers and a case of unrusted nails, dead-mined from my own claim."

"What are you doing?" I asked while the musicians and the owner of the cow conferred.

"Done!" the fiddler shouted, and instantly exploded into the first notes of "The Dragon's Demise."

"Tiring you out, little mage." Audric grabbed my hand and whirled me; I slammed into him. His huge hand secured me to his body as he stepped across the dance floor, fingers splayed on my back. "Dance," he commanded.

Years dropped away in an instant and I found the steps to "The Dragon's Demise," body flying fast, held in check only by Audric and his human speed.

The dance started with a tango of teasing, the story of Adam and Eve, the Pre-Ap, flawless world. It moved into the temptation and the fall, the dance a parody of the beginning moments of the apocalypse, a perfect world annihilated by the Most High, furious at the evil of humans. The pace of the dance sped up with the appearance of the seraphs, minutes passed as we danced the plagues, the wars, and the arrival of the first demons. I fled, keeping the beat, resisting as he pulled me into his arms, whirled me away, faster and faster. I was sweating, breathing so hard my lungs ached. The pace increased as we danced the end of the world.

I could hear the handclap rhythm of the audience, picked out the sound of bets being placed. Knew we were on the edge of giving ourselves away. "Audric," I gasped.

"I know," he said, his face full of joy and passion. "Just a little more." And he followed the music into the final segment of the dance, already too fast, too frenzied. In the sequence of the Last Battle, he added a half dozen steps, forcing the cadence of the music even faster. Mage-quick, I followed. It was an En-clave move, but it looked like improvisation to the humans, and they shouted with laughter and encouragement.

"One more," he said as he twirled past. And I knew what he intended. He was adding the story of the mages into the dance, a version of the Dragon's Demise as told only at Enclave. I stamped my heels and spun in a tight circle, arms over my head, face to the sun.

Audric leapt past me like a runner, toes pointed. In midair he threw up his hand and brought it down, the motion mimick-ing the first recorded action of the Mage War, the signal given by the U.S. Army general as he ordered an aerial bombardment of fifty teenage mages. Midwhirl, I leapt straight at the sky, the symbol of the missile of mage-power that struck at the U.S. troops. Audric fell to the ground in a ball, thousands killed in an instant. I landed and swept a leg over him, turned my back to him and fell backward, toward him. Just as it looked as though I might fall across him, he rose and caught my wrists, letting me down to the ground slowly, body tight with the vision of death and agony.

As I slid slowly, so slowly to the ground, our bodies in tune to each other, the band faltered, a missed note. Triumphant, Audric tossed me upright and spread his arms wide, the story of seraph wings outstretched. I coiled in the air and landed on my toes, arms curved in a circle around me. And Audric, faster than the music could follow, gathered me up and threw me across the dance floor. I landed in perfect position. We laughed, tri-umphant. The banjo player lost two beats. The mage-war and victory were steps they had never seen.

At the edge of human endurance, feet moving so fast it seemed that surely he must stumble and fall, Audric slashed with an imaginary sword and spread his wings again, attacking the unseen enemy, a Dragon of Darkness. The fiddler staggered, lost a full beat. Chasing the error, the guitar player missed a lick. The harmonica player began the chorus too soon. Faltering, the band caught the beat again.

Audric stabbed the beast, roaring as the music clanged to a disjointed halt. He held the position as if frozen, one arm out before him, as if his sword were buried in its flesh. For a long, silent moment, neither of us moved, chests heaving, breath so loud it could be heard over the breath of our audience. Then Audric twisted the sword and pulled it, cutting, from the flesh. He danced on tiptoe around the dragon, wrapping it in chains. I waved my body slowly from side to side, exhausted, the mages about to fall.

The beast chained, Audric turned to me and gently took my hand, a suitor once again. I lifted my chin, sad but victorious. We walked around the circle, hands joined, held out in front of us, a dignified gavotte as mages and seraphs had departed the battlefield together, leaving the field of victory to the few humans still standing.

The crowd shouted and whistled and swarmed us. The band abandoned their instruments and followed. Audric laughed and bowed, pulling me down with him. And as I bent, I saw Thaddeus Bartholomew in the gathering, his eyes on me. But my heat was gone.

As we rose, Ciana threw her arms around my waist, hugging me hard. "I didn't know you could dance like that!" she squealed. "That was so cool!"

Over the head of my stepchild, I met Audric's eyes and knew he had danced away my heat, knowingly. Which meant he had figured out who had triggered my heat and, therefore, what Thadd was. He knew too much.

A kirk elder climbed on top of a table and cupped his hands around his mouth. He shouted, "Thaw rest and sun-day is over. Remember and find solace." Traditional words that meant a return to the real world, a return to school and kirk and work. Except the sun still shone and water still dripped, the resonance of spring.

That night, exhausted but far more relaxed than in days, I sat in a basic charmed circle, the *Book of Workings* at my feet. Beyond the first section, the part I had completed when my gift fell upon me and forced me out of Enclave, I had never thoroughly studied the reference used by all neomages. It was divided into thirds. The first third, titled "Common Things," dealt with incantations for everyday life, heating water, incantations for fire, storing a charmed circle, creating a shield of protection, storing strength. The second portion, "Workings Together," was for midlevel mages, those who had mastered basic incantations, could use their gifts without endangering themselves or others, and could work in concert with other mages, empowering—or even creating—new incantations for specific purposes. Midlevel mages used part two to steer a hurricane to someplace where rain was needed, or to put out a forest fire. Higher-level, individual workings were also here, like the instructions for creating a prime amulet, one tied to one person's DNA, and the guide for creating a glamour, and the incantation for healing a seraph with minor battle damage and burns. The final section of the *Book of Workings* was titled "Warfare." For the most part, it was bloody stuff.

Over the years, I had tried a few incantations from each of the last two sections, enough to be conversant with the more mundane conjures, like the glamour I wore at the swap meet, a few minor painkilling and healing incantations, and the tag I had attempted on the men who attacked Rupert. But I had never bothered with the book as a whole. In my cursory searches through it, I had never seen instructions for an incantation regarding mage-heat.

BLOODRING

Deep in the second section, I discovered a page of love potions. Love potions for mages. Who knew? In with the love potions were pages listed simply as "Heat," distinct conjures that seemed to be for very different problems. Unfortunately, there wasn't an asterisk, or a note, or a big flashing arrow beside them to indicate which was for mage-heat. Because I hadn't been taught how to use the book, it was a guessing game. Well, whoopee.

The incantation that called for a glowing coal seemed to be used to generate warmth in winter, a handy-dandy portable furnace. The one that asked for hay, seeds, and a dead fish could possibly be used to keep the ground warm in early spring to protect crops. The one that called for three ewes to be placed inside the charmed circle may have been intended for use in animal husbandry. At least I hoped so. It called for a randy male sheep to get the ewes in the mood, and three drops of blood acquired from his . . . well . . . Yuck.

The most promising conjure mentioned down, lust, and feathers in the template incantation itself, indicating a direct response to mage-heat, though as usual, the book was maddeningly insufficient in its direct application. It requested that a single drop of dried blood be diluted with the water from a melting icicle. There was no demand that the blood be mage-blood, and no proscription against using animal blood. On a cloth on my knee was a dried smear of Homer's blood, acquired when I treated a hot spot on his shoulders in October.

I didn't need to bleed the Friesian, though I could with a quick prick of a ceremonial knife. I felt terribly guilty bleeding him, but Homer never noticed, always too engrossed in his dinner. Still, I was glad I had saved the bloody cloth.

The incantation didn't require a specific number of mage participants, so I could conceivably do it alone. The icicle only had to melt onto the blood, not be brought to boiling. It might work. In fact, it seemed way too simple to be in the second portion of the book, but the subject matter may have been considered sensitive by mage teachers.

All incantations are pretty general, guides only, because an earth mage would use certain items during an invocation that a stone mage couldn't draw upon, like leaves or roots, or maybe an ear of corn. A sea mage would use shells, or pearls, or kelp. A metal mage would use an iron cross, a silver brooch. Regrettably, no one knew what items would work best for a specific mage until after the conjure was tried the first time. Because I didn't know which stones would be best for this one, in the charmed circle with me was my silver bowl, filled with stones from the storeroom.

Bloodstone might work for me. I had an affinity for the mineral, and blood was part of the rite. Blood. Heat. Bloodstone. It all seemed to fit. In the bowl was a shard of white quartz for innocence and purity, moss agates for growth, a few nuggets of dark green aventurine, and malachite. Cool, earthy, restful colors and stones. On a china plate was an icicle from the eave. Ice and minerals to cool heat, ardor, and lust. I hoped.

I sighed, easing into the proper state of mind for a rite, sitting beside the bowl of stones with the *Book of Workings* at my side. I calmed immediately, the energy employed in the dance having left me tranquil and spent, and I settled into meditation, regulating my breathing, my heart rate slowing. Never before had the proper state of mind been so easy to achieve. I took it as a sign this was going to work.

I opened my mage-sight, seeing the energies of my apartment. I relaxed, my body in a full lotus.

I drew on the bear amulet that stored strength, and placed the cloth with the dried smear of blood on a clean plate. Lifting the icicle with my left hand, I held it over the plate and placed my right hand into the silver bowl of stones. Instantly I felt one warm to my hand, and set it in my left palm, in contact with the icicle. It was the sliver of white quartz. I began the incantation. "Heat and lust and desire too warm. Crown and down and cock o'erfill. Flesh and thigh and breast and wing. End the draw of empty nest."

The first drop of melted icicle fell onto the blood, then another. The quartz heated, growing warm. A second drop of water ran across my hand onto the cloth. The blood in the center softened and ran into the fibers, a rich pinkish red as I continued the incantation, finishing with, "End of need deep in the night, rising need, one day of lust, then be gone."

It was a small icicle, no larger than my pinkie, and it melted fast from the heat of my hand and the quartz, the blood diluting into a faint tint. I repeated the first verse again and waited. The quartz cooled, my hand dried, but nothing else happened. Absolutely nothing.

I pushed the plate away and dropped the quartz into the bowl. Maybe it took all night to actually work, or maybe it would only work after twenty-four hours, as the line "one day of lust" seemed to indicate. Or maybe I'd try it again in the morning. Maybe it needed sunlight, or the moonlight was warping the conjure.

Tired, I blew out the candles, opened the charmed circle, and cleaned up the salt. I crawled into bed and dropped off instantly. I had no dreams, steered into a deep, calm sleep by the sound of dripping, melting snow outside my windows.

Before dawn, the sky a dark gray, stars still shining and the moon still up, I was awake and standing by my front windows. It was the noise that woke me, the incessant crowing and calling of roosters. Up and down the street roosters flew, attacking one another, claiming and challenging territory—fence posts, columns, the eaves of storefronts—fighting and posing, wings spread, dancing for attention. Some were bleeding, feathers missing; one limped, a bloody path trailing after. With the roosters were chickens, gathered in small groups, or running about from rooster to rooster, mating where they stood or fighting off the amorous attention of multiple suitors, making a horrid racket. Angry, noisy, horny chickens.

Other sounds of crowing and frenzied clucking came from the alleys and side streets and from the wooded areas of the surrounding hills. They echoed in the predawn air. Hundreds of chickens, all in heat.

I remembered the words of the incantation. *Heat and lust and desire too warm. Crown and down and cock o'erfill. Flesh and thigh and breast and wing. End the draw of empty nest.* An incantation to bring chickens into heat for twenty-four hours. Oops.

Like most of the rest of the town, I dressed and went into the streets, unable to tear my eyes from the spectacle. Half dressed, half asleep, poultry owners were running up and down the streets corralling hens that had escaped from their coops. Ignoring the skirmishing roosters and their wildly slashing claws, the humans were sliding in the slush, falling into puddles, scraping elbows and knees, getting clawed by lady hens intent on other matters. Still more chickens were back in the coops, some trapped in the fencing, some mating with roosters that managed to find a way inside, some dead from trying to get free to join the roosters, impaled on sharp chicken wire.

When I screw up, I screw up big.

I needed to do something to help alleviate the mess I had caused and couldn't admit to or apologize for, and so I helped Esmeralda Boyles track down her guineas, gray fowl I would never have placed in the chicken category.

When I saw her, Miz Essie had two large pillowcases in one hand, one empty, the other wriggling with desperate pullets. She was bent over chasing chickens when I joined her, her dress bunched at her waist exposing sturdy calves. I emulated her technique of squatting close to the ground and running up to a guinea, grabbing it so the wings were clamped to its body, head and neck in one hand, then dropping it into a pillowcase.

"Thanks, sweetie-pie," she shouted at me over the raucous clamor as I caught my first pullet. "I'm the only one what raises guineas, so any you see are mine." She pointed at a bird perching atop a fence post down the street. "See him? He's my rooster. We'll get him last. And then he's for the stewpot. Horny old bird. Never gave me a speck o' trouble till now. I'll fix up a pot of soup and bring it around for your trouble."

My heart clenched. "I'm a vegetarian, Miz Essie," I said weakly, dropping a second struggling bird into the pillowcase. I didn't want a rooster to lose its life because of me and my ineptness and stupidity. Why hadn't I studied the book better? Or called Lolo about the incantation? Idiot not to have learned.

"So I'll make you a pillow out of its down. Either way, that shameless rooster is for the pot. Open the bag; I got another one."

I took the pillowcase from her and opened it just enough to allow her to drop in a hen without letting the others free. It screamed and the others fought to get out; one distraught bird made eye contact with me, as if she knew I was responsible for her plight, and clawed across my wrist. "Why not wait a day?" I pleaded as blood welled and I secured the birds. "It might regain its head by tomorrow and come home all humiliated and ready to repent." Can birds repent? *Feathers and fire. Could I sound any more stupid?*

But Miz Essie grunted as if she might reconsider the death sentence if the rooster came home. She concentrated on the task at hand and pointed down Crystal Street. "I see one o' mine down there. You got better legs than me, sweetie-pie. You get her. You married?"

"No, Miz Essie," I said. "Not anymore."

"I got me a son by my first marriage what's prettier than a spring bouquet. I'll send him by you next time he's in town. Now, go get my hen. Hurry afore she gets with that rooster."

Another man in my life. Just what I needed. But I didn't say it. Crystal Street was downhill, running with snowmelt, a slippery, flooded mess. Near the old Crystal Place, a four-story stone building leftover from Pre-Ap times, a gray hen was dancing around beside an old rusted Camry. On its roof was a pair of brightly feathered birds, mating in the predawn light. The guinea wasn't happy about having to wait her turn for cross-species rooftop procreation, but her concentration would make catching her easier.

I slid down the street and grabbed her. As I stuffed her in the pillowcase, I saw another hen down the side alley. She was making a nest atop a storage drum, and she seemed quite pleased with herself. Farther up the alley was a rooster who looked a mite worn out. He was being courted by a lady hen but wasn't returning her overtures. He was sitting, head tucked under a wing, body language claiming he wasn't up to the task. How many times in a half hour could a rooster mate before killing himself? What had I done?

For two hours, as my shoes soaked through with water, as the sun rose and the day warmed, I scoured town streets and alleys, and once into the edge of the woods, for guinea fowl. The search did little to assuage my guilty conscience, but it was all I had.

Most of the chickens were caught by eight. The ones that were the least wily were home in repaired coops by breakfast time. The clever ones were still loose at noon, copulating in back alleys or roosting in the low branches of trees in the woods. The roosters that had followed their mates back home were spared the shotguns the mayor ordered out after an angry rooster clawed a toddler who was trying to help recapture his pet. But the mating frenzy of the town's fowl was only a minor matter. Even the death of the licentious roosters was a minor matter. Because while I was at the edge of the woods, I spotted tracks that were distinctly nonhuman, and I scented fresh sulfur and brimstone.

I'd been putting off doing a thorough search of the woods behind the shop and along the base of the Trine. Hundreds of tracks. I couldn't put it off any longer.

Chapter 14

M y own lust was again smothered, banked beneath coals
of chicken hunting. Watching what would happen to
me if I let mage-heat free had been an effective deterrent.
Flapping my arms, chasing after Thaddeus, and begging to be
mounted was not my idea of a fun memory to carry around after
the heat wore off.

At eight ten, while the townsfolk were leaving for work or the
continued early-melt celebration on the far side of the Toe, I
changed clothes. I hadn't worn my black battle uniform in years,
not bothering to practice as I should, hours a day, dressed for war.
There was no one to demand long, exhausting sessions. No one to
care how I dressed when practicing savage-chi alone. I never
troubled to wear either the loose practice dobok or the tighter
battle dobok, never strapped all the blades in place. But the uniform had been created for warfare against demons, the padding
on the tight arms and legs repelling the scrape of spawn claws,
rings for securing blades on arms and shins and along the spine
from neck to shoulders. There were rings for saltwater bombs,
Dead Sea water, seraph feathers, an ax, nunchucks; even places
for holstered guns, not that I had any weapons but blades.

BLOODRING

The battle dobok still fit, though I hadn't worn it in more than ten years. In the mirror over the vanity table, I watched myself dress in the uniform, making certain all the seams were straight, inserting the throwing blades into the straps properly, so they slid free easily. I had a moment of uncertainty about which wrist blade went on which arm, and which were the right and left shin blades, but I finally got them all in place. A blade was strapped into the collar of the dobok, the hilt hidden in my braided hair. The pommel, within easy reach, was protection from being beheaded or chewed on from the rear.

My amulets were fully charged, and I stood over the damaged prime amulet, for the first time regretting the harm I had done it in a fit of temper. At one time it was my best protection, the amulet powerful enough to keep my neomage attributes blanked without continuous effort. Now it was barely alive, only a weak energy pulsing in its heart. I had tried once to charge it anyway, and the power slid right through it into another amulet.

I pulled on layered socks and battle boots, lacing them tightly before securing them with the Velcro straps. I was ready. Gabriel's tears, this was stupid. But I was going anyway. I bent one last time over the *Book of Workings*, from which I had refined two incantations, committing them to memory rather than taking the extra time to load them into a stone. I studied the notations I had made, then closed and shelved the book.

I drank a liter of springwater, hooked a second liter to my belt, and pocketed a handful of stones that had been charged with extra strength from the amethyst. Satisfied, I took up the walking stick and opened the stained-glass window at the back of the loft, the huge window that once was used to swing in hay bales and feed. It faced the woods north of town and the Trine. I grabbed the plumbing drainage pipe and shimmied down to the old alleyway. I checked the time. I had less than two hours to see what was in the woods and still get to work before opening. At a slow jog, I passed the stables and trotted into the trees.

As soon as I left behind areas where humans ventured, I paused, leaned against a tree trunk for balance, and opened my mage-sight. Holding it open, I blended a small—minuscule—skim. The impressions were a barrage, but this time I was prepared, and they didn't overpower me. The nausea I experienced the first time I tried a scan was now more like a case of indigestion than like the need-to-hurl nausea in the church.

The hillside north of town was a glowing fairyland of colors and scents. The snow and sunlight were a sickly yellow. The trees were dark with melt. The rocks that rose from the snow were bright blues, pinks and gold, bright with creation energy. The air smelled warm, almost like spring, with the scents of sap and leaves. The musk of a predator cat was carried on the light wind. The scent of sulfur overlaid it all like smoke low on the ground. I wasn't surprised that the sulfur seemed strongest near my spring. Something was hunting me.

Old brick and stone stabbed up from the earth to mark the ruins of Pre-Ap homes. Rectangular depressions of basements half filled with detritus and soil, made a mad dash almost as dangerous as standing still. Abandoning human speed, I shut down all but the mind-skim, rushing twenty feet uphill, sweeping my sight over the landscape. I was alone, but others had been here. The stones at my spring were fully exposed, the snowmelt well advanced. Around it, the forest was dripping, running with water that trickled like tiny bells, but the ground wasn't completely bare except for where I stood. There were hundreds of footprints, the reek of ammonia, the stronger scent of sulfur and the harsh smell of brimstone, fear, and sweat that clung to the denizens of the deeps. The reek of the netherworld, remembered from nightmares. Cramming the ancient fears deep inside, I searched for the things that were hunting me.

Circling my spring, still angling laterally across the base of the Trine, I counted three trails into the hills, two that led vaguely east and one that led west, all moving north. Shifting my search grid up the mountain, I followed each trail for several hundred yards, coming upon the half-buried, burned remains of an old fire truck, its hose in a pile. Far above, the grade changed from an easy hike to nearly vertical as hill became cliff, foliage thinned, and shattered rock rose toward the sky, the raw, blasted peak the result of Mole Man's battle.

The sun climbed, throwing shadows across the forest floor, through the tangled branches overhead. The snaps and spits that signaled snow melting, and the tinkle of running water were the only sounds. I bent over tracks, several different sets, overlaying one another. As I expected, the tracks were not from a single type of creature, but from at least three categories: one that wore boots like a human, one the pad of a midsized hunting cat, its paws as large as my spread hand, and the others from barefoot, three-toed spawn. Strangely, very strangely, all the spawn tracks seemed to be from a single beast. I knelt in the slushy snow and examined its tracks. It had a V-shaped scar on one right footpad. Both the spawn prints and boot prints reeked of Darkness.

The spawn had spent its time in the periphery of the spring, hiding, its footprints winding behind trees, behind boulders, in depressions of old foundations. When I triangulated its positions, its focus was clearly on the spring, not on the business and loft. It was watching the boot wearer as that creature had watched me. At no point did the spawn shift into a position where it could see my loft window. That made me pause. What could make a hungry spawn ignore the scent of mage and humans? Spawn were always hungry.

I studied the boot prints, thinking about the spelled beings who had attacked Rupert. Second-unforeseen? Humans? My mage-sight had been wide open. Had they been as well glamoured as Audric? Their boots had tracked as human. Was this one such as they, or was this the track of a daywalker?

When I was sure that no Darkness was on the hill, I walked along the treeless length of an abandoned road, back to my spring, and surveyed the ground, looking for clues to my hunter. Resting against a tree trunk, my mage-sight still open, I tried a deeper blended scan and this time nearly fell over. The kaleidoscopic impressions were an avalanche of sights, smells, sounds, and *knowings*. Over it all rode a taste of evil.

At the impact, I dropped the walking stick. Racked with nausea, I fought the overload as a cold sweat broke out on my body. I tied to parse my reactions into fact, intuition, and fancy. I scented, felt, tasted, the spawn, wholly evil, wholly mindless, hunting for prey, wanting to eat, to rend, to destroy. But the Darkness that had lain in wait behind the trees had been watching the other, the shod being, the daywalker, following him here at night. I could feel its purpose. It *had* been spying on the walker.

The daywalker, however . . . With my senses totally open, the daywalker didn't smell like the spawn. Instead of the scent of pure Darkness, the walker was a mad conglomeration of evil and something else. I pulled in the scan, concentrating on that one odd note of reality, and opened my vision wider. And I had it, that *something* that was familiar to me, yet not from my childhood terror. Something I had only recently smelled for the first time, and then I had only unconsciously noted it.

Holding to the tree, I drew the aroma of the beast into my mind, into my nose, knowing that while I used my senses like this, I was totally exposed and vulnerable. If I had missed something in my search, I was open to attack. I was dinner and a mate, maybe both at the same time. I had heard the tales.

Forcing out rising fear, I sought to identify the trace scent. Suddenly I knew. It was the scent of human mated to something else. The something else was seraph. The scent of the High Host. The smell of holiness. Thaddeus Bartholomew smelled like this.

BLOOÐRING

I dropped my blended scan, closing myself off from the energies around me, the influences soaked into the ground, permeating the air. I fell on the wet, bare soil at the base of the tree, landing hard on my walking stick and a root.

The world swirled around me and I leaned forward in a violent retch, emptying my stomach. A sour, horrid taste, but a mage taste, not the taste of Darkness or of kylen.

When my stomach settled enough to allow me to reposition, I pulled the walking stick out from under me and shifted my back against the trunk. Twisting the top off the liter of water, I swished some around my mouth and spat it out, repeating until I could drink and keep it down.

When I could stand, I braced against a large white oak, branches wide and bare, a tree my earth mage friends from childhood would have loved. It made a dandy prop for a stone mage. I brushed the detritus off my uniform, feeling the wet that soaked through to my skin at thigh and butt. It was snowmelt, water that had passed through sky and air. I could feel it draining me, my power evaporating away with the water.

Making my way to the spring, intent on splashing myself with springwater, charged from deep inside the stone mountain, I watched my feet, careful not to twist an ankle or lose my balance again. I wasn't watching where I placed my hand to brace myself.

At the spring, I crouched on a slab of marble, one of several large rocks that ringed the fountainhead, and settled the walking stick across my thighs as I cupped water over my wet clothes. The cold stung like a brand but instantly stopped the leaching of power from my flesh. The temperatures were above freezing and might reach fifty today, but on the hillside, under the cover of the trees, it was cold. When I stood from the spring, I rested my hand on a boulder for balance.

From the stone, Darkness reached out and touched me; claws and silken flesh raked gently down my arm. The scent of blood, drying puddles and violent sprays of old blood, of death and terror, and the cleansing scent of sage snared me. Words, words like music—as if the demented in hell had broken their chains and formed a chorus, all singing notes to a different song. Bizarre words. Meant for me.

"*Welcome, mage,*" it sang. "*I seek you.*"

Its hands slid up my bare arms, daring, wanton. Heat blossomed in my belly.

"*I seek and I desire you, only you. Seraphs will not touch you. Will not love you. In their orderly, mannerly,* obedient *way, they will never offer themselves to you. Never.*"

Unable to move, unable to pull away, I felt the brush of lips along my collarbone, moving slowly up the side of my neck, raising prickles of desire. I looked for the thing that touched me, but I was alone, naked in the woods, on the hillside. A warm breeze drifted across my skin. *Charged stone,* my mind whispered. *Charged with an incantation shaped and formed just for me.* And, *Incubus . . .*

"*I can bring you to heights of passion,*" it said, making me shiver with want. "*I can show you the true power of the* Book of Workings. *I can give you control over your gift without the needless Enclave instruction and practice and time-consuming study.*" The hillside and the mountain above it burst forth with power, the power that was hidden there, waiting for me, the vision supplied by the charged stone. The spring beside me flowed with raw energy, blue and scarlet power from the center of the earth. Below it roared a volcano of power, the sound rocking me to my marrow, the thrum of strength, the force, the raw, raging might, deep in the earth below me. It burned, that molten mantle seeking an outlet. I was nearly overcome. Nearly reached out to it. Nearly took what could be mine.

But it was too much, too strong, an ocean of promise making me drunk on power just viewing it. The image of might developed an imperfection, a minuscule crack. The cold of a breeze over melting snow brushed my face. I forced my little finger to move. The shackles of the incantation loosened. Around me, the vision continued.

The incubus's hands and mouth touched, stroking along my sides and belly. *"Yes,"* it whispered. *"More power and strength and delights of the flesh than you can imagine. Come to me. I desire you, you above all others. I desire you. Come to me. Come,"* its breath murmured on my bare throat. *"I invite you; I desire you. I am here for you. For you alone."*

As it spoke, I eased my hand away from the stone. Reached under my tunic, the tunic I could feel only with my hand, not with the flesh of my body, and gripped the large stone bear. Its back was a hump of greenish jade fading into black at its legs, solidly planted and strong. I placed it over the pocket holding the rough shards of stone and drew strength from them all. I drained the bear and the stones in an instant, paltry power compared to what was being offered in the images. Yet it was enough to draw my blade. The walking stick's sheath fell to my feet. The vision shattered.

From behind came the shushing sound of last year's wet leaves, and I whirled, lifting my blade high, drawing a blade with my left hand as I moved. Before me was a young man, too beautiful and alluring to be mere flesh. Sulfur burned my nostrils. The thing pretending to be human squatted low to the ground. I swept into the cat stance, ready for attack. It was watching me, unmoving, hands limp, dangling between its knees. It tilted its head to the side, demon-fast. I saw all this in a single heartbeat. Time dilated.

In the following heartbeat, I focused narrowly on it. It had long black hair braided into a single plait, stones interwoven in the strands. Loose hair drifted slowly in the cold breeze. It was wearing dark blue, the color of periwinkles, tight pants that molded to every line of its thighs and buttocks. Its shirt was a lighter shade of the same color, tight to its body, but with loose sleeves, the collar open halfway down its chest, fine hairs visible in the deep V. Its eyes were a liquid blue and threw back light like polished labradorite in the sunlight.

My heart beat thrice; time snapped back. I took a breath. The beast smelled *wrong*, but it looked human, in its twenties, its face unlined. And still it watched as if curious, unmoving, clearly considering itself safe.

The heat of battle flamed up in me and I advanced, shouting, blades flashing in the winter sun. Its lips tilted up and I stopped, stunned by the beauty of that smile, the sadness, the melancholy. "Will you go to him?" the daywalker asked. "Will you take the offering?"

"Never," I said. I pulled the last of the bear's strength and transferred it to the bloodstone of the walking-stick hilt in my right palm.

"She didn't think so. She will be pleased." The smile faded. "You understand that I have no choice."

"All beings have choice."

"Not us. We never did." It stood in a single, fluid motion, demon-fast. Faster than a mage could ever hope to move. "I'm sorry," it said. "She said I should say that if I had to hurt you." And it charged.

I slammed the gathered force against him with a single thought. Twelve feet from me, the daywalker staggered and slid to the ground, one knee dragging a long trench through the topsoil and old leaves.

Left-handed, I hurled the throwing blade at its heart, drew the kris in the same instant and raced toward the daywalker. Surprise scored its face. Fear. It opened its mouth. It shifted. My thrown blade whistled past. My sword blade descended.

But the beast was gone. Whirling, blades high, I searched, feet planted firmly in the wet earth. The daywalker with the beautiful face and shining eyes was gone. I strode quickly in a widening circle, blades at the ready. Thirty feet beyond where we had stood was my throwing blade. Sheathing the kris, I scooped up the knife, the wicked point angling back behind me.

The rage beat in my veins, screamed within me. My fighting skills hadn't been enough to kill it. The daywalker had moved faster than lightning, faster than my eyes could trace. Faster than I could react. I wanted its blood. I had let it get away.

I drew on the walking-stick hilt, the power of bloodstone filling me. I touched the rounded rock holding the incantation. Little was left. Yet the conjure that had crafted the enticement was crisp and neat, and I breathed it into my mind. I would recognize the pattern of the temptation if I ever saw such again. It was a powerful, intricate web.

I had no salt but would use what was handy. With the heel of one boot, I traced an irregular ring in the soil, a big circle around the spring, the cistern, and the rocks that encompassed it all. Thumbing the jade elephant that stored a basic charmed circle, I stepped inside, then scuffed the ring closed, feeling the power of the circle snapping into place. With mage-sight, I studied the source of the spring bubbling out of the ground, a little burble of underwater motion, flowing unfrozen to the cistern. It glistened, a crackling blue of purity. I ran my sight across the rocks, the branches, the soil beneath my feet. Only the rounded rock had been polluted. I sheathed my short blade and scooped up a handful of water.

Without my having to think about them, the words were there, the words I had taken from the *Book of Workings* and refined for my own use. On the fly, I changed one of the incantations and added it as a prologue line to another one. I knew the incantation was right. Knew it deep inside where my heart beat with anger. I said, "Cleanse and purify stone from Darkness."

I dumped water over the stone and it hissed with a scent of sulfur smoke. The clean scent of sage followed, as if carried on the breeze. I flipped the sword upright, blade pointing to the sky, gripped the weapon by its pommel, and quoted the incantation

I had prepared. Using the might of scripture, I began, "He shall be for a stone of stumbling, a rock of offense . . ."

With the walking-stick handle, I tapped the stone that had held the incubus's incantation, replacing it with my own. My conjure slid into place as if it belonged there, as if the stone waited for it. I moved around the spring, still speaking, smearing rocks with wet fingers and tapping each stone circling the spring, the powerful water I used daily to restore me, water that could have been compromised, contaminated. Water that was now both protected and set to trap and trace an interloper.

When I had walked around the spring, tapping the snare into place, I reached into my pocket and pulled out a rock crystal, a yellow quartz, as pretty as sunshine. Repeating the incantation, I filled the stone with power. At the last word, I tossed the crystal into the spring, directly into the bottom, where the water moved the smooth soil as it poured in a steady gush. The quartz landed in the center of the movement, jumping once, twice, tumbling across the bottom of the spring, out of the eddy. It lay still, picking up the glint of yellow sunlight, like a promise to me, to defend and succeed. I was going to battle.

I broke the circle and stepped back. Drained, I sat on the nearest rock, shivering.

Back at my loft, I found the energy to climb up the drainage pipe, and tumbled into the apartment, wet, exhausted, and frozen through. I would be late to work, but I had to get warm. I drew a bath, hanging my dobok to dry, placing my weapons in a pile on the table. Sliding into the heated water, I lay there until it covered my shoulders and chin.

Slowly, warmth trickled back, and I found myself reviewing the incident. In a morning filled with weird, the weirdest thing of all was the daywalker. It had smelled of both good things and bad. It had smelled of Darkness and kylen, and kylens smelled like seraphs. It had acted unhappy to be attacking me. It gave me fair warning. And, weirdest of all, it had apologized. I examined the conversation from every angle. Rumors and legend said it took both Darkness and Light to create a daywalker. Kylen and spawn? Some other bizarre combination?

Long after the distant kirk bell tolled the hour, long after ten, I got out of the bath and dressed, sliding into brightly toned clothes that spoke of spring, because I knew that was what the weather called for. But underneath, I layered on silk long johns and an extra T-shirt to combat the cold that clung to my bones. My hair had dried in an ungainly snarl, and I pulled it out of the braid, forcing a comb through it before securing it in a twist on my crown.

I cleaned, oiled, and put the battle blades away in the long black weapons case I kept under the bed. To the casual observer, the case looked like a leather suitcase with special compartments for stones and fine jewelry. In the early years I had used it for that on occasion, taking the case when I traveled to a swap meet or a show, disguising its extra weight with stock. But it was an ungainly shape, it was heavy, and I had never needed the blades, so I had stopped taking it with me and had tucked it away out of sight. Now, I set the case beside the small getaway bag at the front door. If I took off in a hurry, it would go with me.

I paused at the door, my eyes on the case, a faint tremor of vertigo seizing me. I had forgotten about the blade case when I'd packed earlier and was pleased I remembered it. But something was wrong. A troubling dream memory of labradorite and periwinkle blooms. I had thrown a blade. Why? *Something was wrong . . .* That thought too slipped away.

Unforgivably late, I damped my neomage attributes on the doorknob and clattered down the stairs to work. The shop had customers, and flashing an apologetic smile, I rushed to help the one Jacey pointed to, her professional mien never faltering. The warm temperatures had brought out shoppers, and business was brisk all day in both Thorn's Gems and Audric's storefront. Twice Rupert went to the back, ducking through the narrow, low-ceilinged hallway between the shop and the workroom, and brought out fresh stock. Because I had come in late, I worked through lunch while my partners took a break. I drank a fruit smoothie and kept going.

Over the past two hundred years, the building housing Thorn's Gems had been several different businesses. Originally the town livery, it had also been a furniture factory, a store, and a restaurant, among others. Now the shop was divided into sections, with the front third of the old building totally renovated for customers. It had a copper-toned, pressed-tin ceiling, old-brick walls we had stripped and left bare, stained, three-variety-wood wainscot salvaged from a condemned building, and a hundred-fifty-plus-year-old wide-board hickory floor.

The storefront was comfortable, with a freestanding gas-log stove in the center, on which simmered teapot and percolator. Around it were the chairs where customers could sit while repairs were made or gifts were wrapped, savoring a bit of warmth in the logs and a cup of their preference. Along the walls were antique wood-and-glass display cabinets, placed so the partners could easily get behind them to serve customers. The rear two-thirds of the shop were mostly unchanged since the 1950s, when the building had been a furniture factory. Its space was taken up with a stockroom, a door at the back opening onto what had once been a service alley, two kilns, and the cluttered workspace.

During a lull in business, at around three o'clock, I felt a flicker of heat curl tightly within me. I knew the dratted kylen was nearby even before he stepped into the shop. He glanced at me, then at each of my partners, nodding to Rupert, man to man. Something about that little nod irritated me, and I started to steam. Thadd didn't notice my ire, tucking his hands into his pockets as he meandered around. He was dressed in jeans, flannel shirt, and Western boots, soles scuffing the floor as he studied the displays with their busts and acrylic stands shaped like posed hands and feet. Each stand was draped with necklaces, bracelets, anklets, and rings. Small statues and carvings took up corner space in each display unit. Thadd turned over a price tag and his brows went up. Thorn's Gems is pricey, but our designs deserve it.

I finished with my customer, bagged her purchases, and made change. After she left, I leaned across the case, watching the kylen cop. He examined a selection of garnets and a collection of emerald jewelry, the stones dug from the nearby hills, and some carnelian and smoky quartz that was set with red and white bamboo into primitive designs. Thadd lingered over the citrine and peridot and studied a necklace of chunky moss agate nuggets that I favored. When he reached me, he didn't pause, but glanced at leopard-skin jasper and malachite and moved on. That ticked me off again, though I couldn't have said why.

Rupert and Jacey watched the cop, as well, a wary look in Rupert's eyes as he rang up a sale, curiosity in Jacey's. She polished the glass-topped display where her customer had left a smear. Behind Thadd's back, she glanced at me, brows raised. I shrugged in reply.

When he reached the front door again, the kylen cop paused and took in the whole room. His eyes fell on the framed needlepoint above the door to my loft. Few people even noticed it. The frame blended into the brick, and the silk pattern was beige and brown. Thadd stepped to the doorway and studied the saying stitched with fancy letters into the silk. A ROSE BY ANY OTHER NAME WILL STILL DRAW BLOOD: the prophecy given by Lolo when my twin and I were born. The rose and the thorn, working together as a single unit, a warrior unlike any other. Meaningless once Rose was killed and I was unable to live with my own kind.

Thadd stepped aside for the last customer to leave, and

turned his gaze to Rupert. When the door swung closed, I said, "What do you want?"

"To go up on the Trine and search for the amethyst," he said to Rupert.

Up on the Trine? Now? I was pretty sure my mouth dropped open. Rupert looked just as incredulous.

"I know you have access to a horse," Thadd said, "and I've rented one. We can leave right now and be back before dark."

"In case you haven't noticed," Rupert said, "I'm working."

"No one's in the store right now. The girls can handle it."

"Girls?" Jacey and I said at the same instant.

"Girls?" I repeated. "We are not his shopgirls, his children, his employees, or his harem. We aren't just passing the time of day in here between tea and the garden club. This is a business. We all work." I rounded the display cabinet, fighting the heat that was trying to rise, letting it branch off and fuel anger. "Maybe it doesn't seem like valuable work to a big-time VIP, like a Hand of the Law, but it's important to our bellies, our creditors, and our retirements. Rupert isn't going anywhere. *Girls?*" I said, the last word a bit shrill.

Audric stepped from his storefront and leaned against the doorjamb, his arms crossed. I'd been aware of him all day, his shop just as busy with sunny-day bargain hunters as Thorn's Gems. Now he looked bored and amused. I figured the bored part was just for show. "You really shouldn't call them girls, you know," he said. "Partners, women, ladies, maybe, but not girls. They get riled. Now you have to bring them chocolate to make them happy."

"The man has chocolate?" Jacey asked, putting a fist on one hip. "If he has chocolate, he can call me anything he wants."

"What about me? Do I get chocolate too?" Rupert asked. "Queens are girls."

Exasperated, Thadd blew out a gust of air. "I don't have

chocolate. Allow me to rephrase. I need you to saddle a horse and go with me to search for the amethyst."

"On horseback?" Rupert asked, hand over his heart in dramatic horror.

"The shop has a horse," he repeated. "I asked."

"Correction. *Thorn* has a horse. A huge, vicious beast, ten feet tall, hooves the size of dinner plates and teeth that belong on a dinosaur. No way in Habbiel's celestial citadel will I get on top of it. No."

Jacey walked around to the central sitting area and plopped down into the chair she liked, pulled a piece of jewelry from a pocket, and started beading. "Rupert is afraid of horses," she said, eyes downcast.

"I am not afraid of horses. I simply hate them."

"Rupert is afraid of horses," she repeated. "Deathly afraid."

"Maybe a little afraid of them," he conceded. "Take Thorn. That horse likes her."

"Yeah," Jacey said, a small smirk on her face, eyes on the bracelet to hide her amusement. "Take Thorn. She needs a good, hard ride."

Her double entendre wasn't remotely veiled, and Audric tried to cover a laugh with a cough. Rupert snickered. "Hey, wait a minute," I said, mortified, unable to disguise a blush. I wasn't going up on the Trine, not with a Hand of the Law, someone who didn't know about Ciana's visitor, a human who didn't know what I was, didn't know about mage-lust, and yet who had a nasty, unhealthy dose of kylen genes in his makeup. A man who probably couldn't fight worth a flip. With a human along, I couldn't fight either, unless I wanted to face the repercussions. We'd be toast. "I thought this was a business and we were all working."

"If a Hand of the Law wants one of us to go stone hunting on horseback, then it needs to be our rock hound and lapidary, who happens to own the horse in question," Rupert said, still laughing. "Besides, it looks like the rush is over. We can handle the last few hours. Question is"—he turned back to Thadd—"can you handle our Thorn?"

Could he be any more indelicate? I wanted to drop through the floor in shame. There was no doubt in my mind that my best pals had been discussing my sex life—or lack of it.

"Go have fun," Jacey said, glancing up at me, smug. "All the fun you want. Or you can stay here and let us hassle you. Take your pick."

I shifted a humiliated gaze to Thadd, not quite sure how things had come to this or how I had been maneuvered into this expedition. With as much dignity as I could muster, I walked from the room and up the stairs to change. I didn't want to go, didn't want to be alone with the cop, but I figured if I stayed any longer, they'd drop the innuendos, and simply ask Thadd to sleep with me.

Chapter 15

†

By the time I was dressed for riding, with three blades hidden on my body and enough charged stones in my pockets to make a decent stand if my life required it, Jacey's stepson Zeddy had saddled Homer and taken him out front, where he stood in the sunshine, happy to be free of his stall and feeling frisky. Zeddy exercised the Friesian daily except when the blizzards blew, but there was seldom enough activity to satisfy an animal bred to work.

Thadd's mount was a high-strung, dappled gray, a big horse at sixteen hands, but nothing compared to Homer's nearly nineteen hands. Zeddy tossed me up as if I weighed less than his youngest sister. Of course, Sissy had turned nine before Christmas, so maybe I did. Neomages tend to be petite.

Below me, Thadd sat astride the smaller horse, looking perfectly at ease though I had the bigger mount. Part of me had been hoping he'd be distressed by the disparity in heights, all macho outrage, poorly hidden. Not so.

I kept hoping Thadd would grow another head or do something really outrageous to appear less attractive. But, besides being a Hand of the Law whose job description would see to my demise, it seemed he was an all-around nice guy. He sat the gray with the easy comfort of a cowboy, jeans-clad legs gripping the horse's sides. He looked good. Really good. My tummy did that little dip and curl that left me a bit breathless. Which made me even madder.

As if aware of my irritation, Thadd gave me an amused stare, which I could feel, even through the black wraparound shades favored by Hands of the Law. I snapped open my own sunglasses, set them on my nose just like a human, and clicked Homer into action. Extending his long legs, the Friesian lumbered across a mound of snow the gray had to go around, and proceeded northwest at a fast clip. Quickly, I guided Homer directly north, and we moved out at a quick pace, unspeaking, me pushing the speed, nursing an annoyance I didn't fully understand but felt entitled to. The antagonism helped to stifle my awareness of the kylen and helped ward off mage-heat that wanted to rise. I let the anger settle in for the duration.

A silent hour later and five hundred feet higher, Thadd moved up beside me at a fast trot. "So. If you were an undiscovered mine of gem-quality stone, where would you hide?"

"Underground and under the snow," I nearly snarled.

"So you're saying this is a waste of time?" When I didn't answer, he asked, "Or did your friends just embarrass you into this by playing matchmaker?"

I had a sudden vision of Thadd and me in my bed, pillows thrown away in haste, covers sliding off the mattress. A flush burned its way up my neck. *Drat.* "Figured that out, did you?" I said. My words were stiff, my tone even worse. And the rocking of the big horse wasn't helping mage-heat at all, not with Thadd so near. "My friends worry about me, since Lucas took off to greener pastures. I try not to let them bother me with their teasing."

"I think it's cute."

"Cute?" I made an indelicate sound. Homer's ears swept

back and forth, and he curved his huge neck to glance at me, eyes rolling. "FYI? 'Cute' is right up there with 'girls.' " I continued before he could reply. "Last month they tried to set me up with a feldspar miner named Ken. The poor guy showed at the shop on a Friday night with his neck washed, his fingernails clean, and a bag full of quartz rough as a gift."

"Fun date?" Thadd asked, not laughing, for which I was grateful.

"Agonizing." I bent under a low branch and guided Homer straight north, wanting to keep the kylen away from anything charged with power. Homer took a massive leap straight uphill, and I grabbed the pommel, holding on. "Easy, big guy."

"What's that?" Thadd pointed to the jumble of rock and mortar Homer had just bounded over.

"Shed, probably. You can find out more about the mountain from Rupert, but the Trine used to be one fairly small hill until one of the last mopping-up battles. People lived on the slope. We'll see foundations and roads and all kinds of stuff, until we reach the rock peaks. I haven't spent much time here, but ruins are everywhere." I pointed off to the west and to the east, to piles of moldering brick. "After a hundred years, there isn't much left but stone and brick, and even that's starting to decay."

The gray moved up beside me, Thadd visible in my peripheral vision. I didn't look his way. "What do you know about the Stanhopes?" he asked, his tone a hair too casual for the question to be idle.

"Less than I thought I did," I grumbled. I hadn't known about Mole Man, or about Lucas' roving eye. I hadn't known that Rupert's sweetie was a mule in hiding. "Why?"

"There's some indication that Jason has allied with a Power or a Principality."

A tremor of alarm shivered down my body. Below me, Homer reacted, his head coming up fast. I soothed him, stroking along his neck. "Is that part of your interrogation technique? Wait till your victim is calm and unsuspecting and then hit her with a zinger?"

Thadd ignored me. "This case attracted the attention of the Administration of the ArchSeraph pretty fast. You've met the investigator, I believe?"

"Oh, yeah. Captain Durbarge." The little assey.

"He thinks Jason may owe a blood gift to a Darkness, which then would be after anyone in the Stanhope line. Stanhope blood—Mole Man's blood—is important to the seraphic host, which makes a blood-demon doubly likely and doubly dangerous."

I didn't look around. Durbarge had speculated about a blood-demon.

"The AASI spotted signs of devil-spawn in the hills."

"Where?" I asked, my hand still soothing my mount. I didn't need Homer giving away that I was upset at the direction in which Thadd was taking the conversation. If the assey had been to my spring, I was in deep doo-doo. The cistern and pipes were spelled to keep long-distance and untrained observers away. A trained observer, however, would see a great deal.

"On the other side of the Toe River."

I made the connection fast and went from relieved to worried in a heartbeat. If Jason owed a debt to a blood-demon, then spawn would come after Ciana. Looking back at the cop through my tinted lenses, I saw he was watching me. "Where, exactly, and how many?"

"Outside Marla's home. A small pack of five or six."

Spawn travel in packs. If there was a daywalker watching Ciana, a blood-demon, and a spawn pack, then things were a lot worse than I thought. I wondered whether I should tell Thadd about the daywalker. But if I did, they might take Ciana into custody for her own protection. Asseys had no conscience. Any human caught consorting with Darkness, even an innocent, was carted off and never seen again.

A faint sense of vertigo made me totter, as a distant thought battled to rise and was pulled under. Something about stones and flowers? Whatever it was, I pushed it away for later and risked a question. "Is it possible that there's a war in Darkness?"

"A house divided against itself cannot stand," he quoted. The New Testament, the words of Jesus when he was accused of working with the devil.

"What if it's not divided? What if one of them just wants more power than before?"

"If you want to discuss theology, go to an elder." It was the perfect cop answer. I shook my head and pressed Homer uphill, a sharp grade that left Thadd behind. He seemed to realize he had lost ground both figuratively and literally. "Sorry," he said, catching up. "Knee-jerk response. The short answer is, I don't know." When I remained silent, he said, "So. Back to the stone. If you were a new mine of gem-quality stone, where would you be hiding?"

"My best bet is up high, on the bare rock near the peaks."

"And why is that?"

"Because no one's staked a claim or tried to buy mineral rights in years, not even Culpepper, so the find isn't easy to locate. Only a team with ice-climbing equipment could get to the peaks easily, and I can't remember the last time anyone took to the ice cap. And because, so far as we know, the stone wasn't found before the Trine was formed, so it's likely that it came to light during or after the battle with Benaiah Stanhope and the formation of the three peaks." It was the first time I had put all that together, but it felt right. The stone must have been pushed to the surface when the Trine was formed.

Homer tossed his head. Behind me and to the side, the gray danced several steps and neighed sharply. Homer's ears went back flat. The horses were spooked.

The hairs on the back of my neck rose, and I tightened my grip on the saddle horn. Something was watching us. I opened my mage-sight and scanned the area. The world looked strange through the sunglasses, shadowed and sparkly, as if viewed through a prism. As far as I could tell, we were alone, but something was wrong.

Homer came to an abrupt stop, ears back hard. He danced around, facing the town, and bowed his back to buck. I hauled on the reins with all my might.

Thadd was having his own problems. The gray pranced, his head up high, neck arched, eyes wide with alarm. "What's going on?" he asked.

From above us, a scream sounded, long and agonized, echoing down the slope, followed instantly by another. The gray dropped his head and kicked, throwing Thadd forward across his neck.

The angry scream sounded a third time. Some kind of predator cat. I hoped.

Homer bunched his muscles and took four mighty leaps straight downhill. Midkick, the gray squealed, whirled, bucked once, and followed. Thaddeus hit the ground.

I hadn't been able to think of an excuse to bring the walking stick but had charged a malachite ring with a calming incantation and stuck it on my thumb. With a thought, I sent it into Homer. He stopped. I didn't. My body was flung forward, my hand jerked from the pommel. The horn slammed into my stomach and all the breath left my body in a single gasp. I tumbled over his head, across a mound of snow. The world reeled by me. Upside down, I glimpsed the cat, black and white, crouched on a limb, eyes watching me as I rolled in midair.

I landed on one shoulder, my arm knocked numb. I thudded on the muddy ground and rolled, out of control, arm flapping, useless. Into a half-frozen puddle. *Snowmelt.*

Icy cold drenched me. Everywhere the water touched,

power was sucked out of me in a sudden, vicious extraction. The energy in the stones I carried was damped. Lust turned to agony. I may have screamed.

Overhead, far overhead, something moved. It flew, wings stroking, slow and lazy, taking it behind a cloud. I heard a whimper; the sound came from me.

"Thorn!" The sky vanished. I focused on Thaddeus. There were two of him, rotating. Hands of the Law. Kylens. In a sickening lurch his faces coalesced into one, greenish blue eyes wide and a trail of blood at one nostril. He'd lost the shades. "Are you all right?" When I didn't answer, he touched my shoulder. "Thorn?"

"Not so good, actually," I said. But feeling was sweeping back into my body, short, sharp stabs, and longer, continuous waves of throbbing. I rose slowly, pulling my upper body from the puddle. "But I don't think anything is broken. You?"

"The same."

"What kind of cat was that?" *I'm lying in snowmelt. Bruised, drained of power, and feeling like I got hit by an El-truck, and I want to talk about kitty cats.*

"A lynx, I think. It's gone now. Can you stand?"

"Yeah. Maybe." My teeth started chattering. A shiver gripped me in its fist and shook my entire body. "A bit chilly, though."

Thadd chuckled, pulling me upright. "If I give you a hand, can you get on the horse?"

"Homer. Sure. I can do that." Maybe. With a stepladder and winch. The world did a little stutter and wobble. I let Thadd balance me as I straightened my arm, testing my shoulder. I glanced down at my hands. They were gray with cold and energy loss.

"You have a knot coming up." Holding me by my good shoulder, he touched my scalp and I winced. "Headache?"

I nodded and wished I hadn't. "Yeah. And I'm dizzy."

A dull roar pulled our gazes to the sky. "Plane," he said. But there had been something else. Huge wings? Seraph? My imagination? Did I mistake a high-flying bird for something less mundane? The shivers worsened. I reached into a pocket, testing the stones. Most were dead, though several unpolished, uncut agates still held some strength. I drew on them, enough to make the pain bearable.

Thadd guided me to Homer and gathered up the reins, placing them in my hand. He cupped his hands and I put a knee into them. He lifted me slowly. I grabbed the saddle horn and pulled myself into place. Thadd held my foot when I would have put it in the stirrup. "I'd be happy to walk, but I don't think you can stay in the saddle."

A wave of vertigo had me gripping the horn with both hands as I said, "Nope. Me neither." When the wave passed, Thadd eased his hand from my thigh where he had steadied my balance. I wasn't sure I liked him being so nice. It was easier to keep my distance when he was just a cop.

As he adjusted the stirrups, I looked around. The gray horse was nowhere in sight. I turned back the way we had come and realized we had covered a lot of ground, too far to walk before sunset. The town was laid out below us like a model, a scene where a toy train runs through a town, along a river. In Mineral City, the train was pulling into the depot.

Thadd put a foot in the stirrup and swung up behind me. He scooted me forward and lifted me until I was pretty much sitting in his lap. Oh, no. Not good. Not good at all. Except other parts of me thought it was pretty wonderful. Warmth flooded into me when he wrapped his arms around me and took the reins, masculine and heated, with the underlying scent of silver and copper and a subtle cologne. Unable to help myself, I leaned back into him. Warm. Really warm. I closed my eyes and heard myself sigh. Without speaking, without thinking, I placed my hand over his. The mage-heat faded and was gone. I fell asleep.

BLOODRING

I woke when we reached the shop. Rupert was locking the doors, shadows were growing long across the ground, and the sun was a huge red ball resting on the western mountaintops. I don't know how Rupert and Thadd got me upstairs, undressed, and into the tub, but I woke in hot water, all shriveled and wrinkled, Rupert waving a piece of cheese toast under my nose. It smelled heavenly.

I jolted upright. Water went splashing across the tile. "I'm naked."

"I noticed. And if I was straight, I'd be interested. Eat."

Suddenly ravenous, I ate the toast in two bites, cramming a half slice into my mouth and chewing, cheeks bulging like a chipmunk's. "Can I have some more?" I asked as I swallowed.

"When you're dressed, dearie. Can you get out on your own?"

I made a little turnaround motion with a finger and Rupert rolled his eyes. But he complied, turning his back to me, a towel held in the general direction of the tub. Gauging my level of stability, I stood up slowly. When I was halfway upright, the realization hit me fully. I was naked. In the room with a human. I looked at my body, and relief swept over me. My neomage attributes were still hidden, my skin not glowing, the worst of my scars blanked. I still looked human. But someone had undressed me, and that meant they had seen more scars than I had ever explained. And they had found my amulets. I was in trouble. Big, bad, wooly mammoth trouble.

On the small table beside the tub was the prime amulet I had tried to destroy. The circle donut of layered stone, stone fused by a means I never understood, had been moved and was now lying fully exposed. The broken chip was sitting in the exact center of the large stone ring. I looked around the room as I stepped from the tub. No Thaddeus. No assey Durbarge. No whips, chains, knives, red-hot pokers in the fireplace, or other devices of torture. "Who undressed me?" I asked, as I pulled on a robe.

"Thadd wanted to help, but we sent him off, if that's what you were wondering." Rupert crossed his arms, his weight on one hip, his back still to me.

"And?" I prompted.

"And Audric and I took off your clothes and put you in the tub. It wasn't the most disgusting thing I've ever done, but it wasn't fun. I never knew those scars on your arms were *all over.*"

"Yeah." I knotted the robe's belt and went to the kitchen. "You can turn around now," I said as I sat and started stuffing my face with cheese toast and a glass of white wine.

"You *will* tell me all about them when you feel better," he said, fishing.

The alcohol hit my system hard. "Spawn scars. Thanks for the food."

"Spawn scars. Two words." When I didn't respond, he said softly, "Maybe someday you'll trust me enough to tell me your story." Rupert lifted the remote and clicked on the television, SNN with its divided screen. In the top left corner was a familiar video feed, Lucas, lifting his head to reveal his face. My gut tightened.

Rupert sighed. "They're still showing it every day on the six o'clock news."

The screen flickered with images: boxes, a woodpile, a tangle of bicycles half visible at the extremity of the circle of illumination. A shadow slithered across, disjointed and stiff.

I leaned in to see.

Two more shadows resolved into the shape of men running. They collided, and Lucas went down. Arms punched, feet kicked viciously. Lucas fell, covering his head. His body was dragged away, leaving the ruptured knapsack. Blood smeared as they pulled him out of the camera's view. Lucas' blood.

This time, I saw something I hadn't recognized the first hundred times I'd watched. The shadow had wings. A Fallen. A Major Darkness.

BLOOÐRING

Battle rage spiked through my system and died. Grief rose and crested into hopeless gloom. There was nothing I could do. Nothing at all. "Turn it off," I said. "Please."

I didn't look up at Rupert but I knew he was studying me. The TV clicked off. I bit and chewed another slice of toast. It tasted like dust in my mouth, but I ate it all, every bite. After my meal, I shooed Rupert out, turned off the lights, crawled between the layered down comforters and the mattress, and closed my eyes. Again, sleep was instantaneous.

The phone rang near midnight, the witching hour. I knew it was Lolo before I answered, snaking a bruised arm out from the warm covers. "Lolo?"

"What you do you *pierre première*? You amulet?"

"I broke it," I confessed, trying to pull myself from dreams.

"Why you do dis fol ting?"

"I took a maul to my wedding ring when Lucas left," I said, sleepily. "It was an accident."

"*La pierre?* Dat stone? It still a close-up circle? All part still dere? No part lost?"

"Yeah," I said, more awake now. "A chip broke away from the outer edge, but the inner edge is still solid. How did you—"

"Listen good. R'ember."

I sat up and turned on the light. Opening the bedside table's drawer, I took out paper and pen. I ached all over but pulled up a knee to support the pad. "Go ahead."

"Incantation de Réintégration, in you book." Her voice took on the singsong cadence of incantation. French, wouldn't you know it. "*Mais tout à l'entour du moyeu,*" she sang.

I had her repeat all fourteen lines, a rhyming verse that would have been easy to learn had I spoken French. I repeated the incantation, making sure I had the pronunciation and rhythm correct. "Okay, Lolo, what's it mean?"

"No exact translation *en anglais*. Say de Cajun word. Follow de formula. Do it firs' ting as de sun tink to rise." The phone went dead before I could ask how she knew about the damage, but I had a good idea. Audric and I had to have a little chat.

I was awake before the sun rose, before the local roosters—the ones who had survived the mating frenzy and the cooking pots—woke. I was muzzy headed and sore but unable to suppress a small flame of excitement at the thought that I might repair my prime amulet. I found the Incantation of Restoring in the *Book of Workings*. It took up three pages late in the second third of the book, and one section was titled "All Around the Hub." I figured that was what Lolo's Cajun *mais tout à l'entour du moyeu* meant in English.

I turned up the flames on the gas logs and gathered the supplies the book called for—a silver bowl filled with springwater, a clean white towel, candles, salt, a ceremonial knife, several of each of the stones used to create the amulet, and the amulet itself. I put my necklace to one side. As an afterthought, I brought over all the drained amulets needing to be recharged but put them in a separate pile to the side, out of the way of the initial working. I locked the loft door, lit seven candles, poured a salt ring, leaving a six-inch opening, and sat in the middle of the kitchen floor. Instantly, cold leached up through the tile into my thighs.

After I centered myself with deep breathing, I opened my mage-sight and sealed an advanced conjuring circle. I felt the faint pop of energy from my head, down my bruised back, to my toes. Power seized me, the power from the beginning of time, a clear note of energy, a bell that pealed, an echo of the first Word ever spoken. The first Word of Creation. That echo of the beginning was captured in the center of the earth, a constant, unvarying power of stone and mineral and destructive potency.

I shivered as the vibrations rolled through my bones,

pulsed in my flesh. I could *see* the thrum of strength, the raw, raging might deep below, liquid rock seeking a channel. Finding me, rising within me. I was the crucible for the incandescent energy.

Power. The hunger for it rose as well, waves of desire that bowed my entire body, clawed my hands into weapons. *I could take what I wanted.* The might burned below me, writhed inside me, welding me to it. I *was* the strength of the earth, the might, the power of creation.

I slid the necklace of amulets over my head. My need receded and fell away. The energy of creation became manageable, harnessed to my control. I inhaled a breath burning with cold and returned to myself and to the loft, which pulsed with power.

When I caught my breath, I read through the incantation again and made sure I had all the stones I needed for the repair. The prime amulet was a four-inch hoop composed of topaz, peridot, amethyst, citrine, and garnet, five inner layers, with a double helping of bloodstone sealing at top and bottom. Seven layers in all.

Following the directions in the book, I arranged the stones in the water according to the order of the stones in the amulet. On top, I set the prime amulet and the small chip, aligning the broken piece in its gap. When I removed my hand from the bowl, the water started to glow.

I dried my hand and gripped the ceremonial knife. I started the incantation. *"Mais tout à l'entour du moyeu. Mais tout à l'entour du moyeu."* I was pretty sure the next two lines were about knives and blood, and I pricked my finger. Blood welled. The next two lines had something to do with repairing and the Enclave. I dropped the first drip of blood into the water. With each of the next six lines, I added a drop of blood. It swirled and settled toward the bottom of the bowl and the pile of stones.

As I watched, the blood coalesced into a large glowing, shining bead of blood and energy. It fell into the crack of the amulet, sliding between chip and ring as if with an intelligence of its own, or as if the amulet directed the placement of the blood for its own healing.

The process would be slow. A mage working solo could take hours to complete the conjure. I repeated the incantation and added seven drops of blood. On the third repetition of the phrases, I heard a voice, tones full of light and bells. And I froze, a drop of blood about to fall.

"Mage!" a voice called.

"No. Too far from Enclave," a second voice replied.

"Mage, I tell you. Listen."

I couldn't stop the incantation—there was no place for the energies to go. No one had ever told me what would happen if I tried, but I figured it wasn't anything good—an explosion of wild magic, fire; me dead and splattered all over the walls. I had no choice. I spoke the lines as directed, dripping my blood into the bowl.

"I hear her. She's in heat!" the first one said, excited.

"Where? Where is she? I scent her." The voice growled with lust.

The flush of adrenaline was instantaneous, fear and excitement, followed by a sexual heat so strong it arched my back. *Seraphs!* Two of them. *Danger.* Heat welled up in me. I was going to die and I didn't care. So long as the seraphs took me first.

With the twenty-first drop of my blood, the amethyst sealed in metal boxes one floor below blazed into my awareness, a sudden influx of power so strong that it sizzled through me, a crackling energy. Power so vital I wanted to weep with the opulence of it. The water boiled. Steam and light erupted from the bowl. I heard a snap, another, and another, dozens of them, like firecrackers or distant guns, the sounds overlapping, a war of stone and rock. And a final crack, muted, muffled but powerful, that sent water into the air in a geyser of fine droplets. I jerked away.

Mage-heat died. In an instant, the force of the incantation, the voices in my head, the purple light from the storeroom, were all gone. I was drunk, sickeningly, violently drunk. I inhaled a breath tasting sharp and acrid, full of nausea and ozone.

In the bottom of the silver bowl, was my prime amulet. It was whole, a ring of layered stone, fused together with my blood. And below the amulet was a nest of crystal sand. The world tilted.

I caught myself on my clean palm and finished the last two lines of the incantation, not because I wanted to, but because I knew I was supposed to. Something about the cycles of mage energies. I giggled drunkenly as I spoke, but it didn't seem to affect the conjure. After the last word, the final incantation energies settled with a soft splash, like a low wave on sand.

I stared at my bloody hand, transfixed by the slow crimson crawl. It hurt, and the pain brought me back to myself. I took a deep breath and wrapped my bleeding hand in the towel. With my other hand I reached into the water. It was still hot, almost painful. I lifted the amulet into the dawn light and held it close. It felt like it always had, a four-inch ring, a few ounces of rock, smooth, cooling instantly to the temperature of my hand. But there was something different now. The crack outlining the chip was filled with a fine bloodred line like mortar sealing it together. Now the center layer, the amethyst layer, was subtly larger, and it glowed, just a hint, with power that wasn't mine.

I recalled the voices I'd heard while I was working the incantation. I had never met a seraph. Had only heard them speak on television, a medium that was said to dull the purity and melody of their voices. Yet I had no doubt that I had heard seraph voices in my mind until the amethyst stone in the storeroom had taken over the conjure and healed my prime amulet, fast, as if to shield me from the seraphs.

Still reeling from the power that had rolled through me, I fell back, lying supine, staring at the rafters. The amethyst had done something to the amulet, and by extension, to me. And there wasn't a darn thing I could do about it.

Chapter 16

The mage-heat was gone. Once I was sober enough to stand, I cleaned up the conjure implements and dressed in my work clothes, layers of leggings and two sweaters. I laid out more formal clothes for kirk and cooked mixed whole-grain cereal and ate it with yogurt. I needed to run errands: groceries, the laundromat, the library, and the shoe repair shop. I could add all that to my social calendar in place of dating and making whoopee, now that the mage-heat had cooled.

By eight a.m. I was in the workshop, wearing a mask, protective goggles, ear protectors and my well-worn jumpsuit over my clothes, excising and drilling stones for the focal beads and pendants that attracted so much attention in the jewelry markets. In a few days, I would have cut enough to start the tedious process of carving, shaping, and polishing.

The scent of hot metal was a tang in the air, almost obscuring the underlying smells of machine oil, gas logs, and acetylene from the torches. Rupert and Audric were working on settings, bezels, and mountings, production work for the jewelry we sold by the tens and hundreds from the online catalogue. It was our bread and butter, but it was boring work, as boring as drilling and tumbling the smaller stones, which I still had to do. Hardly creative. Not nearly as fun to make as the exclusive designs we created for particular customers or the unique items for retail shops that carried our work. For those, a customer had to shop in Thorn's Gems itself, or in the few upscale retail stores that stocked our merchandise in cities such as Boca Raton and Atlanta, or commission their own pieces. Thorn's Gems could afford to be picky.

Using a diamond wet saw and wet drill, I cut, drilled, and examined for stability four citrine ovals and six free-form peridot pieces that would eventually be buttercups and leaves, stones both delicate and chunky for Emmanuelle Beasley, the film business's newest female action star. She wanted the stones mounted on a gold chain that was shaped like little handcuffs. Whatever. She had money enough to dictate anything she wanted.

By the time I was ready for a break, I was globbed with stone dust and water that splattered whenever I used the equipment. I wiped it from the clock face, satisfied that I still had some time before I had to dress for kirk, and I retrieved the bloodstone I wanted to shape and carve for an amulet. I turned it over, envisioning a cat curled in sleep. This one wouldn't be drilled to hang as a pendant. Rather, I'd wrap it with wire and secure it with leather thongs. The final design of the necklace was coming together.

I clamped the stone into a padded vise, a design of my own, used when I wanted to secure a stone but didn't want to risk scoring it with the hatch marks of the vise faces. Mage-sight half open, I started working the stone with delicate tools.

I placed the chisel against the lower edge where the cat's face and front paws would emerge and tapped it with the hammer. From the storeroom, I saw a soft tendril of lavender energy rise. I ignored it and tapped again. I had been drunk with power already once today and was still feeling woozy. No way was I going to use the amethyst again.

BLOODRING

As if hearing me, the tendril curled away and formed into an eye, which blinked once. The lavender fug of energy wisped flat and then shaped into a hand, fingers long and elegant. It beckoned, pleading.

Surprised, I opened the sight fully and stared at the stockroom. Before, the amethyst had bombarded me with power, as if trying to pound and pummel me with its strength. But now there was a beseeching quality to it, a kind of submission. Offering itself to me as if it had observed my reactions to it and evolved a new approach. Which would make it intelligent. Which was way weird. "No," I said, under my breath. "No way."

Returning to my work, I tapped hammer to chisel, dislodging a fragment of rock and a shower of dust. The amethyst slid closer. A fine strand like a lock of hair touched the bloodstone. Weirder and weirder. I placed the chisel there and tapped the hammer. The amethyst energy brushed my finger. When I didn't freeze or fight it, the lavender light slid over my hand like a glove, warm and faintly tingly. I tapped again. The light flooded over the soon-to-be cat.

The bloodstone in the vise suddenly glowed green and red, like sparklers on New Year's. The underlying crystal matrix of the stone pulsed with the ordered pattern of the minerals. I tapped with more certainty, watching the way the cat absorbed the blow, the way the crystal medium spread the jolt throughout.

Tempering my taps to the strengths and weaknesses of the stone, I began shaping the cat with fast, sure strokes. The face and paws began to emerge from the rock. Time lingered, a languid construct. With the pick, I shaped the toes on one paw, rough work only, but much faster than any I could usually do.

As I worked, I became aware of a soft voice at the limits of my hearing, a voice chanting, a drum beating, the soft, breathy sound of a flute. Lolo's voice, performing a working, singing in her Cajun patois. *"Break dat call of siren's song. Ring dat bell and right dat wrong . . ."*

It felt odd to have another mage in my mind, so different from the brief time when my gift came upon me, and twelve hundred mage-minds fell into mine. Lolo's mind was soothing, as if the conjure was for me. Lavender light throbbed, and Lolo faded.

"Cool. Is it a cat?"

My vision broke. Dressed for kirk, Ciana stood at my side, looking at the cat. My mage-sight was still open. And I saw the mark of Darkness on her neck. I dropped the pick and hammer with a clatter, yanked off my eye protectors and mask, and gripped her shoulders. "Ciana. It licked you?" Her face shuttered closed, her mouth turning down in an annoyed pout. I shook her hard, smearing bloodstone dust onto her dress. "Ciana?"

"He said you'd be mad." She looked up at me, a taut pout on her lips. "He came to my house this time."

"Did you let it in?" Ciana's eyes shifted, just a flicker of movement, but I knew. "Did it lick you?"

"He said I could tell you. I let him in." Her blue eyes lifted, defiant, rebellious. "But there was nothing wrong with it. Really."

Her skin was pale, with purplish circles beneath her eyes. Her hands looked ethereal, blue veins prominent. A daywalker had licked her. Claiming her. Marking her. "Oh, Ciana. Baby," I breathed.

"Get dressed," she said, still not meeting my eyes. "We'll be late."

While Ciana played with my dolls, I showered quickly and dressed. Marla had dropped Ciana off for me to take to kirk, knowing I seldom missed Sunday services. Marla was human. She could brave the elders' wrath, playing hooky on Sundays. While I seldom went to kirk for weekday meetings, I attended at least one of the Sunday services. To skip would result in attention from the elders.

BLOODRING

Wearing flowing taupe-gray robes suitable to the volatile temperatures and lowering clouds that obscured the tops of the mountain peaks, my leather cloak over my shoulders, two blades strapped to my wrists, and the walking stick in hand, I rushed with Ciana into the cold to kirk, following sleepyheads and late-comers for the eleven o'clock service. We made it inside just as the elder closed the doors.

Ciana and I squeezed into the last row and sat on the smooth wood. The preaching had already started, Elder Culpepper reading from the New Testament, from the gospel of Mark, the fourth chapter. "And in the same way, the ones sown upon stony ground are those who, when they hear the Word, at once receive and accept and welcome it with joy. . . ."

I helped Ciana off with her coat, the unheated room almost warm with close-packed bodies. I brushed back her hair and, even with my mage-sight firmly off, I could see where the thing had licked her. I spent the hour of preaching deciding what I could do to protect her.

Thadd bumped into me at the doors after the service. Literally. Without speaking, he moved on, shaking hands with the elder, talking about the uncertain weather, a blustery wind blowing. I started to speak when I realized something had been deposited in my pocket. Instantly, I knew what it was and shut my mouth. I fingered the small bag all the way home.

Ciana had brought a satchel containing enough clothes to last a week, Marla having dropped her off for Rupert and me to baby-sit, while she took off with a new boyfriend. The unhappy woman probably thought she was being a pain, probably enjoyed the thought that she had put us out, sticking us with an onerous job, but Rupert and I were always delighted to have Ciana, and I was especially happy to have her near me now, where I could guard her from the daywalker—blood-demon? the same thing?—that had left a spot of Darkness on her throat.

During kirk services I had come up with a plan. I intended to create for Ciana a prime amulet, a protection from the thing that stalked her. I hoped there was a conjure for human primes in the final third of the book, but I wasn't betting on it. Yet even without a recipe, I would attempt it. It would be easier to accomplish if I had a drop of her blood, but I could use a few strands of hair with roots, which contained genetic material to work into the mix.

After Ciana changed clothes, I brushed out her hair and sent her across the small hallway, where she banged on Rupert's door and let herself in. The unmistakable smell of frying meat had attracted her. Ciana thought my being a vegetarian was way cool, but she liked meat and she really liked bacon and eggs.

Alone for a few moments, I scraped the strands of hair from her brush, wrapped them around my finger, and stored them in an envelope in the armoire with the dolls. Then I fished the bag from my pocket and poured its contents on the kitchen table. Lavender stones glowed up at me, as if warm and contented to be with me. They positively blushed with happiness.

I was anthropomorphizing a rock. I had to be losing my mind.

Dry reddish brown residue coated the cracks and vugs of the amethyst. Lucas' blood. I knew that with his blood embedded in the lavender crystal, I could scry for him successfully. I picked up the phone and dialed Rupert. A few minutes later, Audric entered, carrying a sandwich and reeking of pork.

"She's playing go fish with Rupert and beating the pants off— Spawn balls," he said, coming to a stop and gawking. I grinned up at him, tickled that I had thrown the big man. He forced his features into his habitual, Zen-like equanimity. "It's been a while since I saw one of those used."

From the center of a partially formed circle of earth salt, I said, "I found a recipe for scrying. I tried it once for Lucas and it didn't work, but I used scripture in it." Audric winced. "Yeah. I figured out scripture was for warfare."

"And for ultimate truth. You want me to watch your back?" he asked, understanding. I nodded and he closed the door, pulled my rocking chair close, and sat. "When you blow yourself up or set the town on fire, who do I call?"

"The same person you called last time," I said, a wry tone to my words. He looked confused, and I said, "Lolo called about the prime amulet."

"Ah." He didn't look remotely uncomfortable at being exposed. In fact he looked self-satisfied and sanctimonious, as only the second-unforeseen can.

"I have this theory," I said. "I don't think you just stumbled upon Mineral City and Thorn's Gems. I think Lolo sent you here."

"Interesting hypothesis," he said, voice grave, but lips tilted up. "I've got your six."

Which meant he wasn't going to talk about it. I blew out an irritated breath and told him what I was going to do. When he lifted a thumb, I dropped the final handful of salt, closing the conjuring circle. The fire of creation burned along my nerves and bones, pulling at me, tempting me. But this time I batted the temptation away easily and slipped the amulets over my head, stabilizing the energies I needed for the conjure.

There hadn't been time for Lolo's ancient warning, pounded into me by countless repetitions while I was in training. I was getting good at this. Maybe too good. Maybe practice made perfect. Or the stones in the storeroom did. I was feeling a little uneasy at the way they had insinuated themselves into my life, but I would worry about that later.

My heart beat slowly; my blood pumped; breath moved through my lungs. All glamour fell from me. My body pulsated with radiance, a brighter glow to my old scars. I was my usual luminous coral and pearl, but now with a lavender underglow, as if I sat on a pillow of lavender light. That hadn't been there before.

I opened my eyes, seeing Audric with mage-sight. The sight hadn't worked before. But now, for reasons I didn't want to look at too closely, I could see past the charm of his necklace. He was beautiful, ripe with energies and power. The lightning bolt at his throat glowed softly at me. I figured his father or mother had been a metal mage and the amulet had been crafted at his birth.

My loft shone with power. Every window, doorway, even the floor surfaces, all were charged with pale energy, glowing with subtle shades, their purposes working together to form the harmony that was my home. All were slightly lavender now.

The *Book of Workings* was beside me, opened to the final third, the section dedicated to warfare against Darkness. "Scrying for a Human" stared up at me from the page. I wasn't going up against the Powers; I was just going to look around their domain—trespass, not fight.

I had procured a small sliver of the amethyst from the stockroom and filled the silver bowl with water. Into the bowl, I dropped stones recovered from the scene where Lucas had been attacked. They clanged softly as they hit bottom, touching tip to tip. A soft resonance of energy gathered as crystalline matrix touched matrix. A faint sheen of red emerged. Lucas' blood.

Taking up the sliver of clean amethyst, holding it in my left palm, I stared into the water and quoted the words I had worked out while waiting for Audric.

"Blood and bone, stone and dust, search and find in life and death, Lucas Stanhope, danger dire. Seek and find and show him now."

It was a simple incantation, as conjuring went, and the lack of scripture made it less powerful, but it felt right. Simple seemed best, what with my pitiful level of training, less likely to attract the notice of the resident Darkness. On the third repetition of the verse, the water in the silver bowl began to darken. It didn't cloud or become opaque, but it was as if all the light began to vanish, as if the sun set fast. I kept up the words and rhythm of the incantation, the syllables soft and cadenced.

The water began to shimmer, dark on dark. A human took shape in the unlit space, a man, lying on a thin mattress that rested on smooth limestone, in rock caverns deep in the earth. *Lucas* . . . There were bars over his cell door; they sparkled with Dark energy. They would be cold, I knew. The burning cold of death.

A reddish mist churned over him. I smelled sulfur. An ache started in my old scars, my flesh remembering. Beneath that smell was a hint of gangrene and old blood. Lucas' chest rose and fell; he was alive, though wasted, thin, and limp with fatigue. He was sleeping, heavily bearded, unwashed, and scruffy. He was the only man I had ever known who could spend a week being bled and still be beautiful. No wonder they hadn't killed him yet. And that brought other possibilities to mind, ways they could be using him other than for food. *Feathers and fire* . . .

To his side sat a container, a handle sticking out of it, and a plate. My attention was drawn to the plate and the crumbs left there. They appeared roseate, glowing in the dark, passed over by the cloud that enwrapped Lucas, but remaining untouched. I tightened my focus on them as the red mist parted. Bread crumbs, glowing blue, the hue of periwinkle, the tint of the sky just as the sun set, as the first star appeared. The blue of purity and heaven.

"Who are you?" a voice called, reaching. "Is there a mage here? Mage?"

Something moved in the dark beyond the cell. Realizing I was about to be discovered, I eased back from Lucas, finished the incantation, and placed my hand holding the amethyst from the storeroom into the water. It cleared and brightened, my vision of Lucas dissipating. I reached over and opened the charmed circle, the energies flowing back into me.

"Thorn!" Tone of warning. Audric wasn't in his chair. I followed his voice to the doorway. In its arch were Audric and Thaddeus Bartholomew. Adrenaline surged through me. Fight or flight.

The men stood chest to chest, Thadd with a pair of hand-cuffs in one hand, the other on his gun at his hip. Audric barred his way. They glowed, supernat bright. "Papers," Thadd said, all cop.

I could fight. I could kill him and run. Instead, a strange calm engulfed me, soothing away the adrenaline rush, taking with it the spear of terror. It was like sitting in a warm bath, like resting in a hammock under a summer sun. *How odd.* "I'm un-registered," I said, tranquil and serene. "You can arrest me. I won't resist. But if you turn me in to Durbarge, you'll have to turn yourself in too." That brought him up short. "If you doubt me, take off your ring."

Audric shot a look at me, his eyes shifting from Thadd to me and back. They both glanced down at the ring on the cop's hand. Audric's battle-ready stance changed instantly. The half-breed stepped back fast, paused, and bowed from the waist, one of the most formal gestures of his kind.

Thadd froze, the cuffs dangling, lifting to me, sitting in a salt ring, the implements of a conjure all around me, the *Book of Workings* lying open. His gaze settled on the man who bowed be-fore him. "What . . . ?" The question trailed away.

"Take off the turquoise ring with the angel-wing setting," I said. "Watch what happens."

His face went crimson, blood flowing up from his neck to his crown. A long moment passed as he darted frenzied eyes from his hand to me. "I can't." The words broke from his mouth all by themselves, and his eyes snapped open, then slit into anger. "What have you done to me, mage?"

Stupid humans. Anything goes wrong, they jump to place blame on the first neomage they spot. The mage did it, whatever it was. "I didn't do anything to you. The ring is an amulet. I recognized it yesterday when I touched it on horseback and immediately went to sleep. I think it's a seraph ring."

"Not possible."

"So take it off."

Thadd, still frozen, slowly lowered his head, the motion jerky, as if his muscles fought him. He was dressed in a standard Hand of the Law suit, dark gray and single breasted, white shirt, knotted tie, and a wool overcoat, shiny leather shoes. Slowly, he brought up his hand, extended his fingers, and stared at his ring in horror. The ring seemed bigger, more imposing. It glowed richly to my amethyst-enhanced mage-sight. "I . . . can't."

"Why not?" I asked, my tone mild.

"I've never taken it off." That was a stupid reason, and even he seemed to know that. Behind him, Audric closed the door to the hallway, locked it, and took Thadd's handcuffs, hanging them over one arm of the coat rack, where they swung.

"You've worn that ring for as long as you can remember? Even when you were a child?" Audric asked, watching his face. Something like compassion crossed his features when he asked, "How many times have you had it sized?"

His throat working, voice a whisper, Thadd swore foully. It was clear he'd never had the ring sized. He'd worn it all his life and it had grown along with him. And he'd never once thought that peculiar. "I've been spelled by a magic ring."

Audric and I snorted, and I stood up from the circle. I swept up the salt and dumped it in the waiting bag. Moving with economy, I replaced all the other implements and pulled the kitchen table over the circle site before I plopped down on the couch and curled my legs under me. The couch wasn't an idle choice. The walking stick was in a large basket beside it.

"What have they done to me?" Thadd asked.

"Take off the ring," I said again.

Movements jerky, as if in reaction to electrical shocks or to pain, Thadd took the ring in his fingers and pulled. It resisted for an instant before sliding smoothly off his hand. The skin beneath it was white and slightly wrinkled. He looked at the hand as if he'd never seen it, then at the ring, which he turned over and over, studying the angel wings on the setting. His face relaxed, settling into lines of perplexity. He opened his mouth to speak.

His body jerked, a vicious jolt, as though he had been hit with a cattle prod or a Taser. Thadd's eyes and mouth opened wide. With a silent scream, he tore off his suit coat and flung it across the room. I reached for the walking stick beside the couch, but my hand stopped halfway as Thadd wrenched off his holster and threw it, the gun banging hard and spinning. He ripped at his shirt, panting. Frantic. A soft, high-pitched moan came from his lips. "Help."

I stood, but Audric was closer. He seized the shirt in two fists. With a powerful tug, he shredded the shirt, sending buttons flying, seams giving way at the shoulders and arms. The cloth fell to the sides, still held in place with his tie. Thadd pulled it free, dropping shirt and tie to the floor together. With one hand he reached over his shoulder and scratched a weal. I smelled blood. And flesh. And kylen. Mage-heat swept over me.

Chapter 17

I slithered across the floor, panther grace in my limbs. *Kylen*. His scent flooded me, sweeping into my nostrils, my lungs, converging on the beat of my heart, swimming out through my vessels, weakening my muscles, warming my flesh. His voice a strangled sound, Thadd clawed at his back, his arms up and bent backward, his chest broad, ribs and abs pulling, stomach flat and taut. Scents flooded me, arching my back.

He pivoted and I saw what he was clawing. From the tips of his shoulders, at the top of his humeri, and angled down his back were two wide slashes of swollen, inflamed tissue. Something was trying to emerge from his body.

Wings.

I raced across the room to his jacket and shook it hard. The ring dropped to the rug. It was huge, maybe a size twelve, maybe bigger, I'd never seen one so large. When I picked it up, a tingle slithered up my arm, inviting me to put it on.

Ignoring its siren call, fighting the demand to mate, I launched myself across the room to Thadd, mage-fast, and slammed into him. His hands came forward as if to stop me, and I slid the ring onto his finger. He wrenched and dropped to the floor, pulling me with him. He landed hard, me on top, my hands going for his belt buckle. Audric pulled me away.

We were all breathless. The smell of kylen was so strong in the loft, it was like a bakery, and I wanted a taste of everything offered. Instead, Audric found my prime amulet and hooked it onto the necklace of amulets around my neck. The mage-heat rippled and faded, leaving me drained and empty. I dropped my head onto Audric's chest and sighed. The remnants of heat pulsed once, falling to a bearable itch I could ignore. If Thadd would put his clothes back on. Maybe.

"What am I?" he asked, his voice still tortured, but stronger.

"From the look of your spine, I would speculate that you are a third-generation kylen," Audric said. "And I am yours to command."

"Not possible," Thadd said. For a Hand of the Law he was pretty unwilling to consider possibilities, even with wings trying to grow out his back. "My mother's human. And my father was killed in Arizona, mopping up a nest of spawn. He was a cop."

"Of course he was," Audric said, sarcasm increasing with every word. "Certainly. You've seen pictures? Seen your parents' wedding certificate?" The big man pushed me aside and I caught my balance on the couch arm. "You've watched home movies of your father? Met your paternal grandparents? Been to their house for a *barbecue*?" He stalked closer to Thadd with every question, and Thadd's face paled. "You've met your cousins on that side of the family? Maybe danced at a wedding or two? Been to a funeral?"

"My father was an orphan. He had no family."

"Your mother lied," I said. "You are kylen. Call her." I licked my lips, eyes on his body.

Audric handed him a throw from the foot of the bed. "Put this on or our little mage will try to have you for breakfast.

Mage," he said, drawing my attention. "I knew he was more than human, though not what precisely he was. More important, how could the asseys have been in his presence and not seen him for what he was?"

"Part of the purpose of the ring, I think. It's spelled to be forgotten immediately, like a fragment of a dream. It kept you from identifying him immediately. It made me sleep. Kept the mage-heat from being so strong, until now."

"And now?" Audric asked.

"Not so good now. I can smell his blood." And I liked it.

"This isn't possible," Thadd said again, settling the throw across his shoulders for a moment before tossing it aside with a hiss of pain. The fabric seemed to irritate the raised flesh. "She's a mage. What are you? You're too big to be neo."

"I am a second-unforeseen," Audric said, bowing again, "and yours to command."

Thadd looked him over from head to toe, as if measuring the big man. "Command. Crap." He walked to my dressing area and turned his back to the long mirror, looking at himself over his shoulder. I could see him from two viewpoints. *Verrry* nice. "What . . .?" The words died as confusion warred with duty and honor.

"You have options now, kylen. And you need information to make wise decisions. Do what Thorn suggested. Call your mother." Audric handed my phone to the cop.

Thadd grimaced and set the phone down, pulling a small device from his pocket. It had a little door on front and he flipped it open, punching in numbers. His satellite phone. I stared at his back where ridges had lifted his skin into bumps and irregular crests, some pointed and sharp, ready to cut through the skin. His fingernails had brought blood to the surface in long weals. He smelled heavenly. I wanted to touch him, to run my hands over his raised flesh.

"Mom? Yeah. Okay." He sounded curt, a hint of outrage in

the foundation of the words and a strong trace of disbelief. "I'm . . . fine." He took a breath, preparing himself. "Tell me about the ring. Tell me about my father. No lies, Mama. Tell me the truth." He paused a moment. "Yeah. I took it off." The silence after that was longer. A lot longer.

Audric pulled me into the kitchen to give the cop some privacy, which was fine by me. The ring had pretty much kept me from smelling kylen, but now my whole loft smelled like vanilla and caramel and ginger. I could sit anywhere and enjoy the scent, the view, and the lovely vision of us together that kept flashing into my awareness in full-color, three-dimensional images.

"Little mage," Audric said. "As I said, I had an indication he was more than human. Did you know he was kylen?"

"Oh, yeah. I knew."

"Would you have known had you not damaged your prime amulet?"

I shrugged, watching the cop. "He's been deprived of his birthright. He's like me, an untrained mage."

"Not quite. Because he received no instruction at all as he grew, he is in far worse shape than you. He is half human, the other half a strange mixture of seraph and neomage. Because he was denied his gift at the onset of adolescence, he may never be a powerful spell caster. His gift may be damaged, though that will not matter to the archseraph. He'll be sent to a Realm of Light, for training." Audric slowly shook his head, the bald dome reflecting light from the windows.

"It won't matter if his gifts are ruined and unusable; they will want him anyway. But in a Realm, he'll be lost, an outcast, isolated, perhaps imprisoned. And because he may well be without the ability to use any of his gifts, he'll be worthless to them, useless, as the second-unforeseen were without use until we became warriors. His life as he knew it is over. They will take him. Unless . . . ," he said.

"Unless what?"

"Unless he chooses, as we two chose, to say nothing. To live as he desires, instead of as the archseraph chooses. He may be willing to keep our secrets if we keep his. An association of sorts, with self-preservation as its establishing bylaw."

That sounded pretty good to me. Positively ducky. If he could pull it off it meant no hot pincers, no shackles, no going insane. "Sure." I wondered if that meant I'd get a chance to—

"If he agrees, you will have to give up any thoughts of taking him as your mate."

I kept my face on the kylen, my expression unchanged, though my body reacted to the words. I fully recognized that if I took Thaddeus Bartholomew to my bed, I would conceive and bear a litter of half-mage, half-kylen pups. My mind twisted through the screwy genealogy. It would make my children one-half mage, through me, and through their father, one-fourth human, three-sixteenths mage, one-sixteenth-seraph. They could be powerful, or they could be powerless. That part would be a crapshoot. But one thing was certain. I would be found out and destroyed. My children taken away and raised by the seraphs. "I couldn't have him anyway. They wouldn't let me."

"No. They wouldn't."

Thadd hung up the phone, moving slowly, as only humans can move. I had found the leisurely motions disconcerting when I came here as a child. Now they spoke of safety and home. The kylen should be able to move nearly as quickly as I, however, which had to be another response to the ring's workings. Only a seraph could conjure a ring that could juggle so many different incantations at one time.

He met my gaze. "She lied to me. My whole life." It was an indictment he laid at his mother's door, and equally at ours for revealing the hidden and unknown to him. If not for us, he would never have discovered the awful secret his mother had kept for so many decades. Her fault. Our fault. With Thadd the only innocent party. That his mother had slept with a kylen was no sin in the eyes of the world, that she had hidden the pregnancy and then the child was.

"And what will you do now, kylen?" Audric asked. "Will you turn us in and yourself as well? Arrest your mother? Arrest your father, a being you have never met, but who may wish to meet you, develop a relationship? Or will you take a different path?" At Thadd's questioning look, he said, "Keep our secrets. Let us keep yours."

The air in the loft swirled with anger pheromones as the cop looked at us, at the phone in his hand, and then to the mirror and the wing bone structure that had tried to sprout. I wanted to trace my fingers down the ridges, run my tongue across the red scratches. And I knew I could never take the chance. I hooked my fingers around my restored prime amulet, drawing on its protection.

Thadd placed the phone in his pocket and walked to his shirt, pulling the torn fabric gingerly up his arms and into place on his back. He unkinked the tie and draped it around his neck. Slipped into the holster and suit coat. Audric tensed as the cop touched his gun, but the moment of danger had passed.

Dressed, Thadd extended his hand and stared at the ring, which had shrunk to fit his slender fingers, spelled, both man and ring. A mighty amulet, created for a kylen by a kylen or a seraph. His father? Had to be. "Can you scry for the amethyst?"

My mouth opened slightly. I had no idea. I started to say so, but Audric held up a hand. "Do you agree, Hand of the Law, that we will protect one another? That we will keep one anothers' identities undisclosed?"

Thadd nodded stiffly. "Yes. For now." Audric dropped his hand and Thadd looked at me. "Can you?"

"I never thought about it," I said. "Maybe." I could ask the lavender stone in the storeroom to show me where it came from . . . and gain even more of it. Lovely, lovely purple stone, lovely lavender energies. And it would be all mine. I'd be drunk, gorged on power. That was almost as good as mating with a kylen. Almost. "I'll try. Later."

His tone diffident, Thadd said, "I came here in an official capacity. To tell you that Jason Stanhope is dead."

I was glad I was sitting down. He'd done that little drop-and-punt thing again.

"The body was drained of blood and pretty chewed up. An elder was found nearby, burned to a crisp. You know anything about it?"

"First I've heard," Audric said. "Have you told Rupert?"

"Yeah. Just now. Ciana was listening to music," he said at my concerned look. The cop glanced at the bigger man. "Not a lot of love lost between the brothers, was there?"

"Jason was a drunk, a wife abuser, and a gambler," Audric said. "He brought nothing but shame on the family for the last ten years. Jason had also been branded twice; once for cursing, once for blasphemy. His lack of self-control in front of kirk elders was well known."

I was surprised. I had known Jason was a troublemaker but hadn't known he'd been kirk branded.

"The family had it done privately," Audric said. "The elder who performed them put both in inconspicuous places." Audric looked back to the cop. "When did he die?"

"Last night. We think between two and four a.m. The body was resting on top of El-car tracks in the mud. We know exactly when the El-car went down the road, and the body was discovered at six a.m., already cold."

"Cop El-car?" Audric asked. Thadd nodded, and Audric said, "I'm guessing that the public knows this already, or you wouldn't be telling us so much."

Thadd inclined his head, composed. Except that his shirt had no buttons, he looked like his ordinary self. I was hoping the shirt would gap a bit, but his posture was pretty good. "The body was discovered by an SNN reporter. Her screaming woke half the block. The rumor mill got it all correct except a few details. Even SNN got it right."

"Imagine that," Audric said, the mocking tone again in his voice.

"One of the details they didn't get was the rock dust they found at the scene."

"Amethyst dust," I said, instantly. "Ground-up amethyst."

"And how do you know that?"

I smiled at the kylen and opened my mage-sight. "I smell it on you." I pointed at a pocket. "You put some of it there." He looked at the pocket and scowled at me. "And if you didn't have as big a secret as we do, you'd take me in because of that." I peeled myself off the couch and walked to him, moving slowly and deliberately. "But I'm a mage, kylen. You'd have to catch me first." In an instant I spun and darted across the room. It took him about three seconds to spot me coiled beside the tub. "Catch me, mate me if you can," I sang, feeling the mage-heat flare anew.

Audric sighed. "Go home, Thadd. She'll try to scry for the stone."

Clearly not happy, Thadd left the loft. But I could still smell him.

Audric stalked to a window and threw it open. "I have to go see Rupert. You, little mage, are going to have to watch your mouth."

I stood up from the tub. "What'd I do? He's the one sprouting wings."

The heat hangover lasted most of the day, leaving me with a headache that pounded with each heartbeat and refused to respond to over-the-counter meds. In the intervening hours, Rupert notified his gramma about the death of his brother and made arrangements for a funeral. The service would take place once the police released the body, though that could take weeks. Rupert decided not to feign public mourning for his brother's passing, and refused to speak of the death.

Near dusk, when the sun rested on the ridge of the mountains to the west, I felt well enough to scry for the amethyst. Rupert kept Ciana busy in his apartment making sugar cookies, while Audric and I set up the conjure. This time, Audric locked the door.

Using the excuse of needing a larger quantity of the amethyst to work with, I brought up a double-fist-sized hunk of the lavender crystal, one that appeared to have lain in contact with the ground for long years on one side, but was freshly broken off the motherstone on the other. It was both comforting and energizing to hold so much amethyst. To make the circle, I used clean salt, untainted by the mystic residue of past conjurings. I added the silver bowl and water, candles, my knife in case I needed blood, a small steel mallet, and all my amulets. Satisfied that I had everything I might need, I centered myself and closed the circle.

With the hunk of amethyst beside me, it was easy to gauge the amount of creation energy I needed for the scrying. I was able to resist the pull of the deeps, settling my amulets over my head without difficulty. In mage-sight, I was an inferno of purple light. It was becoming too easy. And maybe Audric thought so too. He said, "You okay? This is . . . odd."

I soaked up the amethyst energy like a drunkard would a bottle of rum, and sighed a long breath that I could follow with the enhanced mage-sight. A purple mist of breath. "Easy as pie," I said. Audric raised his brows, which made me giggle. Yep. I was power drunk, all right. And I wanted more.

Struggling to put on a serious expression, I said, "I'm fine," and waved him away from the circle. I took slow breaths, and when I was calm and wouldn't chortle in the middle of the incantation, I took up the hunk of crystal, setting it into the water in the silver bowl. Fine bubbles of air were trapped along its sides, like perfectly round baubles of light.

We didn't think I needed an incantation for this but hoped I could simply match my body's energies to that of the stone and then use mage-sight to look for a resonance. I pictured the ground, broken gray boulders and snow, a big purple rock protruding. When I was perfectly centered, I dropped a small shard of amethyst into the water. It plunked down, sending clear, concentric rings out from the center of impact. The shard swirled through the water fast and landed with a tap on the larger stone beneath. Without pause, I dropped in a second crystal, and a third. When nothing happened, I took up the knife and pierced my finger. Three drops of blood fell into the water. It swirled and spread, a soft cloud of ruby over the lavender stone. The water darkened as I watched, the vision as lightless as the inside of a mine. Rough walls, dirt with roots protruding. Dark, but with a strange glow, like the color of my blood in the water. There was no purple stone.

"Mage . . ."

I almost gasped but managed to maintain my breathing. I searched the dark vision. Dripped in three more drops of blood. Through the images, *something* reached out, mage-fast. A clawed hand. Bloodied. It ripped through the vision and slashed my face, blinding me. It grabbed my body. My breath stopped. It wasn't mage-fast. But demon-fast.

"Mage," it whispered in my mind. "My mage."

I struggled in the grip, fought for a breath, pulling against it. I forced my eyes open. I was no longer in my apartment. I was underground. Sulfur burned me, acid bright. The claw around my middle tightened. My breath stopped, and I couldn't turn my head. A fire burned in a brazier. Water trickled. Blood splashed softly. A flat-topped stone was in the center of a charmed circle. *An altar.* Lucas was spread-eagled across the altar stone.

To his side, sitting on the ground, was a mage. I was so stunned, I stopped fighting to breathe. The mage was filthy and emaciated. Dark hair hung in lank strands over her face. Her mouth moved in an incantation, her blood dripping fast into a stoneware bowl. Lucas' blood dripped nearby, a steady tink. She was shouting the prophecy Lolo had spoken as I was born. The mage was scrying for me. *"A Rose by any Other Name will still draw Blood."* She repeated. Her thoughts were instantly in my head, beneath the incantation of the prophecy. *"Help me, mage. Help me."*

Our eyes met; she lifted her bleeding hand and wiped it across Lucas' side, leaving a long smear, mixing her blood with his and spreading the mixture on heavy steel links. A short length of strong chain.

The scene darkened. I still had not taken a breath. I pulled against the hold of the Darkness, fought, threw back my head, but I was immobilized in the grip of the thing. The Power. My heart stuttered, missing beats. I was caught underground. By a Power. I heard it laugh. Beneath the grating tone came the beat of a drum, the tone of a flute, and Lolo's voice, too soft to hear.

The Dark mage's eyes widened in shock and hope. *"Lolo?"* she asked.

With mage-sight dimming, I could almost see the mathematical properties of Lolo's incantation, like linked droplets, alternating large and small. Lolo, who was in my mind again, as she had been the last time I had used the amethyst to conjure. That was important somehow, but a problem for later, if I lived that long. My lungs burned. If I passed out, I'd belong to the thing that had trapped me. Almost out of strength, hot coals blistering my lungs, I prepared myself and suddenly went limp, resting in its grip, letting it support me.

A tremor ran through the hand that held me and I could have sworn I startled it. Prepared for the jolt of vertigo and nausea, I took advantage of the Power's surprise and stole a breath of air, converting it into a quick scan.

I could see Lolo's conjure forming round circles of power, like tiny, interconnected diamond drills, a rivulet of them, corroding into the strands of the Darkness' conjure as she wrapped her incantation around it. But as each strand of the dark conjure was cut, another grew to take its place, a spider lace of glowing red and black strands. Desperately, my vision again drawing to a pinpoint of perspective, I drew on the amethyst.

The Dark conjure centered on a perfectly round hole, ringed with threads of power. I directed the amethyst energy through the center hole, pulling the image of Lolo's linked droplets with me. As it passed through, I reshaped the links into a weapon, a talon, a *thorn*. And ripped back out through the hole, taking the strands of the trap with me.

I was pulled from the grip of the thing that held me, up through the limestone cavern, up through the earth. Lavender light, forked lightning bolts of power, flared close around me and far off in bright sparkles of purpose and luminous tones. Two words, sung in a sad, lonely voice like bells: *"Little mage . . ."* Not the voice of the Darkness. Not the voice of the trapped mage, but an unknown voice.

Suddenly I was free, lying on my side in the loft on the cold floor. I pulled in a breath, a golden, glorious breath, that sent pain ricocheting through my air-starved torso. The inside of my charmed circle was filled with glowing lavender, a mist I inhaled and exhaled, a richness of power so bright it tingled against my flesh, along my nerves. The water in the bowl was boiling, a rising fog in a semispherical shape over me. The charmed circle was warm and steamy. And I was drunk, bombed, *plastered* on the energies.

I raised myself up on one elbow, hearing surprise in Lolo's

mental voice. *"What you done, gurl? What you done with dat purple power? What happen you? Where from you get dat?"* Her mental voice faded to nothingness.

With a finger, I broke the circle. All the power looped back into the silver bowl and the amethyst in its bottom, a silent whirlwind of might that vanished with a wet splash. I rolled over onto my back, concentrating on breathing, staring up at the circling ceiling fan.

Audric stood at the edge of the circle, his two swords drawn, eyes wide with bloodlust.

"There's nothing here to kill, big man," I said through lips that felt numb and swollen. "No demons followed me back."

"Something had you." He stepped across the broken circle of salt and stood over me, looking down into my face. "I could smell it. Demon-blood, human blood, mage-blood, a stranger's. And sulfur and acid. Darkness!" he said, his tone joyful. "Where is it?"

"It was a trap. Lolo helped me escape. We left it behind, but it has Lucas." The sense of inebriation faded with my admission.

Audric's face fell, disappointed that he had no demon to fight. "And the amethyst?"

I held up my hand and he sheathed the shortsword before pulling me to my feet. "I can find it. I think. Maybe," I said, trying to find my balance, remembering the lightning bolts in my vision, bright sparkles of purpose answering my call from far away. "The Power called me 'little mage' . . ."

"And?" Audric kissed the blade of the longsword before sheathing it.

"The same words you used earlier." I rested both hands on the tabletop, feeling steadier. "You called me little mage. And you aren't the only one," I said, remembering the bell-like voice from the vision.

Something shifted in Audric's eyes. He turned toward the

door and I snatched at his arm, holding him, though he had the bone structure and muscle mass of his human parent and could have wrenched free easily. "You knew how to call Lolo," I said. "Or she called you. You knew exactly who and what I was before I screwed up in the alley, didn't you?"

Audric inclined his head slowly, the motion regal, doing that weird second-unforeseen thing he did. "You are ready to hear this, I think. Your Lolo sent me to you. Some half-breeds do not wish to be bound to a seraph for war, but rather to live free, choosing their own battles. This is my desire, to be free, always." His lips nearly smiled before sorrow took it away. "There have always been rumors of banished mages, free mages. I searched for such a one and Lolo sent me to you, to fight beside. Next time, you will enclose me in the circle with you. And together, we will battle the Dark."

Uh-huh. Sure we would, I thought drunkenly. Like I was going to let myself get trapped again. But I didn't say that. After a slight hesitation while the room pirouetted around me, I said, "You want to fight. I see it in your eyes. Why don't you want to bind with a seraph or a battle mage?"

The last of the battle lust drained from his eyes, and Audric pulled his arm away. "When you're ready to tell me your story, I'll tell you mine. Little mage."

The thing in the deeps had kept me prisoner for longer than I had realized, time not moving belowground as it did above, in one of the weird little quirks of Einstein's theory of relative time. It was nearly ten p.m. when I broke the grip of the Power and found myself on the floor of my loft, muscles stiff and cold where they had lain in contact with the floor for hours. Ciana was already asleep in the guest bed in Rupert's apartment, and Audric, deprived of the chance to kick ass and bleed demons, went away disappointed. I just crawled into bed and fell into a deep, serene sleep.

Even asleep, I was aware of the amethyst, however—a pulsing, breathing plea of power and might. It offered itself to me,
asking nothing in return except to be used, consumed. And in
my dreams I was filled up, drunk, reeling with the energies it
shared.

Chapter 18

B efore dawn I woke, the sheets warm around me, the air I
breathed frigid, the cold scalding my delicate nasal passages. A noise had woken me, and I quickly sent out scans for
danger. Outside, a scream sounded and echoed, and reechoed,
anger on anger. It was the lynx from the mountainside. It
screamed again. And I knew, suddenly, that it was right outside
my window.

All in a single motion, I lifted my amulets over my head,
rolled from the bed, and drew the sword from my walking stick,
steel swishing. On bare feet that protested the cold floor, I
moved to the back of the loft, pushed aside the drapery, and
looked out over the melting snow. Sitting on the ground near
the stable, its tail wrapped around its feet, looking for all the
world like a prim housecat, was the lynx.

It looked up at the twitch of the drape and opened its
mouth. It spoke, the sound a growl, almost a greeting, nothing
like the sedate meow of its tamer cousins. Its long canines
caught the moonlight.

Scientists had been claiming that predator animals were
changing to fit the colder ice-age environment, growing longer,

sharper fangs needed to bring down larger prey, and producing longer claws. I was seeing the evidence firsthand. The lynx's fangs were more than two inches long. It was staring at the window. I moved closer to the glass. The large cat met my eyes and then looked over its shoulder for a long moment before glancing up at my window again. Suddenly it jumped from its sitting pose, a long arc that took it uphill. In three bounds, it was gone.

Enclave teachers would call it a portent. I shivered in the cold and started back to bed. Halfway there, I stopped and returned to the window, the sword in my hand. Placing a palm by the windowpane, I looked out. Exactly where the lynx had been was a human figure.

My nostrils flared; my hand tightened on the sword as battle instincts blazed. A daywalker. Just as the predator cat had stared at me, the child of Darkness stared. My mage-sight flashed on its own. The daywalker glowed with Darkness and with Light and I remembered seeing it up close once before. Near my spring . . . but the thought flitted away, as insubstantial as an echo. The beast held out its hand, the gesture imploring. Its lips moved.

"Come. Come to my mistress. Hurry. There isn't much time." Its eyes widened, remarkable, shining eyes like labradorite stone, green and translucent blue. It blinked and said, "Please."

A scream sounded and I rose up in bed, the dream shattering, evaporating like fog. The lynx called from the Trine, its voice waking me. I rolled back over and slept.

When I woke again, it was morning. I dressed quickly and was ready for my workout when a chill raced along my arms, settling low in my abdomen. Something was coming. Walking stick in hand, I raced from window to window, looking for danger, for the lynx, as if the dream warning had been real. There was nothing. Just early risers and the crowd spilling out the kirk doors after dawn service. Yet the sensation persisted, like the scent of battle, like the smell of blood. To disperse it, I flew into the forms of primary-level savage-chi.

I was ten minutes into my workout, flat on my stomach starting the cluster of lion moves, when my door rammed opened and rebounded off the wall. Audric stood in the breach in his black dobok, scarlet sash tied at his waist. He had a weighted wooden stave in each hand, the kind used to simulate swords for midlevel practice, when bruises and cracked bones are acceptable but blood loss is not. Before I could rise from the floor or speak, he attacked.

The rods swished the air in violent arcs, the sound like a warrior's dying breath. Placing each foot deliberately, yet moving with battle speed, he was on me in an instant. In the act of rising, I ducked under the first two cuts and whirled across the room, mage-speed my only defense.

"Where are your practice staves, little mage?" he taunted, following me. I spun under one strike and leapt over the next. "Why are you unarmed?"

"A little warning would have been nice."

"Darkness seldom offers such pleasantries." He sent a barrage of blows at me, any one of which would have shattered my bones had it landed.

"I don't have them."

"Lies. No mage leaves Enclave without practice weapons. You're sloppy. Laziness has made you weak." A serious pronouncement from one of his kind. An insult.

"I didn't exactly do my own packing." I jumped behind the couch, landed, and sprang back to the front. "I was drugged and taken to the nearest train station in the dead of night." He stuttered in his steps, an almost certain fatal error had the battle been in earnest instead of play. I marked exactly where my blade would have penetrated beneath his arm. "When I woke up, I was in Mineral City. Whoever packed for me packed my blades but left my staves behind. Ask Lolo next time you talk to her. I'm pretty sure the priestess opened a rune of forgetting over me and sent me here."

Audric didn't respond to the opening about Lolo. Whirling, he slammed both mock blades into my sides, driving my breath from my chest. I strangled a scream and fell to the floor, gasping, arms around my sides. In battle, the scissor strike was used to cleave a foe in twain. Even with staves it could kill. Fortunately, Audric held back, hitting me with half force. In spite of his restraint, the staves cracked some ribs and bruised my lungs.

"This is true?" When I nodded, not yet able to talk, he said, "I will provide you with two sets of practice staves: a weighted set for strength, and lightweight bamboo for speed. Henceforth, we will practice every dawn for an hour." Audric crossed his staves over his thighs and half bowed. With a sharp click, he tucked them together beneath his left arm. "I am pleased to be your instructor. I will attack you whenever and wherever I choose. You will defend. You will work on forms. You will take the written tests. You will fight."

"What if I say no?" I managed from my place on the floor.

"Each morning I will damage a different bone. After a week, you will no longer resist. You will no longer be sloppy or lazy." When I groaned, Audric laughed. Just what I needed, a second-unforeseen using me to assuage his battle lust.

Because the shop was closed on Mondays, Rupert and I turned on the TV in the corner, made hot tea, and tinkered with some new displays that looked like porcelain hands, one white, six others pure black. If he noticed I moved a lot more stiffly than usual, he didn't comment on it. He worked silently, intent, re-arranging items in the cabinets, standing back to judge the visual impact, then repositioning them.

Outside the shop windows, kids playing hooky skated and

played hockey in the streets. El-cars dodged pedestrians intent on errands, all encouraged by the warm weather. A group of sunbathers in thin clothes was lying on wooden chaises, faces, arms, and lower legs turned to the sun, soaking up a winter's worth of vitamin D and springlike warmth.

On the TV overhead, an SNN reporter and two "experts" babbled about the warming trend on the East Coast, with one expert claiming an end to the ice age, and the other insisting that it was an anomaly, soon to be reversed with much colder weather to follow.

I was practically upside down behind the emerald display when the SNN news anchor broke in with a seraph update. I jerked upright. There hadn't been a notable seraph update in ages. Eyes dancing with excitement, unable to sound stern and disinterested, Tom Snead said, "In an unusul turn of events, two seraphs were just seen departing from a Realm of Light." Snead's hands were trembling, and he pressed them on the reporter's desk.

"Zadkiel, known as the seraph of solace and gentleness, was one of two chieftains who assisted Michael when the archseraph fought in the Last Battle. He and another seraph departed before dawn from the only holy region on the North American continent, the island once known as Manhattan." Snead ran out of breath and inhaled noisily. "Zadkiel is known to guard the powers of invocation, the most powerful form of which is prayer.

"Because he was seen departing to the south, wearing his usual dark purple but not carrying sword and shield, some wonder if he has gone to aid the prayers of some of the faithful. Hopeful people are standing on rooftops, gathering in cathedrals and kirks, in synagogues and mosques all over the eastern seaboard.

"The seraph traveling with Zadkiel is a lesser-known warrior of the Light, Raziel, called the revealer of the rock. Raziel is the seraph reputed to have given Adam *The Book of the Angel Raziel*. He is a ruling prince and the chief of the supreme mysteries, the seraph of secret regions."

On the screen, fuzzy video depicted two forms rising into the clouds as the cameraman zoomed in and refocused. They could have been out-of-focus birds, except for a blast of light accompanying their departure.

"As soon as we know more about the mission and destination of these two most senior seraphs, SNN will bring you the latest. Stay with us." Tom smiled, his ten-thousand-dollar orthodontics a searing white. The picture broke back into the weather discussion. But after that, who cared about temperatures?

I remembered the horrible feeling from the early morning. The chill that convinced me that something was coming. I walked from the display case to the front window and placed my hand on the glass as I watched the street. Kids seemed so lighthearted, the adults so blithe. Most wore spring clothes, sweaters over T-shirts, jeans, summer boots. The orthodox women still wore the pale gray dresses of spring.

The seraphs who had departed at dawn were coming south, possibly along the seaboard. If their flight plan deviated to the west, they might fly past Mineral City. Even with the mended prime amulet, I'd know they were near. I'd go into heat so intense I'd attack any male in sight. Even Rupert. The thought of his horrified expression made me smile, though my reflection in the shop window appeared wan.

And if the seraphs came too close, they would pinpoint my exact location. Running could save me from humans, but nothing could hide me or save me from seraphs if they came close enough. Nothing. Feeling itchy, with a fight-or-flight urge trying to take over, I went back to work, keeping half an eye on the TV.

Midmorning, a customer knocked on the door. He wasn't

a local, but with the weather warming, the train had made two runs, bringing strangers to town. Strangers who could afford to travel in winter always made great customers, so Audric let him in.

This particular guy was in his mid-twenties, dressed for the changing weather in a wool business suit, gloves, hat, and periwinkle blue scarf, but no overcoat. He had beautiful eyes, blue-green, like sunlight on water, like labradorite, eyes that seemed familiar. With a businessman's smile, he went straight for Rupert.

"I'm Malcolm Stone," he said, "and I need a gift for my wife. Do you have any mage-stone or mage-silver rings?"

My entire body clenched at the question. Jewelry created by mages and shipped out of Enclave by human traders was fantastically expensive, and Thorn's Gems seldom had access to any. Except all those created by me, but I couldn't quite admit that. I knew I looked guilty, but fortunately neither man looked my way.

"Nothing in stock right now," Rupert said, turning on his salesman's charm, "but we do have some imported stone from Pre-Ap Africa, and some locally mined emeralds. The miner claims that they came from the far face of the Trine, the site of one of the last battles."

I turned away from the men, desperately worried about being discovered. Would my friends suffer for my presence? Would they receive the same fate as I if I was caught? Did I have the right to keep what I was from them?

Malcolm ended up purchasing a ring Rupert had designed, which held a stone I had charmed to provide a sense of calm to the wearer. It was an unusual tumbled amazonite in a lovely mint green shade, set on a sterling band with a wavelike design, and he had the ring gift boxed and wrapped in silver paper.

After he left, the itchy feeling returned, this time with a vengeance. I hadn't noticed that the feeling was at bay, but now it was a burning sensation down my back, on both sides of my spine. Something was coming. Something big. I could have sworn I heard a cat scream.

Near noon, as I was eating a solitary lunch on my back porch, overlooking the stables and the Trine, a shadow crossed the sun. I looked up and saw wings. Huge wings.

Mage-heat slammed into me, a beating, pulsing, sultry lust that drove me off my chair to the porch floor. I moaned, curled into a tight fetal ball on the rough planking, and fought to catch my breath. The heat washed over me in wave after wave of desire and pleasure.

They were here. The seraphs had come to Mineral City.

One's feathers were white and purple, and the nervure, the veins visible through the soft down of the underwing, was a purple so dark, it looked black. The other was pure scarlet, a deeper hue than a cardinal, its nervure a bright teal fading to crimson. Beautiful. Exquisite. I wanted both of them.

Icy water hit me like a frozen fist. Desire morphed into rage. Mage-fast, I came up off the planking and launched myself at Audric. I hit him square in the chest, sending the water bucket he carried flying. Before it could land, I was on him, ripping the staves from beneath his arms and striking a tattoo of blows across his body. I heard a bone in his hand crack and snarled when he jumped back.

Staves materialized in the half-breed's hands, blocking six strikes, eight, fourteen. I backed him around the small porch, hearing soft yips and low growling. The sound, deep and menacing, heated my blood with battle lust. It came from my throat. I wanted blood. I wanted to see the half-breed dead.

Audric laughed. "Fight me, little mage. Fight. Already your heat is waning. Fight!" He advanced on me, sweeping long strikes, moves I had seen as a child on the practice floor but had never tried, let alone mastered. I blocked most. The rest landed, leaving bruises on top of bruises. Pain slowly cleared my head.

"Audric," I gasped, blocking the opening moves of the walking horse.

"Are you back in your own mind, little mage?" he asked, transforming the horse move into the dolphin midstrike. The bamboo staves slapped my thighs, searing pain that brought tears to my eyes. Had they been weighted sword-staves, my femurs would have broken.

I retaliated by sweeping a stave up between his legs. He blocked it at the last moment. I risked a look at his face. "Yes. My heat is gone," I admitted. "Will it stay gone?"

"An hour. If we are lucky."

"An hour." I laughed, the sound wretched. I blocked a swipe that would have dislocated my jaw.

"You fight better when you fight by instinct rather than with your mind. Two levels better. Do we run, or do we tell Rupert what we are?"

"We tell," I said. I broke through the master's stance and touched him hard over the heart with the tip of my stave. Audric jumped back, crossing his staves in an "enough" gesture. I stepped back as well and crossed my staves, accepting the end of the match.

"Rupert and Jacey, both," Audric said.

"Yeah." And if they hated us for it, we could run. But if they wanted us to stay, it would at least be with full knowledge of the consequences. "I like the staves. Well balanced. Small enough for my hands."

"They were mine as a child. I'm glad you approve." He looked down at his broken finger. "Nicely done, mage. I don't suppose you know any healing incantations?"

I shook icy water from my hair and picked up the bowl that had once held my lunch. The bowl had survived being knocked to the floor. The food hadn't been so lucky. Applesauce and cottage cheese were all over the place, ground into the boards by our feet. "A couple of healing chants are in my repertory. You clean up the porch. I'll heal your hand."

"Done," he said. "And after that, we tell our friends what we are. Then we'll go up on the mountain to find the rest of the amethyst. And we will take along your Hand of the Law. What?" he said when I flinched slightly. "I have no doubt you can control your peculiar reaction to the stone and your attraction to the kylen. We need to find the motherstone. It may help us. So may he."

By two—bandaged to keep the mended bones from rebreaking, in Audric's case, and with ribs taped, in my case—we were in the shop with Jacey and Rupert. I had a rune of forgetting ready just in case they decided to turn us in, but I hoped I wouldn't have to use it.

While Audric poured and served tea in the shop's tiny salvaged porcelain teacups, I started the confession. "I have something you guys need to know. Something I haven't told you. Something that would put you in danger if it was discovered." Not able to stay seated, I stood and paced in front of Jacey and Rupert. Jacey was working on a bracelet of green and brown yarn and tumbled amber nuggets, her eyes on her work. Rupert sat back in his chair, legs outstretched, and watched me as I paced, speculation on his face. "If you want me to leave when you hear it, if it's too dangerous for me to be here, knowing what I'm about to say, I'll sign over my share of the shop to you and take off. I'll be gone by nightfall."

"You're a mage?" Jacey said.

I stopped so fast I nearly tripped over my feet. "What?"

"Rupert and I think you're a mage. Probably a stone mage."

Audric laughed, the sound of his chuckles low and astonished. I looked from Rupert to Jacey. She raised her head at last and stared at me. "We talked about what we'd do if it was true. What we'd do if you were caught and us with you. Rupert saw your scars. No human would have survived the venom and viruses from a spawn-attack that severe. You had to be either a neomage or a mule." Jacey placidly returned her eyes to her work as she spoke. "It's not like we're orthodox."

"My uncle on my mother's side," Rupert said. "The one who was elected to Congress? If we ever need to run, I can call him and request sanctuary in an Enclave somewhere. We can move, lock, stock, and barrel, and take everything in the store-room, of course. "Thorn's Gems as an Enclave business would increase our value a hundredfold. If we could advertise that all our stock has mage-stones, we would be rich in five years and could live anywhere we wanted. Jacey already talked to Big Zed, and he agreed. So. Are you a mage?"

Big Zed was Zedikiah Senior, Jacey's husband. Which meant he now had an idea what I was too. And because I hadn't been flayed or tortured this morning, it appeared that he hadn't turned me in to the AAS. "Yes," I said, the word a breath without tone. Tears sprang to my eyes. "Really? You really don't want me to leave?"

"Really," Rupert said. He stood and set down his empty cup, crossed the room, and gathered me in his arms. "We're family. When my brothers and parents discovered I wasn't straight, they dumped me—for years. So did my friends, all except you. Even though you weren't a mountain native and hadn't lived here long, you accepted me."

"And when I got pregnant and wasn't married to Big Zed, you and your foster father took me in, gave me a place to live. Helped me get the paperwork done to get married, even though I was showing and Big Zed was a widower with kids and the eld-ers didn't want to approve it." She smiled softly. "And you got me that dress. That beautiful white dress."

I sobbed once into Rupert's shoulder.

"Because of you, I got married wearing a real wedding dress, with an elder to officiate, even if he was a minor elder and shaking in his boots. In spite of their feelings toward me, my parents came, and I know you had something to do with that. We're family, you and me." Her grin widened, lighting her gamin face. "You're pure flame." It was the highest compliment Jacey could give. She turned to Audric. "And you?"

Audric went still, his eyes on Rupert. "I'm a half-breed. Humans call us mules. We call ourselves the second-unforeseen."

"That explains a lot," Rupert said, his words heavy with meaning. Half-breeds were seldom physically whole, most missing internal and external genitalia.

"Our time together isn't as . . . complete, as what you would experience with a human," Audric said. "You may not choose me for partner now that you know what I am, and now that you know my disfigurement can't be reversed by surgery, as you once suggested."

"Sex isn't everything," Rupert said, his hands massaging my back. I wasn't certain he knew what he was doing, but it felt good on my bruises, so I leaned into him, putting my ear over his heart. It beat with a strong sound, a steady double thump of love. "I don't consider you disfigured," he said to Audric. "Never have. Stay. As long as you want. Forever. As a half-breed, you'll outlive me by twenty or thirty years. Plenty enough time to do something else with your life after I'm gone."

Audric's body loosened as tension eased out of him. "Seraphs are in town. Thorn went into heat, though it's in abeyance at the moment. We may be discovered. You still want us to stay?"

"Yep," Jacey said. "We do."

I pushed Rupert away and bent over Jacey, hugging her. She hugged back one-handed, holding her work in the other, patting me as she might one of her children.

As I stood, my eyes were drawn to a figure standing in the front window. It was a businessman in suit, hat, and periwinkle blue scarf. He had beautiful eyes like labradorite, clear and blue-green, like the gulf. He bowed slightly when he saw me and walked away. He looked familiar somehow, but I couldn't place him.

Long before dark, Rupert, Audric, Thaddeus Bartholomew, Ciana, and I headed up the mountain. We made a motley crew, as if we had been put together from different fashion magazines. Thadd, having traded in his jumpy gray horse for a calm, barrel-chested bay with a black blaze and four black stockings, was dressed as before in jeans and several shirts. A tan cowboy hat hid his reddish hair, and the layered shirts hid his now-deformed back.

He glanced at me beneath the rim of his hat, and I hated it that he looked so good in jeans, sitting on a horse. I hated it almost as much that he seemed to have come to some sort of acceptance of me and our bizarre situation. He tipped his hat, eyes rueful. I had presumed he'd stay angry, blaming me for the incipient wings, but it seemed he recognized it wasn't my fault that his mama slept with a kylen, hid the resulting pregnancy, and then lied to him for his whole life. I didn't want to like him, but I was beginning to.

I had taken time to research incantations for emotional calm and found two that claimed to provide protection from the passion of anger and the passion of jealousy. I had instilled two aventurine donuts with the incantations and now wore them in my bra. While not intended to stop or control lust, passion was passion, and they seemed to be working pretty well. Even when the cop sat a horse like he'd been born in the saddle, butt gripped tight against the cantle, thighs wrapping around the fork, boots solid in the stirrups. I wasn't ignoring him totally, but I wasn't jumping his bones in public, so things weren't too bad.

Ciana—who couldn't be left alone, not with a daywalker, spawn, and a blood-demon loose—rode pillion behind Audric on his Clydesdale. The palomino, like my Friesian, had been bred to work. Clyde had been stable bound too long and was raring to go, bringing excited squeals from Ciana each time he fought the bit. Audric, dressed in black denim from head to toe, and fully armed, gave the horse more rein than usual, laughing happily when Ciana shrieked. We might get lucky and find Darkness to fight. Audric was psyched.

Rupert, goaded with liberal amounts of ridicule into accompanying us, sat on a small mule. He was glum but still made a fashion statement in fuchsia from head to toe, including his boots. I was dressed in dark green, the layers calculated to permit me to wear all my blades, amulets, and charged stones, along with a generous handful of the amethyst to use like a divining rod. I had secured all my stones in waterproof bags in case of a second accidental drenching. The walking stick went into a loop near my thigh, a shovel beside it in case we got lucky and had to dig.

The ground was nearly free of snow, and according to local radio, the ice cap was beginning to melt. Overhead, a plane flew a grid north and south, checking it for stability. Melt ran in sheets. If the temps didn't turn cold soon, it wouldn't be long until something bad happened. Going up on the Trine would be fatal if the cap shifted and created an avalanche. We'd be buried. Of course, the town would be inundated a half minute later, so either way our danger quotient was high. Either way, we'd be dead.

Everyone in the group except Ciana knew I was a mage, so I didn't have to pretend. I opened a massive blended scan, managing to stay on Homer's broad back and not toss my cookies when the vertigo hit. Knowing what to look for, I spotted the lightning and sparkles that had attracted my attention during my virtual trip into the Power's domain. The amethyst in my pockets throbbed in time with the pulsing energies. If the stone had been alive, I'd have said it was excited. Dropping the scan, I urged Homer to the head of the row. "I'll take point. Take our backs, Thadd?" When he raised a thumb, I slapped Homer's withers with the reins and let him have his head. Straight uphill.

The ride was fast, wet, and exhilarating. Opening my mage-senses on the careening ride caused my control over my neo-mage attributes to slip, and by the time we were five hundred feet higher than the town, I was glowing faintly. Audric, who frowned at my lack of restraint, kept Ciana's attention on things to the sides so she wouldn't notice.

By late afternoon, when we reached the place that had drawn my attention, we were all mud caked and tired, and some of us were ornery. A snow-covered, oval glen on the mountain-side was marked with runnels of snowmelt and animal tracks, grass peeking through. The land to the east fell away in a long gulley, and the trench was running with a waterfall full of de-bris. To the west was a mound of broken rock overgrown with hibernating trumpet vines, honeysuckle, and ferns. It was an idyllic spot, and boulders protruding from the earth glowed with a soft resonating power. I rode Homer across the glen to the tall mound, composed of overgrown, shattered granite. It had to be a remnant of the battle on the Trine.

I damped my neomage attributes and tossed the reins to the ground, sliding after them, taking the shovel and the walking stick, one in each hand. Homer looked down at me and snorted into my hair. "Thanks," I said. "I really needed a head full of horse snot." Taking me at my word, he nuzzled my shoulder until I gave him a sugar cube from a pocket. Hearing the others reach the glen, their horses neighing softly, the people talking, I left Homer munching spring grass, tucked the walking stick into a loop on my belt, and climbed the mound. It glowed more richly on the far side. A strong pulse answered from my pocket. I was pretty sure I'd found the motherstone.

BLOODRING

Brushing snow, ice, and detritus away, I positioned the shovel and put my back into digging. The soil wasn't tightly packed, but it was heavy with snowmelt and fracturing ice. I felt the activity in my bruised back, biceps, and thighs. I knew the instant Thadd joined me. He put his shovel on the north side of the mound, as far from me as he could get and still be digging in the same piece of real estate. Audric joined us with his own shovel. Rupert, complaining about saddle blisters, pulled Ciana to a pile of rock and watched.

I uncovered the first cracked fragment of amethyst, a shard about the size of Homer's foot, traced with a fine network of shattered, high-grade quartz. It was damaged, and when I looked at it with mage-vision, its rhythm seemed offbeat from the glow that pulsed from the earth. But it still contained power, oddly undiminished by being exposed on all four sides to soil and groundwater. I set it gently aside, knowing it might crumble into pieces if I handled it roughly. Audric placed a brittle shard beside mine.

As he set it down, a rumble sounded. We all turned our eyes uphill and froze. A loud crack, like cannon shot, echoed through the nearby peaks; a groan followed it, tortured, as if the earth itself were in pain, the worrisome signs of avalanche. But they faded, and silence settled in. Slowly, we returned to the backbreaking work. From the corner of my eye, I saw Rupert climb from his perch and lift something from a crack in the rocks, but my attention was snagged by a shard, this one a perfect crystal.

We began to uncover amethyst in every scoop, picking the smaller pieces out of a shovelful of soil, drawing larger ones out by hand. This was not a typical stone formation, but loose and jumbled together. Whatever it was, it wasn't a mine.

An hour later, I took a water bottle and a fist-sized hunk of rock and walked to the top of the mound. Out of sight, I marked a small circle in the soil and sat on a dry boulder in the center of it. I'd be drunker than ten monkeys attempting to scry here, but I hadn't forgotten Lucas or my promise to Ciana to try to get him back.

Putting the new stone, freshly dug from the ground, in front of me, I set a tiny shard coated with Lucas' blood on top and drew on the amethyst, chanting softly, "Show me Lucas. Show me Lucas. Show me Lucas. Show me Lucas." My heart rate slowed, as did my breathing. I felt a sensation of falling swiftly, then, with a jerk like a prisoner at the end of a hangman's rope, I stopped.

I was hovering above Lucas in his cell. He was emaciated, sinewy, as if hunger had stripped away fatty tissue, leaving well-developed muscle. His beard was long, his eyes closed, but he still breathed. Again, I smelled old blood and gangrene, and saw a place on his neck where something had fed.

He didn't have long. We had to find him soon. I knew from personal experience that once spawn started to feed, dinner died. I used my newfound ability for a blended scan to pinpoint Lucas' whereabouts. He was deep inside the left peak of the Trine. The smell of limestone came to me, indicating that the entrance to the pit was nearby. But Lucas was far, far underground. And he was still in the claw of a Power.

I opened the charmed circle. I was useless to help my ex-husband. Dismay welled up in me and, sighing, I stood, surprised at how steady I felt. I had used the amethyst power, but I wasn't drunk. I paused, considering why.

Hairs along my arms lifted in warning.

Chapter 19

†

The shot was so close that the round whizzed right by my ear. I dropped into a crouch and leapt. The sound of the rifle came an instant later.

"Gun!" Thadd shouted. "Get down!"

"No kidding," I shouted back, ducking behind a tree. More softly, surprised, I added, "It went through my hair." Shock sizzled through me. I fell against the tree, breath rasping.

Four more shots sounded. One plunked into the tree that hid me. Another landed near my foot. Fear went through me like a missile exploding. I rolled, somersaulting behind a rock. A small gulley running with snowmelt trickled beside it and I landed in the bottom hard, jarring my bones, splashing in the runnel.

Silence as the snowmelt permeated my clothes and drenched my flesh. I didn't feel the cold. A soft alarm sounded in the back of my mind at the anomaly—my body wasn't reacting as it should. I couldn't stop to think about that now.

"Where are they?" Audric shouted.

"Uphill and to the right," Rupert said, his voice shaky.

Two more rifle shots sounded, neither landing near me. I

guessed there were at least two assailants, one firing at me, one at the others. Only humans used guns. Darkness didn't depend on such puny weapons.

No one had claimed the site, so why were humans attacking us? The ground hadn't been disturbed. Not in decades. A barrage exploded from uphill. I heard the horses scream and the sound of hooves as they stampeded. Two gunshots sounded, closer—Thadd returning fire with a handgun. *Sweet seraph.* Ciana was in the line of fire. Shock blossomed into a white-hot anger. Someone, some *human*, was endangering her.

I rolled mage-fast through the mud and sheeting water until I was behind the bole of a mountain maple. Two shots followed, plowing into the soil behind me. I hadn't tried to activate an amulet through plastic before, but with wet, shaking hands, I couldn't open the bag. One thumb and forefinger squeezing the white onyx fish, I called its incantation up from memory. I had made the amulet when I thought scripture was used for all incantations, and I edited it on the fly. If the amended conjure didn't kill me, it might work to protect us.

Breathless with terror, I said, "For my soul takes refuge . . . in the shadow of thy moving wings . . . with the shield of faith . . . able to quench all the fiery darts." It wasn't scripture-perfect, but with the amethyst to back me, it should do in a pinch. I thumbed the fish, and the shield snapped into place with a shockwave of might that left me reeling. In mage-sight the shield looked like a big bubble layered over with purple feathers. I touched it and the feathers gave around my finger without breaking, like a balloon. The shield was markedly larger than any I had ever produced. Drawing on energy from the amethyst, I might be able to shield us all.

I stepped into the side of the shield and it moved with me, fluttering like a wing. Adrenaline pumping, I leapt ahead and over the hillock, down the side of the mound. The shield kept pace with me, enclosing and releasing trees, rocks, and the ground beneath my feet. Gunshots sounded above me; the rounds landed behind me in soft spats of sound. Battle lust welled up in me, fueled by fear and too much power. As I ran, I chanted. "My soul takes refuge in the shadow of thy moving wings."

I tumbled down the mound toward Rupert, Ciana, and Audric, taking cover behind a boulder. Audric's eyes widened as he spotted me. A rifle shot sounded an instant after something struck the shield.

"Close your eyes!" I yelled, running toward the pile of rocks. There was a blast of lavender light as the shield absorbed the cairn and two humans inside. Ciana screamed at the sensation of it closing over her and rolled to the ground. A bigger detonation rocked the clearing as the shield closed over Audric. He was knocked to his back on the wet ground. Ciana slapped at her body as if ants were crawling all over her. "Make it stop!"

Audric's eyes traced the shield over his head. Tiny lightning bolts of power raced through it, visible to mage-sight. "What have you done?" he breathed.

It was an accusation. He should have been thanking me. "Saved us all," I snarled, wanting to hit him, wanting to draw blood. I controlled the urge with effort and turned my back on him. "Thadd! Can you get over here? I've activated a shield."

"I see it. Will it take me?"

A human couldn't see . . . no. Thadd knew he was kylen. He had taken off the ring once, enough to begin the process of mutation. He was probably going to see a lot of things. "Yes, it'll hold," I said. Combat readiness and bloodlust had overtaken fear. They thrummed through me, twin flames. I drew two small throwing blades, wanting to fight, but my enemy was too cowardly to face me. Too *human* to fight face-to-face, might to might.

With each breath I smelled cordite from the gunshots, the stink of human panic, the smell of kylen like caramel and brown sugar. The peppery scent of ginger was growing stronger. With each blink of my eyes, I saw the landscape in rich shades of purple and green and opulent tints of stone. Far uphill, behind a rock outcropping, I saw black and red, a sinuous cloud of Darkness—human and half-breed. My entire body clenched.

Battle rage spiked in Audric. Swords overhead, he roared with the need to race uphill and draw blood.

"Shut up, Audric," I growled. Faster than human sight, I ripped off my outer shirt and gathered up all the bigger pieces of the amethyst we had unearthed, wrapping them in the T-shirt and tying the arms into a sling. In an instant, the power of the stone melded to my body.

Ciana had stopped screaming, her face now cradled against Audric's chest. Thadd ducked and ran to us, blasting into the shield. Light sparked and forked like lightning across the shield. "Let's go," I said. "Downhill, back toward town."

"What about the horses?" Thadd asked.

"Took off. I smelled blood," I said. Homer was hit. Rage ripped through me. I threw back my head and screamed my fury. The sound echoed across the mountainside. *They hurt my Homer.* I gasped, drawing in drafts of air across my tortured throat. "We'll have to walk back," I said, my damaged vocal cords making the words grate.

"We've come miles," Thadd said.

"Unless you sprout wings and fly us down, we don't have much choice," I said, heedless of his face hardening.

"They've stopped shooting. Maybe they're gone," Rupert said.

I looked at him, his face white, hands shaking. Rupert could fight. Normally, Rupert wasn't afraid of anything. But suddenly Rupert was petrified. Something was wrong. But the thought was swept away when Audric said, "Let's go."

I moved to the head of the shield, needing to rush the enemy, to draw blood. I laughed, the sound as harsh as breaking stone. Great time to learn I was one of the unlucky mages who got trapped in battle lust.

We moved out downhill, a ragged group of humans and supernats. I ground my teeth at Rupert's slowness. The others could have come closer to my pace, giving me the release of speed, but my best friend had no such hidden traits.

Our progress was slow. Uphill, the swirl of Darkness followed for a time before it stopped, moved a few yards, and stopped again. I watched them over my shoulder, drawing on mage-sight, switching to mind-skims, terrified of trying a blended scan while on the run. They weren't following us. Which was very strange.

I navigated over a fallen tree, around a snow-covered depression. Full night would be on us soon. We had traveled north for two hours on horseback and climbed more than a thousand feet. We would never make town by nightfall. I wasn't certain I could maintain the moving shield for long. Already, the lightning bolts overhead flickered and blinked.

The shards in my shirt pulsed. A single blast of light erupted from the amethyst I carried, from the ground, from all around us. I dropped to my knees, blinded. The energies around me bucked, twisting in a spiral that stabbed with pain. All the might arching over us wrenched in a whirlpool spasm. And was yanked out.

The shield was sucked into the ground in a sudden rush. My back arched in agony. I tried to scream, but my breath was sucked away. Half an instant later, an explosion rocked the Trine.

"Thorn!" Audric shouted.

I fell to the ground, hitting hard, my breath knocked out by the explosive concussion. I couldn't see, but I knew the shield was gone. My power was gone, all that astonishing might, stored in my body, stored in my amulets. All drained. All empty. The amethyst I cradled was muted and vacant, its energies pulled through the ground, back up the hill to the motherstone. I screamed.

When my sight returned, I was flat on my back, staring at the sky. Exhaustion flooded me, as fatiguing as a plague. I sheathed the small blades and lifted my walking stick. The act of drawing the longsword left me exhausted. My hands fell to my sides. Fear rushed in to fill the rage gap. I had lost it all. All that power. Nausea gripped me and I rolled to empty my stomach on the earth. The groundwater soaking me began to burn, an acid tincture on my entire body. I screamed, gagging.

I had gorged on the amethyst stone. I had drunk it down until my body was full. The power had permeated my flesh, pulsed into my bones. I had been near it for days, had drawn on it, used it, been intoxicated, drunk, stoned, on the power. And now it was gone.

I was in withdrawal. I gagged again, the taste bitter with bile. A tremor rippled up my body. It was like the DTs. My insides wanted to climb out of my skin.

A shot exploded. Another. My friends scattered. More shots sounded. I lay on my back, acid snowmelt burning and freezing. This was my fault. This trip up the Trine, this attack, this danger, all my fault. I had wanted to find the motherstone, the lodestone of amethyst, of power. I had succeeded, bringing us to this destruction.

Risking being shot, I lifted my head to spot my friends. Thadd was farthest uphill, lying with his weapon in both hands, returning fire. Rupert was squatting behind a rock, looking at his cupped hands, seemingly calm. Audric was curled on the ground, Ciana beneath him. He was bleeding. The smell of half-breed blood came to me, mingled with the cordite. *Audric's been shot. He was shot protecting Ciana.*

And then I smelled the scent of Darkness. Using the last of my energy, I opened my mage-sight and focused tightly on Audric. A tendril of Dark energy curled from his wound. The round buried in his body had been infused with Darkness. Audric groaned in agony. Rupert didn't look up at the sound, but knelt, face slack, holding the thing he had picked up earlier, cupping it in his hands—a perfect target. A cloud of Darkness swirled about him. He had fallen for a trap.

Above us, the Darkness moved, swarming downhill, mostly humans, but several moving demon-fast. Toward us. One of them moved like the wind, dancing in savage-chi, like a mage. Others moved like half-breeds. Hundreds of them. We were going to die.

I looked at Audric. He was near death already. Near "dire," that mystical word. His blood, spilled defending a child and a mage, the severity of his injuries, meant I had a way to salvage some of this. I looked down at the town. Mineral City was far away. Enough distance to allow the humans there some safety. The Mole Man's blood would—should—protect Rupert, and Ciana's age meant additional security for her.

I had no choice. I forced myself into a stable sitting position and pulled out my drained prime amulet. I set it on the earth and dumped all the amethyst I had on top of it. I could hear the approaching Darkness, screams and thump of feet. Shots peppered the earth around me, missing such easy targets. They wanted us alive.

Moving too slowly, tired beyond imagining, I pulled an earring out of my ear and stabbed my hand with the pointed ear wire. Pain shocked like an electric jolt. Blood welled in the hole, and I held my palm over the amethyst. Three drops fell as I chanted a traditional call for help, the nursery rhyme call created by the earliest mages, teenagers attacked by humans and their nuclear weapons in the Mage War. There were seraphs nearby. If they heard me, they would come. "Mage in battle, mage in dire; seraphs, come with holy fire."

I repeated the phrase. And again. Audric howled in agony. Ciana, protected beneath him on the ground, screamed with him, terrified. I kept repeating the phrases as shots infused with Darkness peppered the earth, and the swarm of Dark soldiers churned down on us. I would die today. Either by the Darkness that was only yards away, or at seraphic judgment.

Innocent blood had been spilled. I had claimed "mage in dire," the time-honored call for help, to be used only after an innocent's or supernat's fatal wound, administered during a struggle with Darkness. The words reverberated in my head. *Mage in battle, mage in dire; seraphs, come with holy fire . . .*

A shadow fell over us. Wind whipped the air. He landed, toes touching down, body clad in battle armor, red-gold overlapping scales that caught the coruscating light. Twenty-four feet of scarlet seraph wings formed a canopy over us. My entire body clenched. Dread and wonder replaced the fear in my veins. He was utterly, beyond words, beautiful. "Down the hill," he said, his voice indescribable—like music, magic, an orchestra in heaven.

I brushed tears away and pointed at Rupert. "He's innocent but has been spelled."

With a flick of his wingtip, the seraph knocked Rupert off his feet. My friend crashed to the ground, dropping a rock. It tumbled into a gulley and exploded. Rupert shook his head and stood on unsteady legs, looking at the smoke from the explosion and at the seraph.

"Down the hill," the seraph said. "Quickly."

Thadd, appearing from behind the seraph, ducked under the wing and pulled a still screaming Ciana from beneath Audric. Murmuring softly to her, he handed her to Rupert. When she saw the seraph, her screams ceased, her lips in a perfect O. Looking over his shoulder and wing, the seraph scanned the hill. Thadd holstered his weapon and hoisted Audric to a fireman's hold. He nodded once, sharply, to the seraph. "Let's go. Shut up, Audric," he added. The huge half-breed's scream gurgled off into tortured moans.

BLOODRING

Under the protection of the seraph's wings, I gathered my amulets and the amethyst and followed the others. We made it a hundred yards down the mountain. Two hundred yards. I looked back. Since the seraph appeared, there had been no shooting, but Darkness still stood on the sharp grade, supernats, watching: several half-breeds and a mage. *A mage, willingly helping Darkness. A mage whose mind I hadn't sensed.* I stumbled across the terrain, my overloaded senses reeling, a seraph's wings spread over my head.

When exhaustion had stolen my last breath, the seraph looked back. "They are gone," he said. He furled his wings with a sound like a storm-laden wind. A deep cloak, the color of old blood, swirled around him. His war armor glowed with the power of the High Host.

I fell against a tree, my muscles cramping. Breathing heavily, Thadd eased Audric to the ground. He hissed with pain, clutching his chest. Blackness shifted beneath his skin. Blood was everywhere, across Audric's back, his chest, smeared over Thadd's clothes. Thadd unbuttoned his top shirt and threw it away. To me it stank of sulfur, and by his expression, to Thadd as well. His ring glowed softly to my mage-sight.

The seraph knelt by me, bringing his face to my level, jaw carved of marble, eyes as pellucid as the finest ruby, red irises in a tawny-skinned face. "I heard your call, little mage. I am here, as I promised, in life and battle and love." They weren't the proper words a seraph spoke when answering a mage-call in battle extremis. They sounded personal, almost intimate. He lifted a hand to my palm, where blood still flowed. At his touch, the wound clotted over. Strength flowed into me from his fingertip. My body shuddered hard and the shivers stopped.

The proper phrases came to me from lessons learned long ago and forgotten. Voice scratchy with exhaustion, I said, formally, "I thank thee for thine assistance. And for the touch of seraph healing."

"I scent Darkness on your companions," he said, one hand moving to his sword hilt.

Fear was an icy blade pricking my skin. I pointed to Audric. "The bullets were coated with a Dark conjure. And he"—I indicated Rupert—"picked up a spelled trap."

"Foolish," the seraph said. He lifted a chin to Audric. "He will die."

My body quivered with the pronouncement, my legs folded, and I landed hard on the wet earth. Rupert settled beside Audric. Ciana, who had been watching the exchange with wide eyes, wriggled from Rupert's arms and twitched the seraph's cloak to get his attention. "So, fix him," she said. "You can do it. I can tell."

The seraph smiled. "And how can you tell this, little human child?"

"I see it there." She touched his hand.

The seraph flinched back, his eyes wide with shock. Humans did not touch the Host. But instead of reacting in anger, he looked from his hand to Ciana. "Mole Man's blood." He touched fingertips to her head as if to make certain. "You carry Mole Man's blood in your veins."

Ciana's dark head bobbed. "Yes, sir. He was my bunches-of-great-grampa. You gonna fix Uncle Audric?"

"You wish this?" he asked.

"Yes. Please," Ciana said, folding her hands politely. "And then you can save my daddy. He's been kidnapped."

"One of Mole Man's blood is in danger?" the seraph asked.

"Yes," I said. Cautious in the presence of such a volatile being, I searched for words to tell him where Lucas was without giving it away to Ciana. "He's in a . . . pit."

"Ah," the seraph breathed, his face lighting with what looked like joy. He turned to the Trine and breathed in deeply, as if pinpointing the entrance to the lair with a breath. "A quest. And you too," he said, looking at me, "wish this injured one to be healed?"

"Yes," I said. "He's my friend."

"But he isn't a bound warrior," the seraph said, looking Audric over. "He is a free being. If I heal him, I bind him."

"Do it," Audric said. Darkness lumped under his skin like pustules. It swirled black in the whites of his eyes. His body was wracked with cramps, limbs drawing up in a spasm. I could feel the heat of fever from where I stood. "I'm dying. Do it. Make me yours."

"Audric?" Rupert said, his voice thin.

"Fear not, progeny of Mole Man. Though mine to call in war, he will still be as he was." The seraph bent and lifted Audric away from Rupert, cradling him like a child.

Instantly, Audric sighed and pain smoothed from his face. But as he touched the seraph's chest, anguish carved the corners of his eyes. "I am yours for beck and call," he said, voice so low it scarcely breathed into the air, "my blood and bone and sinew." The words were traditional, but his voice grew ineffably sad. Audric would no longer be free. "With sword and shield, in battle dire, I'll follow your behest. Never to fail, and never to falter, for the length of my life." Hot tears seared my cheeks, scalding on chapped skin.

The seraph touched Audric's chest, over his heart, completing the binding. "Feathers and fire, in time and without, I accept the gift of yourself. I will answer your call, guard you beneath my wings, and carry you into the Light at the end of your days."

The seraph turned to me, his red irises strange but not unpleasant. "There is no need to grieve for your friend, little mage. He is now a rock in my river of time. He will not be forgotten nor held in disdain." Which did nothing to help. Audric was bound. A slave to the High Host. I willed Audric's eyes to open, but he kept them shut, as if shunning certain pity.

The seraph's eyes moved over me, changing from kindness to puzzlement. With a single finger, he lifted my jaw and turned my face from side to side. "You have no heat, nor do I. Only magnificent battle and great use of creation energies can forestall it. We are blessed."

With the same hand, he bent and touched Ciana's head. "Your desire is fulfilled. The seraphic promise to Mole Man is remembered unto eternity." He tilted her head, staring at the mark of Darkness on her throat. He tapped the agate necklace on her chest, then lifted the pendant to peer closer. "Ahhh," he breathed again, "a Power would harm Mole Man's blood." He smiled widely, battle lust lighting his eyes. "It is well that I have come. This trinket is not enough to protect you, little human girl. But this—" He shifted Audric as though he weighed nothing. Feathers brushed my shoulder and I closed my eyes as pleasure and heartache washed over me in equal measure. The seraph removed a brooch from his cloak and pinned it to Ciana's chest. "This will protect you for as long as you shall live."

"Way cool!" she said, fingers tracing the winged shape of the red-gold ornament.

"Yes. It is." His eyes settled on me. He cocked his head. "You do not recall."

"Recall what?" I asked, swiping at tears with my sleeve.

"You too are a stone in my river of eternity. When the *time* comes," he said, a peculiar accent on the word *time*, "you *will* remember." It was more command than assurance. He carried Audric to an outcropping and spread his wings, easing them between the trees. "Soon it will be night on the face of the earth. Darkness will swarm the moment the sun falls below the horizon. Even now, they mass on one peak of the Trine. Hurry." With a single thrust of his wings, he shot up into the sky, dodging branches. And he was gone from sight.

"Seraph stones," Thadd whispered, cursing even though a seraph was still perhaps close enough to hear.

"Fire and feathers," Rupert said, less dangerously.

"Sweet seraph," I mouthed, a sense of awe finally stealing over me.

"I like him. He's cool," Ciana said. "And you're a mage. That's even cooler. Don't worry. I won't tell."

My first thought was to release a rune of forgetting over her, but taking away a first, and perhaps only, encounter with a seraph seemed a cruel punishment. And then I remembered. A seraph knew I was living among humans. I wouldn't be around long enough for Ciana's memory of me to matter.

"I see the horses. Let's get out of here," Thadd said, his face tired, his eyes on the town below us. He glanced at me as he swung Ciana up in his arms. There was compassion there. "He'll be all right. All the accounts say so."

But he'll be bound, I wanted to say. Instead, I was silent, fighting tears made worse by his sympathy.

Rupert and I followed the cop down a steep incline, scattering shale, and helped to reclaim the horses, who were grazing on a patch of grass. Homer's flank was blood caked, a jagged flesh wound, but not reeking of Darkness. We mounted, Thadd riding point, Rupert taking up the rear, and Ciana and me on Homer between them. Silently, we headed home.

As we rode, I realized two things. The seraph hadn't recognized Thadd. The ring he wore had fooled a winged warrior. And the seraph hadn't wrapped me in chains. Hadn't made me go back to Enclave. Hadn't condemned me. He even seemed to recognize me. *You are a stone in my river of eternity.* What in heaven's name did that mean?

We made it back to Mineral City not long after the sun set, and I spent nearly two hours in the small stable with Zeddy, grooming the two oversized horses, and Rupert's mule, and cleaning up Homer's injury. The bullet that grazed his haunch left a deeper wound than my quick inspection on the mountain had revealed. Zeddy, who worked with the town medic and who could pass as a skilled assistant in a pinch, sewed up the four-inch gash, a layered closure that really needed the town veterinarian or a healing amulet. Doc Hampford, however, was on his honeymoon, and wouldn't be back for a week. And my amulets were totally drained.

The wound across Homer's beautiful black flank would likely leave a white scar, which brought me to tears as Zeddy worked. I sniffled, collected bloody rags, passed over cleanser, antibiotics, and sterile thread, and cried like a tot over my horse. Homer, who glanced back in curiosity several times during the procedure, ignored us except for an occasional quiver, the kind used to discourage irritating flies.

The energy gifted to me by the seraph lasted until I showered, ate, and fell into bed, when it drained away in a wash of misery and heartache. I couldn't stay here. Not anymore. The seraphs wouldn't allow it. I could run from humans; I could take my packed bag and my blade case and disappear. But not from seraphs. Once they had scented and located a neomage, they could follow the trail anywhere. Any minute now, they would descend on me and take me away from my friends. Forever. As the minutes ticked away toward midnight, my last hours here, my tears collected in my ears, dried on my face, and my grief intensified. In the dark of my home, I sobbed.

Exhausted, yet unable to sleep, I wallowed in my sorrow, staring at the rough-hewn rafters over me, brokenhearted over losing my home, my bed, my stuff. I loved my home, loved its rich history, loved every rafter, every slate shingle, every board and tile on the floor. And I was going to have to leave it. I was going to have to leave Rupert and Jacey. And I was going to have to leave the child of my heart.

The winged brooch the seraph had given her marked her as protected by the High Host. It was a better amulet than anything I could have created for her; I knew that. Yet, near midnight, I eased from the covers, dressed, and made my way downstairs to the workshop. My feet ached as I walked, my spine was stiff; every muscle cried out for the return of the amethyst energy I had hoarded to myself. Out of curiosity, I opened one of the metal cases the amethyst had arrived in and discovered that the stone within was dull, somnolent, with only a bare spark of the vibrant warmth it had once contained. Part and parcel of my total defeat.

Closing the ammo case, sealing the metal strips back in place, I turned on lights and found the remaining bloodstone. Half carved into a cat shape, it was lovely, a rich green periphery with a bleeding heart of bright fuchsia, a curious hue for bloodstone. Turning the nearly fist-sized piece of rough, I studied it, considering a curved triangular section, vaguely sickle shaped, that could become something else. A second cat? I flipped on the wet saw and slid into my coveralls. Goggles and mask in place, I secured the partial cat into the saw and carefully excised the sickle shape. The piece of rough had contained a second sleeping cat.

Two hours passed, my body relaxing into the rhythms of working stone. Under the attention of the saw, the drill, and various picks and tools, the cats began to emerge. Ciana's cat was longer, more narrow than mine, lying on its side with paws and legs curled into its body, green along the spine, with a pink tummy. Mine was a fat, tight ball, smaller than originally planned, with paws just visible beneath its chin. Predominantly pink, my cat had green paws, jaw, and nose, a mottling of green across its back.

When I had the basic shapes ready, I set them together on the counter. They looked like mother and child napping, and the comparison brought tears to my eyes. I had to finish them both tonight. I might not have a tomorrow. The polishing alone would take hours. As I worked, I noticed that Ciana's cat had one eye partially open, just begging for a hint of lavender. Turning the larger cat, I found a place on its neck where a nugget of amethyst could be inserted, as if part of a collar. I had plenty of lavender stone that no longer performed like it should, so I went to the storeroom and gathered a small lump for working.

I teased off a single crystal shard, and, still holding the amethyst in my left hand, I lifted both bloodstone cats in my right. Suddenly, I was outside, sunlight dappling the ground all around me. I was disoriented, feeling the stone in my hands, the bloodstone and the amethyst. I raised one elbow and it hit the workbench in front of me, a workbench I could no longer see.

I was standing on crushed granite and tortured grass, blackened and wilted. The sun was hot, too hot, on my shoulders. Far below me was Mineral City, Upper and Lower streets black with asphalt. Between my booted feet and the town was devastation, houses and sheds that had imploded or been blasted into debris. Cars were overturned and burned. I smelled cordite and sulfur and the reek of my friends, recently dead.

I turned away from the town and looked uphill, toward the Trine, felt my surprise that the hill was no more, that a mountain stood there, three-peaked, barren rock over two thousand feet higher than only a week past. I put out my hand and touched the low mound of rock and wreckage rising up from the ground at my feet. I saw my hand rest on a single broken piece of lavender stone, felt myself respond to the amethyst. Below it, hidden in the rubbish of bomb-blistered rock, I saw the gold glint of navcone. Navcone, here and not-here, seen and not-seen. There was no one to find it. No one to report it to. Not now. Perhaps never again.

Around me were a dozen ordinary granite rocks and boulders, sharp edged, ripped from the heart of the mountain. Decision made, I lifted a small boulder, felt the strain in my shoulders and back as I carried it to the navcone and set it over the bit of shattered amethyst and glinting gold I could see only when the light hit it just right. Sadness welled inside me, but I pushed it away and lifted a second stone, placing it near the first. I was making a cairn of stones to hide the remains. What else could I do?

I saw my hand as I lifted it away, the odd shape to the long fingers, the index extending past the middle, tapered, like my father. My father, whose bloodstone ring I now wore. I saw the ring on my finger, a small green stone with a single fleck of red, the setting a pitted nugget of raw gold. After a moment of rest, I went back to work. The scene blurred and returned, crisp and clear.

I had finished the cairn and buried a series of mines along the ridge over the pile of amethyst. Pushing a small button on a black box, I triggered a sequence of explosions. The resulting landslide hid the wheels. My work was done.

I was lying on the workroom floor, cold, more stiff than when I'd crawled out of bed. I had dropped the bloodstone and the amethyst. They rested near my hand, pulsing with lavender warmth, even the bloodstone. Using my heels, I scuffed myself upright, sitting with my back against the leg of the workbench.

Had it been a true vision? A prophecy? A memory? I recalled the image of the town, with its paved streets, and realized that there had been no sign of snow, not anywhere. It had been hot, hotter than any summer had been in decades. I had been sweating as I worked. A memory, then, gifted me by the amethyst when it touched the bloodstone. Bloodstone, like the ring on the man's hand.

I had seen that ring once, worn by Lucas' grampa. Had he been buried with the ring? I didn't know. I only knew that once upon a time, bloodstone had come in contact with the amethyst on the Trine. And I knew a golden navcone—whatever that was— was buried near the mound of amethyst we had found today, the smaller mound, the cairn of stones built by the man in the vision. Rupert had sat on it today. I had to go back to the site of the vision. Soon.

I picked up the bloodstone cats, pulsing with dim lavender energies, and inspected the amethyst. Some of its power had been restored, yet something was different now. After a moment, I realized that the beat of its energies was subtly altered, as if its heart rate and rhythm had changed. I pressed the larger bloodstone cat to the small lavender crystal, opened my mage-sight, and let myself slip into the matrix of the rock, down into the quartzite hearts, where light and matter danced and moved and swirled. I realized that the amethyst was harnessed to the bloodstone cat, under its control. That shouldn't be possible.

Curious, I went back to the storeroom and opened the case I had inspected earlier. The rough within was pulsing weakly, softer now, a steady, delicate rhythm that matched that of the bloodstone cat. Sudden fear made my heart skip a beat and then speed up.

The rhythm of the stone matched my heart rate. The stones pulsed with it. At a dead run, I raced upstairs and grabbed my necklace of amulets off the bedside table. Each amulet vibrated softly lavender, in time with the steady beat of my heart. Except when I used them in a conjure, they never pulsed. Until now.

"Glory and infamy," I swore. The amethyst wasn't harnessed to the bloodstone; it was harnessed to me, acting just like a prime amulet. I dropped to the rug beside my bed, intensely aware of my heartbeat, of the feel of my blood throbbing through my veins and arteries. "Saints' balls." I was tied to the amethyst.

Something had happened on the Trine; something weird. I remembered the explosion of light when the conjure I was working was sucked into the ground, when I was drained of all power and left gasping. That was when it happened, I was pretty sure, whatever *it* was, the explosion that drained my heat away.

I turned my prime amulet over, scrutinizing the mended place. The fine line of bloody stone that had filled the crack now glistened like faceted rubies set with lavender diamonds. Like scales or cells of a living thing. The melding of the bloodstone and the amethyst had given me power over the stored amethyst in the storeroom. And over my heat?

The seraph—Raziel, I remembered his name from the TV reports—had touched my chin. Nothing had happened. No heat, no wild rapturous mating on the mountainside. No instant death from the Most High. Raziel had been surprised. He'd been curious. Seraphs hadn't been curious about anything, not once, in all the decades of their presence on earth.

I separated the stones, turned off the machinery and lights. I had to polish the cats, but later. After dawn. I showered off the bloodstone dust and crawled naked between my sheets, taking with me the amulets and the half-finished cats and the amethyst.

Chapter 20

T uesday passed in an agony of anticipation and worry. No seraphs appeared to take me in. No cops arrived with handcuffs, leg shackles, sharp knives. No one ran me off or arrested me or suggested I should undergo torture. No lynch mobs gathered in the streets. The day passed slowly; the weather continued to warm, and snowmelt to race downhill. The Toe River grew until I could hear its roaring as I worked. Early spring? *In February?* An end to the ice age? SNN was rife with conjecture about the weather and with speculation about the seraphs reputed to still be near Mineral City, the reporters giddy with excitement at the sightings. Seraphs had been filmed in Asheville, in Boone, in Linville, and in Black Mountain. Two other seraphs had been filmed leaving the New York Realm of Light, one smoky gray, one teal. I kept the overhead TV on between customers, one eye on the screen, and I turned up the volume for each update.

After lunch, Jacey filled Internet orders, Rupert stared out the window worrying about Audric, and I took care of customers. When Rupert tired of window watching and shooed me away, I went to the back to polish the cats. I couldn't tumble them; they were too big. I had to polish them by hand, starting with a sixty-grit wheel to remove the surface scratches, progressing methodically to the hundred-grit wheel, the two-twenty-grit wheel, the two-eighty, the six-hundred, and finally twelve-hundred-grit paper and the loving movement of my hand.

It took most of the afternoon, but by four, I was satisfied with their gloss. Ciana's had a small space between her front legs for a fine, thin silver chain. Mine was secured with copper wire to depend from a leather thong or chain. I didn't string it with my other amulets or create the necklace I had envisioned, but kept the pieces close together until Ciana got home from school and I could surprise her with them.

For the second time today, I peeled out of the jumpsuit uniform and ran upstairs to wash off stone dust. I stepped from the shower, dripping wet, and my back arched in reaction to a bolt of power. My hair stood on end. My skin crawled. I *felt* him enter the shop.

Though my body pulsed like it had in heat, this wasn't heat; not at all. But I *knew*. A seraph was here. Although I had been expecting it, misery and anger gushed up in me, an artesian spring of grieving. I bowed to the sink, resting my forehead against my fist. If I begged, perhaps they would allow me to stay long enough to say good-bye to Ciana.

I dressed in my battle dobok, placed each knife in its loop, braided my hair, and pressed it around the hilt of the neck blade. I draped my amulet necklace over my head in plain sight, the mended prime throbbing in time with my accelerated heartbeat. I put on my wide silver wrist cuffs and huge hoops in my ears, and dumped my jewelry into a small travel bag. I tossed the leather cloak over the bags and pulled them all, thumping, down the stairs.

I propped them at the door, beneath the prophecy Lolo had made at my birth. I'd have to remember to take that too. If

I survived the punishment I would receive following my return to Enclave and the subsequent insanity from so many minds open to me, I would want it. Jacey, standing in a corner, stared at me, eyes blank with panic, face in a rictus of terror.

Straightening, my heart fluttering like a trapped, feral animal, I walked with my back straight and my head held high into the shop.

In human guise, he stood alone at the counter, silent, no aura of power, no chains, no shackles. No wings, no sword of justice and retribution. But there was no doubt he was an angel of punishment. The sigil of his office was a pale gold disc on his chest, the sigil that allowed him long minutes in contact with a neomage without generating his own heat. Rumors said the time was as long as an hour. An hour of torture for the mage he questioned. He turned glowing turquoise eyes to me and stared. Minutes went by; according to the beat of my racing heart, long, silent minutes.

"Little mage," he said at last, his voice like mellow brass bells rather than the tolling gong of doom I expected. "Come to me."

Knees quivering, stomach in a knot, blinking against tears, I walked to him, my battle boots loud on the wood floor. I stopped three feet away. Like all seraphs, he was beautiful, but his was a terrible beauty, a slash of mouth, jaw excised from cold marble, brow tall and wide with a widow's peak and dark hair curling like wood smoke.

He cocked his head, studying me, his glowing eyes moving up and down my body. With his left hand, he lifted his sigil and pulled it off, over his head. He stared at it a moment and looked again at me. Then, as though the action was of great significance, he set it on the counter with a soft clink.

Peripherally, I was aware of Rupert standing in the doorway to the workroom. Of Jacey's fear, mutating to something else. Of the silent crowd that gathered at the display windows of the shop, staring in, too fearful to enter.

The angel of punishment—one of the few seraphs to use the term "angel" in a title—looked at me. His eyes were already glowing with fierce energy, and the turquoise light slid out like tears, over his cheeks, his lips, up over his forehead, down over his body like a second skin, growing like mist, swirling around him, over him, with a clockwise spin. When it covered him from head to toe, he reached out a misty hand and brushed his fingers over my face. The pulsing energy slid from his fingertips across my cheeks, over my eyes, and down across my jaw, brushing my lips. I closed my eyes, feeling his energy, a lover's caress, tracing down my throat, around the nape of my neck, into my hair, and slowly, so gently, down my spine.

It was as if my clothes were nothing more than a cloud, and he touched me through them, the teal mist brushing my breasts and down my thighs. The mage-heat I expected from such an intimate seraphic touch didn't rise. My body remained cool and at rest. Surprised, I opened my eyes and stared at him through the mist.

The seraph finally smiled, a slight lessening of the tension in his narrow lips. He sighed and the mist that touched me boiled and swirled with his breath. I scented cinnamon and cloves and pomegranates, spicy and sweet. The swirl of the mist stopped. "It is true," he whispered into the mist. The words formed waves that crested between us and splashed down my body. "Finally. As it was prophesied. 'It shall be thus, blood to blood, bone to bone, flesh to flesh, in battle and before the throne.'" He touched a layer of bloodstone on my prime amulet. I felt a sizzle of power to my bones.

"Bloodstone," I said, as if that were important. The mist slid away from me, and now it smelled like lemon mint and sage, cool and light, parched, like dried herbs.

"Yes. Bloodstone. It has happened," he said again, so softly I could scarcely hear. I felt the weight of the necklace resting on my chest. "Welcome, little mage."

With that, he swiveled, picked up his sigil, and walked from the shop. The crowd gathered in the door parted, and he moved through them, every eye following his progress. In the center of the street, he stopped. A flash of light burst from the sigil as he placed it over his head. The brilliance was dazzling and I turned away, blinking in the glare. When it cleared, the seraph had transmogrified. Fully winged, his feathers were a lustrous teal, edging to black at the tips. He lifted and spread his wings, exposing smoke-colored down beneath. One wingtip touched the window on the far side of the street. "Wait," he said to me. "I will return." With a snap of feathers like a battering wind, he leapt into the sky and was gone.

The crowd stood silent after the seraph was gone, motionless, as if frozen. Finally, a little boy turned and looked into the shop window. I damped my neomage attributes, which were glowing richly, and hid the amulets beneath my tunic. I met his eyes as human to human, but I knew it was too late. His mouth opened and I read the word in it. "Wow."

The crowd turned toward the shop, one by one, and then the entire group, as if pulled by a string. Their expressions were stunned, uncertain, growing angry. Elder Jasper was in the crowd, robed from kirk. I had gone to school with Jasper. He had performed Jacey's marriage ceremony. He was compassionate— usually—but now his eyes were full of terror. My heart plum- meted. Terror in a human is not a good thing. In an elder it was deadly.

The little boy who had said "wow" was jerked away. His mother, Sennabel Schwartz, ran the library, and we had always been friendly. Now she stared at me, fear twisting her features. I caught sight of Durbarge and Thadd in the crowd. The assey was using a sat phone, his eyes on me.

Murmuring started far back in the crowd and rolled toward me. I caught sight of Ciana, looking from me to the crowd. Fear and horror etched her face. Fear for me. A hand swiped her back, out of the way. The little boy was pushed in the same direction and quickly swallowed by the crowd.

"Mage!" someone shouted.

Oh, no. Adrenaline flooded my veins.

Mage-fast, faster than human eyes could follow, I whirled and grabbed my luggage at the door. Behind me, I caught sight of Durbarge breaking into a run. Rupert slammed the shop door and locked it, shouting, "Run! Out back!"

I shot through the shop, into the stable. Zeddy stood there, saddling Homer for exercising. "Zeddy. Out of the way," I said, pulling my blade, advancing.

The huge boy looked from the blade held across my body, to the dobok, to the suitcases, to Homer, understanding dawning. And something like awe. "I ain't adjusted them stirrups yet. Whyn't you let me give you a leg up?" He cocked his head, listening. "Hurry, Miss Thorn. You got company coming." He laced his fingers and bent his very broad back, ready for my boot.

I hesitated only a moment before trusting him. I dropped the cases and placed my boot in his hands. As he tossed me up, I said, "Tell them I threatened you."

Zeddy handed me the cases and helped me tie them in place. "I reckon I can handle them people just fine, Miss Thorn. But Homer, he ain't warmed up." He opened the door and looked out. "They're coming. You best go!"

I kicked Homer into a lumbering trot. His long legs took me from the grooming area into the daylight and rounded the stable. I caught a blur of movement and color. Humans. They shouted in concert. "There she is!" "Stone the mage!" "Leave her alone!" "Get her!" "Keep her! Make her save the town!" "Gut her!"

Breath stuck in my throat, I kicked Homer again. Mentally, I found the fish used for the shield, and spoke the incantation that had amended its original conjure and allowed it to move as I moved. The shield, shaped like purple feathers to my mage-sight, snapped into place over Homer and me. The big black horse shied quickly left, then right. I controlled him, urging him uphill, my bags banging into my knees, hard. A shot sounded. Another.

"Where'd she go?"

"Tracks! She's headed up the Trine!"

A lucky bullet pinged off the shield. Quickly, I outdistanced them, Homer's long legs eating up the yards. But I was leaving a clear trail through mud and snow.

I moved Homer into a runnel. His hooves sank into wet ground still covering a layer of permafrost. The huge feet threw mud everywhere. I slowed him to a walk to keep splatters from creating a trail as easy to follow as spoor or hoof prints, and maneuvered him into a stream. The movement of water hid his tracks and would throw off his scent if they brought out bloodhounds. And they would.

Alternating between a bone-jarring trot and Homer's ground-eating walk, I planned. I would head north to the amethyst mound, uncover as much as I could carry to help me fight past the Darkness and over the peaks to the far side. With the amethyst, I might be able to reach that town of Ledger by tomorrow night. The stone had undeniably been damaged by the explosion that stripped it of power, but a quantity of it would still be more than all my amulets combined. I hoped.

The voices fell behind. I was safe. For now. When I licked my lips, I tasted salt. It was only then that I realized I was crying.

It took an hour of hard riding to reach the oval glen with its high mound at the west and the smaller cairn thirty feet beyond. Homer's wound packing held through the climb. If I needed blood for a working, I could rip the bandage off and create a fresh flow.

BLOODRING

Above me, the ice cap groaned, all around me water plashed and trickled, and overhead a cold wind whistled off the Trine. It was like a symphony composed by half-mad humans. That the Most High had composed it was scary.

This time I didn't leave Homer in the meadow, but brought him around the mound to the far side, tethered him to a low limb, and loosened his saddle girth. I climbed to the top of the mound and surveyed the area with mage-sight, studying it intently, instead of doing a general sweep. Except for a weak pulse in the depression of the recently disturbed ground, I saw nothing that would indicate the presence of the amethyst lodestone. There was even less to designate navcone. Of course, it might have helped if I knew what the heck navcone was.

I saw Ciana's distinctive footprints mixed with larger ones and my heart wrenched. Was it only yesterday I had a life, people to love? Tears threatened again but I forced them away. I'd grieve later, when it was safe. Much later. Steadying myself with a deep breath of the cold air, I leaned against a tree and combined a skim with mage-sight. Vertigo swelled and crested in me; gorge rose. I forced myself not to drop the two divergent senses, and slowly the nausea settled.

With the scan open, I again studied the surrounding terrain. Above the lavender light of the buried amethyst, I spotted a delicate tracery of something else. Not the red and black of Darkness; not the delicate rainbow tints of mage or seraph workings. But something else. Something I had never encountered in my interrupted studies. It appeared to be both here and not-here. It was a fog, a mist of energies that pulsed not at all. A golden vapor of . . . something. Like the final breath of a dying godling.

I couldn't quite bring it into focus, couldn't quite get a sense of its smell or structure, as if it was created just for the purpose of camouflage. Keeping it in sight was impossible. It kept slipping away. Struggling to follow the shape, I finally decided it was strongest at the disturbed side of the mound and at the cairn of stones, the cairn I was pretty sure a Stanhope had built. He had lifted the stones in my vision.

I had come to the mound for three reasons—to get some amethyst, to see what the cairn hid, and to see whether I could use it to flee. But the need to be on my way worried at my mind like fire ants, keeping me on edge.

I moved down the muddy mound, pulled off my gloves, and started digging barehanded. If only I had brought a shovel. Water. Food. I laughed sourly and the bitter sound echoed off the rocks. I quickly found a dozen stones and, because snowmelt didn't seem to affect them much, set them in a puddle to clean while I worked. When I had all I could carry easily, I filled in the hole in the hillside, so no one could say whether I had been back. Knuckles abraded, hands dangerously chilled, I risked drinking a mouthful of snowmelt. With the amethyst close, it wasn't so bad.

I retrieved the weapons case from the saddle, opened a velvet bag designed to hold a blade, and tumbled the amethyst in. I put one crystal the size of my fist in my chest pocket before closing and hanging the case across the saddle horn and sliding on my gloves. I thumbed a shield of protection over Homer, took up my walking stick, and climbed the cairn to its center.

I was close to where Rupert had sat the day before. Stretching my shoulders and back to relieve the strain, I thumbed a charmed circle and opened my scan. The crevices in the cairn and the ground around it were littered with black pebbles of energy, glowing opals of power I hadn't seen until I was directly on top of them. The cairn was booby-trapped. I pulled in my legs, circling them with my arms. The motion brought on vertigo and the world swirled around me.

The sun shifted in the sky, falling to dusk in a heartbeat. The *otherness* of the scan I had noted earlier had taken over. In vision-memory, I saw a young boy standing at the base of the stones, his face slack. His eyes were unfocused. He moved with the erratic, shuddering motion of a puppet as he opened a bag and lifted out a handful of the black opal stones. Walking around the cairn, around and around, he placed the booby traps into the fissures of the rocks. It was the daywalker, I remembered, but much younger.

As he walked, one of the opals rolled and fell a few inches onto the bolder below. A massive explosion followed. The daywalker ignored it, as if he hadn't seen the boulders blast apart. I understood that he slept, clearly under the control of a being not present, that I saw a vision, a record, from another time. Rupert had survived picking up one of the booby traps. We had been more than lucky not to have tripped one.

I checked around me, noting each of the opals, and focused on one. It glowed, a hot ball of brimstone, but was wrapped in a tiny net that coruscated. With gloved fingers, I lifted one, and it tried to push me away, like a magnet would push another away. Was that how we hadn't activated them? Because they resisted us?

The opal flared softly in my fingers, blue over its red heart. The opal was a Dark conjure, overlaid with a tracery of Light. A Darkness that had been amended in some way, just as I had amended the conjure of the shield, I thought. But this was a much more difficult alteration. I had never seen such a thing. So far as I knew, it wasn't possible.

I carefully set it down, wiped my fingers, and crossed my legs yogi fashion. I set the walking stick in my lap, breathed in deeply, and looked down, through the boulders of the cairn. Below me was a soft golden glow. Here, not-here. Present, not-present. Nausea swirled through me; gorge rose, hot and acidic. Just in time, I rolled to the side and vomited.

The blended scan dropped me, sickeningly fast, through the rocks, into the deeps. The smooth walls of a cavern appeared. No roots protruded from them, but a dull red glow permeated the limestone. A man was lying on a thin mattress on the ground, a worn blue blanket over him. *Lucas*. I smelled death and old blood and caught my breath, but his chest rose and fell. He was alive, barely. Beside him was an urn of water with a metal dipper. Nearby was a tray with crumbs on it, crumbs that glowed faintly blue.

I could feel cold rock under my palms, smell the stink of my last meal. With that to center me, I tried to pull back from the cell where Lucas was held, but dizziness snared me.

A form entered the cell through a crevice in the rock. It was the same boy who had bespelled the cairn, but older now, a young man, black hair in a long braid. The daywalker, dressed all in black. A small diamond brooch glimmered on its shirt, a rune weaving its tracery through the faceted stones, the working of a conjure visible with the blended scan. A rune of forgetting. That was why I kept forgetting him.

The bloodstone hilt warmed in my hand. Mentally, I passed the vision of the daywalker and its rune into the stone, storing the memory. I'd not forget, this time.

The creature knelt beside Lucas, placing an object near him. I concentrated on it, falling closer. It was a small black leather shoe. Ciana's shoe. My heart clenched. "It won't be long now," the daywalker said, stroking back Lucas' hair, tenderly, as a lover might. "Soon we will have all of you. And enough blood to bring our creation to life."

Lucas moved in his sleep, as if his dreams pained him, as if he battled monsters. The daywalker soothed Lucas' limbs to stillness, murmuring softly. It tilted Lucas' head back, cradling him tenderly, bending as if to share a kiss. As it opened its mouth, small fangs unhinged, snapping forward from its palette, like a serpent's. With a vicious motion, it sank the fangs into Lucas' neck. With one hand, the walker stroked Ciana's shoe like a talisman as he fed. With the other, he stroked Lucas' body.

No! Battle instincts flared. I tried to pull my blade, fingers on the surface gripping uselessly. Lucas sighed. I struggled, sliding away from the cell where the foulness was taking place. The *otherness* of the blended scan pulled at me, and my sight divided with a sickening lurch. Distantly, I heard the sound of my retching. In the visions, Lucas still slept, the sound of lips muted at his neck.

In the divided scan an earlier Lucas was carried, screaming, bleeding, fighting, from the surface into the earth and along the tunnels, showing me the way. Without thought, I stored the path in the bloodstone.

Near Lucas' prison was a second cell, this one glowing bright blue and red. Inside, a seraph lay on a bed of seraph feathers, his wings clipped to the wrist bones. He looked up at me with green eyes, glowing with red flecks like Christmas ornaments. *"Mage,"* he mouthed, struggling to rise as I swept past. In a third cell was a sleeping woman, the dark-haired mage, her limbs twitching, her dreams troubled.

"To me," a voice like bells whispered in my head. *"To me, little mage."* A tendril of blue reached for me through the walls of the prison, like the bluish light in the crumbs of food Lucas had eaten. It wrapped around my wrist in the here, not-here, and pulled. I was towed down, and down, until I saw a single glimmer of bluish purple. Far, far underground. *"To me."* The blue brightened and pulsed, just once, with hope, with desperate need. The tendril of energy beckoned, entreating, begging. I could hear sobs of relief. Of pain. *"Help me!"*

No. I'm being chased. I'm running, I thought back. A wailing fear erupted, the sound of *bells, bells, bells.* I retched again, my stomach empty, but the nausea overpowering. The blue holding my wrist tightened.

I was dragged toward her, through cubic acres of old stone, through the heart of the mountain. I jolted to a stop, slammed against a barrier of sticky red material, like a web of steel threads. It arrested my downward passage, halted and trapped me.

Just below, a handsbreadth beyond, was a glowing blue chamber. In the center was a bizarre and fearsome creature. I had expected a mage. Or a seraph. This was neither. This was unlike anything I had ever seen before. Unlike anything I had heard of before. This being, enclosed in a cavern guarded by an impenetrable tracery of Darkness, was a being of *Light*. It was one of the High Host, I was almost certain, but no seraph. Unlike the High Host, this one felt female. On the surface, my body curled up on the icy stone into a fetal position, the blade half freed in my hand. Below, I was watching *her*.

She had four faces on one head, each pointing in a different direction. One was human, one a cat face, one a bird of prey; the fourth face was the chiseled features of a seraph, softened into female curves. The entire rest of her body was feathered in pale lavender, a mishmash of body parts, demi-wings, hands, feet, breasts, all secured with reddish black chains that had seared into her flesh. And every part of her body was covered with eyes.

Eyes. Held in demon-iron chains. I blinked. Somewhere in the depths of my memory came a portion of scripture, from Ezekiel. "And every one had four faces: the first face was the face of a cherub, and the second face was the face of a human, and the third the face of a lion, and the fourth the face of an eagle." . . . "And their whole body, and their backs, and their hands, and their wings, and the wheels, were full of eyes round about."

That was it, whatever *it* was; this thing, this glowing being, was something unseen since ancient times. No mage had ever seen such a creature.

There was no question that she was a Power of Light, a member of the High Host, but an unknown being, unknown except for the four faces and the eyes . . . something about eyes . . . She turned those eyes up to me. All those eyes, begging. I focused on her chains. Huge demon-iron links bound her to the spelled heart chamber, a cell that had been carved out of the mountain just for her. *"Trapped,"* she belled. And I understood.

About me, the web thrummed. The vibrations grew stronger, faster. Coming toward me. *"You have been discovered,"* the bells whispered. *"Flee."* But to where?

I tried to pull free, but the strands held me fast. I tried to take a breath, but there was no air in the heart of the mountain. Like the being with the eyes, I was ensnared.

I knew what had happened. On the surface, I had forgotten to breathe. There, I was still lying on the cairn of stones. And someone had broken the charmed circle. Someone, some*thing*, was inside with me.

Wrath of angels, I was trapped. And I was dying.

A claw appeared beside me. It was more than six inches long. It plucked the red strand securing my face. I felt the thrum of the vibration through my whole body. Yet my body was on the surface. I wasn't here, not really. But the sense of my body was fading. My sight was telescoping down; I was passing out from lack of air.

Above the claw were barbs, the barbs of a spider's leg, though the leg was jointed differently from a spider's, with six joints that I could see. At each joint was a hooked claw. I was glad I couldn't see the rest of it. The strands vibrated again, and I realized that something else was heading my way. This one was bigger than the first. A lot bigger.

I felt a distant twinge on my face. Another. Thinking that the thing had touched me, I fought against the strands. The pain on my face came again, stinging. Another. Somewhere, someone was slapping me. It came from above me, on the surface.

Suddenly, a breath of air filled my lungs. Wonderful, moist, warm air. A breath had been forced into my body. Someone was beating my face and performing mouth-to-mouth on me, up on the surface. I wanted to laugh—someone was killing me and saving me all at once.

Pain could be used as a tether. I could follow the pain. Using the energy of the slaps, I pulled from the web that had caught me, slipping myself free of the strands. The claw reared back and plunged down, spearing through me. I wasn't present bodily, but my energy was there, and I felt something, some vital part of me, rip.

The pain of the beating forced the red strands to part, and I moved up through the boulder-heart of the mountain. Faster, I moved up and up straight toward the air and the sun and the sky. My scan was still open and I remembered to draw in energies from the stone, age-old energies from the time of creation. The energies that had sustained me once, before the amethyst gave itself to me. *"Yes, amethyst,"* the bells sang, far beneath me.

I burst into dying sunlight and high into the air. Saw my body, supine on the cairn of stones. A man bent over me, one hand holding the back of my head, his mouth on mine. I was sucked into the dark again with a horrendous pressure, into my body, a tight, stiff, unforgiving place. I took a breath. Opened my eyes. Looked into Thaddeus Bartholomew's face, flesh sparkling with kylen might.

His mouth was hard on mine, sealing my lips shut. It was his breath I had taken. Another filled my lungs. He pulled away and slapped my face, sharp ringing slaps. Three of them before I grunted, "Stop," and tried to lift my arms to defend myself.

He rocked back on his heels, face flushed, breathing hard. "Thank the Most High," he said, winded. "You weren't breathing." He looked at his hand, and the seraph ring was glowing, a bright light that faded quickly.

I blinked the scan off, seeing with only human eyes as I

groped both elbows under me. I pried myself into a half-sitting position. The smell of vomit was strong on the air. I wiped my mouth with a hand that felt as though it weighed a ton. The touch of the kylen was fresh on my lips. Faint heat trickled through my veins.

Thadd stood, eyes widening. A look of horror crossed his features and he backed away, down the cairn of stones. He wiped his hands down his jeans, as if to get the feel of me off his skin. "What are you doing?" he whispered.

Mage-heat. Once he took off the ring, the transformation of his body by his kylen genes had begun. Now, even with the ring in place, he felt the touch of a neomage, felt it in parts of him that had their own little minds. He thought I was doing it to him on purpose.

Gasping still, I chuckled at him, a breathy little laugh. His face suffused with color, growing even more red than when he bent over me. "It's not a love spell, you idiot," I wheezed. "If you got hot and bothered, it's because I'm a mage, you're kylen, and you used your ring to break a conjuring circle. You're going into heat." *But my own heat is subdued, subtle.* A thought for later, when I was sure I would keep breathing on my own.

"Keep heading north," he said, backing away, his feet missing all the little opals, as if they slid just to the side of his boots. "When you get over the Trine, disappear. I'll head them away from your trail." Thadd turned and strode to his horse, the bay he'd ridden before. With a single leap, he was mounted and heading down the Trine.

I looked around. He had come alone. Broken away from the searchers, or come before they could organize. He had come to help me, I realized. Thaddeus Bartholomew was a man of honor, even to a mage. And he had used an amulet with no training, no preparation. I wanted to call him back, but the taste of kylen burned on my mouth. It would be unkind and perhaps dangerous to call him. Legends said kylen youths, when they came into their gifts, could be treacherous. How much worse could a grown male be?

By the time I managed to get my knees under me, he was gone, and the sun was sitting on the peak of the mountain to the west. Sunset. I had to get out of here. But Ciana's shoe . . . Where had the daywalker gotten her shoe?

The memory of Rupert being accosted in the street, dragged away beneath a gray cloth, was brittle in my mind. And the daywalker's words, just before he bit into Lucas' neck. He wanted blood. Stanhope blood.

I could do nothing alone. But I wasn't alone. Not anymore. I remembered Raziel's words when he learned Lucas was in danger. "A quest," he'd said, with what looked like glee. Seraphs would protect Stanhopes, when they got around to it. Or if a mage called them in dire.

Against Thadd's good advice, I wouldn't be going over the Trine. I wouldn't be running away. Ciana was in danger. A daywalker wanted her blood. My fist circled the hilt of my walking-stick sword. I was going to war.

Chapter 21

†

I half crawled off the cairn, watching the booby traps. They slid slightly to one side for my feet. A wonderful conjure. I would have carried some with me, but I didn't know how they worked and didn't feel like exploding if I moved wrong.

When I stepped on the earth, the backlash of energies from the broken charmed circle snapped up my calves like static electricity, stinging. In the distance, I heard voices. Fear skittered up my spine. I ran to Homer, who stood dozing, safe beneath the shield. I broke it and tightened his girth before leading him to a sturdy branch. Climbing the limb, I jumped into the saddle and guided the Friesian uphill through the dusk.

Only when night fell did I look back. The voices had vanished. No lights were visible. If they had found my trail, they had lost me in the gloom. No sane human would spend a night on the Trine. They had gone back to town.

Feeling me shift in the saddle, Homer stopped and stubbornly set his feet at the edge of a clear, ice-rimmed pool that glowed sickly of air and water to my mage-sight. The big horse didn't like walking without a path, up an unknown mountain, after dark, navigating by moonlight. And though he trusted me, he didn't know I could see in the dark. I kicked his sides. He looked back at me, the white of one eye showing, clearly saying, *I ain't walking in the dark, lady.* Homer had a sense of humor, but bad timing. I kicked him again. He huffed a breath and bent to drink.

"Oh, all right," I said, hungry, feeling the cold wind through my cloak. "How's this?" Quickly, I threaded two tiny quartz rings to a saddle thong, thumped them on, and hung them down along Homer's legs. They brightened the ground enough that he gave a chest-heaving sigh and started uphill, his ground-covering pace faster than I could have walked for any length of time. I patted his massive shoulder. "Thanks," I whispered.

Two hours later, I caught a whiff of distant brimstone and sulfur. I opened my mage-sight and spotted the origin of the stink, still far uphill, the trail across broken ice. We had reached the ice cap and Homer had gone as far as he could.

I had discovered several things on the long ride. The silk-lined, padded leather cloak wasn't insulated enough for temps near the ice cap at night. A battle dobok wasn't comfortable riding gear, and battle boots didn't stay in stirrups well. I had blisters on my backside and my ankles hurt from being held at an unaccustomed angle. And I had been really, really stupid to have neglected to bring food for Homer and me. I was frozen through, thirsty, and hungry.

I let the Friesian drink icy water from a small creek, his haunches at a thirty-degree angle lower than his head. "This is it for you, old boy," I said, patting his shoulder and sliding to the ground. "I wish I had thought to bring you some feed. The water should hold you for a while, though."

I led him to a spot that was nearly flat and pulled the bit from his mouth. Looping the reins once around a twig, I loosened his girth and pulled an amulet containing a shield of protection. Spawn never turned down a free meal—they would stop and eat even in the midst of a major campaign. If they hunted tonight, I wanted them to bypass Homer.

"When you get hungry, pull the reins free and head home," I said to Homer. "You can break the shield anytime you want from the inside." Almost as if he understood me, Homer took a deep breath, relaxed onto three legs, letting his left hip go lax, and closed his eyes. I chuckled, the sound sad. "Hope you get to enjoy the nap." I lay my head on his warm shoulder and ran my hand along his side, fixing his scent and form in my mind. Tears stung, but I blinked them away. Leaning into him, I silently reviewed the last-ditch incantation I had come up with while on the ride.

There was nothing else to keep me with Homer. I secured all my weapons and draped myself in every amulet and charged stone I owned, emptying the jewelry bag, sliding the three crucifixes over my head for the help they might give. I patted the amethyst piece inside my dobok shirt, near my heart. Thumbing the shield over Homer, I pulled my leather cloak tightly around me, turned, and took the first steps uphill, north, toward hell.

It was near dawn and colder than winter when I reached the opening in the left peak of the Trine. Below me, Mineral City was invisible. Above, only a few stars still dotted the sky with hope. In front, the opening in the earth glowed a foul reddish shimmer visible only to mage-sight. The smells were sulfur, blood, old death, and brimstone. There were no sounds except the cracking and groaning of tortured, softening ice and the whistling wind.

Bracing myself on the lip of the pit, I stared inside and down. The ground near the opening was marked with the prints of many kinds of feet. The smell of death grew stronger as my gaze traveled in and down.

Old fears, kept at bay on the trek uphill, when every thought and sense was focused on the half-frozen ground and melting ice at my feet, reared their heads. I had been in a place like this. Four years old? Three? Too young to fight. Too small to get away. Weaponless. Bleeding. Lost in the dark.

Horror rippled over my flesh. The memory of spawn claws, tearing my skin. The smell of my blood. Under my dobok, my scars flared with white-hot pain and light, a tracery of old agony.

I remembered the sound of licking lips and gibbering, echoing off the rock all around me. Memories I had buried for decades arose, bombarding me. Standing in front of the entrance to a hellhole, I shivered uncontrollably.

I didn't have to do this. I could mount Homer and move laterally across the Trine and through the gap in the peaks. Ciana had a seraph amulet. She'd be safe. If she had time to call for help. If a seraph was nearby and heard her. If . . . But even if they were close by and answered in a heartbeat, she would likely be injured, and certainly terrified. And humans seldom survived a spawn attack.

I knelt and drank from a runnel, splashing my face in snowmelt. There was a time that would have drained me. Now I felt nothing—except the icy certainty of failure and death. Even with the amethyst to supplement my energies, I wouldn't win here. Not alone. And this time, whether help came or not, there would be no respite, no mercy. This time when I called "mage in dire," I would probably die, whether fighting alongside answering seraphs, or after, in Enclave. If they answered. If they heard me from the pit.

When I tried to stand, vertigo gripped me. Suddenly I was underground, in a hellhole, trapped in the blackness of eternal night, in the past. Something held me there, as if I were pierced by a massive claw on a corkboard of dark threads. The cold stone had been rough at my back, a measure of safety in the fissure of rock. *Help me,* I prayed, hearing my child-voice. *Help me. Seraphs of the High Host. Seraphs of stone. Help me.*

The spawn passing by in the dark had laughed. My thirst grew, and my pain. I slept and waked and slept again. I called on the High Host, over and over, even as my voice gave out and hope died.

A bright light speared me, glaring through the tears in my eyes. *"Revealer of the rock,"* a voice said, a voice like bells and wind chimes, tender and full of love. *"I am here, little mage."* And then I was free, on the surface. In the healing hands of Lolo. That was all I remembered of the time underground, a prisoner. All that I remembered of my rescue. Except this time there was one more line, one new canto in the old memory. *Revealer of the rock.* I had heard that phrase before, recently, but I was too tired to remember where.

The dark and fear and horror had branded my entire life. I would do anything to save Ciana from that.

With the heel of my boot, I drew a small circle in the frozen mess of the pit entrance. Settling my cloak, I sat on a flat stone in the center of the conjuring circle. I placed the hunk of amethyst on the stone between my knees and the charged stones in a ring around it. I removed the necklace of amulets, laid them in the ring, and upended the walking stick, tip to the sky, with the bloodstone touching the mended prime.

With a finger, I closed the circle. Mage-sight opened. The stench of evil intensified. The peak glowed the ailing greenish yellow of snow, overlaid with the red and black of Darkness. Though I had never been to war, I had been taught how to prepare. I closed my eyes.

Swallowing, my throat still rough from retching, I began the ancient chant. "Stone and fire, water and air, blood and kin prevail. Wings and shield, dagger and sword, blood and kin prevail." Calm descended on me, as soft and gentle as the down beneath Raziel's wings. I chanted, breathing, feeling my heart beat, my blood pulse. I centered myself. Preparing for death.

The stone under my thighs dried and warmed, offering its strength to me. The stones and the amulets in the pile soaked up the strength of the mountain. Nothing came from the deeps to hunt. Nothing disturbed me. The last hours of the night passed.

The time in the circle with stone had restored me. Strength thrummed through me, almost as if I hadn't spent the night in the saddle. Almost as if I had rested the night before. Almost as if I had eaten. Almost as if I weren't terrified. I paced toward the opening to the pit, nimble as a dancer, muscles moving smoothly. I knew it wouldn't last. If the seraphs didn't hear me when I called "mage in dire," if they didn't come, I'd die. But right now, power slammed into me, coursed through my veins, and with blades held in a perfect lion rampant, one blade vertical, one horizontal, I entered the hellhole.

In mage-sight the lair of Darkness was bright with scintillating energies, red, the dull yellow of lichen beneath the glow of small crawling things. I moved down, into the heart of the pit. The smell of sulfur grew stronger, the air more dense. I coughed. And heard a soft click just ahead. Followed by the skittering of padded feet on stone. Outside, though the sky was bright gray with dawn, the sun was still below the horizon. Spawn were still awake. Now or never . . .

I sang out a battle challenge as I advanced, placing my feet carefully on the downward-leaning stone floor. "I, the mage which goeth to war, I, yes I, the stone mage, I join battle with Darkness! Battle in the mount of the Trine! Battle which the Lord commanded!"

Three spawn appeared in the tunnel before me, reddish Darkness with heads like insects, fanged and pincer-clawed, bodies like moles, human-shaped hands but mailed with scales and six-inch claws, three-toed feet. One sniffed, a wide smile breaking across his maw. "Mage," it mangled through its many teeth. They all sniffed. And attacked, howling, screeching, piercing cries for blood.

I lifted both arms in the swan, slicing, blades in clean arcs. A forearm reached for me and I drew first blood. Spawn bones jarred the blade, but the hand fell, twitching to the tunnel floor. With the longsword, I cut higher, prepared this time for the bone jolt. The spawn fell, head rolling, spine severed. Another, his blood a spurting geyser. The third, bodies left writhing like snakes, all beheaded. Darkness could heal of anything except beheading.

Dozens more replaced them. Hundreds screamed from the deeps. Sword and blade slicing and hacking, I moved down into the pit. It was a simple plan. Fight until they wounded me enough for me to call "mage in dire," close enough to need help, and yet far enough from death for me to survive. A dicey position. I laughed, and the sound echoed off the limestone, louder, more harsh than the yowls of spawn. The hoard paused, shifted, as if the laughter frightened them far more than the battle challenge I had issued. So I laughed again. And beheaded two with a single strike.

Ichor splattered, burning my face. My gloves were slippery with spawn blood, reeking of death and battle. It tried to eat through the leather to my skin. But the dobok and leather were mage-touched, conjured against their spawn fluid.

The smallest, braver and more stupid than the others, ducked in under my blades and bit into my thigh. Its teeth ripped through the cloth and the flesh above my knee. With a single swipe, I cut it in two. It fell at my feet. The dobok stopped its saliva, but the scent of my blood filled the channel as it trickled down my leg. Spawn licked their chops and chattered with hunger. I cut off the leg of one who leaned too close. When I danced back, the spawn nearest tore into it with ravenous teeth, blocking the tunnel for an instant. Until now, I hadn't noticed, but they were eating their own fallen. The smell of blood was too much an invitation for them to resist.

Ahead, the tunnel forked and I recognized the one to the left. It was where they had taken Lucas. I shouted and spun, racing to rescue my ex-husband, the man who had betrayed me. The father of the child of my heart. A Stanhope the seraphs owed a blood debt. His scent was on the air, remembered, beloved. An ache started in my chest. The amethyst throbbed in time with the pain.

Spawn chased behind me, their breath foul on my neck. From a junction of tunnels, more spawn poured. I took a blow to my left arm, and only the thong around my wrist let me keep the kris as it dangled free from my numbed fingers.

Cutting, slashing, a revenger of blood, I cleared a swath before me. Passageways opened left and right and ahead. I sensed Lucas, one level below me. With his cell fixed in my mind, I turned left and down. Teeth and claws lacerated me. Sulfur and acid filled the air. My lungs burned. My cloak smoldered. My exposed flesh seared. I cut and sliced and hacked. My left hand tingled as feeling returned to it.

I veered again, forced right by hoards of spawn, my left arm held to my waist. The scent of Lucas faded. The battle entered more narrow burrows. My left hand ached but I lifted the blade, removing a spawn's arms with a single strike. I had lost my way, off course in the smoke and dark. Ahead, a form took shape. I knew him, even in the night of underground, knew him by the smell of his spelled blood. The half-breed who had attacked Rupert.

"Mage," he said. "You take my blood and enter the deeps. I claim you."

Without a word I met his blade, knowing that only speed would save me. Remembering his strength from the alley, I twisted and brought both blades down as if to scissor his torso.

As his weapons swept up in defense, I pivoted on my left heel and ducked under his arm. I stabbed between the third and fourth ribs, aiming for his heart. But the blade slid along his rib cage, and he was suddenly behind me. His boot caught the back of my heel and swept up. I was falling.

I hit the ground with a whump that blasted the air from my lungs, leaving me breathless, stunned. The half-breed laughed, standing over me, feet to either side of my waist, staring down at me, his blades poised over my heart. "You're sloppy, light mage.

"Back!" he shouted when a spawn dashed in, teeth gnashing down. His sword took off its head and the others pulled it back to feast.

I found a breath—blessed, wonderful air. It scoured my tormented throat, filling my lungs with life. In the millisecond his attention wasn't fully focused on me, I shifted my grip on the shortsword. I might have a—

His eyes met mine and he touched the point of his sword to my throat. In what sounded like a sloppy holiday-card poem, he chanted quickly, "Blood for blood and life for life. Yours belongs to my battle knife." He thrust down. I spasmed beneath him, shock tightening my entire body in a single contraction. My blood gushed from the wound I didn't yet feel. But I was still breathing, still seeing. Still—

The half-breed bent and collected my blood in a small cup. Demon-silver burned my flesh. I arched to the side, mage-fast, and brought my blade up between his legs, cutting through, cutting deep. The blade stopped, buried in bone. He howled and fell back.

The spawn scattered as he fell, cursing. I stepped over him and killed a human raising a sword behind him. The spawn raced away, squealing. The human fell. The half-breed was gone in a trail of blood.

For a moment, I was alone. I rested against the wall of a

tunnel, sucking in deep breaths, wishing I had a gallon of water. Wishing I could call a seraph, tasting blood in my mouth. Feeling it running down my leg. Knowing it wasn't enough to call "mage in dire." The lost little girl I had once been whimpered deep in my mind, sapping my strength. I forced the sounds of her—my—fear and pain away.

In the harsh atmosphere, my throat was raw, my voice gone. The rush of energy from the time in the circle had faded and my arms were heavy, the strength drain far more intense than I had projected. Or had I been underground far longer than I thought? The recent past was already half forgotten, blurred with blood and pain and fear. My sword blades dropped, no longer a fast swish of mage-brawn. They touched the ground at my feet.

Something bit my shoulder through my cloak, teeth snagging on the leather. I knew it happened, but I felt no pain. I felt nothing. With a backhanded fist, I knocked the thing loose and spun to take its head. The horde had rallied and swarmed at my back. I killed two. Three. The bodies were dragged back, but now the swarm kept coming. I heard whimpering with each sword thrust, nightmare whimpers, my own whimpers, remembered from so long ago. I clamped down on my vocal cords to stop the sound.

Spawn sniggered and slashed with claws and teeth. None of the cuts were deep, but I was losing blood from each shallow wound. My old scars ached. Fear had grown and solidified. And still I fought. What else could I do?

I lost track of time. I was hopelessly off course, Lucas' prison cell entrance somewhere behind me, below me, in the earth. Maybe. Surely I hadn't moved lower than his prison. I killed another human, his eyes glowing red with willing possession, a Dark human, bred in this hellhole. As he died, a black cloud poured out with his blood, gathered, and drifted away along the floor.

BLOODRING

Again, the spawn paused and withdrew. My blades dipped, points grinding on the stony ground, slippery with spawn blood, human blood, my blood. I panted, heart racing. Sweat and blood had mixed into a noxious mire on my skin. My battle lust was used up. The bloodlust, dead.

Spawn giggled at my side and I lifted the short blade, cutting off a clawed hand. Without the lust, I slung the blades without grace, a slowing metronome. I killed another. Killed a half-breed. Killed another human, stepping over his body as if he counted as nothing. Once more, I found myself alone, uncertain where I was or how I had gotten there.

I had taken a cut right through the cloak to my left arm, up high on the deltoid. Fresh blood caked my clothes and flesh. I was gasping for breath and stumbled hard. One knee hit the stony earth. I had lost blood. A lot of it. Enough of it. I managed a cold smile. Forcing myself back to my feet, I took a breath that ached and lifted my arms and began calling, "Mage in battle, mage in dire; seraphs, come with holy fire."

The spawn went mad, attacking in such great numbers, I was forced into a crevice to protect my back and sides. Chanting the lines of calling, I beat back the attack, severing limbs. I took another wound, this one along my right forearm. Long minutes passed. I had no breath to continue the chant and fell silent. Seraphs hadn't come. They weren't coming. But I was too stubborn to just stop and let the spawn kill me. I hacked and cut, breath heavy.

Sometime later, they withdrew. I smelled Lucas' scent, the reek of blood and sickness, yet cleaner than the gore-tainted air. A glimmer of an idea sparked in my mind. Drawing on my prime amulet, I spun from the fissure and around a corner toward Lucas. He was close. And he was a Stanhope, whose blood was precious to the High Host.

As if they knew what I planned, the spawn returned, enraged. With the strength of hope, I fought on. Twice my shortsword caught on bone and I paused to pull it free. Each time teeth shredded my body, but I used the instant of time to draw and loose throwing blades. When I reached the fallen spawn, I retrieved the blades, but they weren't going to be enough to save Lucas. Not alone. I was going to die here. Torn apart by spawn. Eaten. As glorious deaths went, this one sucked Habbiel's pearly, scabrous toes.

A whirlwind knocked me down, into the pit wall, bruising my shoulder, scraping my palm. I landed on my knees. Blinked to clear my eyes and head.

Wings, long feathers of white and purple, soft down a pale lavender, swept past. The nervure along the underwing was a purple so bright, it glowed to my mage-sight. *Seraph . . . Wrath of angels*, it was a seraph. The wind and dust of his passing beat at me, filled the channel with the scent of pepper and mint. In his wake were left spawn bodies, smoldering into ash. Hoarse, I coughed, covering my eyes, hearing wings beating, a sword clashing from deep in the pit. I was the only living thing in the underground corridor.

The noise of war and death rose to me. The screams of spawn swirled on the air. His name came to me as I clawed my way up the pit wall to my feet. Zadkiel, the righteousness of God, the seraph of transmutation, the seraph of solace and gentleness, the right hand of Michael, had come to do battle. I laughed, the tone more croaking sob than joy.

The scent of holy fire and demon-blood filled the air, a mix of flowers blooming and spring winds, and a sulfurous stench, acidic and burning as if the odors themselves fought. Brimstone and smoke were carried on a swirling spring breeze, the smell of death, rank and moldering, and bright like copper and pepper.

I could sense the opening to the pit behind me, but I couldn't see anything in the smoke and the dark. Minutes passed as I rested against the wall of the tunnel. The sounds of battle changed, growing intense and fierce. Triumphant calls, like deep bells, resonated through the rock and the air. I rolled so my back was to the wall and gulped what air there was, though my throat ached with the effort and the passage of smoke in my lungs.

"Little mage," a voice tinkled in my mind. *"Fight. Call for mage in dire yet again."*

"Why?" I gasped to the voice. "The seraph who fought next to ArchSeraph Michael is in here, fighting."

"He is wounded," the voice breathed, a susurration of silk and melodious brass bells. The voice of Malashe-el's Mistress? *A trap. Call mage in dire.*

The High Host had to be getting tired of hearing from me. How many times could one unlicensed witchy-woman call for help? Was there a limit? I chuckled, the sound counterfeit, but tougher, stronger than I would have thought. My amulets throbbed once, renewed with lavender light, though dull in comparison to their original strength.

Sounds of scuttling raced toward me. *Spawn. Seraph stones . . .*

Energy seeped through me, burning life in veins blistered by war. Power, strength from the Mistress, though she had hardly any left to share, hoarded strength she gave to me. I pushed away from the wall where Zadkiel had tossed me, and called a battle cry, a croaking challenge. On legs like rubber, I ran through the dark to meet them, toward Lucas, chanting, "Mage in battle, mage in dire; seraphs, come with holy fire."

The words made me laugh, and in some small part of my brain, I knew toxic fumes were making me crazy. Nothing happened in response to my plea except that spawn surrounded me, this time forming a ring just outside my sword's reach. One darted in behind, and I swiveled, blade just missing him. He cackled as he scurried back to safety. "Devious little buggers have figured out how to stay alive, haven't you?" The only reply was the red eyes that watched me, hungry.

"Use the mountain," the voice said.

"What mountain?" I asked. And then I knew and laughed again at my own blind stupidity. I was underground, under tons of rock—my element to call. Lost in battle lust, linked to the stone against my chest, I hadn't had a brain to think with; trapped in fear and memory nightmares, I hadn't recalled what I had become since that time as a child, when I was prisoner and alone in the dark. "I've never done this before," I croaked aloud to the unknown voice in my head.

"Call . . ."

I spun in the whirlwind figure, my cloak flaring out, blades slashing, slowed from injuries. It was a fancy move, seldom useful except to gain time against numerous opponents. To make them pause. The spawn jumped back. Planting my feet firmly, I crossed the swords at my torso with a soft clink. Pressed the bloodstone handle of the walking stick into the blood caked on my thigh.

I threw open my senses, mage-sight, and mind-skim, and that something else, that *otherness* I hadn't known I possessed, the sense I couldn't name that was part of the blended scan. With it, I drew on the power of stone. Tons of stone, the entire bloody freaking heart of the Trine.

Colors detonated in my mind and I stumbled to my knees. Smells of Light and Dark blasted their way through my head and lungs. Strength exploded through me. As teeth tore into me, I called again, a *sending* with all the power of a stone mountain at my disposal. "Mage in battle, mage in dire, seraphs, come with holy fire."

The clash of wings and steel and the screech of dying spawn were instantaneous. Scarlet plumage and golden battle armor flashed past. Reddish irises locked to mine a bare moment. A sword rose and a hand shoved me against the wall, out of the way. *Raziel.*

Behind him were other feathered forms, armor glowing with Light. Winged warriors, swords held high. Screams ripped through the air, and a wind like a tornado, a gale that smelled of lilies and honey and chocolate and roses, an explosion of Light in all the hues of the rainbow. The smell and might of seraphs, many seraphs, filled the passage and dropped me again to my knees. Mage-heat called to me.

"Go, little mage," Raziel called, his voice a caress on the air. "The sun is high. Back to the surface. To safety. I have lighted the way."

Voice nothing more than a grinding whisper, I said, "Lucas Stanhope, the progeny of Mole Man, an unwilling mage, and other beings of Light are here, prisoners." Raziel screamed, a sound of challenge, demand, and death to his enemies. In an instant, he vanished.

Blinking slowly, my eyes gritty and aching, I looked around. The spawn were gone, even the blistered corpses that had littered the floor of the cavern. The scent of sulfur was a faint taint, the air blowing with spring and bakeries and candy. The mage-heat that had waked at the presence of so many seraphs wilted and died, along with the last of my borrowed energy.

To my right, a trail of blue mist rested on the floor, coiling slowly as if contained in an invisible tube. I lowered my weapons, too tired to sheathe them. My hands had gripped the hilts so long, they were cramped closed, skin of knuckles showing white through torn gloves, soot, and dried blood.

Every skin cell, every strand of muscle, every tooth, nail, ligament, and sinew hurt. My bones ached. My nerves thrummed with exhaustion. My pulse slowed to a dull, despondent, irregular beat. Each breath I took burned. Each wound throbbed. I looked down at myself, mage-sight showing me the dull glow of my own blood and devil-spawn blood, and dried daywalker blood and human blood and half-breed blood. Blood everywhere.

My hair hung in straggles, caked with it. My dobok was a burned and slashed tatter, my skin showing through the scorched places, a fiery blistered red.

I sighed, and from somewhere, some deep inner spring of resiliency, found the strength to lift my right foot and take a step. After that, I took another, and another, all uphill, following the blue marker back to the surface.

Chapter 22

†

I stepped through the opening into the glare of noonday sun, so bright it blinded me. And was shoved to my face in the dirt, cheek ground into the earth. I caught a whiff of human. A knee landed in the small of my back, driving my breath out with a grunt. My lungs wheezed as my cloak was torn away and my hands were twisted behind my back, wrists secured in handcuffs, ratcheted tight. *Seraph stones. Humans.*

I was patted down with rough, crude, groping hands and yanked to my feet by my hair and my injured shoulder. I yelped. And came face-to-face with Captain Durbarge, AAS investigator.

With a balled fist, he ripped away my amulets. The other fist, he buried in my gut. I bent over, retching. Pain spiraled out, settling in each cut, each burn. My flesh glowed so bright even the humans blinked. Durbarge lifted the crucifixes from a fold of my dobok and stared at them, burned and crusted over. I had forgotten I wore them.

"A Christian mage? Not possible." He let go the crosses and they bounced on my chest. They too were clotted with blood. He spotted the lump in my shirt and took a knife—one of mine, the bastard—and cut open my dobok. The amethyst fell out and bounced on the ground. It was pale, drained, almost colorless, like the quartz that filled the mountains all around. Had I used that much of its strength while underground? Yeah. Likely. Durbarge kicked it away, and it rattled a few feet down the slope.

"Lock her up," he barked. I was lifted off my feet and half carried, half dragged to a helicopter. A cruel hand jerked me up inside by one forearm, wrenched behind my back to my shoulder blades. Pain spiked through my shoulders and chest. Inside the helo was a steel cage, about three feet on a side. The door swung open and I was thrown inside.

I landed hard, face on cold mesh. I smelled dog and cat and mage and human, smells mingled, full of waste and pain. I was in a dog cage. I was so tired, I slumped down and—amazingly, astoundingly—I fell asleep.

My world rattled, waking me. I opened my eyes to find steel frozen to my face. Cold had stiffened me into a tight ball. I tore surface skin on my cheek as I lifted my head and sat up, legs cramping as I scuttled upright. A foot kicked the cage again. Bleary-eyed, I craned my stiff neck up and met the face of a stranger, callous, fleshy features, blue eyes, blond hair. He squatted down to me, inspecting me like the dog he had made me.

"What's your name, mage?"

I tried to form words, but my throat was too dry to speak. Thirst undulated through me, snaking after pathways of pain. Shivers gripped muscles already tortured with combat. "Water," I mouthed. When he frowned, indicating he had no intention of giving a neomage anything, I affected a shrug and rolled back down, closing my eyes. He stood and kicked the cage again and again, rattling my teeth, sending the dog cage bounding across the floor.

With my arms bound, I couldn't protect myself. The most I

could do was brace my legs and shoulders. Gritting my teeth, I kept my eyes slit nearly closed, ignoring the treatment. If that was all I got from an assey today, I could count myself lucky. Red-hot pokers and sharp blades would be next.

"Stop that, Richards!"

I swiveled my head and watched through matted hair as Durbarge called off his toady.

"Give her some water. And leave her alone. I have plans for her."

I was sure none of those plans called for treating my wounds or feeding me or letting me take a bath. A water bottle was passed through the food slot, a narrow space where a pet's food tray would normally have been passed. No one bothered to take off my shackles so I could drink. Bastards. As if hearing my thoughts, Richards laughed softly and walked away.

At the sight of the water sloshing gently in the bottle, fury flamed in me, a tiny wick of warmth. Weapons. I needed weapons. Anything stone. I shivered in the cold, my entire body shuddering, teeth clacking. I looked down at the crucifixes bouncing on my chest with the motion. All were caked in blood and gore. One was partially melted and nicked. Another was charred and tarnished, crusted over with a white film. It was a tigereye and sterling Jesus on a wooden setting. I grinned, baring teeth at Richards' back. Stupid humans had left a stone mage a weapon. I looked at the bottle again and could tell it was well water. "Well, crack the Stone of Ages," I whispered, swearing on Saint Peter's head, a branding offense, if an elder should ever hear me.

I bounced against the back of the cage once, and again, rattling the tiny cell, letting the silver chain twist and twirl with the motion. The crucifix bounced with me, flipping over. The body of the dead Christ landed on my burned and lacerated skin, squarely on a cut crusted over with my blood. The tigereye flared. I closed my eyes and sank into the stone, ad-libbing under my breath. "Body shaped and formed of stone, fill my flesh and ease my pain. Make the power from before time answer to my call."

The tigereye warmed on my skin, the trickle of energy soothing a bit, just enough to take the edge off pain and thirst, like a handful of aspirin might take the edge off broken bones. But it was enough for me to think, and my shivers eased.

Neomages are smaller than humans. A lot smaller, in my case. The size of the dog cage wasn't as much an impediment to me as it would have been to a human. I turned onto my back and nudged my arms down, below my hips. Muscles abused in fighting, and then shackled in an unnatural position, tore and pulled, hurting like I was being beaten again. I ignored the misery and strained against the handcuffs. Muscle-ripping moments later, I got my hands under my backside and paused to take a breath. Though I couldn't see him through the mass of hair that had loosed from the braid, I heard Richards chuckle again. "She's a feisty one, ain't she?"

I shook my hair away and saw the man standing near a bench along the side wall of the helicopter. Beside him sprawled another human. I remembered him instantly from the dance, where his eyes met mine in challenge and heated sexuality. Eli. The miner. His mouth quirked down in a frown at Richards' words.

With a booted foot, Richards nudged my cage, staring at the slice Durbarge had made in my dobok, retrieving the amethyst. The upper curve of my breast was exposed, skin prickled in cold. He spoke so it wouldn't carry. "Durbarge has plans for you, witch. And when he's done, you and me are going for a little ride."

I didn't think he meant a carriage ride through the park. I blew my hair from my face and grinned up at him, showing my teeth, spearing him with my eyes. "Good," I said, voice scratchy with thirst. "Because I'll use that ride to turn you into a mule. And I'll eat the severed parts."

BLOODRING

Eli chuckled. Richards paled and stepped back, before kicking the cage with enough force to send it into the rear wall of the helicopter. I laughed and wanted to add, "With fava beans and a good Chianti," but I couldn't remember the exact quote and I figured he wouldn't know the Pre-Ap movie reference anyway.

When Richards had left the chopper, and as Eli watched with a modicum of interest, I pulled my backside, hips, and thighs through the cuffs, bent my knees, and slid my booted feet through. Taking the bottle in my stiff fingers, I opened it and drank, finishing off half the bottle in three swallows. My wrists were bleeding, fresh trickles running down my forearms. Fresh blood, water, a nugget of stone. I was practically free. I drained the water except for a swallow I might need for a later conjure, and resealed it. The twist cap was made of thin metal and might make a good pick if I could figure out how to roll the metal small enough.

The helo began to shake, a fine vibration through my skin and teeth. I rolled to my side, face to the icy mesh, and looked out the chopper door. Seraphs burst from the mouth of the hellhole, scarlet Raziel in the lead. Five seraphs followed.

Each seraph shouted a victory cry, and each carried a body. Raziel carried Lucas, fulfilling his promise to Ciana and to the memory of Benaiah Stanhope's sacrifice. The second seraph carried a dark-haired mage, as did the third, and the last. The fourth seraph carried a human child. No one carried the many-eyed being trapped in the heart of the mountain. No one carried the seraph with clipped wings. My shoulders slumped, my eyes on the sky. Six seraphs. I was certain of my count by the smell of Lucas' blood and by the mage-heat beginning to swell on the breeze. And by the gibbering insanity that pierced me as the neomages' minds thrust into mine. *"Fear, rescue, healing, death, horror, horror, horror, rescued, saved, saved!"* I curled into a ball, hearing a thin mewling. *No. Not again.* The thought was swept away, into the minds of the mages in the sky.

One mind was lucid, still sane, and I followed her thoughts. *"High above the pit of hell, we hover, wings beating the earth with wind. Seraphs throw back their heads, shouting in a language of tinkling cymbals, the gongs of church bells, the blare of a ram's horn. With a sweep of wings, we tear straight up toward the sun, the glorious sun. We fly a complicated pattern, a Celtic knot in motion, dizzying, euphoric. We separate, dive toward a city low on a mountain, a city with a river running through it. We are cradled like babies in their arms. . . ."*

And they were gone. I returned to myself, remembering that cry, that paean of victory. And I remembered Raziel, his beautiful face, the feel of his smooth arms and his down-covered chest beneath the battle armor. His smell, like honey and chocolate. I remembered being carried, a child, safe in his arms, when he rescued me from the deeps. Raziel, the revealer of the rock, the seraph who most often went underground, taking the war to the Darkness in its lairs. He had saved me once, when I was a child, lost underground. Now he deserted me.

The sky cleared. Durbarge jumped into the helo, landing on a bent knee, the other out behind him. I watched him, waiting.

"We're done here. Let's get going."

"What about Zadkiel?" I asked.

Durbarge's face was colder than the air. "Don't sully a seraph name with your mouth, witch. All the seraphs are back to the surface. All of them."

"Six of them. He's still below. He came through first, didn't you see? And where did you ever hear of seraphs doing anything in groups of six?" *Fool,* I wanted to add, but didn't. Maybe I was finding wisdom before I died.

Eli quirked that fast grin at me and slouched deeper into the hard wall of the chopper. "Lady's got a point," he said. "I counted six."

Doubt flashed across Durbarge's face before he turned away. "Belay that. Get me a sat phone." And he was gone. Which was a good thing. I needed time to get away. Once I was in a se-cure cage, a real jail cell, back among the asseys, I was dead.

The helo emptied except for Eli. The miner let his amber eyes trace over me and settle on the crosses against my chest. His lips pursed with amusement and he met my eyes once as he swiveled along the bench, lay down, and settled his hat over his face. Cocking one leg against the chopper wall, Eli laced his fin-gers across his chest and released a deep breath. "Next time we meet, think about whipped cream and a saddle. It could be fun," he said. "Long day. Think I'll take a nap."

Whipped cream and a saddle? I was too tired to laugh. I took the small cross in my hands, pressing the charred tigereye against the cage lock. The spit of energy that had followed the water and the use of the tigereye was gone, and I couldn't think of a single incantation to open the lock. I wasn't even sure that there was one. How did you tell a rock to stick its head into a tiny opening and turn the tumblers? *Were* there even tumblers in this tiny lock? Or only in a combination lock? There was too much I didn't know to risk an incantation.

"Okay," I said, abandoning words. I focused my mind on the tigereye. It flared, hot against my gloves, and melted into the locking mechanism. Hissing followed. I was glad the back of the cross was wood and not metal, or I would have been forced to drop the setting. As it was, the wood backing heated and charred again, smoking. A moment later, liquid metal dripped to the floor. And the lock clicked open.

When I pulled the cross back from the padlock, the stone and silver Christ were gone. Only scorched wood was left, still smoking in two places. I waved the wood until it cooled, and then tucked it into my shirt against my skin. As a memento, I'd make another tigereye cross and would place the setting into this damaged wood. If I lived.

I pressed the door of the mesh cage open. Rolled slowly out, into the body of the helicopter. It wasn't graceful, but it was sufficient. I was free. Eli snored softly, though I thought it sounded strangely like laughter.

Mind-skimming, I set all the locations of the humans firmly in my mind. I paused, body drawing up in surprise, at the scent of kylen. On the periphery. Thaddeus Bartholomew. I'd know his smell anywhere. *Coward.*

I closed off the skim and opened my sight. A strong glow wafted from a locked container on the floor. My weapons and my amulets. Stupid humans had put them together in one place. My cloak was there too. I heard Durbarge's voice from the rear of the helo. His telephone voice held the tone of a subordinate to an officer of higher ranking.

Lifting the box of weapons, I wrapped it in the cloak and grabbed a candy bar from the pilot's seat. I smelled Thadd on the candy. He'd left it there. For me. If I happened to get away. The smell of his small help was as clear as the sky outside. "Thanks," I muttered. "You're still a coward, but not totally *human.*" A compliment, to my way of thinking, especially after the last couple of hours.

There were three bottles of water too, lying haphazardly on the floor. I stuffed them into the wrapped cloak and slid out the open door to the ground on the far side of the chopper. I moved noiselessly into the brush, heading lateral to the cave. If I could get around the hellhole over the peak before dark, to the far side of the Trine, I could make it to safety. Then only a seraph could find me. In a quick sprint, I made it to cover.

Chapter 23

†

When I was a thousand feet lower on the mountain than the searchers, I stopped, dropped the box holding my blades, and pulled the blood-encrusted cloak over my chilled body. I drank two full bottles of water, braced against a tree, relieved myself and found a big rock to beat the locked box into smithereens. I took all my fear and frustration out on it, and it was a twisted, shattered mess when I stopped. I only quit then because I was afraid I'd damage my stuff inside.

Once it was open, I slipped the amulets around my neck, which had a soothing effect on the nerves vibrating in my flesh. More calm, I considered the handcuff chain. All I had that would weaken the steel was my fire amulet and the simple mental trick I had just discovered with the tigereye crucifix. I picked up a small pebble from near my feet, wrapped it with the fire amulet in a corner of my cloak, and pressed them together against the handcuff lock, heating the stone and directing it inside with a simple mental push. The granite melted, bubbled, and folded itself into the lock with a hot hiss that burned a hole in the conjured leather and blistered my fingers before I dropped it. The lock didn't open so much as dissolve and separate, liquid rock and metal dripping on the ground.

Hands free, I tossed the steel cuffs, pulled off the ratty battle gloves, and sucked on my fingers. When they hurt marginally less, I ate the candy bar while inspecting my weapons. The walking-stick sheath had suffered a long slice down the inlaid wood and was missing a small garnet cabochon that had decorated the tiny ring near the hilt. The blades were crusted with dried blood and needed cleaning and oiling, and also some time against a grinding wheel in the hands of a sword master. The longsword was nicked in two places and the kris edge had slivered, ready to form a two-inch-long chink.

I whirled both. They made a satisfying sound in the cold air. "Not great, but not bad."

From the landing site, I heard the cry go up. I was found out. I wondered how long it would take Eli to "discover" my trail. "A saddle and whipped cream?" I asked. My teeth showed in a grin at the images that suddenly came to mind. "I owe you, Eli Walker," I said to myself, "but maybe not that much."

I whirled the longsword again and knew if I needed to defend myself, they'd all better be clean, at least. I rinsed the blades one by one in snowmelt, scraped them with moss I found beneath a tree, and polished them on the cloak's lining. As I worked, the sugar high from the candy bar and the adrenaline flare from my escape burned out, leaving me exhausted, in pain from hundreds of small lacerations, bites, claw cuts, and bruises, groggy headed, and teary eyed. I was worn out, hungry, dirty, blood caked, and hurting.

Eventually, I could find and heat a springhead pool with an incantation, could steal food when I got near humans, could go among them wearing the glamour I had used at the swap meet, could start over somewhere new. If I got away. But where should I go? What in the name of the Most High would I do? I was trapped from above by men with a helicopter and guns, and from below by the town. I'd have to move at night. On foot. I couldn't make my way to any of the nearby roads or trails, as every traveler would be searched. Heading south meant passing close to the town—not the brightest thing I could do this week. It would take me two days to circle around the Trine and head back north, on a mountain where the resident Darkness had already had a taste of my blood, a thought that caused a soft gong of warning to sound in my head. But I could deal with that— whatever that was—later. Either way I went, I needed transportation. I thumbed on a healing amulet to lessen the ache of my battered body. I really needed two or three, but they might make me sleepy.

Homer's scent was carried on the breeze blowing down the Trine. He seemed to be on the move, as his scent was touched with sweat and hunger, but he was too far away for me to get to him, and suddenly I missed him. Loneliness slid through my ribs into my lungs like a demon-iron stiletto. I couldn't go back to my apartment for more supplies, because that was the first thing they would expect. If I stole a horse anywhere, they'd know it was me. And night was falling. I was toast.

But below me, only an hour's travel time away, was the mound of amethyst. Power I would need. I sheathed each of the weapons, pocketed my gloves, tied the strands of the dobok together at my breast, tightened my boots, threw on my torn cloak, and struck out south.

I reached the site of the mound just before sunset. I could hear voices on my trail. Eli the tracker hadn't promised not to chase me down, only to give me a head start. Generous of him, under the circumstances. I knelt near the mound and started to dig.

When I had seven fist-sized chunks of amethyst, each pulsing so slowly I feared they would stop between beats, taking my heartbeat and life with them, I stood. After rinsing them off, I tucked them into my dobok and drank more water. With the stone against my flesh, the pain of my myriad hurts lessened to bearable, and I felt more lucid, more prepared to strike off west and circle the Trine. First, however, I leaned against a tree and opened mage-sight to position each of the searchers.

There were twenty-one. Three carried charmed objects, making them asseys, one was out in front, moving downhill fast, likely Eli; and one glowed bright rainbow hues. Thadd. The kylen was just behind Eli. My own personal posse, chasing an armed and dangerous mage. I could smell them on the wind, human sweat and kylen blood, like a bakery. My stomach growled and I chuckled at my body's confusion; I patted my stomach, saying, "I'm supposed to mate with him, not have him for dinner." Though that presented interesting possibilities. I dropped the sight and took a deep breath.

Sulfur. In a single motion, I threw back the cloak and drew my sword from the walking stick. Adrenaline pumped once through my heart, slammed into my muscles, nerves, and bones, and my mage-sight reopened. I saw it. Saw them.

Where before there had been twenty-one forms, now there were dozens. They hadn't been there only a moment before. They *hadn't*. And then I saw a glimmering tracery of red fading from the hills. Half-breeds and humans bound to Darkness had been using a moving shield much like mine; evaporating red strands, shaped in a semicircle, corresponded to an ambush of the group chasing me. I hadn't seen them, smelled them, or sensed them. If I had blended the senses into a scan, would I have spotted them?

A shot rang out. And then hundreds, reverberating through the peaks. Screams echoed. The smell of anguish, blood, and death touched the breeze.

I stood in indecision. This was a perfect chance for a mage on the run. I could be miles away by the time they . . . The thought dropped away as I looked at the sun propped on the nearest peak. It would be dark in less than a half hour. Swarms of spawn would join the attack. By dawn, there would be noth-ing left to chase me. And humans couldn't call "human in dire," because they had souls. If they died, it was no skin off a seraph's back. They'd just go to heaven in a blaze of soul-bright glory or to judgment in a tuft of smoke. No one would help them. No one would help Thadd. Or Eli.

I almost swore, stopping myself just in time. Drawing on the amethyst next to my skin, I turned and raced uphill toward the battle. Overhead, I heard the rotor of a helicopter blade and felt the wind of it in my hair just as I spotted the conflict. The battle was a thousand yards from the mound and the amethyst. They had been close to retaking me.

The posse was situated on both sides of a small, twenty-foot cliff, a precipice I had skirted, but that they were rappelling down, making good time. Until someone shot the human who still hung, dangling midway down the cliff face, gently banging against the rock wall. Two more humans were dead at the crown of the rock face. The rest of them clustered at the base of the cliff, all except for Thadd and Eli, who were now behind me. The smell of human fear and blood was hot and pungent. The underlying scent of bowels that had released in violent death wafted through, dropping with the cooling air.

The Darkness was circled around them, three at the cliff top, creating cover fire as the rest darted to both sides closing in a pincer move. I dashed left, hard toward the heart of the Darkness. I jumped a fallen tree, rich with lichen. Splashed through a small, whitewater creek, breathing hard and deep. I saw the first Darkness.

They looked human, wore human clothes, jeans and flan-nel shirts and boots, but with mage-sight wide open and battle lust burning bright through my bones, they glinted red and black, swirls of Power and intent, black-fire eyes and mottled skin. All were spelled. Three carried demon-iron blades at their sides—daywalkers, leading the attack on this side, three in a cluster. They would move in groups of six if possible. That put three on the other side, closest to Thadd. One of them spotted me and grinned, showing pointed teeth.

Unlike the one with labradorite eyes, these walkers' eyes were untouched with blue, gleaming agate red. I filed this little tidbit away for later consideration. Fear pumped energy through my veins, riding adrenaline bareback. I sucked a breath and screamed, a loud, long battle cry. Without thought, without plan, I raced toward them. They leapt toward me, blades high.

Time dilated, slowing to a thick syrupy consistency, and I saw every movement with complete clarity; each shift and its consequences flitted through my mind, with time enough to consider and discard dangerous repercussions. I threw the walking-stick sheath at the first one, tangling his legs. Pulled a throwing knife and spun it at the second one. The blade caught the light, glinting.

The walker in the middle leaped high and past me. My sword clanged against his blade, throwing sparks. An instant later, I heard the throwing knife hit home and the leaper land. I drew my kris. Battle lust raged up and through me.

I shouted, blades ringing, paraphrasing a battle chant, "And they joined battle with them in the vale of the Trine! The men of war went to battle. Behold, I have given into thine hand the Dragon of Darkness, and his land: Begin to possess it, and contend with him in battle." The words were like bullets filled with holy water, like the hand of God himself wielding a weapon.

The daywalker who had tripped on my walking stick writhed on the ground at the scripture. I danced over him, slicing him along his sword arm. The smell of sulfur and acid filled the clearing, harsh and burning.

The other daywalker spun beneath my longsword, laughing, and he shouted back, paraphrasing only one name, "And the Lord said unto me, Distress not the Moabites, neither contend with them in battle: for I will *not* give thee of their land for a possession; because I have given Ar unto the children of the *dragon* for a possession."

Fear welled up in me, a deluge of terror. I faltered, hearing scripture from his foul mouth. A cut scored along my knuckles and down across my elbow. Deep in my mind, I heard a voice, the bell-like tones of another. *"He dares to profane the holy words!"*

It was the Being of Light in the mountain. "Even the Dark One knows scripture," I shouted, hearing her voice in my mind, meeting his blade with every clash. *"Yet now be strong . . . says the Lord; be strong, oh, Thorn, enfant de Lolo, the high priestess; and be strong, all mages of the land, says the Lord, and fight: for I am with you, says the Lord of hosts!"*

Riotous energies boiled up through me. I screamed with all the wildness of my heart. And I stroked and cut, sliced and hacked, moving from the swan into the clawed lion rampant, into the eagle. The clash of mage-steel and demon-iron rang through the clearing.

I heard the voice of bells in my head and repeated the words she gave me. "When thou go out to battle against thine enemies . . . be not afraid of them: for the Lord thy God is with thee. Be not afraid of the king of Dragons . . . be not afraid of him, says the Lord: for I am with you to save you, and to deliver you from his hand."

I drew blood with a reverse Zorro, scoring my blade across his thigh, over his ribs, and up across his face. For just an instant, he staggered, black blood on his clothes and flesh. "Die, demon. Die!" I shouted, thrusting with the kris. The curvy blade ripped through his shirt and into his chest. It hung there, the long nick caught on a rib. I spun away, letting momentum force the blade from his bones with a hard, grating rotation. Something snapped. Bone parted and broke. Muscle ripped. The hilt came away empty. The kris blade was gone, broken off inside him. Blood frothed with bubbles. It splashed my face, burning, and I roared with laughter, the sound like trumpets on the hillside.

The daywalker who had tripped thrust up with his blade. I drew a throwing blade and countered, sweeping his weapon up and away. With a single thrust of the sword, I pierced his heart. Disconnecting the throwing blade from his ribs with a twist, I whirled, cutting high as he fell. The sword took off his head in a gusher of black blood. Letting the momentum of the blade continue, I stepped forward and removed the head of the one I had disabled, the one who had chanted scripture at me.

They looked proper that way, headless and twitching. A black mist of sulfur and brimstone filled the clearing, burning my delicate nasal passages and the pathways to my lungs. The breath caught in my throat.

"Yet now be strong . . . says the Lord," the bells said in my head, *"and fight: for I am with you, says the Lord of hosts."*

I cut off the head of the last one. Blood was everywhere. It had splattered the ground where I stood, my chest heaving with exertion. It had sprayed my clothes, which steamed with acid. Burns and sword wounds slashed my skin. I screamed a cry of victory, blades outswept at my sides, head back, mouth to the sky. My cry echoed all along the hills. From high up, hidden in the rocks, the lynx screamed with me.

As the sound of victory died, another sound followed. From the hillsides all around came scream upon scream of challenge. I sucked in a breath and looked up. Dusk had fallen. Devil-spawn ringed the hills all around. Three-toed, clawed, scaled spawn with built-in blades in place of fingernails.

A snap sounded behind me. I whirled, bringing both blades up and across, a defensive move. It was Thaddeus. "You are one weird, crazy mage, you know that?" he said, a gun in each hand, eyes blazing chrysocolla, still angry. More than angry. Raging. "Do you know how many there are on the hill-sides? Do you?"

I laughed, the sound ripping through my chest, full of despair and challenge, both. "A lot. Too many. Your bullets filled with holy water?"

"Yeah. From the Dead Sea. We all carried special ammo. Not that it helped much."

"You're still alive, aren't you?" I said, chest heaving, lavender light blazing from my amulets. Beneath its palliative and strength was a growing, distant pain. "How many bullets?"

I followed Thadd's eyes around the hills, long shadows striping the ground, the sky a lovely shade of navy above. One star showed, hanging over the waning moon. All at once, the spawn's screaming stopped. An eerie silence fell on the clearing. Half a hundred of their eyes watched us, hungry. I counted the human and half-breed attackers. One walker was still alive, and fifteen Dark humans. Of the original posse sent to capture me, ten were left.

My fear, which had lightened for a moment, was a heavy stone of terror. Time, which had been so fluid, felt unyielding now, as ungiving as granite. As one, the spawn leaped down the mountain toward us. "Not enough," Thadd said, slamming his back against mine. Three shots sounded. "Call a seraph."

"I can't. Not yet," I said. "*I'm* not in *danger dire*. The posse isn't innocent. They struck an unarmed mage. If I call, you'll all die too."

"Gabriel's tears," he hissed. "We'll die anyway." Spawn reached us. Blades whirling, back-to-back with the Hand of the Law, I shifted into the move called the winged warrior. I drew blood and screamed a battle cry I hadn't remembered. "*Jehovah Sabaoth!*" echoed through the hillsides. "*Jehovah Sabaoth!*" For a single instant, the Darkness paused. And then they fell on us.

There were too many. Analytically, I knew I would die.

On another level, I was quaking with fear. On a third level, the demented level of a maniac, I was raging with fury. I *would not* give up. Not to these *things*. Three went down as I took their heads. The ground beneath us was perilously slippery with demon-blood. My battle boots smoked with the acid.

"Over there," Thadd said, pointing his blade south to the cairn of stones. "Up high."

"Yeah. But step where I step," I shouted as I ran toward the mound. "It's booby-trapped."

"Of course it is," he said, tone caustic. "Why not?"

Thadd raced at my left, shooting two spawn fast. As he changed clips, I took their heads, opening a path. As one unit, we raced to the cairn. Eli stood atop it, bleeding in a hundred places. I jumped up first, landed high, finding footing at the tracker's back. Thadd landed beside me and set his feet. His riding boots were smoking and made sticky sounds on the stones as he positioned himself. My battle boots instantly cooled and sealed against the acid of blood. I hadn't even noticed their protection until now.

Thadd fired three quick shots, dropping three. The hoard was upon us. I stabbed the first that bounded up the cairn, sliced his head from his torso. When he fell, he landed on a booby trap and his body exploded. Blood flew. Spawn screamed. And we fought. From uphill, Durbarge and six others raced. As I cut, I saw one more of the posse fall.

Time seemed to drag, as if it had a weight and pressure all its own. My arms tired, muscles growing heavy, slowing with fatigue. I was weakened, and hungry; adrenaline could fuel me for only so long. Though I had been partially restored when Raziel saved me, partially healed when I called on the Mountain, that healing was long gone. And still the Darkness came, humans and half-breeds in the mix. The height of the cairn slowed them, forced them to move up one by one or in small groups. Two humans triggered a booby trap and pieces went flying, taking with them a dozen spawn. That helped. But it wasn't enough.

"Why don't they just shoot us?" Eli shouted.

"Don't give them ideas," Thadd said.

"They have plans for us," I said. "Really, really bad plans."

"Well, crap," Eli said, shooting a human.

The mild expletive seemed wildly funny. Laughing together, we fought the pawns of the Power of the Trine as my fear gathered and throbbed and the night deepened. Shots rang through the peaks nearby. Blades flashed in the gathering night. We cut, and hacked, and killed. The air was full of the stench of Darkness and death, of rotting spawn meat and sulfur. The mountainside pealed with the screams of the wounded and the dying and with the ring of steel. Four more booby traps exploded, scattering body parts.

"I can't see," Eli shouted. "Where are they?"

Without answering, I thumbed on four light amulets and tossed them to the ground.

"Remind me I owe you a hot-oil massage and sex in a hot tub, mage," he said. I felt Thadd's reaction but didn't look around. In a circle around us, six spawn attacked as one. Spawn were fast but stupid, easily dispatched. They won in battle through sheer numbers, *not* tactics. By one battle estimate, a thousand spawn died for every mage.

When a lull came in the combat, Durbarge and three others reached us, jumping up on the lower stones of the cairn. I dropped my arms, too tired to hold the blades at ready. My breath was an arrhythmic pain, my heart ached with each beat. My skin stung from splatters of acid blood. With my mage-vision, I estimated fifty bodies.

"Is it true that mages can call for seraphic help?" Eli shouted as rock shards fell.

"They hit her when she was unarmed," Thadd shouted

back, shooting two more, again changing magazines. "That makes us evil or something. And this is my last magazine."

Durbarge looked around at that. He had taken a blade in his right eye. It was gone, his face engraved with agony, gore spilling down his face.

"What about me?" Eli said. "I let you go. Doesn't that make me innocent? 'Cause I'm bleeding like a stuck pig over here."

"Yeah, and I put your things in easy reach," Thadd said.

I laughed, the sound wheezing. Durbarge computed both comments. I could see an intent to shoot me form, and I spun my longsword. The thought entered his mind and passed on through. Any mage was a better warrior than he, and he knew it. Self-preservation saved him. I whipped the sword in an arc, back under my arm. Belatedly, his eyes widened.

We would all die without seraphic help. I needed to call on them, even if this time it meant I'd die, but I couldn't. No innocent was near death. I had to wait until Thadd or Eli was mortally injured. Compulsion held my tongue.

"They will take you in a single rush this time. You must call on my wheels." The words belled in my mind.

"Your what?" I said, as spawn circled us.

"Call on them. Call on the navcone. Call on my wheels."

"That helps a lot," I muttered raising my blades. "They're going to hit us all at once," I said. No one refuted me. Eli sighed and drew a hunting knife. Its blade was nearly as long as my shortsword had been. "I have an idea, but I need to . . . meditate." I had almost said conjure but caught myself at the last moment. I didn't think Durbarge would "suffer a witch to live" if he caught me at my gifts.

With a weary sigh, I folded my knees and sat on the cairn. A black opal was near my boot, but I was too tired to move. Blood and pain throbbed in my veins like vinegar and whiskey, dulling and enervating. I closed my eyes and opened a mind-skim on top of the mage-sight. The world ducked and spun around me. The hot taste of acid and chocolate rose in my throat, but I swallowed it down.

To my side, the mound pulsed once, here, not-here, a lavender energy I didn't understand but had used. Had made my own. In time with it, my amulets pulsed, and energy flowed into me. Guiding the tempo and rhythm, my blood beat at one with the mound. I breathed, and my breath blew out a lavender mist. Beside me, Thadd glowed all the shades of tourmaline, and I smelled the reek of kylen excitement and fear. He could suddenly see the amethyst too. I felt his lips press together to stop whatever he wanted to say.

The rest of the scripture that described the creature trapped in the bowels of the mountain emerged in my mind. She gave it to me, the words belling clear and ringing. *"And there appeared in the cherubim, the form of a man's hand under their wings. And when I looked, behold the four wheels by the cherubim, one wheel by one cherub, and another wheel by another cherub: and the appearance of the wheels was as the color of a gem stone. And as for their appearances, they four had one likeness, as if a wheel had been in the midst of a wheel. When they went, they went upon their four sides; they turned not as they went, but to the place whither the head looked they followed it . . . And their whole body, and their backs, and their hands, and their wings, and the wheels, were full of eyes round about, even the wheels that they four had. As for the wheels, it was cried unto them in my hearing, 'O wheel!' And every one had four faces: the first face was the face of a cherub, and the second face was the face of a human, and the third the face of a lion, and the fourth the face of an eagle.*

"Use the otherness of the blended scan," she said. *"The otherness . . . "* And her voice fell silent.

My mind was still sluggish, my fatigue marrow deep. I was close to collapse. I struggled to find the moment in my memory when the sight had changed, to isolate the *otherness* I had experienced when I blended the mage-senses.

"Blasphemy," another voice tolled. *"Humans and mages cannot do this. Only the archseraph and his senior winged warriors can do this thing. And only after they are paired with a cherub."*

"She has bound herself to my wheels," the Mistress' voice rang.

"Foolish, she," came the answer.

The world fell away. Light, sound, smells, textures, blasted at me, smothered me, flailed me like barbed chains, rolled me like rapids, and trapped me there, dying. I fell, retching. My heart beat once.

And I fell and fell and fell and fell. My heart beat a second time.

On one level, in one place, I landed on the stone cairn. Felt the bones in my hand break, shatter, splinter, into hundreds of calcite shards. Purple light flared. The rocks beneath me shook, vibrated, and began to slide. One shifted and slid over my broken hand. My heart beat a third time.

In the other place, I glimpsed a river of lava, heat, energy, life, and death, and blood, and birth. It flowed to me, through me, and was gone. *What are wheels?* The boulder ground my shattered bones. Pain spiraled up, pulling me back. My heart beat twice more.

Below me, I saw a glimmer, a shine, a gold so pure, it was self-sustaining energy, trapped, hidden, shielded, beneath a layer of *otherness*. The *otherness* stood outside the world where my hand was broken, secluded, isolated in a sea of calm. A sea so black and textured it was like black velvet viewed on a moonless night. A place, but not a place. The next universe beyond this one? The space between universes? Between dimensions? The next dimension beyond where I existed? It wasn't within my understanding. My brain wasn't equipped with the necessary synapses to appreciate or comprehend it.

I threw up. Instantly I was back in the world I knew, my

BLOODRING

hand trapped beneath a boulder so massive, no mage could have moved it. Pain, a lissome agony, streaked up my arm, paralyzing me. My heart beat a sixth time. I gagged again as the pain reached new, unheard-of peaks of torture. I realized the earth was shaking. *Earthquake.*

On the hillsides, Darkness raced at us, streaking blobs of reddish black. "Tears of Taharial," I whispered, not caring that I was heard. I was trapped.

The cairn below me shifted again. The boulders slid and tumbled. The flesh of my hand was shredded, the bones ground to dust. I screamed. Time shifted. Thadd picked me up and threw me across the clearing. I landed in a tangle of spawn, sending them bowling away.

I cupped the remains of my hand against my chest and pulled the blade from my nape, whirling it once over my head, spitting stomach acid and partially digested chocolate. From beneath the cairn, navcone rose into the air. Navcone was gold, tons of gold, twisted and spiraled in perfect circles, hoops of energy that sparkled and spun and sang with joy. If pure energy could laugh, it roared with laughter. And I knew what it was. It was part of a machine.

As if moving in slow motion, Durbarge flew through the air and fell beside me, bones broken. Thadd landed at my other side, nimble footed and reeking of kylen.

From the mound only yards away, and from the oval glen beyond, lavender light pulsed, throbbed, pounded, a beating heart of life pouring through the soil and grass and trees. The ground shifted. Fire erupted like lightning. The earth rose and the accumulated soil of decades, rolled from the top of the new hill and tumbled to the ground. And still the mound and the glen lifted.

Amethyst, a single, narrow, pulsing, faceted amethyst the size of a football field, appeared through the falling soil. It sang, it choraled, a paean of joy and hope and life.

And its eyes opened. Glowing amethyst eyes, like the eyes along the Mistress's body. That was her name, the Mistress. Mistress Amethyst. Holy Amethyst. And these were Amethyst's wheels. I quoted the rest of the scripture from Ezekiel about the cherubim. "Their whole body, and their backs, and their hands, and their wings, and the *wheels*, were full of eyes round about."

The eyes, hundreds of eyes, thousands upon thousands of them, blinked and looked at me. The weight of the stare was the weight of the world. The song of the wheels changed key and hummed a softer tune, an audible caress I could feel across my skin as if I lay naked in a summer field. It felt alive.

Above me the navcone rolled, altered its plane, and slid through space as if it weighed nothing. It impacted the lavender stone. Cracks showed through the amethyst, shattered fragments as useless as my hand. The gold navcone settled around the damaged stone tip with a soft, broken snap.

The navcone was the navigation nosecone of a ship.

Sweet Hail Mary. The amethyst I had been drawing upon was a ship. The eyes smiled at me. The ship crooned, pianissimo, a gentle lullaby melody. The lavender stone behind the nosecone clicked and separated into two hoops. Purple light discharged from the skin of the stone like lightning. It separated again and formed four, again and became six. A seventh circle lifted from the center and whirled and whorled. The other wheels began turning, gyrating. Each wheel within a wheel sang a different harmony, a chorus, a hymn.

Tones of blessing enwrapped me, brushed my skin, penetrated to my muscles and nerves and into my bones. And even deeper, into my cells, my very genes, my spirit. I closed my eyes and threw back my head. "Darkness attacks," I told it, speaking aloud.

Behind my closed eyes, I saw the ship fire weapons into the hillside, into the attacking Darkness. The weapons were light and heat, yet neither, the fine, laserlike beams a gavotte across the mountainside. The ship rose, still firing, and altered its plane, climbing over the blasted ground of the sepulcher where it had lain, land that had once been a clearing.

Yet the earth still shook and the rumbling had grown. Suddenly, I knew what I was hearing. An avalanche. The ice cap had shifted. Broken. It was racing downhill, thousands of tons of ice and rock and debris, to bury the town. "Thorn! The ice pack!"

Mistress? I thought.

"It is of no matter. You are safe. The rest is of no importance. They are humans."

Shock swept through me. I raised up from the ground. Even in the night, I could see the avalanche approaching, a thunderous roaring of white and death to my blended scan. There was something I could do. I could call "mage in dire" now . . . But there wasn't time.

I threw back my head, flung open my arms, dropping back into the *otherness*. And once again, I heard my heart beat. Lavender light pulsed. Power lanced me, speared me, damaged me as it passed through me. I studied the wheels for two heart-beats. Light, brighter than the sun, sang inside me.

"What are you doing, little mage?"

"What I have to," I yelled back.

I called on stone.

In a place that was here and not-here, I understood how the wheels, the ship, worked, what directed it-them. The eyes, all the eyes turned to me. My heart beat a fourth time. On the hillsides all around, I saw Darkness dying. Being burned and drained and killed all around me, their energies warping, bending, shattering, as the bones in my hand had shattered.

The ground vibrated beneath my feet. My heart beat again. I looked into the eyes on the wheels and *twisted* with my will. Wordless. Without incantation. With only my need and desire and fear for the town, for the people I loved. With only my knowledge of stone. The wheel gyrated. Pulsed once in time to the beat of my heart.

A light brighter than the sun reached out from the nav-cone. *Navigation cone*, my mind whispered. In a single sustained burst, it melted the ice cap.

The thunder of avalanche ice became the rushing of Niagara. An entire sea of water, a tsunami of destruction raced toward the town.

My heart beat again. A second burst of light followed the first. Steam, hotter than the fires of hell, rose and hissed and divided and separated. The avalanche of snow that had become a sea now steamed into a cloud. My heart beat. Rain started to fall. Heavy, drenching sheets of rain. My heart beat.

I was suddenly back in the clearing. Beside me, Thadd stood, his gun sweeping. I smelled battle and death, blood and spawn, ozone and sulfur and rain.

I felt, I knew, the thoughts of the Darkness, the spawn, the few remaining humans, the walkers . . . and the Dragon standing in the mouth of the cave. My heart beat. The Dragon that smelled of Lucas' blood. The chain it held in its hands. Links from Mole Man's chain . . .

The wheels turned and fired again, the energy of creation gathered, braided, wove itself into a single beam of Light and otherness. Darkness howled with anger, shrieked with pain as the Light weapons of the wheels killed them by the thousands. My heart beat.

My chin rested in wet, chilled soil. Rain pelted me, forming runnels and creeks and currents that sparkled and gurgled. I found the energy to lift my nose out of the water and roll over, my face to the heavens. Darkness fled and died. The smell of death and defeat and victory and rain blew over me. My heart beat.

Mage-heat blazed up in me. Need and want were colors, rich and glorious and yet, somehow, meaningless. Desolation welled up in me. I sobbed, once, as my heart beat.

BLOOÐRING

I released the ship, Holy Amethyst's wheels. We had won. We had won.

Suddenly, the sky above me was filled with seraphs. They shouted and sang, a song of a thousand bells. I felt, more than saw, Raziel settle beside me. I took a breath. We had won.

My heart beat. And I knew no more.

Epilogue

†

The world was dark, a clouded, cold, empty place. I stood in a meadow, a glen, my dobok whole, my hair free and blowing in a chill wind, my cloak tied around my shoulders, my amulets throbbing with power. My blades, the longsword and the kris, were crossed before me, steel on steel. I was scarred, my face disfigured with a tracery of glowing white, stark, yet beautiful.

"Help me, little mage," a voice belled. But the sound fell away. Holy Amethyst's voice, caught once again by the heart of the mountain that trapped her.

Malashe-el stood before me, smiling, older, darker than it—he?—had seemed once. Its hair whipped back in an unseen wind, free of its braid, flying and tangled and lustrous.

"You survived. You will be called," Malashe-el said, its voice a lower tone, abrasive and coarse. "You are desired. You will not refuse. I have your blood." Turning, it raced away toward the night.

I have your blood.

In the vision, feathers and down brushed along my sides, down my legs. A hand cupped my head and lifted my lips for a

334

kiss. Raziel peered through his wings and smiled at me. *And I have your heart.*

Three days later, I woke. I eased up on my elbows and looked around. No cell. No hot pincers. My loft was as neat as a pin, clean, windows sparkling. Outside, a snowstorm howled, but inside, gas logs whispered and fans circulated warm air overhead. Scented candles burned, flickering in glass votives.

I had been bathed, shampooed, slathered with sage-scented unguents. Despite a strange, hollow ache though my torso, and an empty stomach that growled its displeasure, I felt . . . pretty good . . . nearly ducky.

I had survived. On a mountain, at night, in a battle with the AAS and Darkness. And . . . wheels. Amethyst's wheels. And a burning river. But the river seemed to slide away, hard to hold on to, impossible to recall with any detail. Stranger and stranger.

I inspected my hand. I expected to see a stump. Instead, four fingertips and a thumb, red and delicate with new skin, peeked from a gauze dressing. I flexed the hand. It hurt, but not like I expected. My fingers moved, bones and tendons contracting painfully. Seraph healing here, combined with mage-conjure.

Mage-conjure . . . Like the links of a chain. *Mole Man's chain. And the Mistress, injured, in pain, still trapped belowground.* I tried to hold on to them, but the thoughts slid away. I flexed my hand again.

Above the scent of candles I caught a whiff of something sweet. Vanilla and caramel, brown sugar and just a hit of ginger. Kylen. My belly did a little dip and curl. The susurration of cloth on cloth drew my eyes to the rocker. Thadd sat slouched in it, his hands draped over the carved lion-claw arms, legs outstretched, his head rocked back, mouth slightly open. He breathed slowly and steadily, the sound not quite a snore. A bruise colored his cheek, and both eyes were black fading to green. His knuckles were scabbed over. I wanted to reach out and touch him, but he looked so tired. I dropped my head back to the pillows, hearing a soft clink.

Around my neck hung my amulets. I had muzzy memories of seeing them each time I woke. On the steel chain were new talismans. I picked them up, letting them dangle. A half-melted silver and gold crucifix, a burned wooden cross, a second cross so disfigured I didn't recognize it.

An additional amulet hung with them, touching the mended prime—a four-inch ring of watermelon tourmaline. Surprised, I lifted the ring and studied it. "Seraph stones," I whispered. It was a sigil, a carved and shaped article of intent. On its surface were runes and characters that flamed like torches and ran like water. The flames were characters of a once-dead language, saying three numbers and one word. 106 ADONAI.

The angel of punishment had ordered me to wait for him.

Almost afraid to look, I lifted my left wrist. On it was a solid copper and gold bracelet, one too small to slide off over my healing hand. It too was inscribed with 106 ADONAI.

Glory and infamy.

106 ADONAI, carved into a stone of promise, and a metal band of bondage. They were the sigils and GPS locator device of a licensed witchy-woman. I had been given one year.

About the Author

A native of Louisiana, **Faith Hunter** spent her early years on the bayou and rivers, learning survival skills and the womanly arts. She liked horses, dogs, fishing and crabbing much better than girly things. She still does.

In grade school, she fell in love with fantasy and science fiction, reading five books a week and wishing she "could write that great stuff." Faith now shares her life with her Renaissance Man and their dogs in an Enclave of their own.

To find out more about Faith, go to www.faithhunter.net.